The Bin Brigade

Fergie

Hey L!

Hope you enjoy!!

F ☺ x

The Bin Brigade

Fergie Robson

Published in 2014 by FeedARead.com Publishing

THE BIN BRIGADE

1. **FOOTSTEPS IN THE STREET**

The school gates had been opened, one of them less than the other, it had stopped in front of a pile of stones and rubble which was preventing it from going back any further. Some cars stopped for a bit on their way in, and drivers looked out their windows, maybe winding them down to stretch their heads out and watch the gap between the front of their cars and the gate before proceeding through.

A pupil, a boy, ran in front of one car waiting to go in, and tried to open the gate further, to force it. He jumped when the car horn went, and the driver shouted something from inside, shaking his fist through the window and waving the pupil out of the way. The boy held his hands up, sorry sir, and walked away shaking his head, joining another pupil, talking to him, and pointing back with his thumb at the teacher's car, which followed him into the playground and then turned to head towards the car park.

In the playground, some more pupils stood about, they were in groups of three or four, maybe five or six. Some pupils stood on their own, not looking at anybody. One boy walked from the gates to the entrance to the school building, and turned round to face outwards. He took his schoolbag off his shoulders and dropped the strap down, holding it by the handles and allowing his arm to hang by his side, then began to swing his arm backwards and forwards, making an arc in the air with the bag.

Two boys walked past him, laughing, one of them saying something to his companion before stretching an arm out to the side and flicking a piece of paper at the boy's face as the boy was watching his bag

1

rise and fall. The boy stopped swinging the bag and put his other arm up in front of his head, and lifted one leg up as he leaned back, balancing, his foot shaking in the air before resting on the ground.

He said nothing as he watched the two boys walk away, then started swinging the bag again, this time making a parabola with it, by lifting his arm when it had reached the bottom of each arc. All the time he was looking at the cars coming in the gate.

The cars passed the sign saying Staff Car Park, and teachers got out, sometimes a few teachers got out of the same car, waiting on each other, lifting bags or boxes out of the boot, before walking into the school via the entrance with its signs, notices and a plaque.

A few pupils were walking around and picking up pieces of rubbish that were lying about, crisp packets, chocolate wrappers, putting them into rubbish bags and taking the bags in through a door which had a No Pupils sign on it.

One of the teachers, opening the door to follow the pupils inside, turned and then nodded his head back towards them, and said see them son, they're the Bin Brigade. Some of the other teachers nodded, smiling. The teacher laughed, see if you ever visit another school, you'll not see anything like them son, wouldn't be allowed. Then, still laughing as he spoke, I'm telling you, if the inspectors ever found out about them we'd be shut down, and that's for definite!

The other teachers around laughed as well, and continued to file through the door, carrying books and briefcases, each holding the door open for the person behind with a foot or an elbow.

…

2

He could be heard whistling Mr Tambourine Man before he came into the room or if he was going down the corridor, sometimes it might be Blowing In The Wind or maybe something else, not always Dylan, but mostly Mr Tambourine Man.

He would sit in the staffroom telling jokes. The other teachers would laugh, and say aw, you're making me feel sick man, or they'd say god sake, you're sick man!

He was always the first to the staffroom at breaks and dinnertimes, and sat at the same table and played cards with whoever sat next to him. There was a sort of rota going on, everybody got a game in at least once a week with him. He always dealt the cards, that was kind of a rule.

All the time he was dealing, and during the game, Mr Tambourine Man would talk and create laughter amongst people around him with the things he would say. He said och, effing this, and ah, effing that! People who weren't playing listened to him as well, and looked up from their marking or newspapers if he said something, and they hooted, aw man, you're really sick you!

...

She came into sight with one of her hands in the air, speaking to the boy she was with, I'm not upset, I'm just, okay, I am upset. He leaned towards her and she kissed him. She stopped kissing and said to the boy they shouldn't be doing this in the buildings, aw my god, we shoudni be doing this. Then she said, and it wasn't a question, what about the teachers!

They were just coming into the classroooom, the two of them, she pushed his hands away, my god, you've been with me all break! The boy said aw, don't

3

not kiss me, kiss me! And then he said he had to go, alright, alright, I'd better go to my class anyway.

Then as he left, the girl turned round to face into the classroom and spoke again, hiya, my name's Kelly sir. She turned the top of her body sideways and smiled, and stood with one leg crossed over the other, her arms folded, where d'you want me then? Then she smiled, I mean, to sit, sir!

Some of the others already sitting down were giggling a bit and looking at each other, holding their hands over their faces and glancing to the front of the room. Kelly said d'you want me to sit here? And sat down. Before a minute was over she looked around the class and then to the front again, stating, not asking, em, you're new aren't you.

Somebody else, a boy, threw a rolled-up piece of chewing gum wrapper at her, he's the student Kelly, and Kelly turned towards him and said wow, my friend's brother was a student!

During the lesson she kept turning round and smiling to the rest of the class, she had bubble gum which she kept pulling out of her mouth and then lifting her head back to guide back in, making urg urg noises as she did so, and laughing when it got back into her mouth. For a while she stared ahead at the front of the class, always smiling.

At the end of the lesson she waited for the others to go out, and then walked to the door and pushed it in front of her, it didn't close, and she kept the fingers of one hand wrapped round the part of the door above the level of the handle.

Then she turned around, then she crossed her legs, and she folded her arms again. She looked and half-smiled, you wanting it then sir? Then she laughed,

4

reached out behind her body for the door handle, she was still facing into the room, and when she got hold of it she said okay then, see you again, then turned and went out.

The boy she had arrived with was outside, you still upset? She kissed him, naw, not anymore, I wasn't upset anyway, I was just, okay, I was upset! And they put their arms round each other and walked away, his hand in her back pocket.

...

The rooms in the corridor with the sign saying Staff Social Area included one that was divided into three sections, one for men that had a sign saying Staffroom at its door which the men kept shutting, one for women saying Female-Staffroom, and one for anyone, a mixed staffroom, which was called the Mixed-Staffroom. Some staff commented on the separation, my god, isn't it ridiculous, this day and age and all, others said well, that's just the way it's always been but.

The staffroom tended to have ten or fifteen men in it at any one time, the female about three or four. The mixed might have ten or fifteen women, and maybe three or four men.

The staff tuck shop was located in the Mixed-Staffroom, so men ended up having to talk with the women if they wanted a can of something, or a Penguin or packet of Quavers.

The woman who ran the tuck shop, as well as filling the three urns, one in each of the staffrooms, talked to the teachers when she was spoken to, she called some of the men sir. She did a bit of tidying up too when break was over, or after lunchtime. Hoovering, dusting, crumbs, spillages.

5

Her grandson was in the school, people liked him, said aye, he's a good kid, not the brightest but a good kid, always polite in my lessons, no a peep out of him.

At the tuck shop she would comment on the weather. She walked to the school each day, so she would know about the weather, the weather she had walked through to get to school. She said that more than once during the winter she had ended up having to walk to school in the snow, she didn't drive. Staff would always say, she walks every day, they passed her as they were driving in to work themselves, saw her walking, and they commented later in the day, she was walking in the snow, aye!

At the tuck shop teachers would look down at the sweets as they asked her how's it goin, and Walks In Snow would say fine thanks Miss Whatsit, or very well Mister Thingmi. Then she would look out the change for them and tell them to have a good day, you have a good day sir!

…

Every so often, usually in a lunchtime but sometimes during a break, the deputy rector made a visit to the staffroom, just to see how you're all getting on eh! Or his words were, checking you're all not planning a mutiny! Palace revolution wasn't it, that right? Eh? And he would look at someone in the History department.

People looked up at him when he came in, he could be seen out the corner of an eye someone said, on account of him always wearing his graduation gown around school, like some kind of ghoul or phantom, other people said. The Phantom would talk to a few individuals, although generally everybody heard him, or

6

at least they looked like they thought he might turn and talk to them next, so they'd need to be paying attention.

Sometimes when he spoke, people would say to him eh, you're quite enthusiastic about the thing! He could be stamping his feet about, clasping and clapping his hands together as well as he talked, aah, yes indeed, aah, dear boy, my good man, aah!

Folk either called the Phantom by his name, if they had known him for a while, or just said deputy, it depended. Some of the time he would mention an anecdote about a rector from the past, or talk about something that was happening soon, a PTA thing, or school show. Events outside of school as well, like the football. Folk would raise their eyebrows as they looked at him, if he was looking at them.

Teachers he talked to with direction stayed in their seats and said aye! Or, that's right aye! There would not be any specifics to have to say in reply to him, nothing in particular was required, and then he would turn and leave, smiling.

Eventually, eventually, people would start talking again.

…

Kevin wouldn't even say much to the person he was walking with on the way into the room, but once the lesson got going he'd say nothing at all. He wouldn't offer an opinion amongst his friends if there was a group of them and a kind of talk or discussion was initiated.

If he did speak though, answering a question, the rest of the class never interrupted him at all. After he spoke and the lesson went on, he would hold both his hands over his whole face and blow out, and when he took his hands away he opened his eyes and seemed to keep opening them as much as he could before blinking, and then he said no more.

People usually spoke to him first though, he didn't start conversations himself. Often if he was asked a question he would reply with the question, em, what was the question?

…

Standing in the staffroom, usually standing, was the staff union rep, scratching his armpits, or cupping a hand under one armpit. Often there would be a stain on his armpits from sweat, on winter days as well as when the sun was out. He might run one finger across the stain and then wipe the finger on his shirt, smiling at whoever happened to establish eye-contact with him at the point of wiping.

Armpits watched as the Phantom left the room. He coughed and then bit his lip. When he turned round he pointed his thumb back at the door, he's a fucking cheeky bastard that one, for definite, eh! Saying that about me eh, Christjesus! He was laughing now though, Armpits, folk around him were too, smiling at him.

Armpits indicated the door again, and said hey, see him son, and spoke about how he had been a pupil of the Phantom, no kidding son, I was an actual pupil of him, he fucking taught me English! People around smiled. And he continued about the fact that although he, Armpits, talked about it if asked, you couldn't ask the Phantom about it. Armpits nodded, seriously son, the old bastard wouldn't want to give his age away, know? You know?

Some staff had said Armpits must have known the deputy rector for about twenty-five years now, and they looked at him, that right? Minus three for college but, know?

Aye, said Armpits, he's a good man our deputy rector, despite for the fact that we all know he votes Tory but says he doesn't, fucking hell. He turned, but dinni listen to anything I tell you son. Or anyone else for that matter. Just do what you think is right while you're here, eh. You'll be fine. Do what you think is right.

Armpits smiled at the people who were sitting down, and exclaimed eh, what you lot fucking thinking eh!

…

Aw shut up Sam, just because you want to join the army, you think you know everything about battles and things!

Sam turned and looked at the boy who had spoken to him, shut up, no I don't! He faced the front again, I am gonni join the army, me. But it's true though sir, every time we study Wallace or Bruce sir, you hear Moray mentioned a few times, or not at all, and then it's nothing after he died, like he never did anything that counted, know? You know? He scratched the piece of paper on his desk with a pencil, I always thought that Moray's more of a hero than any of them, but his name gets mentioned a couple of times and then it's nothing, sometimes he doesn't get mentioned at all. Sir, was he a lieutenant or a general? All the History we've done never tells you much about him, just Wallace and Bruce.

The class giggled, someone said listen, listen to soldier Sam! Sam looked to the side and then the front, then went on to explain that they had learned about Wallace and Bruce at school every year, for years now, sir. Not every year, other people said, you're wrong Sam, ya liar! Well, just about, Sam replied, it feels like

9

it sometimes, there was that big project we did in primary six, and we had that visit to Stirling in primary seven, plus whatever we did in first and second year here.

Ah, but we weren't taught it last year, in third year, someone said. Naw but, but, and Sam went on again to tell of how all the pupils in the school had to do that mural thing on the wall of the Maths extension that got built when they were in third year, he folded his arms, all that had something to do with it didn't it? It was all about Wallace and Bruce, see? He nodded, and somebody drew Wallace with a blue cross on his face instead of a white one and got told it was wrong, as if Wallace ever had a cross on his face at all! I'm telling you, it's all made up, the History they want you to learn. I'm telling you, it's all made up.

A boy started to tap his fingers on the desk. Another boy did the same.

Sam continued, now we're doing this stuff on Wallace again, so that's every year for five, no six years. I'm just saying, all I was saying was that Moray seemed like a good guy, too, I'm no saying Wallace and Bruce weren't, obviously I'm not 'cause obviously they were, but just, wasn't it his soldiers who backed Wallace up early on after the Lanark thing, Moray? And, that probably never happened the way they said it did either, Lanark! It's all made-up, History.

The class looked at Sam, listen to know-it-all, how do you know what happened or not? And how it happened or not!

Sam shook his head, if Andrew Moray hadn't got killed at Stirling Bridge, he wouldn't ever have let Wallace fight the English at Falkirk, that's all I'm saying.

10

A couple of pupils chanted, soldier Sam, soldier Sam!

The class put away their pens and packed their bags as Sam kept talking, I'm just saying, nobody writes books about Andrew Moray, or films.

The bell went and someone said well done, you got us to the end of the lesson, Sam!

…

A group of three men took the same chairs in the staffroom every day, ones with cushions on them, and did crosswords from the papers that were always lying around. They didn't say much to other staff, staff other than themselves, and on occasions were referred to as freaks by another group of four or five men who sat elsewhere and just told jokes amongst themselves all the time, or laughed, or mocked people, or issues, or related stories about pupils' answers in class or pupils they had found out had wet themselves in school in the past, maybe at primary.

No-one else sat with the Joke Club, there was no membership or anything, but still.

Amongst the Crossword Freaks, Crossword Freak Number One was bringing up his Open University work again. Crossword Freak Number Two listened. All the while they were interspersing their conversation with helping each other with the crosswords. Crossword Freak Number One shut his eyes as he nodded his head, of course, it wasn't until I started this degree that I had such a perspective, that is, a sociological perspective on education in an ordered society.

Hmmf! The sound came from Mr Tambourine Man, who didn't look up when he made it.

Crossword Freak Number One turned his head towards Mr Tambourine Man, and then back away from him, and continued, I mean, I teach Geography, sometimes the basic concepts, perhaps the finer points even, it depends on the class, obviously, but really, am I really delivering individual needs?

Crossword Freak Number Two was nodding his head, holding his pencil to his mouth, em, three down, you get that today?

Eh, no I didn't, Crossword Freak Number One said, but do you see what I'm saying? With a class of thirty, maybe thirty-two in front of me, can I truly foster individuals at all? That is, am I, as the liberal school of thought would demand of me, creating a situation in which individual school-leavers can achieve mobility within society through academic success?

Armpits burped in the background.

The Crossword Freaks looked up and across and back and down again. Crossword Freak Number Three said nothing. Crossword Freak Number One shut his eyes and nodded again, if I teach about shanty-towns in Brazil, the pupils acquire knowledge, and, hopefully, eventually a qualification, but, oh I don't know, and he twisted his face up and held his fist under his chin.

D'you philosophise like that in front of your classes mate, asked Armpits, who half-burped again, and do you pardon me for being so rude?

Crossword Freak Number One smiled, of course not, I mean, what I do in class. I'm just saying. I'm doing this course, you see?

I see, I hear and all! Armpits sat a bit up and looked at Crossword Freak Number One before speaking. Are you trying to work out if by instructing the kids on how to use fucking Ordnance Survey maps you're attaining some kind of fucking bargaining position for the working classes in a country where there's inequality in the bloody schooling system and poverty fucking still in existence? Armpits stared at Crossword Freak Number One.

Well, em, I don't think we've covered that in the course yet, Crossword Freak Number One was looking back at his newspaper by now.

Because that's what the liberals say mate, that's essentially what the liberals say, Armpits was sitting up now, and the Marxian view, they told you that yet?

Em, I don't, em.

Armpits shook his head, what they say is, in the Marxian view, that is, is that the education system provides a workforce for capitalism, prepares the kids for fucking exploitation. What's your view, your actual opinion, Armpits challenged him.

Crossword Freak Number One shifted his position on his chair, em, we're just commenting on the general views at the moment, you see, that is, theory.

Theory?

Theory.

Theory. Well, see when you've got a view, an actual original thought yourself, then you can talk about it in the staffroom, until then shut the hell up man, it's bad enough that the system might be crushing us all without you showing us that you haveni got a clue. Back to your crossword man. Christjesus!

Crossword Freak Number One kept looking at Armpits who said again, don't not go back to your crossword, go back to your crossword!

...

Mr Tambourine Man said, if you're doing an essay on moral education son, you should speak to the

13

head of R.E., he'll help you I'm sure, though you'll need to listen carefully, speaks really quiet and doesn't say much, used to be in the police, big guy, and hard as bloody nails, never seen a class as quiet in an R.E. lesson as in his, ha ha! Or in any lesson, whatever the subject actually. Kids love him but, though they're bloody petrified of him too, eh! He nudged Armpits, ex-cop isn't he, that right?

Armpits shook his head and whispered, would you know it, here he is now. Then Armpits didn't say anything, but nodded towards Ex-Cop who was walking in at that moment. Mr Tambourine Man lowered his voice to say em, not now though son, don't ask just yet, he spoke in a half-whisper.

Ex-Cop went over to the classroom desk that had been put in the corner of the staffroom to allow people to work if they weren't teaching but someone else was using their classroom, and picked up some papers off it, saying right, too much stuff lying around here, I'm going to do this somewhere else.

Mr Tambourine Man nodded up at him, alright eh, how you doing, I mean, aw still doing your first year reports, what a pain eh. Ex-Cop looked at Mr Tambourine Man, you're asking me? Mr Tambourine Man blinked. Ex-Cop said aye, aye, a pain, I suppose they are, em, are you two gents okay? Mr Tambourine Man and Armpits both nodded, Armpits folding and unfolding his arms whilst doing so.

Ex-Cop got up and left.

See what I mean, Mr Tambourine Man nodded in the direction of the door, doesn't say much about the thing, doesn't say much at all.

Armpits agreed, aye, talk to him about the moral education essay when you've got a moment though son,

then he said Christjesus, imagine giving up the police with its pension, and all for this place and all, eh!
…

Teachers who talked about pupils who didn't say much in class maybe said see him, that pupil, he doesn't say much, he's a quiet one, or perhaps see her, she's a quiet wee soul that one.

Maybe a teacher would point out that a pupil they had been speaking about in the particular, a pupil who was the subject of staffroom discussion, was currently overcoming some difficulty, aye, there's something personal going on at the moment for that pair, him and his big sister, best just to leave them alone. Or maybe staff would have received a note giving information about a bereavement or another kind of situation, a domestic, for example.

Somebody else, a teacher in the staffroom, would always point out that something going on at home was no excuse for rudeness, in the case of pupils who didn't speak much when they were spoken to, or another teacher would say it wasn't an excuse for indiscipline, in the case of pupils who ignored or disobeyed instructions. The argument from a teacher might be, I mean, you try to see the kid's point of view yeah, or the kids', plural, you try to be the bigger person, but sometimes, ach.

Sometimes, once people got to know a bit more about some pupils, it emerged in the staffroom from a teacher in the know that perhaps those children labelled as daydreamers were really in a state of desperation about something affecting their lives outside of school, those that seemed to allow themselves a luxury of contemplation were, in actual fact, in despair.

15

Teachers talked about how they themselves had worries, troubles, but they said they didn't let it affect the way they spoke to pupils. Someone might indicate concerns from his own life outside school, exclaiming, Jesus Christ, I've got a house to pay for, and another kid on the way! Perhaps a guy would say look at me, I'm tutoring every hour I can in the evenings just to buy a bigger car so I can fit an extra bloody baby-seat in, but I'm not swearing at the pupils, and some of these pupils say they've got problems to whichever do-gooder will listen to them, and so then they think it means they can do and say what they bloody well want in my bloody lesson!

Other teachers would be nodding and agreeing about how they, pupils, because they were children, really couldn't know what desperation is, in the sense of the word that represented truth, and one teacher would conclude by saying kids, they think they can do and say what they want!

…

The class asked Marie about things, everyone did, the ones who never said a lot, and the ones who spoke more than anybody else, or could be heard above everybody else, they all said to Marie, can you please help me Marie? And when they asked her, she did.

When she talked it was usually about something none of the others in the class would bring up, but they always paid attention. If she talked about something she liked or something she was looking forward to she said aw, I just love thinking about it. Kelly always looked at Marie and smiled, aw, do you Marie? And Kelly kept looking at Marie, aw!

One time, Marie gave her tie to someone who had to go and see the rector. The pupil had said aw naw,

I'd better no go with this tie, look at the writing on it, Marie, gonni lend me yours? The boy started to say please, but by that time Marie was slipping off her tie, and she passed it over, and then when he said och, I canni get this right, she stood up to walk behind the boy and put the tie on for him. He left the classroom smiling, aw, cheers Marie.

And more than one pupil in the class would smile at Marie.

…

So you're saying that the arts are more important than social subjects? History? Armpits was arguing with Mr Tambourine Man, it had started somehow. Armpits shook his head, humanities, man. We teach humanity, a humanity, you are looking at a teacher of compassion!

Armpits was looking at the teacher who was sitting beside him, the two of them were laughing, then he was looking back at Mr Tambourine Man who was in the process of stopping what he was doing and starting to reply, saying away, away ye go man, I'm talking about the performing arts man, and I wasn't saying they're more important than social subjects. He shook his head too, a place for everything eh, that's all.

Armpits began to nod, there seemed to be a kind of accord, but then from Mr Tambourine Man came the words, but of course, if you want my opinion, then at least Music, and I mean the proper study of it, allows the kids the chance to appreciate something more than just who fought who in which war, and when and why, and how it happened all over again, just to prove that we don't learn from the past, no matter how much our best teachers of compassion try to make the effort, mind Bruce and the spider in that MacCaig poem, eh!

17

The person sitting next to Armpits looked at him. Armpits stood up and took one stride towards the door and stopped to say aw aye, playing Yesterday on the keyboard, that's gonni teach them a lot of fucking appreciation, I've heard your second year classes, and then Armpits was singing, wouldn't you agree baby you and me got a groovy kind of love! Armpits was hooting along with a couple of other folk.

Mr Tambourine Man paused a second before starting what he was doing again. Armpits leaned down and nudged the teacher who had been his neighbour, he's got no answer now, that one!

Mr Tambourine Man put something away in his briefcase, and sighed, man are you serious? Armpits said aye, sat down again, pulled his trousers a bit up at his knee and sat back and folded his arms. The two continued.

Okay then, how come it was Music that was the first subject to be taught in schools then?

What you talking about!

I'm saying, Music.

Your arse man.

My arse?

Aye, Music, your arse man!

Alright, so-called History expert, who was it who ran the first schools in Scotland?

Armpits paused, shut up man, if you're talking about the Reformation period then education round about then was all about History, not Music, History, John Knox looking at Scotland's Catholic past, teaching all the young lads about discipline and fucking godliness, so we wouldn't go back to those wicked days of Popery!

That's when education started is it? Mr Tambourine Man folded his arms.

Fifteen-sixty-ish aye, or fifteen-sixty-one some people say, aye, how, you know different?

Mr Tambourine Man opened his arms, man, song-schools, medieval song-schools!

Song-what?

Song-schools, pre-bloody-your-Reformation man, of course. It was still the church that ran education in those days wasn't it, monks. Look at you now, I can see it in your face, you're admitting you didni know that, a History teacher and all!

Armpits smiled and shook his head, aye aye, naw, I was talking about formal education but, I knew about the fucking song-schools, man, I know about them for definite, we used to teach about them to the first years before the primaries hijacked all the best topics.

Mr Tambourine Man began to wave his arm in the air towards Armpits. Armpits was sitting forward by now, so was Mr Tambourine Man. Then the pair of them looked around at the people who were looking at them and listening to the conversation. Some teachers had put down newspapers or marking, they didn't take their eyes off the two arguing, Armpits and Mr Tambourine Man.

Mr Tambourine Man and Armpits, the two of them looked at each other. At the other folk. There was a pause.

Then Armpits said, do either of us give a fuck? They both sat back, laughing, naw!

…

Sometimes the pupils in upstairs classrooms would look out the window and watch a dumptruck in the distance drive up a slagheap on the outskirts of the town, the pupils would sit and use their watches to measure the time it took for the dumptruck to get up to the top of the hill.

They commented on the dumptruck's speed at the end of each ascent, it's amazing sir, pretty much on the minute exactly, every time! This could pre-occupy them for some time, if allowed.

Some pupils said the sixth years in the common room put bets on whether the dumptruck was going to make the journey in over or under the minute. It was also said the sixth year factored in the quantity of muck the dumptruck had to carry, they had to screw their eyes up to examine how much of a load the digger at the bottom of the slagheap put onto the dumptruck. Then a judgement would be made.

Staff gave out punishment exercises if they caught pupils looking out the window towards the goings-on at the slagheap, and when the pupils spoke about such instances as the issuing of punishments, they opened their eyes and kept them like that as they talked, and shook their heads, a punny just for that sir! Then they turned back to look out the window.

At the dumptruck.

…

Eh, me sir, Billy sir, he looked at the person sitting next to him and pointed at himself, me? Billy sir, your star man. He smiled, you gonni tell us your name then? And he waited, and then he mumbled to himself, eh, sorry sir. He looked down and fiddled with a pencil or ruler.

After the lesson had been going on for a while, Billy said you're a student aren't you, is it the uni you're at then, aye? He said that his primary had been there once, at the uni, to see a pantomime done by the drama students, he laughed as he spoke about it, it was crap sir, and all the actors were drunk, perfecto!

Later on in the lesson he asked, d'you want to be a teacher then, and then he said me, I'd never be a teacher. Someone else said Billy couldn't be one anyway, he'd never get the qualies. Billy laughed and then looked at the front, what qualies is it you need to be a teacher anyway sir, d'you have to be dead brainy? And then he scratched his head, think I'll just go on the broo, it sounds easier!

There was some laughter. Then, again from Billy, no, I'm gonni get a job, definitely. He was holding some piece of paper and looking at it. He looked at it still. When he put the paper down his eyes faced the same direction as where the paper had been. He smiled, and said he didn't know what job yet.

A couple of other pupils in the class laughed, Billy laughed too, still looking at the space in front of him where the paper had been.

…

On the train there were a couple of boys, hey, there's that new teacher, he's a student isn't he! Naw, he's a proper teacher. Naw, student! Then they ducked down, woops!

They were in the carriage a few rows down from the door, two double-seats then two lots of doubles facing each other with tables in between, then the boys' seat, a double-seat. In the carriage as a whole, there were only two double-seats left that had no-one sitting on them, they were on either side of the aisle, facing each other. It worked out.

The two pupils looked over their seats again, aye, naw, he's definitely a student. Shoosh, he'll hear you, hee hee! They turned and faced the front, talking to each other now. You going to football tonight? Aye. My mum'll take us. Aye. Pick you up at half six yeah? Yeah.

Someone came from the other end of the carriage and sat in one of the double-seats that didn't have anyone already sitting in one of them, there was just one left now, but the imbalance might be evened up soon, another stop was coming up.

…

Some folk called him Willie but most of them called him William. He sat in the class, usually beside another boy called James. He would come in the class with James, William, but if he didn't then he would still go over and sit with him. A lot of the time, some of the time, William was mocked by the boys about his size, you're a fat barrel William!

He mostly laughed at that as well, himself, William. He would look at James but James would not be laughing. Sometimes the situation was that the other lads would say aw, you're thick William, and sometimes it would be that they said hey, you haveni got a brain William! Leaning back on their chairs, bending their necks to look round at him, smiling at him, haven't you no William? But James wouldn't laugh.

William always looked at them as he smiled back at what they said, whatever the joke was. Least I'm gonni get a job, this was what he often replied, I'm gonni be an upholsterer when I grow up! And he talked of how that was more than any of them would have, he nodded as he spoke, aye, so stuff yous! Then he smiled and put the end of his pencil in his mouth and didn't say much more. James never spoke, he never said anything.

There would be some days when William didn't reply to anything the others said though, he looked away when they spoke, or he would be staring at the wall before they started. Or if he did say something it would make the others laugh and say ah, he's in a huff now, ha ha! And point at him.

William pushed his glasses back up the bridge of his nose and folded his arms, he would mutter about his assumption that they didn't have a chance of getting a job, the other boys. And he would stay in the huff, and he would keep looking away.

James wouldn't say anything.

…

In the staffroom Crossword Freak Number Two had just asked Crossword Freak Number One if Harry Lauder had ever been knighted. Crossword Freak Number Three wasn't involved, he was getting on with his own newspaper.

Crossword Freak Number One looked up and adjusted his glasses on his nose using his pencil, which he then pointed at Crossword Freak Number Two as he asked him, em, Harry Lauder, that is, Sir Harry Lauder?

Crossword Freak Number Two nodded, yes, yes, I meant Sir, Sir Harry Lauder, aye that's who I mean, of course.

Crossword Freak Number One looked back down at his lap, sighing, well, there's your answer then, Sir, Sir Harry Lauder. And he carried on with his crossword.

Crossword Freak Number Two paused a bit, and then looked down too, and then he looked back up again, no, I'm asking the question about Sir Harry Lauder, about him. Crossword Freak Number Two blinked, was he ever knighted?

23

Crossword Freak Number One took his glasses off and half-held them, half-hung them off his lip, you're asking was Sir Harry Lauder ever knighted, that is, Harry Lauder, who became Sir Harry Lauder?

Yes, and Crossword Freak Number Two tutted, it's for sixteen across, you're obviously not at it yet, I need to know, was Sir Harry Lauder ever knighted?

Crossword Freak Number One looked around the room, and then stared back at Crossword Freak Number Two, Crossword Freak Number Two looked at him and then at his newspaper and then started to whisper to himself, tapping his pencil along the paper, one two three four five six seven, then he did it all again, one two three four five six seven, and said och, one two three, no, it doesn't fit.

Crossword Freak Number One continued to stare at Crossword Freak Number Two, you do realise what you've just asked don't you?

And Crossword Freak Number Two replied, without looking up, saying that he did know, aye, I was just asking if Sir Harry Lauder had ever been knighted, but it doesn't matter now, it doesn't matter anymore, it doesn't fit, even if he had been.

Crossword Freak Number One sat up, yes but, Sir, Sir! Sir Harry Lauder! Was he ever knighted? Sir!

Crossword Freak Number Two replied yes, see if I think about it, then I do think that he was knighted. He pursed his lips and shut one eye before opening it again, in fact, wasn't he the first Scottish entertainer, or Scottish singer or actor or whatnot to be knighted, something like that? And he nodded, yes, yip, I think he was, aye. He looked back down at his newspaper, but I've just seen, looking at it again, it won't fit now, so.

24

Crossword Freak Number Two didn't look up again, and just got on with his crossword.

Crossword Freak Number Three said nothing.

Crossword Freak Number One rolled his eyes and glanced around at people sitting nearby, including Armpits, and then looked back at his own crossword again, re-adjusting his glasses, crossing his legs and waving one foot up and down in the air.

Armpits laughed into his coffee mug and then looked at Mr Tambourine Man, saying to him hey, what position did King, that is, King, Zog of Albania hold!

…

The head of History cycled into work every day. Staff said aw, see him, he's a good guy, good man, solid worker, liked by everyone here, the kids and so on, and they all agreed, the staff, aye, good guy, your head of History, good guy, he is.

He would wear his socks outside his trousers and have bicycle clips around his socks. He wouldn't take them off when he came into the staffroom, he would make a cup of tea first. Anyone he talked to would always speak back to him about the thing, and he would say de facto, de facto, de facto, about anything, in whatever context he was talking about. And the conversation would contain lots of agreement on both sides, nodding and such, aye you're right, aye it's such a simple idea. Bicycle Clips offered conclusions, saying ergo this, or ergo that, and whoever his companion was would say aye, aye you're no wrong, yip, aye, aye, yip. Bicycle Clips would smile and raise his eyebrows and nod, aye.

Bicycle Clips sometimes went out of the staffroom in the morning with his trousers still in his socks. The Joke Club occasionally had a snigger about him, see him, bet he never takes these clips off at home! Then they might say aye, bet he wears socks to bed, keeps them up with his clips, and tucks his pyjama bottoms into them, hee hee!

And the guys in the Joke Club would congratulate each other on the extension of the image of Bicycle Clips wearing his bicycle clips everywhere he went, Bicycle Clips coming out the womb with bicycle clips on, wearing tartan clips at his wedding, ha ha, aye, the Royal Stewart of course! Keeping them on to have sex with his wife, aye, he'll still have them on when he's lying in his coffin, eh!

And they recalled once, hey, mind that time he told us about those burglars that woke him and his wife up in the night, and he went out the house to shout at them when he saw them raiding his garden shed? You can imagine him running down the stairs and out into the garden, pulling off his clips and hurling them at the robbers hitting them on the head and the clips returning to him like a bloody boomerang!

There was much hooting at this. Not from anyone outside the Joke Club, only from those in the Joke Club. Some people would stand and stir their coffee looking at the Joke Club, but they wouldn't say anything, there was a kind of looking down if someone in the Joke Club tried to catch their eye.

Everybody else said other things in relation to Bicycle Clips though, aye he's alright, a good guy, you won't hear anyone say a bad word about him, for definite.

…

On the way into the building, Armpits said alright son, didn't see you there, you got a minute? Come on up to the department, I'll show you that stuff on the First World War that I told you I've got. He had said in the morning that he had received some stuff from Bicycle Clips on the First World War, he said he never really wanted it, or hadn't asked for it, but the circumstances were just, I don't know, I was just asked if I wanted some posters and wee booklets and things and I said yes without thinking, it was easier than giving a reason for not wanting them, and it meant I wouldn't get asked again, eh!

He looked at his watch, so, anyway, you and your wee pals in the Bin Brigade can have them now eh, the posters and wee booklets, I mean.

Armpits coughed, bent over and coughed again, and stood up, I heard you talking about the wee poster project on the First World War you're gonni be doing with them, you can get them to cut things out of this stuff if they want, it's all sorts of I don't know what, photos, poems, pictures of poppies and things, know. Just stuff, you know. The kids'll love cutting stuff out of it all, they love cutting things out, know? And stuff!

There were two flights of stairs up to the History department and one had twelve steps on it and the other had fourteen, which meant jogging up one step at a time for four and then two steps at a time for eight, then singles for six and doubles for eight.

Armpits stood at the bottom and watched for a second before starting to climb.

Or it could mean counting out two footsteps before hitting the stairs, and then going up the twelve in doubles which would then lead on to counting one footstep before going up the fourteen in doubles. It all added to eight steps. Whichever way, whatever method was employed, it worked out.

You training for something? Armpits asked.

...

A set of headphones was being shared by Armpits and Mr Tambourine Man. They were agreeing about the music, in voices that were raised a bit on account of the two of them listening to music in one ear each.

Each had just discovered that the other shared his opinion, Mr Tambourine Man smiled, aye, I used to listen to this album all the time, and Armpits smiled, aye, Aztec Camera, fucking magnificent! Armpits frowned for a second, pursing his lips. nineteen-eighty-three was it, High Land, Hard Rain? Mr Tambourine Man nodded, mm, aye.

Then they went on to bemoan the fact that the follow-up album didn't achieve the same level of excellence, Armpits nodded, aye, naw, it wasn't as good, I mean, Knife had the same touches of magic, but they were only dotted here or there, it lacked consistency across the whole piece though, eh.

Mr Tambourine Man said hey, you sound like you're quoting from the press you bloody plagiarist eh, ha! Some music hack would be contacting his lawyer right now if he heard you!

Armpits hooted, but still insisted, if it's right it's right though eh. And added, not that they'd make much out of me in court anyway, with not a bean to speak of in my bank account!

Conversations in the staffroom continued around them, although the Crossword Freaks didn't speak, instead occasionally looking up at Armpits and Mr Tambourine Man before looking at each other, and then there was the raising of eyebrows, as well as the pointing of elbows, the shaking of heads. And the sighs.

Armpits and Mr Tambourine Man never looked at the Crossword Freaks once.

When the Crossword Freaks looked back down they weren't writing anything, there was only the tapping of the rubber-ends of pencils on newspapers whose folds rested on the knees of crossed legs, with feet twitching. Then one of the Crossword Freaks might look back up at Armpits and Mr Tambourine Man, who still never looked at the Crossword Freaks once.

The conversation between the two continued, Mr Tambourine Man enthused about the thing, aw, but High Land, Hard Rain man, listen! And an earpiece would be passed over so Armpits could listen in stereo, he smiled back, thanks, aye, I know!

Armpits sniffed and coughed and scratched his arm, it's strange the way the album started with Oblivious, know, and The Boy Wonders was second, know. Because of how The Boy Wonders contains the actual words high land hard rain, the lyric. Armpits then used the word eponymous.

Armpits and Mr Tambourine Man talked for the entirety of the lunch hour about this, the tracklisting, the placing of songs next to one another, contrast, matching of themes, Armpits used the word juxtaposition.

The discussion would be between the two of them, but sometimes one of them, maybe Armpits, would look at somebody else and say Christjesus, listen to us aren't we the fucking pop intellectuals eh! Mr Tambourine Man would agree, saying ha! He laughed and shook his head at the same time, Oblivious but, see just listening to that, it is quite the perfect acoustic pop song, and with key changes and harmonious

29

background vocals, with the virtuoso guitar-playing of a genius at work behind it all.

Another guy in the staffroom joined in, Oblivious eh? It was another teacher, and he leaned towards Mr Tambourine Man and Armpits, I know that song you're talking about, aye, it's a really catchy tune, I love it, it's my daughter who plays it, don't know where she got hold of it from, but she's playing it in the house all the time at the moment, must be off a film or TV programme or eighties collection or something, aye, catchy tune! The teacher finished talking and looked at Mr Tambourine Man and Armpits.

Armpits nodded, aye.

Aw god sake man, Mr Tambourine Man was smiling, of course your daughter likes it, of course she likes the tune, the effing tune! He grinned, but I'm talking about more than just a melody though, don't you think there's something, I don't know, transcendental about the whole experience of listening to the music? The whole song, the thing!

Armpits stared at Mr Tambourine Man.

Mr Tambourine Man stared back, well?

And Armpits said well, I was talking about the fucking great melody too, Oblivous, it's got a great melody!

The pair of them laughed and the other teacher went back to what he was doing, saying he didn't know the song was called Oblivious, he'd always thought it was called I hear your footsteps in the street. Mr Tambourine Man and Armpits ignored him.

Melody, aye so you were, Mr Tambourine Man shook his head and looked at Armpits, you need to look deeper into what you're hearing man eh! Armpits leaned back, burped, scratched his stomach and said don't let me puncture your pomposity mate.

The pair smiled and the bell rang.

…

There was an English teacher who was saying he had a girl from England who had just started in his class in the fifth year, he looked at the staff he was standing with, it'll give me an excuse to start teaching a bit of Shakespeare again, her being English, she says she studied Romeo and Juliet and The Merchant of Venice at her old school, aye, she's just new, some of you might have taught her already, nice lassie she is, and he nodded, aye, Shakespeare, that's what it's all about. A few other heads nodded, aye, yeah, I know her, yeah, seen her around. Shakespeare bit into his biscuit and continued, anyway, it's been interesting to see our kids' reaction to her, asking her about England and what she thought of Scotland and so on.

People looked at him, oh aye, what was she saying to it then? Shakespeare said well, the girl hadn't really said much, just about this town looking a wee bit different from where she came from, Nuneaton she's from, Warwickshire yeah, I asked her if she knew about George Eliot but she didn't. Anyway, and he went on, she didn't say a lot about Scotland being different from England, just about this town being different from her old home, her old hometown, as if there was no difference between Scotland and England, know?

Shakespeare continued talking about what the girl's situation had made him think about, aye, imagine how any of our kids would survive if they went to school in England and they were the only Scottish person there! He nodded, suddenly they'd be in the minority yeah, they'd think of themselves as being

31

Scottish in amongst loads of English, some of them would practically have a nose-bleed, and yet this girl hasn't batted an eyelid once, she doesn't feel different, know? Or at least, she says she doesn't, just gets on with it, know?

A few people joined in the discussion, though most didn't. Somebody said something about being in a group that gets called the others by everyone else. Somebody else mentioned otherness.

Aye, people agreed, otherness.

…

Crossword Freak Number One and Crossword Freak Number Two were discussing whether Prussia was still Prussia in the seventeen-hundreds or not, and if it was, then could Kant be called a German writer, Crossword Freak Number One qualified the question, that is, a German philosopher and not a Prussian one?

Bicycle Clips was brought in to settle the thing but he just began on the notion of nationalism in Germany, the history aspect, and about the idea that when Kant was writing, there was no such thing as nationalism, at least in Germany, he shook his head, eh, sorry Prussia, tss! Bicycle Clips clasped his hands, or any of the German states for that matter, they numbered around three-hundred at that point, Napoleon still had to invade and whittle them down to thirty-nine, Beethoven hadn't yet written his symphonies, the Grimm brothers weren't even near collating their folk-tales, Bismarck hadn't forged the Emms telegram. He drew breath, ergo, em, hee hee! Bicycle Clips stuck a couple of fingers up to his mouth and placed them between his lips, tapped his teeth and shook his head as he laughed.

Crossword Freak Number One challenged him, but you said the German states, German, not Prussian. He crossed his arms, so he was a German, Kant then, that is, German, as in a German philosopher, thinker? You did say the German states. Could Kant be described as German then?

Em, I meant, aye, I see what you mean, but I mean German-speaking, I meant German, as in German-speaking, Bicycle Clips said he thought Crossword Freak Number One had understood that, that Bicycle Clips hadn't been talking about German identity as such, just the language, it was a language thing. He reached under his sock and rubbed his leg, so, he was a de facto German, Kant, possibly, tss!

Crossword Freak Number One said he did, he understood, he had understood. Crossword Freak Number Two looked from Bicycle Clips to Crossword Freak Number One and back to Bicycle Clips again, does that mean we can have Kant as the solution?

Crossword Freak Number One looked at Bicycle Clips as Bicycle Clips kept talking about the growth of nationalism in Germany to someone else who had just sat down amongst the group of them, and nodded to Crossword Freak Number Two, who scribbled the answer down.

…

As the man stood there, he would be saying, once again, that pace is what it is, aye, pace is what you need nowadays if you want to make it as a whatsit, a professional, it's all about pace. He held his mug and watched the steam come out of it, every so often raising it to his mouth to blow the steam away, he would stick his tongue out of his mouth a bit before doing so, almost touching the rim of the mug.

People speaking about him said he was a talent scout for Dundee, or had been at some time, then they questioned themselves, or was it Dundee United? They would nod or shake their heads, aye, naw, but anyway not one of the lower league teams, and not a top side, at least not a top side anymore, not these days, but a well-known one, still. Or anyway, he used to be, he maybe still did a bit every now and then, they thought, the way he spoke made you think he went to games with somebody from a football club, it was a thing like that.

Somebody would be sitting next to Scout but not looking at him as he stood drinking his coffee.

See, it's pace boy, that's all managers look for nowadays, pace, and he blew over his mug again, in young players that is, boys, schoolboys, the talent-spotters get sent to look for fast runners, that's all. Scout didn't say a thing for a minute, and neither did the other person, then Scout looked out of the window and back in again, the skills and that, that can be worked on later, that's what managers seem to think.

He lifted his mug to his mouth and opened his lips, then screwed his eyes up. He paused, and blew again. He waved his arm slowly in the air as he talked about skills not being needed that much anymore, naw, not required in the modern game anyway in my opinion, if you just look at all the most successful sides, in Europe as well like, not just in Scotland and England, and I mean consistently successful, they've all got three or four massive guys just stuck in the team for their speed, or physical presence, no kind of ability or anything, just big whatsits, know!

When Scout finished his sentence he looked at the person sitting next to him, eh? Aye I know, bad stuff, the other guy said, and put his mug down and said to Scout so, how's the world of Modern Studies anyway these days, eh?

And before Scout replied, before he could respond in actuality, the other teacher said well, I'll have to get to my class now, wee buggers'll be running around the room if I'm too late.

Scout continued as his colleague got up, I mean, I'm not saying there aren't skilful players around the now. Just. He watched the teacher get up and leave. He nodded after him, aye sure, don't let me slow you down now, and Scout waved him towards the door, then smiled for a second before looking at his coffee, blowing across the surface and drinking it all in one go.
…

One of the posters made by pupils and displayed on the wall outside the Music department, on the way out the back of the building, had a cut-out picture of a sculpture of Bruckner's head stuck on to it, beside a drawing of Bruckner's head as well, with his name written above it and 1824-1896 underneath it. There were other posters too, Wagner, Schubert, and a heading in bubble-writing over the whole of the display, saying Composers and Musicians by the Third Year Standard Grade Music Class, under which pupils had written bits and pieces about a variety of composers and musicians.

Look at that, him over there, Bruckner, Bicycle Clips indicated the poster, and he spoke about how he'd read that Bruckner had numeromania, did you know that, tss? And, he raised both his hands in animation, aye, Bruckner, he did, some of his writing showed the obsession with numbers, and the numbers on the bars, know, the bars in the music, were significant in a way, some kind of way, there was no hidden code or anything for anyone else to work out when they hear the music, the listener doesn't have to decipher anything, just listen to the music I suppose, but the numbers on the bars, they meant something to Bruckner. Bicycle Clips reiterated the point, adding that what he said would mean more to musicians, he didn't even understand himself what he'd read about Bruckner.

There was no answer that was given, or no response to the thing, from anybody in attendance.

All the time Bicycle Clips was staring at the poster, he had stopped walking and was standing, staring, commenting, fierce looking isn't he, that baldness as well, doesn't help. Bicycle Clips turned, makes him seem a real hard man eh, even in a pupils' drawing eh, and he turned to the other side, saying aye, numeromania that right? Your man there, numeromania, Bruckner?

Mr Tambourine Man had just appeared, and he stopped and looked, who, Bruckner? Aye it is, aye, numeromania, you're right. He raised his eyebrows, aye, Bruckner, bit of a maniac alright. Mr Tambourine Man blinked, aye, I play a couple of his pieces to the kids sometimes, that one with the hunting horns, they love that eh! He looked at the poster, I've had the music all lined up a couple of times in the past for difficult classes, and just release the pause button and blast it out at them if they're getting noisy, jump out their effing skins, so they do, looking around at each other like frightened animals, for definite!

Bicycle Clips said of course, and the fact that this picture's a sculpture doesn't help soften the image, something about sculptures, eh, tss!

Mr Tambourine Man continued to look at the poster, hands in his pockets, lifting his toes up and down, aye, well.

Bicycle Clips turned and looked, and then turned again and looked at Mr Tambourine Man, I'm saying, sculptures, they make people look awful hard, don't they, even if they're not, it's just, sculptures.

Mr Tambourine Man said mm, and then he paused, then, there was that other guy who was obsessed with colours, and when he wrote his music, em, who was it now? There was a pause. Bicycle Clips reached inside his shirt and scratched his stomach, I don't know, I haven't heard of anyone like him. Mr Tambourine Man answered his own question, saying he forgot but he'd remember soon.

Bicycle Clips turned, right then, we'll head up to the department eh.

And Mr Tambourine Man walked away, away from Bicycle Clips and into the Music corridor, whistling It's All Over Now Baby Blue.

2. THE FALL OF HONEST RAIN

The sign saying Senior Management Office had the words Open Plan written underneath it, these words were in brackets. And the office was in that style, the Phantom sat at a desk that had at the front of it a placard saying Deputy Rector, propped up on either side by a paperweight with the school crest on it and a box of reminder notes.

The Phantom said his seat, the position of it in the office, allowed him to look out the window, into the rector's office, or at least towards the rector's office door so he could see who was coming in and who was going out. It also let him speak to the other assistant heads in the office when they weren't teaching, and it would be them that would have to turn round in their chairs to have the conversation with him. He said that assistant heads is what they get called at the moment, aah, their job title keeps getting changed, you see!

This morning he was smiling, come in, come in, dear boy! Coffee, tea if you want, I can get one of the office ladies to put the kettle on, though we'll just be a few minutes so it's not really worth it, aah, yes, well let's just leave it then, the coffee. Now, got your name here somewhere, and he was lifting bits of paper up and swapping one pile of letters with another, now then, where are my glasses, I must stop, em.

And he found them, aah, here they are, aah, here we are, yes, I thought so, History is it. He held a piece of paper halfway off the desk and looked up, History? Yes, of course it is, eh! Then he said em, now, em, aah, the reason I wanted to have this little chat was to explain why your timetable has had more of that class of fourth years you've been teaching recently put on to it. And he looked beyond his office door.

The Bin Brigade yes, though you won't hear me calling them that, they are a proper class, and they do get taught proper lessons. He lifted the back of his hand to his mouth and coughed on it, excuse me. Em, we, aah, don't have a group like it in the third year, decided it wasn't the best way forward, but once we had this group started, well, you see, it was easier to carry on with them than try to re-integrate them back into normal, aah, I should say, timetabled, classes. He fidgeted with his Deputy Rector placard. It's also, really just that we're a bit short-staffed at present, and, well frankly, it's good experience for you.

He paused, is that alright? The thing is, we could give them to somebody else on the staff, but again, quite frankly, their expertise would be wasted, we need our best teachers creating heady atmospheres in the classroom, put all our resources where they'll be most effective, you see?

So, you'll still have plenty of History, don't worry, and this is a big responsibility, I won't forget to include it on your final report when your ten weeks are up, what is it, just before Easter yes, the Wednesday before?

Anyway, and he looked up as one of the women who worked in the office came into the room with a cup of tea, there was a biscuit on the edge of the saucer. Aah, thank-you, and he turned and said aah, wonderful ladies we have in our office, yes, aah, I'd asked for this shortly before you came in. He took a drink, and as he sat the cup down he half-whispered aah, that's better!

He banged both hands on the edge of his desk, it was the front of his fingers that made the contact, and said right, so that's us got that sorted out, if you'll excuse me, I now need to make a couple of announcements on the tannoy and then go and see a few heads of departments about timetables, and he sat back and took a bite of his digestive.

…

Billy wrote on his knuckles sometimes, with a marker-pen, the writing on them wasn't there every day. He told some people that he had tattoos, folk who maybe didn't see him a lot or who hadn't met him before. He didn't have tattoos, he could be seen drawing on his hands at times. His knuckles said 1873 GERS if he clenched both fists and held his arms out.

He always smiled at whoever was looking at them, and he spoke about Rangers, aye, says right there, see, formed in the momentous year of eighteen-seventy-three, the greatest football club in the world, I'm telling you, it's been proved, it's been proved they've got the biggest support worldwide, I'm telling you, Scottish people who live abroad, they support Rangers and not Celtic, it's been proved. And he nodded.

Then he looked at his mates around him and sang the words or lines that opened a song, any song, about Rangers. He smiled, the teddy boys eh! And banging his knuckles together, hitting his fists off the table, hullo, hullo! His friends would smile back but they wouldn't join in. He looked at his knuckles, aw, look man, perfecto!

In the class sometimes Billy would lean back on his chair, pushing himself away from his desk with one hand while looking at the tattoo on the other, then swap and look at the hand he'd pushed himself backwards first with. He grinned at whichever pupil was sitting next to him and showed him or her his knuckles.

40

Then he would lean forward and take part in the lesson, taking part in the discussions that went on, saying a lot about whatever subject the class was being taught, offering his opinion and asking questions. He might take a moment to examine his knuckles again, and then re-enter the lesson.

…

Mary Queen of Scots got her head chopped off! Some of the pupils in the class laughed together, aw, aye, mind how we used to do that at primary with a dandelion or something and you could hold the stalk and do a karate chop on the flower and the head would snap off?

The Bin Brigade could all remember, ha! Most times it didn't fall off, it just hung off by a thread, didn't it!

They were learning about Mary Queen of Scots after they had said that they had all heard of her but no-one knew anything much about her, one of them had a cousin in England who had been up for the weekend, and she'd said she'd learned about Mary Queen of Scots at school there, in Coventry.

Man, imagine that, Billy said, isn't it rubbish that the English get taught more Scottish history than Scottish pupils, ourselves! The rest said that's not true, we learn plenty, just no about Mary Queen of Scots, and we canni learn everything! Billy said they knew what he meant, he shook his head, know, never mind, forget it. The others said so, you're still wrong anyway. Billy ignored them, squinted his mouth, as well as one eye, and looked at the wall for a second.

And so, they began then, a couple of lessons of work on Mary Queen of Scots. They couldn't understand the connection with France, how come she was queen of France sir? But they did enjoy her life story, the names of the Dauphin, Darnley, Riccio, Bothwell, they all got written down, and the pupils hooted, my god all that marriage and lovers stuff sir, nae wonder she couldni manage to run the country, aye too busy in the bed, or just knackered, heh heh!

The Bin Brigade looked at each other, I wish we'd learned about her every year instead of William Wallace, at least she got to be queen! And then they studied her stay at Carlisle Castle, being taken prisoner by the English, just as she was enjoying their hospitality, man she well got taken in there sir, didn't she! Then there were the letters, the poetry, all in French, eh sir, she must have been well brainy!

But they didn't take to James VI. They never liked him, especially after they found out he hadn't done anything when Mary Queen of Scots did in fact get her head chopped off, my god, his own mother sir! And he just went and made an alliance with England, just like that!

Billy said to Kevin, imagine that Kev, hey, wake up Kev, listen to this man, James VI, his own mother, executed, and he does nothing, not much of a star man there, eh! Kevin rubbed his eyes and said yeah, it's terrible. Then he didn't say anything more. He looked Billy in the eye.

Billy half-punched Kevin's arm and said eh, sorry Kevin I didni realise. And then he said, I mean I do realise but I just forgot, I just forgot, for definite I did, honest.

Kevin said it's okay, forget it Billy.

…

They were called the Bin Brigade because they sometimes emptied the bins around the school, bins outside, or ones in corridors. Not everyone called them the Bin Brigade, usually teachers referred to them as that, and some pupils had picked up on it and sometimes referred to them as that, but people, teachers and pupils, generally didn't have cause to refer to them a lot, so the words Bin Brigade weren't heard that much. But it was known that this was who they were. The Bin Brigade.

They were a class, in actuality, staff would speak about the group as the Bin Brigade. They might say aye, that lad's in the Bin Brigade, or see that lassie, Bin Brigade. Or it could be, aw Christ I've got the Bin Brigade next period, shit. Maybe a comment would even be hey, there they go, the Bin Brigade look at them, bunch of wasters!

People agreed on the origin of the Bin Brigade, it had been during or right after the last time the school was inspected, over a year ago, when some third year pupils who had dropped some of their exam subjects had been found at a variety of times during the week walking around the school doing nothing, and something had to be done to keep them from disrupting classes they were no longer taking, or at least they had to be kept out of sight, or at least be contained somewhere where they couldn't affect the other pupils. Teachers would say you know son, the normal ones!

So then the class was formed and the pupils were given books and things to help them work on whichever subjects they were still doing. There were about ten to fifteen of them, it wasn't a matter of the definite, mostly boys, only two maybe three girls, attending some classes but not others, and for the most time being together in whatever classroom was not being used by other classes at the time. They didn't all

43

stay as one group all the time as a necessity, it depended on which classes were on at the time, though as much as the timetable could manage, they were all kept together, a unit.

Some staff said see this, it's not right. They said these pupils were getting denied an education, having to work on their own with teachers just taking it in turns to be supervising them. You can't deny it, others might say, but here, would you want them in your class! And the reply would be aye, naw!

Most staff said they didn't want the pupils of the Bin Brigade in their classrooms, as individuals or as a group.

The Phantom would say though, in staff meetings, that, you see, keeping them together as a unit will develop their social skills, they'll come to rely on each other, you see, develop, develop a sense of cameraderie, you see? Staff nodded and looked at each other and stopped nodding.

During and at the end of such staff meetings, Armpits would say hey, see the Bin Brigade, they're just mad bastards, and then hoot with laughter along with whoever he was talking to.

Then there would be a silence around him as he would develop a point, aye, but they're okay, honest kids, decent too, no like some of the stuck up wee shites we have here eh, and those stuck up wee shites just say anything they want to the Bin Brigade because they can't say anything back, if they get into trouble they're out of school, that's it, goodbye, dropped from any subjects they might still be doing, won't get presented for exams or anything, and some of them might need a couple of qualifications, basics, Maths or English but, just to get into a wee job or something, a training scheme maybe. Armpits sighed, so they just have to take any abuse that gets hurled at them from the stuck up wee shites, or it's goodbyee, wipe the tear from your eyee.

Some people who were still hanging around nodded as Armpits shook his head, aye, their parents don't know even know that its even going on, or if they do they don't know that it's probably violating their kids' human rights, Christjesus.

Then Armpits said to the last person remaining, if there was one, nah, I like teaching and all, I like my classes, overall, but give me the Bin Brigade over any of these stuck up wee shites we have here. Then he turned, I mean it, if you get more chances to take them son, make the most of them. And when you get the kids in a room, don't give them something to do while you get on with your marking or redrafting your university essays, teach them, actually teach them, they'll work for you, they understand. Don't not teach them son, teach them.

…

When the bell went one day and the Bin Brigade came in, a few of them were teasing William about his dad being a bin-lorry driver. William was saying shut up yous, how, what's it to yous anyway? Aw, never mind William, Billy ruffled William's hair as he passed his chair.

William pushed his hand away, there's no need to patronise me on the head Billy!

Ha ha, patronise me on the head, Billy repeated, and he hooted, you're so funny William! Billy looked around the class, you mean just, there's no need to patronise you, or there's no need to pat you on the head, how can I patronise you on the head! William turned

45

the other way, get lost, he caught a couple of other pupils' eyes and turned away from them also, sitting with his chin resting on his hand, alternating from one hand to the other and and then back again with his arms, leaning them on the desk with his elbows.

Billy then turned away from facing William and shouted out hey sir, was it Ronnie Donegan who sang My Old Man's A Dustman sir! William took his hand away from his mouth and started smiling, he turned to Billy and said aw man, it was Lonnie, Lonnie Donegan, sure it was sir, wasn't it, and he looked across at Billy, remember we had to listen to him in first year Music!

The others in the class remembered, aye, and second year, that stand-in guy that kept playing it to us, ha ha! William continued, aye Lonnie Donegan, what else was it, Elvis Presley, Cliff Richard! The class were smiling at William, and he continued, and mind one of the days when the normal teacher was off, how we had to draw those posters advertising a fifties night for an old folks' home or something like that, with rock'n'roll and skittle bands. That old supply teacher loved making us do that!

Billy said aye, remember! Hee hee, the fifties night posters! And it was skiffle ya daftie! He grinned, that right sir? William was laughing now as well, aye, skiffle it was, and then the next lesson when the supply teacher was there again, James got given lines as a punishment, just 'cause he'd drawn a picture of Elvis Presley wearing a tartan shirt and holding a washboard, the teacher took the huff, thought James was taking the mickey!

The Bin Brigade looked at James and laughed, William smiled at him, at James, and you'd just got mixed up, hadn't you James, ah James, hee hee! James

46

just smiled. William patted him on the head, ya big daftie James, and James parried William's arm away.

Billy continued the story, looking all around the class as he spoke, yeah, then when James did the lines and handed them in the next lesson after that, he got given even more because the supply teacher had found another picture he'd done and it was a drawing of Lonnie Donegan in a kilt with his hair greased back, with Lonnie Donegan the Scottish Elvis Presley written above it in huge letters, perfecto! The class giggled as Billy continued, the teacher went mad, saying how rock'n'roll and skiffle were completely different, and anyhow it was the Irish hillbilly James should have written! Billy shook his head and smiled, he was furious, the teacher, like it was important! Billy looked at James, ha, James thought he was being dead clever with the Scottish Elvis thing, but the supply guy just went on about how anyhow even though Lonnie Donnegan was born in Glasgow, he was more or less English in the end, because of his parents moving to London, nae luck James!

And the class laughed while James smiled and shook his head. Billy looked at James, aw sorry James, star man though! William was digging James in the ribs with his elbows, then when James tried to deflect William's arms or to shove him away, William poked his fingers into his chest, ah James!

…

Sir why've we got to learn about this? Faces looked up, looking at where the question came from. The question was repeated, the question, it was from Sam, he looked around the class before going on, I mean sir, why are we learning about this whole James VI and Andrew Melville thing, James VI versus

47

Andrew Melville, I mean who cares! How come we have to do any history anyway, all that was three hundred years ago, what's it got to do with anything, with today!

Aw Sam, just because you've got chucked out of History man, Billy waved his arm at him, you've had something against it ever since, ha ha! Then from another part of the classroom someone said aye, shut up Sam, anyway can you no count? Four hundred, not three hundred years ago man, at least that!

Sam said well, I'm gonni join the army, me, for definite, and I won't be needing History or anything, so there, just shut up yourselves.

Then William sat up and started to participate in the class now, taking the conversation back to Sam's question about History, aye how come sir, what's the point!

History, it was, History, that was what Sam and William wanted to know the point of, they wanted to know the point of the thing.

From Sam there came the question, sir, I don't know how people say there could be two kingdoms in one country with just one king, how was that? Then he looked about at the pupils around him, sitting near him, but anyway, who really wants to know anyway! Eh? Hands up who wants to know! He looked around the class, see sir! Nobody! Sam looked down again, aye sorry sir.

A few laughs were heard. People were looking around, not really saying anything.

Sam then continued, it's just, I mean, two kingdoms, or what was it, the twa kingdomes, twa! More laughter again was heard. Billy said aye, twa kingdomes man, how come they say it like that, it's written like that on the poster on the board sir, look! They all looked at the front of the room, yeah, yeah, twa kingdomes sir!

A couple of pupils got pen and paper out of their bags and stared scribbling things down, then one of them leaned on his hand and stared out the window.

Sam sighed, so are we just gonni keep on learning about that again, now? And he kept going, look at the poster on the board, what's it say? And he screwed his eyes up and read it out, the struggle, for, control over, education, in Scotland in, the, 1580s and, 1590s, James VI, James VI versus Andrew Melville. The struggle for control. In the fifteen-hundreds? What about the struggle for control now? Is there no a struggle for control now? Doesn't that have something more to do with our lives, know? He shook his head, plus everything in History's made-up anyway, they just make it up to sell books and make people believe things about stuff that never happened, or happened differently to what it says in History books, eh.

Billy told Sam to shut up, stop being such a moaner Sam, then he announced, two kingdoms in modern day Scotland! Eh? Aye, my dad's always saying there's two halves of the country, it's a divided country, don't know if he's talking about a struggle over education though. Just, well, rich and poor. But he says one half's bigger than the other though.

The conversation fizzled out, and then someone else in the class said Sam, Billy, can we no get on, come on, sir's waitin!

…

Did you hear about that MP dying, he's the guy for this place yeah? Someone standing in the staffroom had heard on his car radio at lunchtime about an MP's

49

death, it was news that was just breaking. Another teacher said no, never heard that, em, been in here all lunch mind, so. Someone else said, aye? Our MP? You mean the school's?

Then there was a bit of a debate going on about the thing amongst the three or four people in the staffroom, the guy who died had the same name as another MP, or sounded like it. The teacher who had heard the news on the radio was unsure which one had died.

So it became the talking point for the staff, they're both from round here aren't they eh, the guys with the same names? Well one's from around here, and the other's the MP for here. The one from round here is an MP in Edinburgh isn't he? Don't ask me, I'm from Glasgow, and I don't even know who my own MP is, man!

Then they discussed the effects of the death, if he is from here there'll be a by-election, yeah?

There'll be a by-election wherever he's from!

Aye I know, I mean, just, just that the by-election would mean a day off, for us!

How?

Well, doesn't the school get used as a polling station?

Aye, so it does, it does! And it's used for the count, aye, you're right, a day off!

Only if the guy's from here though.

Naw, only if the guy's the MP for here. If he's just from here, then he's the MP for somewhere else, that's where the by-election will be, and no day off for us, just some lucky bandits in an Edinburgh school.

What party was he anyway?

Which one?

50

The guy from, the guy who's the MP for here.

Och, I don't know, does it make a difference but?

Hmmf!

There was a bit of a silence, then someone half-burped, excuse me.

Then they started talking again, hey, you heard they're asking for half a million pounds to pay for the rebuilding of the science wing eh? Aye, they could bite the bullet and rebuild the whole place if the council had the bottle. Maybe the new MP will push for something like that. Aye. Maybe if there's a few ambitious candidates they'll mention it in the campaign eh. As long as they don't veer off the party line eh!

And if it's our guy who's died, ha!

…

Aw, you're always going on about getting a job, William! As if none of us are gonni get a job eh! The class were sitting on the chairs all round the room but William was at the centre of the conversation, a kind of subject of the debate. They berated him about his claims to be the only pupil in the class who had the chance of employment.

William was shaking his head and saying aye, he was gonni get a job, and they could just wait and see. His brother would sort it for him, aye, and I'll be an upholsterer when I grow up, yous'll see alright! I'll be an upholsterer, you'll see!

Someone in the class asked the question, had William's brother not been chucked out the house the week before, has he not William? William said naw he's no! It was just that his brother had moved out. Billy said aye, your mum's boyfriend kicked him out, I heard.

And people stopped smiling and looked at him, some said Billy, hey, Billy, come on Billy.

Just shut it man, William looked at Billy, just shut it Billy, will you.

Billy smiled and looked round at everyone, then leaned back on his chair, wobbling a bit, and said okay okay, I'm sorry William, sorry.

William said again, just shut it, only now he wasn't looking at Billy, he wasn't looking at anyone in the class, he was looking at his desk.

…

Armpits asked so, have you joined a union yet son? Folk laughed at him after he said this, asking how, can you not give the boy a chance yet, and god sake, straight in there isn't he, doesn't hang about!

Armpits said Christjesus, and said that if it wasn't for him, the place, or the staffroom here at least, it would be like a morgue, aye, he nodded, or more like one than fucking it is already! Then, naw seriously son, and he said to come and see him, he looked around and then back again, if you do think about it, know, joining the union, and just ignore they bastards and all. The rest of them went hmmf, exchanged glances for a second and then went back to what they were doing.

He went on, I've got all the necessary shite like, leaflets and crap, all the stuff I'm supposed to give you, know, but you just fill in a form basically, and they send you lots of bumf through the post anyway. He pursed his lips and sighed, but I can give you the literature if you want. You're still a student aren't you, bound to be willing to join in the great fight eh, you students, well, I say great fight, more a wee skirmish of a lost cause, but you students though, always ones for a lost cause eh!

People around said god sake again, and spoke about how Armpits thought everything was a fight, aye, you're always saying everything's part of the great fight, but doesn't being a History teacher mean you know that great fights are never won? Some were laughing.

Armpits said aye, I know it, I know it, don't I fucking know it, and if some of you hadni voted for Thatcher in seventy-nine or the fucking nineteen-eighties, fucking aye, aye, and he nodded at them and smiled and turned his head, look there son, look at them, well may they hang their heads in ugly shame, Christjesus, aye. And I'm fucking right am I not, eh? And now! If it wasni for fuckers like me! See what I mean son, fucking ashamed so they are, look eh, ashamed, and so they should be! He grinned as he raised his voice and indicated his colleagues.

You're a poor soul said someone, people were laughing, shaking their heads.

Including Armpits, aye, fucking poor's the correct term there, Christjesus, you're no wrong!

…

A criticism that was made by some teachers of the Bin Brigade pupils was that they looked after their own interests, they didn't realise the part they had to play in the scheme of the school, or where they should fit in. Teachers would comment, aye, the pupils in the Bin Brigade are selfish.

People would say look, look at them walking through the school, swinging those rubbish bags about like they own the place, they're basically bloody selfish them, that group of pupils, they haven't got a clue why they're doing what they're doing, swinging those rubbish bags about like they're something special.

Some people thought that when the Bin Brigade walked around the school tidying up, they gave the impression that they thought they were above everybody else, because of the fact they got to walk around the school tidying up, and this made them think they were above everybody who didn't get to walk around the school tidying up. Then some people would say aye, that lot should try and remember where they fit in to this place, and realise that what they're doing now is what they're going to be doing for the rest of their lives, eh. Walking around, swinging their rubbish bags about like they're special, like they own the place, like they're better than everybody else.

However, sometimes in the car park, sometimes, but not often, someone might suggest something about a boy or girl in the Bin Brigade, something along the lines of em, you know, do you not think that boy might have to be selfish because of not having a lot getting thrown his way in life, or having a lot taken away from him, know, maybe a lot of them in the Bin Brigade are like that, they have to look out for themselves 'cause no-one else ever has, or they think no-one else ever has.

And while the other teachers hearing this would just stand and not move, holding the car door handles as they listened, the guy speaking might continue, I mean, we don't know, but, just, given their condition, know, they might have to be selfish, know?

As the other teachers looked at each other, considering the point that anyone in the Bin Brigade would need to adopt some subjectivity sometimes, the teacher might go on to venture as to how it would be a necessity for the pupils of the Bin Brigade to possess a self-interest, and staff would prepare to get into their cars speculating on the idea of William or Billy

54

examining their own place in the world, ignoring the place of all others around them.

But such a teacher as one who would venture to speak up for the Bin Brigade in this way would have their thoughts greeted by the derision of the other staff collapsing into driving seats and passengers seats and back seats, aw, come on listen to you man, speaking up for them, the Bin Brigade, Jesus Christ, you think any of these kids would even look at you as they cross the street to avoid you once they're old enough to leave school? And you're speaking up for them!

There was nodding and agreement, aye, they opted to leave some of these classes, they could've chosen differently, they've all made their choices, however stupid they were, now they have to live with them.

The thing was also though, that everyone getting into a car would be aware that many teachers had said at one time or another that whenever they had the Bin Brigade in their class, or some of the times, they had acquired quite an impression of the way all the pupils got on with each other, the teachers would report oh aye, they take the piss and everything, and you've got to keep on top of them, but they do stand up for each other, it's like, they maybe do know what their place in society is going to be, so the last thing that's going to happen is that they have a real go at each other, they won't condemn each other, to be philosophical about it!

Nobody really said that they accepted the notion that the Bin Brigade didn't ever have a go at each other, or each others' actions, but for the few minutes while people put briefcases in boots and piled themselves into cars, nobody had any criticisms to make about them.

…

On the wall there were notices about union meetings. It was always Armpits who put them up, and he always told people what he was doing it as he did it, he would stand on a chair and put the notice up and say aye, that's me putting a notice up, and he would look at the person he was talking to and then look at the notice. The person would then look at the notice, then walk away, still glancing at it, then sitting down and not looking at it anymore once Armpits turned to face the wall again.

When he was putting a notice up, Armpits would turn his head round as he stretched his hands to put the drawing pins into the noticeboard, and he would see that in the staffroom no-one was looking at him. Maybe he didn't have the number of pins required to hand, so he sometimes located a pin on the salary-scale sheet that was up on the wall, took it out and doubled it up on the meeting notice too, so that one pin was holding two posters up.

Then Armpits said fuck if a pin fell onto the floor, and he would have to ask someone to get it while he held the notice or the two notices onto the wall with one hand, the other stretching down to reach the pin whenever it was going to be passed up to him. He might look around to catch someone's eye in order to indicate that he needed assistance with the thing.

Someone might come by and help him out, then ask him what he was doing standing on a chair, and he would say well, as well as trying to be the bigger person in this place, I'm just putting a notice up.

…

The school social worker had been doubling up as the school's attendance officer, in the car she said that the school's attendance officer had hurt her back

56

falling down some stairs, she'd been visiting a truant's flat while the pupil had been dogging it. Now the attendance officer was off school.

The social worker said her job was a bit like these guys who drive around in vans catching dogs in America, though she laughed saying darling, the only thing is I get paid better mileage than them, know, travel expenses! Half the kids I see in my line of work are doggers anyway, so, so I'm talking to them about the same stuff, mostly anyway. Just like the dog-catchers in America, me!

The Dog-Catcher looked at her watch, got a meeting tonight back in the school, just have time to put something in the microwave at home, I'll drop you off at the end of the road, that okay? Thanks darling, I'm just in a wee bit of a rush, need to be better organised, always telling myself that, this okay here, end of the road?

As she was about to pull away she put her Coke can down on the seat between her legs and wound down the window, shouting out, the other thing is, it's that they vote for the dog-catchers in America, don't they, though I don't think the kids would vote for me, and that's for definite!

…

When folk were talking about the by-election coming up, people tended to bring Scout into the discussion, if he was around, sometimes, often, just prior to leaving the discussion themselves.

Or Scout would come and sit in on the discussion, then begin participating at a point in the thing. Someone would say something about him being a Modern Studies teacher, and how he would know a bit more than everyone else, you teach it, I mean, you'll naturally know a little more than us so, so, and they asked if he could answer this, or if not, could he answer that.

Scout would look ahead before offering answers to their questions on the by-election, and after some debate he would bring in sub-topics, maybe by way of using a football analogy, a question of the rules of the game, or the notion of loyalty from a football player, the issues of professionalism, and loyalty shown to a team which gives a footballer his first wage, or perhaps he would expound upon the issue of dilemmas faced by referees when confronted by cheating, the morals involved in the thing, these were linked to issues, Scout would say aye, it's all political, boy.

Folk would sip their coffee or tea, and take more sips, and take yet more sips as Scout spoke. Some might walk away. Sometimes Scout would end up talking about football to the person who'd asked him the question about the by-election in the first place, and he would comment on the conversation itself, hang on, were we not talking of electoral law, or local representation or parliamentary whatsit? And the others around, in other parts of the staffroom, would continue the debate of politics themselves. This would be if they hadn't moved onto another subject. Or if the bell hadn't gone.

Scout would finish by looking around, getting up, not saying anything, walking over to the sink and stand still before leaving his cup there, still, steam rising from the drink still in it.

…

If the staffroom conversation was about Celtic and Rangers, people might talk about the fact that the next match would be a title decider, aye, mark my words, a six-pointer. Then someone would say hey, you see that eejit on the telly last night? Talking pish, eh, talk about an easy life, a has-been, or never-has-been more like, making money out of talking pish! Not enough that he spent his entire career playing pish football, now he has to talk pish about it! People nodded, again.

Or the thing might be the cost of petrol, aye man, recent events in the Middle East will be pushing it up bloody further, and when it's all over, or at least subsided for a week or so, they'll no be as quick pegging the price back again! Bloody religion man, cause of it all, that right, eh? That right?

And they'd look at Ex-Cop.

They would look at Ex-Cop, and Ex-Cop would would look up, and he'd first say eh, you're asking me? Then after one or two people who might still looking at him would blink a couple of times and maybe one of them might nod, he would say yeah, and clasp his hands and not say much more and they would all stop talking about religion.

The conversation could perhaps be about the school and what needed done with it, how the management ought to be working together, people complained, och, they've all got their own agenda, bloody senior team, aye, team, team, that's a joke eh, stabbing each other in the back, and stabbing all of us plebs in the chest and all, how can that ever be good for the school eh.

Football, petrol, religion, the school, the staffroom conversation at morning break could be about any of these things, or all of them, all of them in the space of fifteen minutes.

…

Kelly always asked if there was anything needed doing, or if there was a message to be taken to the office or anywhere, aw, I'll be disappointed if there isn't, isn't there anything, sir, no? You sure sir?

A lot of the boys in the class made jokes about Kelly during the lessons, and sometimes she turned round and said shut up to them, although she was still smiling and laughing when she faced the front again. She would sit there and sometimes tell the boys not to say anything, this was before they'd even said anything at all. So in response then they would say hey, we never even said anything yet Kelly! Their hands would be held out, eyes opened and not blinking.

Aye, yous were thinking about it, Kelly said, she said she could tell if they were thinking about it.

Then they would ask her if she was a mind-reader. She smiled and laughed.

There were other times when if somebody said something about her she didn't say anything back to them, she just asked excuse me sir, gonni tell them to shut up please, they're really bugging me. Then before anything could be said to the boys, she would turn round and scream stop yous! I'll kick you out of the building at lunch, you know I will so just shut up! Please, please, shut up, please.

If she spoke like this, perhaps with one tear appearing in her eye the boys would shut up, or talk amongst themselves, aye, naw, no let's give it a rest lads.

Kelly would smile at the girl sitting beside her, and talk to her while the boys settled down, I'm not really upset, I'm just, it's just. And she would sniff, aye, I suppose I was upset, and she would half-laugh, half-sneeze, and face the front as she wiped her nose,

60

then turn round and smile at the boys again, giving a
giggle as she did so.

…

Aw man, what a plook! Man! William was
talking about how much he admired the spot he was
pointing at on James's forehead, he looked at James,
aw, are you not tempted to burst it James, look at it, it's
a cracker! Any of you girls got a mirror! And William
looked around the class, telling them, look at it, what a
plook!

James shook his head and then waved his head
away from William's arm that kept stretching out
towards him, James tried to thrust his own arm out at
the same time to deflect William's. William laughed
and said come on James, let's go to the toilets now and
you can burst it onto the mirror, ha ha!

James waved William away again. Aw, come on
James, William said to him, you know it's the right
thing to do, you know it, aha! Do what you think is
right, James, do what you know is right!

You're disgusting William, leave him alone,
Kelly looked at William and shook her head once to the
left and once to the right, all the time keeping her eye
on James, then she looked down at her desk, then
looked up again and shook her head once to the left and
once to the right again, squinting her eyes and looking
at James's forehead.

I'm just saying, it looks like he's really looked
after it, know, William was laughing, yeah? He kept
laughing and looked across at Billy, what word was it
you said Billy, from the farmers, in that Geography
lesson once? Cultivating, Billy replied, grinning at
William. William replied aye, cultivating! William was

bouncing on his seat now, James has been cultivating his plook! Ha ha! And now it's ripe for the squeezing!

Billy was looking through his bag at the time, but could be heard to say aye, star man James, without looking up.

Kelly said again, just leave him alone, that's terrible, everybody gets a really bad spot now and then, I get them, and I've seen you with them William, so just shut up.

William kept laughing, and screwed his face up at Kelly, och, it's only James, Kelly!

Billy looked up, he was still grinning, and spoke to Kelly, aw Kelly, go and have a really good look and you'll think differently then, go on Kelly, have a look! But Kelly refused, and said to Billy naw Billy, don't you think it's embarrassing enough for someone to be walking about with a huge spot on their head without having their friends, or should I say so-called friends, all pointing it out to everybody and drawing attention to them, no way am I going to be staring at James and embarrassing him any further, I'm not that type of person. You should feel terrible, the pair of you.

Billy sighed, aye alright, and looked down. William shrugged his shoulders at Kelly and half-giggled. Billy smiled and shook his head and started to fidget with a pencil. William stared at his desk.

Then Kelly leaned over a bit and looked at James and away again, and then back again at him, she opened her eyes and kept them open, aw god, look at that, aargh! And then she was screeching, aargh! And leaning over her desk to hide behind the girl she was sitting beside, holding the girl's shoulders and leaning round to look at James.

William and Billy were hooting at Kelly now, she was putting her hands up to cover her eyes, peeping through the spaces between her fingers, aargh, get it away from me aargh! Other pupils started to laugh now, as Kelly kept screaming, aargh!

James said nothing as the class all laughed. James still said nothing.

William and Billy hooted even more at the thing as James sat and continued to say nothing and just looked at Kelly. And Kelly kept screeching, aargh, aargh! Get it away from me, aargh, mammy daddy!
…

Shakespeare was in the staffroom, saying there had been an article in the paper by an ex-pupil who'd left the school five or six years ago, he was writing about his experiences when he was at the school. Now he was living somewhere else, he'd made a success of himself in some field, research and such, worked at a university, taught mostly, but was writing books as well, according to some staff.

Here the ex-pupil was commenting on the school, it was part of an article he was doing for one of the nationals, a feature for a daily, someone said. Shakespeare and others spoke about the ex-pupil, he had passed all of his exams at the school and many had predicted that he would do the kind of thing he had ended up doing, everybody knew he would become a leader in his field, nobody expressed any surprise that here he was, in print.

People in the staffroom had all read the article and they would ask each other, have you read it? Aye, have you? Eh, you read that article in the local paper yet? Aye, have you? Interesting eh! You'd think the school was some kind of experiment, the way he speaks about it eh!

The Crossword Freaks conducted conversations about the article amongst themselves, though others could hear. Crossword Freak Number One related much of what the ex-pupil had written to his Open Uni coursework, that is, the ruling class requires labour, that is, something of an efficient workforce to perpetuate its own position in the hierarchy of society, and it is schooling that creates this workforce. That's the way I look at it, and I think that essentially that's what he's saying in his article, using the school as a microcosmic example.

Crossword Freak Number Two nodded and asked for an anagram of something.

I mean it's probably just what I've always thought since I started teaching, Crossword Freak Number One went on, and he continued to talk about how his view now was that the education system taught an ideology of morals, and that this view of his had developed over a period of time.

At this point both Armpits and Mr Tambourine Man looked at each other and shrugged their shoulders, and then continued to play cards. As he looked down, Mr Tambourine Man said that's his view, he's developed it over a period of time! Armpits laughed.

Crossword Freak Number One looked at them. Do you want to take part in this conversation gentlemen? Armpits laughed again, conversation? Sounds like it's a lecture, the ideology of morals man! Crossword Freak Number One looked at Crossword Freak Number Two who didn't look up.

Armpits challenged Crossword Freak Number One, do you even know who you're quoting there, the ruling class requiring labour, a workforce created by schooling, an ideology of morals? Crossword Freak Number One muttered that it was from a course textbook, written by one of the course leaders.

Well, if it is, and he's claiming to have come up with it, then it's fucking plagiarism, replied Armpits, because you my friend, you have been reading from a book written by somebody who knows they're plagiarising Althusser, but is pretending, badly, not to paraphrase Althusser.

I don't think so, Crossword Freak Number One started to shake his head, then stopped. You don't think so, eh, ha, Armpits looked back at Mr Tambourine Man and then at Crossword Freak Number One again, and what does your course textbook go on to say that the ideology of morals encourages?

Mr Tambourine Man looked at Crossword Freak Number One, and then looked away, back at the table, then looked up at Armpits. Crossword Freak Number One clicked the pen he was holding so the nib came out and in, out and in, em, I don't think, and he raised his eyebrows but didn't continue his sentence.

All the time Armpits had kept staring at him, and then he said submission, my friend, submission, is that not right, that's what it says? And he folded his arms, you read that bit of plagiarism yet?

Crossword Freak Number One said em, no.

Well, and Armpits talked through Crossword Freak Number One's answer, submission is encouraged, and not only that, but the schooling system which encourages that submission also manufactures young people who willingly participate in the perpetuation of the encouragement of that self-same submission, it actually creates politicians to be agents of capitalism in the future. You get it?

Armpits moved his neck outwards and his head towards Crossword Freak Number One. Crossword Freak Number One nodded and start to mutter something, he said he could see what Armpits was saying.

But Armpits interrupted to continue, this time turning away from Crossword Freak Number One and looking at Mr Tambourine Man, of course, Althusser doesn't provide enough evidence to convince me, but when he says stuff like agents of capitalism you can't help but admire his style eh, smug bastard!

…

So you wouldn't say this is a big country then? Billy kept asking about the size of Scotland in relation to Holland. Someone in the class, a boy, had said, or he'd seen it written in a football magazine, that Holland, the Netherlands they called it sir, it said it was a big football team, or one of the big football teams. And Billy couldn't understand, eh, how come Scotland isn't a big team or doesn't get called a big team, when Scotland's just about the same size as Holland?

William looked round, who were the other big teams Billy, in the magazine? Billy took the magazine off the boy's desk and looked at it, Germany, Italy, France, Spain, Holland, they're all the big countries, or each of them is a big country, there might be more, but how's Holland one?

You're a big team if you're a good team, I think, someone else in the class said.

Billy was looking at a map of Europe on the wall now, he got up and walked towards it, how come Belgium isn't a big team then? It's the same size as

Holland, look, they're right next to each other, and they're good, Belgium are, or they get into World Cups at least. And look at Russia man, the size of it! I never knew Russia was that big, it goes off the bloody map! Perfecto for Russia!

The class looked at him. He said, sorry sir.

The class looked at the map, and a few people commented, oh aye, I've never noticed that before either, Russia is big, aye, I thought Russia just stopped where the map stopped!

Someone else said they'd seen Russia on a world map and it was three times the size it looked on the map of Europe. The Bin Brigade looked at each other, and some exclaimed man, three times!

Billy said he remained in the same position with regard to the issue of football team, I'm still confused sir, sir, if people in Holland live in a big country, then so do people in Belgium, but then how come we don't live in a big country too?

They're not that good a football team, I mean Belgium, a boy said, not recently anyway. And Billy said well, they're better than Scotland.

Kelly said everybody's better than Scotland

And Billy told her she was being a traitor.

…

From the bus stop some pupils could be seen towards the back window, half-standing up, half-sitting, some would be in between standing and sitting as the bus pulled up, and they were just turning from looking out the window to face into the middle of the bus as it slowed to a halt. Pupils looked to be sitting in pairs, with perhaps one pupil on his own at the front, this would be evened up by the likelihood of five pupils sitting on the row of seats across the back. There would be a balance, so it would work out.

They would keep turning, the pupils, their hands supporting them on the back of the seat in front, and their heads would turn about three hundred degrees to look out the window, they would turn their bodies to follow.

There would be pointing and laughing and avoiding of eye contact. One pupil might bang on the window, though it would usually be just a hand that could be seen from the bus-stop, but no arm or body, or anything. At the steps just going into the bus the noise that could be heard would reduce.

For the rest of the journey there might be giggles, or a piece of scrunched up paper flicked forward.

The driver would look in his mirror and then complain, these bloody kids get the service bus because they're too lazy to get up in time for the school bus, then I've got to bloody put up with them.

And he would go on to say that they were a danger to the health and safety of the other passengers, aye, decent people paying their way, and as he drove along he would turn round in his seat and establish eye-contact with any passengers who looked as if they were nodding in agreement with him.

…

See that bit at the end of The Boy Wonders, Armpits began to gesticulate, when the guitars start strumming away really fast, you can't believe they could be any faster, then they speed up again just before the song finishes!

Mr Tambourine Man smiled, aye, that's the kind of thing you like eh! Aye, Armpits was smiling, I know

I don't know much about music but I know that's good guitar playing, fast, and I'm right, eh? Aye, Mr Tambourine Man nodded and said it is, it effing well is. Then he said but, you know what I really like about that song? And he paused.

Armpits waited, then laughed, ah, come on man, you think I won't understand eh! Am I just a fat bastard who just likes melodies, hee hee! Mr Tambourine Man smiled back, aye, and fast guitar strumming heh heh!

The two of them laughed. Aye, ya snobby wanker, Armpits half-scrunched up a piece of paper and chucked it at Mr Tambourine Man across the card table. Mr Tambourine Man shielded his face with his forearm, ha ha, aw pal!

Armpits stopped smiling, looked at Mr Tambourine Man, aw pal what? Mr Tambourine Man shrugged his shoulders, and Armpits raised his eyebrows and leaned up in his seat and smiled again, aw pal your fucking cheeky arse, I'll give you fucking aw pal, ha ha, patronising bastard so you are! So Armpits then insisted that Mr Tambourine Man tell him what he liked most about The Boy Wonders.

So there was then a monolgue from Mr Tambourine Man about how major-sevenths dominated the verse with the bass driving the rhythm, he tapped on the desk, aye, you have to listen out for it though, and then there's the way there's a single guitar strumming each new chord, just once, right at the end of the bar, right before any other instruments play the chord, and I mean right at the end of the bar, you have to listen closely just to hear just when it comes in.

He looked up at Armpits and nodded at him, you know, yeah?

Then he kept going, plus the bridge into the chorus is different at the end of each of the two verses, and in the second verse even changes keys and then changes back to the original key just before the chorus, and I mean that's really clever, really clever what he does, going from major to minor to major again, and also, the chorus soars halfway through, just on the third line, just after he sings when he'll feel the fall of honest rain, and just, the way it just comes back in the fourth line to repeat the melody of the first two, I mean it's a proper structure, the boy knew what he was doing when wrote all that, he knows what he's doing with the structure there.

When Mr Tambourine Man had started speaking he was looking at the table, then as he continued to speak he was staring at Armpits, then he was looking at the window and gazing up and out of it by the time he stopped talking.

Armpits was opening a biscuit wrapper as he listened but didn't take a bite of it, at first looking between the biscuit and Mr Tambourine Man and eventually just resting his wrist on the table, holding the biscuit up with one hand, scrunching the wrapper in the other, staring at Mr Tambourine Man.

Mr Tambourine Man looked at Armpits, see what I'm saying man, I don't know if people can truly say anything's beautiful when they're talking about music, I never use the word much myself about anything, and I try not to use it about music, at least certainly not with my pupils, but some things, you just have to use the word beauty, if nothing else fits, know?

Armpits paused.

Mr Tambourine Man looked at him, know?

Then Armpits gulped and said em, can I eat this Penguin now? It's melting down my fingers.

Ah ya! And Mr Tambourine Man threw the piece of paper Armpits had thrown at him back across the table, och, it was you that told me to tell you what I liked about the song, I asked you and you said to tell you, you fat effer, ha ha! Armpits smiled, ah you're no wrong, I did, he was laughing back, and I didni have a fucking clue what you were talking about man, Christjesus!

Mr Tambourine Man sat back in his chair and breathed in, aw pal.

Ha ha, aw pal you're right, Armpits continued to laugh, still, it has got a nice melody!

…

Bicycle Clips said he was no expert on philosophy, not at all, he grinned, me? No, he answered himself and then asked again, but hadn't Kant started off his working life as a minister, or he'd gone to study for the ministry? Armpits breathed in and said here's your man, and breathed out as Ex-Cop came in and sat down at the classroom desk in the staffroom.

Didn't Kant used to be a minister, Bicycle Clips was looking across and asking Ex-Cop, who looked up and saw that it was Bicycle Clips talking to him, and he put his pen down and clasped his hands, you're asking me? And he said aye well, he went to university in order to study Theology but gave it up and turned to Maths and the Sciences, clever guy, ha ha!

People looked up when they heard Ex-Cop laugh, and looked down when he stopped.

Bicycle Clips said it was a wonder anyone could study anything at that time, em, wasn't Kant around when Frederick II was king! It was all about de facto education decrees and all that, no chance for many people to make a thing of it in at school or uni around then eh, tss!

Ex-Cop said well, Kant started uni in seventeen-forty, the same year Frederick II became king, but he never actually graduated till the seventeen-fifties, because of taking so long to pay for his teaching, it was just, his mum and dad had died, and everything.

Armpits looked across from where he was standing with his folder under his arm, people had gone quiet while Ex-Cop and Bicycle Clips were talking. Armpits grinned, see? No government funding for education even then!

There were a few laughs, a few, and Armpits tucked his folder under his arm again and waved his other arm towards Bicycle Clips, allowing him to continue talking, aye, the University of Konigsberg was deprived of funds at that time but of course that hadn't halted the advancement of philosophical thinking in Prussia, no, tss!

At that point Crossword Freak Number Two looked up, Prussia, not Germany? Then he said never mind when Crossword Freak Number One looked at him and shook his head, and they both went back to their newspapers.

Ex-Cop agreed with the point Bicycle Clips had made about progress in Prussia, and said that the Berlin Academy of Sciences got more money under Frederick II than it had ever done before, under Fredrick William I even.

In the middle of the room, Crossword Freak Number One looked at Crossword Freak Number Two and Crossword Freak Number Three, and shrugged his shoulders.

Ex-Cop picked his pen up and continued, saying anyway, Kant started off wanting to become a minister but he changed direction at uni, and that's how he ended up doing philosophy.

Crossword Freak Number One then leaned over and asked Ex-Cop, em, wouldn't it have been called metaphysics in those days, philosophy I mean? And Ex-Cop said it was called logic and metaphysics, logic and metaphysics.

Bicycle Clips sat back in his chair and clasped his hands round one knee and lifted the knee up into the air, I knew it! Ergo! And he looked round at Crossword Freak Number One and said you know, I've been thinking about it on and off for a few days now, and you could probably call Kant a German, aye, tss! Crossword Freak Number One nodded back at him.

Crossword Freak Number Two said oh aye, it was in the paper the next day, Kant was the answer, so it must be right to call him German.

Crossword Freak Number One said nothing.

Crossword Freak Number Three said nothing.

Bicycle Clips said nothing.

When they looked up, Ex-Cop was leaving the staffroom with his stuff under one arm.

…

People were talking about the rector of the school, and also about how he carried out his duties, they agreed about the thing, aye, he's making an arse of the job, arsehole.

A couple of folk had worked at other schools where the deputy rectors there had been respected by many, aye, they were good guys them, could have done with them here. They had been interviewed for this school's rector's job a few years ago, these deputy rectors, but didn't get it. The rector must have known someone on the interviewing panel, it was concluded, aye, a fix for definite, old twister.

Heads nodded, there was more agreement about the thing, yeah, even our deputy rector would have been better, at least he knows the school, and more people nodded, raising their eyebrows at the same time. Two people who were standing together at the window looked at each other and nodded too, it seemed everybody thought the Phantom should have got the rector's job, at least ahead of the guy who got it.

Then the Phantom walked in, and people didn't say anything, not anymore. He looked around, aah, talking about me, were you, eh, aah!

He laughed, looking around the room, seeing someone and throwing his head back, aah there you are, and clapping his hands together and going over to kneeling down beside the guy, not sitting on the chair that was there for him to sit on if he wanted, and he spoke just to that guy, lowering his voice, no-one else was involved.

A few conversations began around the room and then the Phantom raised his voice, which then drew everyone into his discussion, which had been about something or other, but then became something else, and something else after that.

When he left, people looked around the room at each other. The two people standing next to each other at the window looked at each other, shaking their heads, on second thoughts, hee hee!

…

William was sitting at his desk as the class filed in. He had been first in, with James beside him. William had a packet of crisps and was just finishing it.

74

Billy laughed at him as he walked behind his chair, you had one of them earlier William you fatso, and he slapped the back of William's head.

William half-laughed, and his words were no I didni, no I didni, then his words changed, to being so what though, so what if I did! Just, Billy kept talking as he sat down, what did I hear your mum say to you once about you and crisps, remember, eh! And William told Billy to shut up. William started to put the crisp packet in his pocket and faced the front, what are we doing today sir?

But some others in the class asked Billy what William's mum had said to him, go on Billy, tell us, what did she say to him?

William protested to them, shut up yous, let's get on with the lesson sir! Billy looked at William, then looked at the class, then when there was no noise he turned to William and said, in a woman's voice, William, William, you know what crisps do to you, William, the wind! The wind!

The Bin Brigade hooted, the wind the wind! William huffed, he turned away from them all and huffed some more.

The laughter subsided, and they were not all laughing so much anymore, and the lesson started and continued for some time.

Later on in the period, William ended up interrupting what was being discussed, Kelly had been reading out to the class from a book about the trysts that used to happen in the Middle Ages, she read about the droves from the Highlands down towards the central lowlands, the journeys with the cattle, the lesson had been moving the class towards reconstructions from their imaginations of the passage from the islands to the mainland and then south to the big markets. They had all been given a couple of minutes to write down ideas as to how they could perform some kind of re-enactment of conversations that would take place on the journey south to the central lowlands.

But then William just turned round, leaning one arm on the back of his chair. The lesson came to a silence and William then smiled as he said to Billy sitting behind him, smell that, then he was laughing, saying again, smell that!

The class laughed with him, have you farted William, it's those crisps you, ya wee, there was a pause, and some of the class looked at each other and then back at William, you have haven't you! William was still laughing, he used his two hands to scoop the air in front of him backwards towards his friends, ha ha, smell that Billy!

Then the class were talking back at him, some of them pulling their jacket collars over their mouths and noses, aw man, William you're a dirty bandit, so you are. Billy was sitting in the seat behind William holding his nose, ya wee fat smelly, god, I don't know. Billy screwed his face up.

And William looked Billy in the eye and waved his arm from his chest out towards him, all the time smiling and saying, in the voice of his mother, the wind the wind, ha ha!

…

How you doin son? You the student, yeah? Shakespeare was at the next urinal, and he turned his head away without waiting for a reply, and he faced the wall, and stood for a while before starting, he looked at a point in the wall just above his head-height, exhaling,

76

sighing, aw, I'm needing this, been waiting for it all last period, aw man, whoo, ah, that's better!

Then he stopped and said shit, I knew this would happen. He zipped up and then turned and went into a cubicle, taking more than one go to get the door locked. Some money jangled in his trousers, they could be heard getting pulled down as he continued to talk, he was instigating further conversation, asking questions about this and that, wanting a discussion about the thing.

Eventually he said em, it's okay to go pal, you don't have to hang around, I'll be a while here. He grunted, em, yeah, I'll definitely be a while.

Someone else came in at that point and shouted hey, is that you, he was shouting to Shakespeare in the cubicle, these wee size sevens are a dead giveaway in there, you not got rid of that curry yet! The reply from Shakespeare inside the cubicle came, aye, naw, aye, it's the last time I'll go out for a nosh-up the night before I've got fourth years period one, I've had to leave my classroom twice this morning, plus I had to hang on all the way through those wee first years just there before this visit the now, and then, wouldn't you know it, know how sometimes you're doing a piss and it turns into a shite just like that!

Aye, the entrant agreed, and he also pointed out aye, and it always takes you by surprise and all, when pish comes to shove! He had been standing, leaning against the cubicle door, but he now approached a urinal. Then he said naw, and turned and went into a cubicle himself, no taking any chances!

And the two continued their talk. After a minute or so, from Shakespeare came the words, going to be late for my top set third years now I think. The reply was aye, better two minutes late though than having to nip out halfway through, I'll just shut up mate, let you concentrate. Shakespeare could be heard, aye, cheers, talk to you in a second!

…

A couple of staff were standing by the window, one of them leaning on the sill. The other was looking at his watch, shaking his head and saying nah, it's not gonni beat the minute, he looked up and out of the window at the dumptruck, then down again, shaking his head, aye, naw, nope.

The first one would say when it was time to stop the clock. The second one would press a button on his watch, announce that it had taken maybe a minute and four or a minute and five seconds, aye I said it wouldni beat the minute, I knew it wouldn't, and then look out with the first one at the dumptruck as it poured its load onto the top of the slagheap and came down the slope to meet the digger again.

One of them would ask if the other thought it was worth waiting to see the truck go up again before the end of break, the other one would raise his eyebrows, and there would be a discussion about whether there would be enough time for the digger to load it up first, what do you think eh, think it's worth it, the wait, the way she's going today?

The watch would be examined again and the staffroom would be surveyed to see if any of the others were looking at their watches, and if there was anyone doing so, it would be surmised that morning break was almost over, and the two would move away from the window, maybe bumping a knee against a chair or someone's elbow as they gazed back out at the digger

and dumptruck at work, one of them re-affirming their views, aye she's not gonni do anything special today.
...

In the classroom on the board were the words, written across the top of one panel of the whiteboard, Please Leave On. It was a couple of pupils in the class that spotted it and said aw sir, you've wiped all that work underneath the sign off, aw sir, ha ha, Miss Whatshername's not gonni be happy!

William looked around the class and laughed, aye sir, what a temper she's got too, better watch out!

Others joined in, aye you're no wrong fatso, aye sir, she's a wee nippy sweetie that one, she'll have you! Aw sir, better watch out!

There was much merriment amongst the class as they discussed the reaction of the teacher who had left the request to leave what she had written on the board, and whose work had now been wiped off, they predicted an outcome that involved the teacher taking some form of action, aw, sir's really gonni get it, ha ha!

When they all came back to the classroom later in the day the teacher in question had written her work up on the board again, this time leaving a message above it which just said Leave On Stupid.
...

As well as being a guy who could make people in the staffroom laugh, Mr Tambourine Man was in charge of the paper club. He collected money off folk once a month, if they were in it, the paper club, and every day people would have a choice of five or so papers to read when they had time between classes or at break or lunch, there were a couple of periodicals that appeared as well. Someone just had to say, and Mr

Tambourine Man would order a journal or paper of their choice.

Mr Tambourine Man walked round the staffroom when it was pay-up time and ticked folks' names off on a list when they gave him money. Sometimes a person might say they didn't have any change on them at the minute, eh, can I give it you the morrow, eh, the money, I'll have it the morrow, that alright? Or they might say och shit, I've left my wallet at home, tomorrow okay? And Mr Tambourine Man would always say aye sure, he always accommodated the request, and he'd walk away and mark something in his book.

If a person said they had already paid for the month, he would always check in his book before saying oh aye, so you have sorry, my mistake, or perhaps he would say em, maybe I didn't think you paid 'cause it would be shown down here on the list and it's not, I usually write it down, know, you know, em, but it's alright don't worry, I'll mark you down as having paid, don't worry, it'll be me that's forgotten.

He would still point at the book and show the person his payment list.

…

She looked at people when they talked to her, Marie, in the eye. Her answers didn't say much, she didn't ask many questions either.

She was only in the Bin Brigade's lessons some of the time, she hadn't opted out of all or even a lot of her exam subjects, the other pupils said it was just the ones they said her dad had picked for her to do, they were subjects that she never wanted to do, there were two or three of them, she'd never wanted to do them in the first place.

80

Though this was just what other people said, maybe pupils in the Bin Brigade, sometimes teachers might be heard to say this about Marie too, if they happened to mention her.

She was going to leave school at Easter, but would come back to do her exams in the subjects she was still sitting. That was her plan, she said, yeah, then I'll go to college to continue studying, don't know what sir, but something. I can't wait to go to college, I just love thinking about it, college, then university!

She smiled if she was being spoken to, inclining her head to one side, then maybe the other. The girls would say to her more than once aw, Marie, you've got such a lovely smile, no wonder the sixth year boys all fancy you! Or one girl might say aw Marie, I wish I could have a figure like you Marie, how can you eat chocolate and keep having such a wee waist!

Marie didn't respond to this talk, she would just say, changing the subject, well, this is just me, so, I'm not going to finish any of my courses before I leave at Easter, but I'll do the extra work at home. And she said that her mum was going to arrange to get her a tutor.

…

A teacher who had been teaching for less than a year waited until everybody that had a class after the break left the staffroom, then went to the wall and put up a thank-you note from his wife saying to the male staffroom, thank-you for the lovely sandwich toaster you gave my new husband and me as a wedding gift, it was so thoughtful of you.

He put it up with one pin stuck into the middle of the top of the paper. Then he went to the shopping bag sitting beside his briefcase and got a tin out of it and put the tin on the coffee table in the middle of the

81

room, just in front of where the Crossword Freaks would sit, clearing some papers out of the way before placing the tin in the centre.

He opened the tin and left the lid beside it, upturned. Eh, got married just after the Christmas holidays, know, ach, weddings, eh, heard it, speeches, heard it eh, understood!

He looked down, then up again, em, wedding cake, he looked around the room, just take some if you like, let them know at lunchtime please about it, eh, the cake I mean, I'll not be here, cheers.

A couple of people came into the staffroom, one turned and went back out again, and the other sat down before getting up again and also leaving.

Sandwich Toaster headed back to his chair, saying the male staff had got him and his wife a sandwich toaster, so, anyway, I'm going to be late for my class, need to get off then. And then Sandwich Toaster picked up his briefcase and left the room, throwing the shopping bag towards the bin on the way out, it fell on the floor and he had to stop to pick it up and place it in the bin before leaving.

…

Where is he today?

Kevin wasn't in school, again, and when this was mentioned, somebody raised the subject of Kevin having come top of his registration class in first year, he did sir, he was brainy, Kevin, sure he was.

An agreement existed amongst the class about that, oh aye, Kevin, he was brainy sir, he was always the brainiest in primary and all, teachers loved him, he got to choose all the different projects we had to do, dinosaurs, airports, sharks, space, different countries, he knew everything about all of that stuff.

There was a kind of consensus amongst the Bin Brigade, head-nodding and other signals, did he not even win a prize in second year too?

Billy looked around, hmmf, Kevin! Then he said but hey, he must still be brainy, you can't be brainy one time and not brainy the next, can you not sir?

There was a second of silence.

After another second of silence, someone else said aye, and see if Kevin had come to school more he'd have been allowed to do his exams, he'd no be sitting in here with us lot, eh sir, that's true isn't it? Again there was more agreement from around the class, they said aye, aye he would.

And again there was a second of silence.

Then another.

There were some sounds from the playground, the top bit of the window was open, hanging on a hinge that was half-fitted and coming off the frame.

There was another second of silence, again, and again.

Then some more playground noise.

It was another few moments before someone spoke, so, where is he today then?

3. CHILL WILL WAKE YOU

Mr Tambourine Man stood, on his own and smoking, at the window of the staffroom, which was opened outwards, and he half-leaned out. When he exhaled out the window itself he watched the smoke rise and disappear into the air outside the building before drawing on the cigarette again. He looked inwards, and asked so, you got fixed up for August yet, with a post yet I mean, after you finish your practice?

And he continued, yeah, it's much harder nowadays trying to get a job when you're starting out, to get your first post, know. He remembered when he had first started teaching Music, man, it was dead easy getting a job, you practically chose your effing school, it was like you were interviewing the schools rather than them interviewing you, god, hee hee!

He stubbed out his cigarette on the window ledge, flicked the butt down into the playground, watching it fall, nodding, of course there weren't enough teachers then. He leaned out of the window, now but.

Somebody popped their head and one hand round the door of the staffroom and leaned in to see who was in, then put his hand up and waved at Mr Tambourine Man, sorry it's okay, and went away.

Mr Tambourine Man looked at the door and smiled and made a hmmf noise and then said aye, and again said yeah, it was pretty easy in those days, a lot of people were going into teaching but there still wasn't enough, the government was really pushing it then, education. He grinned and then stopped grinning, whereas now, aye, words. He got out another cigarette and said hmmf to himself, again.

As he lit up the cigarette, he looked up and said you, you don't smoke do you? He leaned back and took a breath, looked at the cigarette and took a succession of drags, about five or six, and said aye, better not to. You'll be alright here, and in teaching, it might just take a bit of time.

Then he said aye, shaking his head, things were easier then, back when I was starting out, he then nodded his head and started shaking it again, aye, in a lot of ways.

…

The foyer at the entrance to the school always had examples of pupils' work on one noticeboard, and at the moment there was some R.E. stuff that Ex-Cop's classes had done, posters about Hinduism, words about its practices, and pictures, and writing about other religions of India. There was a heading above one set of drawings which said Ganesh, and a lot of the pupils had produced a variety of illustrations of the elephant god, some had shown men playing sitars or women dancing as well, there was a lot of food being eaten too.

On the way into the building, as she was opening and shutting her briefcase, and after only a glance up at the wall display, the Dog-Catcher had mentioned that there had been something about Indian music on telly the night before, she nodded as she looked in her make-up mirror, on the news I think it was, did you see it, darling?

And also in the staffroom, a teacher had walked in and said to Ex-Cop that he had seen Ravi Shankar on the news the night before, the teacher half-punched Ex-Cop on the arm, and Ex-Cop turned his head to face the guy. The teacher apologised, sorry mate, but em, hey, see those drawings on the noticeboard outside the main

85

entrance that your classes have done, aye well, there's a picture of a sitar, and I saw Ravi Shankar on the news last night, or somebody like Ravi Shankar, he was taking a sitar round some schools up in the Highlands, showing it to the kids, playing it for them, giving them a go like, it wouldn't be Ravi Shankar right enough, now I think about it, somebody like him though, a sitar player, yeah?

Ex-Cop looked at the guy, yeah what, yeah the guy was a sitar player? Yeah?

People looked at the guy. The guy looked at Ex-Cop, em, sorry for hitting you on the arm. People looked at each other and started to move again.

Ex-Cop was now getting asked by everyone about sitar music and Hinduism. Mr Tambourine Man came in and then he was getting asked too, about the sitar, and he nodded as he listened and nodded as he answered. Ex-Cop didn't say anything in reply, Mr Tambourine Man was doing the talking, answering everyone.

Someone asked, hadn't George Harrison been into the sitar, or he was at some point, wasn't it Donovan that got him into it in the sixties? Ex-Cop looked at the person in the eye, if you're asking me, I'm not the man to ask about pop music, me. The guy who'd asked the question said okay, aye, and looked away from Ex-Cop, blinking.

People then just looked at Mr Tambourine Man, and from someone came the question, hey, could you no get the kids to learn a bit of Donovan instead of playing them Bob Dylan eh? Folk agreed, aye Christ, there's enough bloody American films on telly, for definite, without the kids having to sing American songs at school! Hmmf, Bob Dylan!

86

Mr Tambourine Man asked if people were finished, and then said, actually I do work on a bit of Donovan with the pupils, actually, you ask any of them, they'll tell you they learn a basic version of Mellow Yellow when they do guitar in first year, and not only then, but older kids too, learning finger-picking for their practicals, Donovan, I play a bit of his stuff to them, so, I do play them Donovan, to pupils, aye, some of the boys who em, you know, all they want to do is thrash on the electric guitar all the way through third and fourth year, they suddenly fall to pieces when they try to finger-pick in fifth year, the thing sadly is, you canni get Higher Music just by learning the chords to a Ramones song. And Mr Tambourine Man then repeated that it was a fact that he never got the kids to learn or sing Dylan songs. People nodded, oh right? Sorry.

And then some of the staff discussed for a minute the thing about Donovan maybe having written Blackbird, aye, I've heard that too, is it true? It was off the White Album was it, or wasn't it, was it? Anyway, they agreed that an acoustic was all the Beatles had in India and Donovan was out there wasn't he as well, teaching McCartney to finger-pick at the time, wasn't he? During the discussion there were looks towards Mr Tambourine Man at times of uncertainty.

Then the conversation didn't continue anymore, and one person said och, you never hear Donovan these days, your hear plenty Dylan though. Mr Tambourine Man said that wasn't his fault, he couldn't be blamed, because he played Donovan to the kids.

Ex-Cop sat through it all and didn't say anything more. Mr Tambourine Man turned to him and said hey, how come they interrogate me and leave you

alone! Then he repeated, if young Scottish kids grow up unaware of Donovan, it certainly isn't my effing fault.
…

Is that how England rules us now then well? Billy furrowed his brow.

England doesni rule us now, Sam said he knew this, I know about how Britain, or the United Kingdom it is, how it's ruled, I had to learn it for one of my army interviews, it's the British Army I'd be joining, not the English one, which there isn't one anyway, an English army.

Aw Sam, you'll never join the army! Billy swung back on his chair, holding on to the desk behind him with one hand and putting his pen between his teeth with the other, you'll never pass that running test! Look at you, you've hardly got the build of an athlete eh, don't worry, you're still a star man though!

Sam said shut up, I am gonni join the army, me, and anyway Billy, sir's trying to teach man, Scotland and England becoming the same country, well not the same, but one country, a single country. If you listen you might learn something Billy, this is useful History for once, so instead of telling me what I'm gonni be or what I'm not gonni be, why don't you listen to the lesson sometimes, eh!

Billy smiled and raised his eyebrows, aye maybe.

The lesson continued. The Bin Brigade listened, and during the lesson asked questions about oaths of allegiance and the Glencoe Massacre, listened again to what they were told about Scottish landowners taking money from English lords, and enquired about James VII, yeah sir, how come it is that James VII was called James VII even though he was never king, plus sir, if he wasn't ever king how come he even got called James III by some people as well!

As the lesson wore on, Kelly could be seen writing 1692 and then 1707, numbers that stretched from the top of the sheets she was drawing on to the bottom of them, then she shaded the numbers in, using dots or stripes or other patterns, and then she shaded them, giving them the effect of having three dimensions, before turning round and showing them to the pupil sitting behind her.

At the end of the lesson the bell rang and the pupils got up and went as soon as they heard it. On the way out Sam asked how come it's even called the Act of Union sir, surely if Scotland didn't want it, or you say a lot of the Scottish people at the time, how can it be a union, you said a union's when two people or groups of people agree to join together, surely it couldn't be a union if there wasn't two groups that wanted it, only the English, and not even all of them either?

Billy tugged at Sam's jacket and pulled him towards the door, aw Sam, who cares man, who cares, come on man it's lunchtime!

…

Pupils called each other by their first names, or surnames, or variations of their first names and surnames, or even nicknames. Teachers called pupils by their first names, not surnames, and almost never nicknames. Though the teachers sometimes, often, knew what the pupils' nicknames were, and these might be talked about in the staffroom, they were recognised as being a kind of code, just for the pupils. One pupil got called Nipples by his friends, and no teacher ever found out why. So, staff saw fit not to intrude upon pupils' sensibilities and stuck to first names.

This was not the case with Ace, Ace got called Ace by everyone, pupils called him Ace, and the teachers all called him Ace, Ace.

Ace didn't appear to be in school a lot, sometimes coming in every day in a week, sometimes away for ten days, sometimes in and out during one day. People, pupils, teachers, said he was going to be an actor, or he was an actor already even, he had been on the television a few times since he was very young, adverts and such at first, but now in programmes, and not just walk-on parts, extras, but characters with names, parts with lines. A child actor, that was what people would say Ace was, and they all called him Ace.

Ace talked about how he went to Glasgow for theatre classes twice in the week, with groups of school students from all over. He had this thing in Edinburgh at the weekends too, some workshop, there seemed to be school leavers and college and university students at this one too. At the moment Ace had been telling the Bin Brigade that he was going out with a girl from one of his acting courses who was seventeen, about to turn eighteen, Ace said, and with him being fifteen, about to turn sixteen, he didn't see her a lot, so it was a kind of on-and-off thing, this is what he said.

Ace could be seen around school with sixth year girls sometimes, it would either be them or the boys from the Bin Brigade, they would walk about with him if he was in school, he didn't really hang about with anyone else, not boys his own age nor his girlfriend's age. He sometimes held Marie's hand if he was walking into school with her.

A film was being made in Scotland in the summer, pupils and teachers had been talking about it being in the papers, news of the production, there was an excitement about the thing, aye, it was on the telly the other night, it's gonni be a big film, Ace'll be working alongside some big names, there's some famous actors going to be in it and all! The pupils mentioned John Hannah and Robert Carlyle, who Ace had met before, Robert Carlyle, Ace said that he could call him Bobby now that he knew him, Ace spoke about Robert Carlyle and said aw, Bobby, he's supercool. Ace was going to be in this film when it started getting made in the summer, or he'd been asked to audition for it anyway, one or the other was the case.

Ace said this to the Bin Brigade on the days that he was in school.

…

Walks In Snow said hello there, or some sort of greeting, to everyone who came into her bit of the staffroom. She would always remember what people had said to her when they'd last been in for a drink or bar of chocolate, and she would inquire as to how people were getting on, asking about their families and cross-referencing the teachers' answers with other events in their lives that they had told her about at other times, how are you doing son, aw hen, how did your thing at the weekend go, did your friend find out about that job, is your wee boy better, and other questions.

When someone cracked a joke she would laugh, ha ha, I know, I know, but if somebody said something about somebody else, another teacher, a joke about the other teacher that made other teachers laugh, she would just smile and maybe laugh a bit if the person who told the joke caught her eye, she tended not to become part of such conversations.

People asked Walks In Snow about herself or her family or her life, and sometimes a teacher might ask her a question her or she had already asked at the break, or the day before or a week before, but the question was asked again.

Walks In Snow would give the answer she had given when the question had been asked before, and she would smile when they said oh is that right, or if they said oh, that sounds great, or oh aye, you told me that earlier didn't you! She smiled as she put some coins in the teacher's hand, saying aye never mind love, or she just said thanks, there's your change, twenty pence love.

The teacher would be turning away in the other direction by that time, and nothing more would be said.
…

Armpits was questioning everyone who walked past him in the staffroom about the logic of a decision made that week by the rector about how some arrangements for reporting in the future would be carried out in the school, first years were going to get reports given out six weeks into the school year, from the next session onwards, Christjesus we'll be reporting on kids we've not even learned the names of yet, won't we!

Somebody said well, you might have a little bit of knowledge about them to be going on with, it stands to reason doesn't it? Reason, Armpits shook his head, reason! The other person smiled at Armpits, aye, reason, then to someone sitting beside him, here we go, he's off on one about another thing, there's always some, em, thing, for him to spout forth about when the moment takes him, eh!

Armpits stared at his colleague, I'm just saying, you're saying that we get given extra work to do, extra paperwork on top of our already huge workload, and it just stands to reason, so that makes everything okay!

Crossword Freak Number One interjected at that point, sitting forward to say em, if you ask me, it's simple, don't you see? You just write what you know of the pupil by then, and if you don't know much, don't write much, it is, in fact, simple, simple reasoning, and he looked back at his paper, he hadn't been looking at Armpits when he said about it being simple, he'd been looking out the window from his chair in the centre of the room. He nodded and said logic, it's logic.

Armpits walked over to Crossword Freak Number One, hey, simple! There were a few people sitting around them, looking at the two. Crossword Freak Number One now looked up from his newspaper and said that from what he'd been learning in his Open Uni course, or at least according to what he understood from what he'd been learning, the argument was what could be described as a dialectic, you know, that is, and he stopped talking as Armpits blinked and coughed and interrupted him

Armpits said look, listen, again, again, I've just spoken about huge workloads and unreasonable expectations held by managers, employers, employers of employees, and you start trying to talk to me about dialectics, reasoning? Crossword Freak Number One said yes, and then laughed, saying the power of reason is god-given so anything that you could say about reason, you, and then he stopped again.

Armpits spoke over him before he could start again, that's shite! Crossword Freak Number One laughed again and said that's a compelling argument, my friend.

Don't you my friend me, Armpits sat down. Look I'm lowering myself to your level just so you feel equal to me, you want to talk about dialectics, 'cause I'm fucking ready for you. People walked away.

Crossword Freak Number One said ah well, wasn't it Descartes who said reason was given to man by God. There you are.

There you are? There I am? There you may be, but there I am my fucking arse, Armpits stood up and walked away. And then he came back, shouting hey, can you not work it out for yourself, do you never read beyond the introductions of any articles you're given for that course of yours? Descartes! Even Descartes himself acknowledged that if you use your mind to prove the existence of a god, and you use the existence of a god to say that you've got the power of reason, then the whole thing, the whole fucking shazam, it's all questionable! He kept shouting, because it's like, I don't know, it's like bloody saying that a reporting system that hardly tells you anything still makes sense simply because it manages to impart some information to parents, even though that information doesn't make sense in itself, fucking hell! You don't see it, do you?

He paused and took a breath.

Then he said between breaths, Christjesus, anyhow, Descartes was a fucking, math, mathematician, what would he know anyway! And he coughed, and coughed again, then he walked away, coughing, ach, dialectics!

94

Crossword Freak Number One shook his head and said em, my friend, if you have to raise your voice then you've already lost the argument, that is, conceded the point.

And Armpits kept walking till he was out the door of the staffroom and shouted back from the corridor, his voice carried in, aye, and if you're a pompous twat at the start of the argument, then, ach!

…

Armpits was talking about Ex-Cop, saying he'd given up the police after being in it since he was twenty or something, had served twenty years and got out, gone to uni and studied Divinity. Divinity, aye, and twenty year in the police before that, almost!

He looked at the staffroom door, ah, though he admits to the kids that he doesn't believe in god, he says he just has an interest in religion in the context of its place in history, tells the kids about religion in relation to its place in the shaping of the world as we know it today. Armpits nodded and kept his eyes staring ahead without blinking, it's true and all, what he says, and he's a complete atheist, or agnostic, em, god knows what he is eh!

Armpits looked out the window, wars and that, that's what he teaches, everything, from about the Crusades onwards, and before! And he's no wrong about religion either! Like I said, he puts in in a context, aye, like always telling the kids that it was true that Richard the Lionheart loved killing Turks or Muslims or whatever, but actually he loved killing anyone and so when the time came to return to England to restore order and kill a few local troublemakers he was more than happy to forget the Crusades, religion wasn't everything! Armpits went on to say that he

95

sometimes wished he knew more about religion in that way, the kids liked getting taught R.E. by Ex-Cop. He scratched his crotch, aye they never feel he's stuffing religion down their throats, and he keeps bloody good discipline too, no mucking about in his room, no siree!

Then he went hmmf, all the same, and again he went hmmf, think I'd rather have the policeman's pay and pension. The guy must be mad, giving that up, getting into teaching, mad! Then he said aye, and I bet he'd have been a bloody good copper too, I bet you anything eh, scares the shit out of half the staff here, let alone the kids!

Aye, must have been mad.

…

I'm gonni get a job sir! I'm gonni be an upholsterer when I grow up! William had his arm up, holding his elbow with his other hand, looking around at the others who weren't saying anything. Then he looked ahead, you don't need any qualies to get into it either sir, the job.

Somebody shouted out, excuse me sir?

William turned and shouted back to the pupil, sir's listening to me so just shut up will you. Me? Aye you. The other person said how, what is it that you're gonni do about it William? William thrust his head forward, he was still sitting on his chair, scowling, speaking to himself about how he'd show them what he'd do about it, he clenched his fists and then unclenched them.

Then a few others laughed and told William to shut up and get on with what he was saying. The Bin Brigade were all smiling at each other, aw William, how are you just gonni walk into a job man, you've got no qualies, and you're unlikely to get any!

I would so get a job, said William, who then smiled and laughed at the other pupils, they were making faces at him. William smiled and laughed again, aye, get lost yous lot! Then he turned, sir I will get a job, my brother's an upholsterer and he says I can work for him after I've finished school, William was beaming as he spoke.

Somebody mentioned the issue of possibly needing to go to college, do you not have to do that, or something like that, William? Someone else said aye, I thought the same, or at least if you didn't have to go to college, d'you no have to do a course or something? Then someone asked, hadn't your brother done one William, a course?

No, William said, it's only if you want to, my brother did it right enough, I think he had to, you had to do at the time when he left school, but he'll let me work for him anyway, without doing it, you don't need to do the course anymore, only if you want to get an apprenticeship. I'll just get straight into the job me, special case!

Aye, that's only 'cause you're his brother, someone said. And William replied, well, how come my other brother isni working for him then, eh? And he grinned, aha, take that eh! The other pupil said em, 'cause he's always in jail, isn't he! Everyone else threw their heads back and hooted, pointing at William, ha ha, aye, that's right, he's in the jail half the time William, that's how he can't ever get a job with your other brother doing the upholstery!

William scowled.

Then he started to grin, saying so? So what? And then he stopped grinning, no he's no, he's not in the jail half the time, there was just that once!

97

Nobody said anything more, and the laughter subsided when there was nothing more to be said.

Then William told them what his first pay packet would be if his brother had a full week's work. See! That's more than yous'll ever get, ah, you're not laughing so much now!

The children looked around at each other and some of them looked at their desks and re-arranged the pens and other things that were on them. Someone coughed.

…

Ace was in school, and he said sir, wasn't there going to be an Anglo-Teutonic alliance, it says here, with Britain, Germany and America? And it was one of them that proposed it, Germany?

Listen to Ace! The class laughed, they smiled at him, he smiled back.

Some of the Bin Brigade had been working on a poster project on the First World War, they were writing and drawing, looking up books, copying diagrams. They occupied themselves for the entirety of the lesson, taking an interest in pictures more than other sources, writing, letters, diaries, it was photographs or illustrations that they concentrated on, hey look, look at that cartoon, it's another one from Punch! Punch! Imagine having a magazine just full of cartoons back in those days! You don't get that now do you sir, Punch?

They collected their thoughts, based on pictures and other pieces in text books, and were always asking questions, on the variety of possibilities regarding the alignment of the Great Powers alongside or against each other in the period before 1914, the forging of alliances, the entente and other half-agreements.

Sir, how come all the countries ended up on the sides that they did, it practically says here that they all hated each other for years before the war, France and Britain, Germany and Austria! Sir, if the war had happened twenty years earlier might Britain have been on Germany's side! Or would Germany have ever fought against Austria?

So Ace said look sir, and he indicated some diagrams, tables that were on the page of a book, maybe the Germans' proposed Anglo-Teutonic alliance could have worked, if America could have ever gone along with it, do you think they could have? Ace replied to his own question, I don't, for definite, nah, it definitely wouldn't have. And he looked over at Sam. Sam looked up, sounds bloody mad! Sorry sir. The class laughed at Sam. They carried on with their work, and talked on the theme of the proposition of an Anglo-Teutonic alliance, aw man, Germany and Britain and America! Imagine them all on the same side, nobody could beat them, eh!

Then from someone else came the question, weren't they all really old guys in the government then sir? I mean, they're all old today, but they were practically ancient then, look at them in the photos, they're all coffin-dodgers, decrepit! The Bin Brigade asked how it was that this was the case, Ace leading things, aye sir, if they were all old guys then, and they supposedly got elected in those days because people thought they were clever so they could run the country, and maybe that's because they were old and people thought they were wise, then how come they nearly marched into war on Germany's side, if the same guys were going to just say Germany was the bad guy a few years later!

99

Ace answered himself again, aye, then again but, maybe there wouldn't have been a war at all if the British and the Germans, the old guys in the governments of the two countries had been on the same side, or at least talked a bit more. There would have been no Triple Alliance, no Triple Entente, or what was it, Entente Cordiale, men would have just said hey, why should I go off and fight against Germany, I mean, what did the Kaiser ever do to me, I've got nothing against him! And there would have been no army to fight with, or armies to fight against!

Listen to you lot, Billy said, sniffing and shaking his head, there's been a hundred wars since then anyway, and that just proves, they'd have all just ended up fighting amongst themselves some other time, taking turns at fighting as allies, enemies, whatever. And it's over now, it's history, it doesn't matter anymore!

And the Bin Brigade looked at each other, and went back to copying Punch cartoons.

…

Sandwich Toaster would often sit close to the Joke Club and laugh along with them and their jokes, looking away if one of them turned to look at him.

A couple of times someone in the Joke Club would turn to him and catch his eye, and then make a joke about him having just got married and how he would be having sex all the time, hey boy you look worn out today, you having sex again last night eh! An all-nighter I bet, eh! Sandwich Toaster went along with it, aye, heard it, and he would say aye, I am indeed worn out, what with having sex all the time, and yeah, we do have sex all the time. And various members of the Joke Club would tell him aye, you're a good boy,

100

that's right mate, make the most of it when you can, new brides eh, see you, young just-got-marrieds eh!

Sandwich Toaster maybe sat in with the Joke Club if there was a spare seat, but he got up and made a drink or went to look at the notice board if someone else in the Joke Club came in late. That person would then take the seat Sandwich Toaster had been sitting in. Sandwich Toaster looked back at the newcomer to the Joke Club's seats.

Sandwich Toaster would then take a sip of his coffee, or put his finger on the notice he was reading and slide the finger down the piece of paper, and look round at the Joke Club, then go and take a seat somewhere else. Then he would talk to whoever he was now beside, making a glance towards the Joke Club whenever they laughed.

...

Kev! Billy nudged Kevin on the arm.

Kevin kept staring, not answering the question. After it was asked for the the third time he was still staring, but spoke too, sorry? The question was asked again and a couple of the class hooted but fell to silence quickly. They were being shooshed by other pupils.

Everyone looked at Kevin again.

Billy said, give him a second sir. Kevin rubbed his eyes, what was the question?

The class collapsed with laughter.

Billy said, aw Kev, star man!

...

Armpits laughed, so, you writing about education at uni then, aye? What about then, what stuff eh? Usual shit yeah? He laughed again and then coughed up, Piaget, all the usual crap! He approached the urn, aye, those kids that say a wee beaker filled up to the brim full of water contains less than a big fucking beaker only filled a wee bit eh, Christjesus, what the fuck does that say to anyone!

He poured his cup of coffee, you wanting a coffee yeah? He grinned, health freak eh, no caffeine to infect you! He walked away from the urn, well, my body is most definitely not a temple, and he sat down. So, that's what they've got you doing, Piaget, yeah? No? Armpit raised his eyebrows. Obedience? Alienation? Christjesus, deep stuff for uni students, eh! Who they getting you to read these days, as well as Piaget then? Bowles and who? Gintis? Don't know them, must be new guys, or maybe just stuff I was given to read when I was at uni but I just pretended to!

He bit into his biscuit and continued talking while he crunched, what did you say it's all about? And he half-spat crumbs as he spoke, well, if education is, as you say, meant to foster conscious, and he coughed again, 'scuse me, consciousness and behaviour, patterns of behaviour you mean? Is it? Well, whatever the case, I don't know if that's what's taking place here, fostering consciousness, fuck!

He sat back a bit and put one finger up a nostril, you think? Well, the union line would definitely be that all teachers are being exploited, the whole workforce is being exploited, even the kids are being exploited.

He looked out of the window across the playground to another part of the school, and burped, pardon, what was that, unknowing, you say? Being exploited you mean? Whether it's unknowing or not depends on the individual I suppose, is that what these guys are saying, Bowles and whatshisface yeah?

Armpits looked out the window again, then at the door, then out the window again, don't you suppose

102

that a lot of people, workers, teachers, must get motivated to work hard, do well at what they do, put a bit of fucking extra in at the end of the day, and that maybe what they're motivated by is wanting to avoid the threat of unemployment. Then he asked, does that start at school do you think? The threat of unemployment? He coughed, spluttering more biscuit onto his hand which he wiped with his handkerchief, woops, sorry about that son.

He gazed out beyond the school grounds, I mean, learning about the idea of working hard for someone else, the importance of it? I suppose the education system awards high grades for fucking subordination and discipline, teaches obedience doesn't it? Even amongst the teaching staff, get promoted if you play ball with management eh!

Armpits looked upwards from his seat, he stretched one arm out and put his other arm on his chest, placing his hand over his heart, and said, me, my lack of fulfilment mirrors the kids', let alone theirs reflecting their future alienation in the workplace. I thank you! Ha ha, aw never mind me son!

There was a silence, then a pause just as Armpits was opening his mouth to speak.

So, he concluded, inequality then, they all like to go on about that don't they! Inequality being simply just, I don't know. Aye, fucking meritocracy, an illusion, write that in your next essay man! Armpits straightened up. Wouldn't it be better under a socialist regime like in Cuba? Soviet Russia? He laughed, I haven't got a fucking clue!

...

Aw sir, see the rector, my dad says he just sits in his office and does nothing, it was Billy who was

103

talking about the rector. The class nodded, aye, see that rector, he does, he just sits and does nothing sir. Billy went on, actually sir, in fact my dad says if the guy was a half-decent rector that's all he would do, sit around and do nothing, in fact he says that a good rector would just come in every morning, hang himself up on the coathook and let the office staff take him down when he's needed!

The class all laughed. A few more comments started to get made, aye, stuck up as well, so he is that rector, won't even say hello to you when you pass him in the playground. Aye, crosses the street if he sees pupils coming the other way in the town too, when he's got to lower himself to go in for a meeting or something, practically covers his face up so you think he doesni see you, big snob so he is!

The Bin Brigade said that outside the rector's office on the wall there was a traffic-light system going on, he controls it from his desk sir, aye really, red means he's not to be disturbed because maybe there's a meeting or something going on, orange means you can knock and wait to be asked in, if he's doing some work or on the phone but he'll allow you in in a minute when he's finished, and green means just to go in, like as if the door's already open, although it never is.

The class looked at each other, then at the front, bet you've never even met him yet sir eh, he wouldni want to be wasting his time with students eh! Have you sir, have you met him? Tell us what you think about him, you can be honest with us, eh! Don't not tell us, tell us! And they laughed together.

…

It was the MP for the school's area who had died after all, people mentioned that the date of the by-election had been set for a few weeks ahead. There was a bit of confusion in the staffroom as to to the question of Wednesdays and Thursdays, and whether the by-election would be on one or the other, therefore bringing in the issue of the by-election taking place on the same day as a Scotland football match, em, that not the week of the Scotland game, the international? Day after, the Thursday, I think, they're always on Thursdays. Aye, but isn't there something else going on that's gonni mean the match has to get moved to the Thursday as well though, was it not on the news? Aye, so it was, you're right, it was that big, what was it?

Nobody spoke for a second.

And then from someone, aye, that big conference thing, the conference taking place on the Tuesday and Wednesday, or the Wednesday and Thursday, the European environment thing, in the same city as the Scotland game, the police will have to be at the conference in big numbers after the trouble at the last one, can't remember where it was held, Clermont Ferrand was it? Mm, don't know. Well anyway, so the football's bound to be moved a day back so they're not dealing with them both at once, the police. Wouldn't want politics and football to mix eh!

Aye, bloody Eastern Europe, canni handle a student protest let alone an international football match, god knows how they'll manage that conference. They'll be recruiting hooligans off the streets and kitting them up in riot gear as we speak, eh. Bet the British police'll be over there too, just keeping an eye, two jobs to do and all, they'll have the video cameras out for known eco-terrorists and football hooligans, eh. Mind that guy with the tattoos on his teeth at one of the World Cups a few years ago, ha ha! Or whatever it was, paint.

Someone said aw shit, bugger that if the election's on the same day as the football, my brother usually gets me a gig at the count around here, he knows the folk running it. I've already said I'd help out as usual, it's usually okay for an evening's entertainment, a bit of tension and such like, get to see the big knobs from the local parties behave like spoilt kids, they're even worse than those jokers in the House of Commons, asking for recounts and so forth, em, but I don't really want to be sitting down earning paper-round money when I could be watching the game, ach, shit, 'cause I've already told him I'd do it, ah well, they'll maybe have a TV showing the highlights in the corner, hope it doesn't distract me when I'm counting, eh, wouldn't want that!

Someone else laughed, aye, woops! Hee hee, was that one thousand or two thousand I'd got to? Bugger it, let's call it one and a half and raise a glass to democracy!

…

William and James came into class after lunch, and James was holding one hand over his eye, it was his right arm, his right eye. The Bin Brigade burst into laughter, hooting at the sight. James had his elbow against his side, against his ribs, and the rest of his arm was pointing towards his face, his palm and fingers were resting on his eye and forehead, holding a patch onto his eye, it seemed to have been secured on by a kind of adhesive, though he was still holding his hand against it to keep it on.

Sam looked up, god sake James, what a numpty, you're such a numpty James, look at you, what a numpty! James shook his head, and walked to his seat, feeling the desks between the front of the class and where he sat with his other arm, the left, half-crouching down as he walked, not bending over, nudging into a few chairs as he went, making an attempt to fix them back into position with one hand before moving on.

The Bin Brigade giggled at him, Christ sake James, look at you, god sake! Ha ha, look at him! Numpty! The class were standing up to see James, the ones at the back were, stretching their heads.

William smiled as he helped James to his seat, holding his chair out for him, he guided James by putting the palm of his hand on his back, and put the chair in once again, once James was almost in the sitting position. William stood behind him and looked at the class, he was still smiling, looking around at everybody, catching people's eyes.

So what happened then, people were asking, smiling at each other, ha ha, this'll be good!

William said it was something James had drunk at lunchtime. The class reacted, alcohol, the drink! Naw naw, William put his hand up and waved it about, as some people started saying how they were surprised at James, god, James, drinking!

Billy said man, James, I never had you down as a drinker man, aw James, perfecto, what a star man eh, James! James smiled a bit and shook his head at Billy. He still had his hand to his eye. His other hand waved at Billy. Billy laughed, and James waved again. Billy laughed still more.

William said James had been drinking some juice using a straw in the canteen, aye, and you should have seen how fast he was trying to drink it, eejit, anyway, it went down the wrong way and he choked on it, aye, choked, I thought he was gonni die for a minute, or a second anyway.

Choked! Billy said eh, how can you choke on juice, did it turn solid on the way down James! The Bin Brigade were half-standing up now, grinning towards the scene where William was still standing over James, the other pupils were leaning on their desks with their elbows, knees up on their seats. Billy hooted, ha ha, it's a cold day, did the juice turn into ice in his throat William, did it James! James shook his head. William half-smiled.

Billy had placed his own hand over his eye now, attracting the attention of the class, hey look at me, I'm James! And he stretched his other arm out, banging it into the chairs and desks beside and around him, I'm James, I can't see properly! A few others were hooting, do it again Billy, do the thing with your hand over your eye!

William said don't be stupid Billy, it's possible to choke on liquid, juice, and he said the class knew what he meant. He carried on speaking through their laughter, William did, anyway, the juice must have ended up behind James's eyes, or inside his head anyway, it was definitely coming out his nose, aye, streaming out of it, it was.

The class was in uproar now. William laughed and patted James on the head.

Then there was another voice, aw William, stop it, aw James, are you okay, James? It was Marie who asked James if he was okay. James turned to look at her and nodded. He smiled at Marie and she smiled back.

William said he'd taken James to the school office, he'd had to take him, the canteen staff told him to, aye, they said it's health and safety, you canni be in the canteen if you're ill, it looks bad for the food. Billy shouted, was it coming out your eyes by then James, is

108

that how your eye's sore! The class were collapsing, and nobody listened much for the next couple of seconds, then they died down.

William carried on, let me finish the story, yeah? Then he said em, one of the office ladies told James to tip his head backwards and tell her what was up with his nose, and he did that, tipping his head backwards and pointing at his face, but as he was pointing he accidentally poked himself in the eye with the straw that he was still holding, the straw from the juice carton, and his eye started watering, and he's not been able to see out of it properly ever since, the office lady gave him an eye bath and sent him to class for the afternoon with that patch, or a kind of patch, to hold over his eye till it got better.

Aw, perfecto! Billy was crying, star man James, star man!

As the class came to order for the lesson to begin, there were still some sniggers.

And during the lesson, whenever there was an opportunity to turn round to the class and put his hand up to his eye and emulate James, Billy took it.

…

The Dog-Catcher was talking about how she'd been at the school for nearly four years now, and it was getting to her, the school, the journey, the job, the intensity sometimes, the difficulty of succeeding, disappointment when she failed sometimes, so she was looking for something else now. She pulled out of the school gates, waving to a couple of pupils as she did so, there they go, little angels.

Then she paused, so, I was saying, I mean, I do want to do social work, but I think I'd prefer working more with adults, know. I mean, I've done all the training, specialised in children's work, and I really enjoyed my placement in a children's home a few years ago. But this.

She stared at the road ahead.

Then she started speaking again, watching the cars on the other side of the road, I find now that when I'm doing home visits I'm more interested in the pupils' parents and how they're coping with whatever problems they've got that inevitably cause problems for their kids. It's what I think about when I drive home, when I'm writing up my reports in the evening or in the office the next day, the parents.

She took a drink from her carton, one of the first cases I had when I came to the school was a girl, just turned thirteen, she'd just discovered she was pregnant, I mean, talk about being thrown in at the deep end darling, me I mean, teenage pregnancy in my first week!

Anyway, this girl, nice lassie and everything, her mum was saying to her just to do what she wanted, and she'd support her and everything, and I was saying to the mum to make a decision herself about what was best for her daughter, and then tell the lassie what the best thing to do was, just tell her, I was practically crying out to the mum to take control, but mum was just so incapable of making any decisions, I think she'd had the girl herself when she was fifteen, sixteen, what can you do, it just turns full circle.

So I just sat the girl down myself and said, listen Kelly darling, you've got to get an abortion, you cannot have this child, look at you, you've not even got hips yet, how're you going to give birth!

The Dog-Catcher turned to the side, woops, sorry, I shouldn't have said her name there, then she

110

looked back at the road, but you'll forget it yeah, I mean, there's hundreds of Kellys in the school anyway!

She took another sip of juice.

So anyway, she continued, I said to her, the girl, that I could take her to the doctor, sort things out. And she just seemed so glad that someone was actually doing something and not just flapping about and telling her to do what she wants, and everything will be right, when she didn't have a clue what to do. She just wanted someone to make the decisions, she wanted to trust in someone, an older person. Mum was useless in that respect. Oh, very nice, for definite, pleasant, brought the girl up to know right and wrong, but, well, just useless, ineffective.

Then I talked to mum after talking to the girl, and she was happy as well to have someone else to take all the thinking work away from her. We sorted it within a fortnight, the girl went into a clinic and everyone lived happily ever after, well not exactly, but you know what I mean darling.

The Dog-Catcher stopped at lights, ah, so, but anyway, all through that case I couldn't help think more about the mother's condition, more than the girl's, I felt if mum could have sorted her issues out, whatever they were, then the daughter would have had a more stable background, and maybe she wouldn't have gone out and got knocked up by the first spotty seventeen year old boy she came across who couldn't get a girlfriend his own age.

The lights changed.

So, she smiled, it's pub-quiz night tonight for me and my mates, I'll be alright if there's questions on abortion yeah!

…

111

Ace was the guy. That's what pupils said, Ace, you're the guy!

Ace wasn't in all the time. He wasn't in today, but the pupils were talking about him.

He was the guy for films. In the film period that the Bin Brigade were sometimes allowed if they had been behaving in their classes, if teachers reported that they had been behaving, or one of them had been singled out for praise for one reason or another, Ace brought in films and the class watched them. Ace always decided what to watch, it was his choice, and the class sat back and watched, nobody would argue about the thing.

If he wasn't in, Ace, then there was an English teacher who always had a supply of the kind of films that the rest of the Bin Brigade said they liked to watch. This teacher got given English classes to teach with the pupils who had issues in relation to their behaviour, and sometimes their learning, and he always did what he called media units. This allowed the pupils to watch films because they were part of a media course, and his classes talked about the topics covered in the films before, during and after watching them.

The teacher was said to be liked by many of the pupils because of the fact that they got to watch films a lot in his class, aw, he's a great teacher, you don't have to do anything in his lesson! Or they said aw, he's a great teacher, he lets you watch films and then you have to write about them and your writing gets better. These were the two views, one was based on a workload thing, the other on a learning thing.

The other teachers all said they liked him too, because if you wanted a film for a class to watch if you had to take them for a colleague who was not in school,

and you only just got told about it, and there was
nothing set for you to teach, you could send a pupil to
this guy with a note about the class you had, and he
would supply you with whatever film he thought the
class would be suited to, you just had to say what kind
of class it was, subject, age group, levels of
concentration and so on, and he would select a title
within a genre that matched the audience, to fit in with
the market.

But Ace. The guy. The Bin Brigade said they
liked Ace, nobody said they disliked him, but if he
wasn't there for the film period they said great, Ace isni
here today! They said they disliked his choice of films
and that they liked the English teacher's films better.
They said things like aw, see when Ace insists on
flicking through his films and showing you the good
bits and stuff, or what he calls good bits, I canni stand
it! Aye! All that stuff he says, supercool for cats, I don't
know what he's on about, supercool for cats!

Plus, all that Italian stuff he's made us watch the
last few times, man, these four ones about the war,
three was it? Boring, eh!

William smiled and said aye, what was that
other one last week about that guy and his son, know,
with the guy stealing the bike and running away? Man,
I canni stand foreign films, black and white too man,
rubbish! The class laughed, aye black and white,
rubbish!

And they all remembered bits of The Bicycle
Thieves, someone spoke about how Ace had told them
the film was, aw I canni remember, what was it he said
sir? They all looked to the front of the class. Aye, naw,
that's it sir, realistic, aye, naw, that's right, aye, neo,
neo-realistic, neo! Ha ha! The Bin Brigade laughed,

neo-realistic! Neo-rubbish! Neo-shite! Woops, eh sorry sir, well I'm neo-sorry! They all giggled.

Someone else said ah sir, I bet you didni even remember that word, you just looked at Ace's posters and stuff on the wall, look there, ah! And they all looked up at some work Ace had done for the wall on neo-realism.

Then they went on about the bit in the film where the guy just about gets hit by a car, and how Ace had told them about the time when the film was being shot, aye sir, he said it actually happened to the actor when they were filming him crossing the street in one of the scenes, the car wasn't meant to be there, the actor had to dodge it, and they just kept it in the film, him jumping out the way. The class looked at each other, and Billy said isn't that rubbish, sir, I bet it was rehearsed, wouldn't it have been eh! A few eyebrows were raised, aye, and it was a crap ending!

Then the conversation changed to being about how Ace kept showing that bit with all the guys lining up in queues in the morning, aye, remember, they were all looking for work and taking the first job they could get, prepared to fight even, prepared to fight they were, just to get a job, man imagine that, crap jobs too, someone said, you wouldni find me doing that! Billy nodded. William nodded. Sam nodded.

The discussion continued, mind Ace told us the film was relevant! Relevant! And a few people said aye, right! Thank god Ace is no in today! Aye!

What is it we're watching today then, Billy inquired, anyone been to the Media classroom for a film? Sam said aye, I've been, I knew Ace wasn't in 'cause he wasn't in my Maths group period one.

So, Billy looked at Sam, what you got then?

Sam held up the slip case, Indiana Jones!

Whoa! Billy punched the air, Indiana Jones, perfecto! Star man Sam!

…

Marie was in school, she tended to come in every day, but this day she had her head on the desk, a couple of girls said sir, she's been like that all day sir, please don't force her to do work, she'll manage some when she feels like it, she's got a note sir, want us to get it for you?

One of the girls tapped Marie on the elbow that she was resting her head on, her hair was draped over her elbow. Marie looked up from her desk, used one hand to clear her hair that had now fallen across her face, and she smiled a bit and wiped her eyes, I do have a note sir, I'll just get it for you, it's in my bag.

Naw it's alright Marie, it was Kelly who spoke to her now, sir doesn't need it, do you sir, and she didn't look up as she said it, it's okay Marie.

Some boys looked at Marie but said nothing. Then one boy spoke to Marie, are you okay Marie, you gonni be alright Marie? Kelly told him to leave Marie, just leave her alone eh, can you no see she's upset about something? The boy spread his arms out, what's up, I was just asking!

Marie looked at the boy, she smiled, I'm fine, really, thanks for asking. And the boy smiled back at her.

Some of the other girls went up to Marie and pulled chairs up to sit either side of her. Kelly put her arm round Marie and told her it's okay, it'll be okay.

The boys looked on without saying anything, some of them just looked at their desks.

…

115

In the staffroom there was a poster up. That wasn't there before, folk were saying, who put that up? I haveni seen that here before, what was it that was there before, before that?

I'm sure it was a health and safety notice, Shakespeare declared, this isn't right, not correct, you can't take down health and safety notices, I know about this, look, I'm the health and safety person for this building, and I know that if you take the health and safety notice down, it's actually against actual health and safety rules, as well as being illegal into the bargain!

Discussions were held on what it was that the poster had replaced. Something about where you could buy second-hand books, it was mooted. Council stuff. Staff activities information maybe?

No, Shakespeare said, it was health and safety legislation, it was me that put it up in the first place, and I hope for all our sakes they've not taken it down and chucked it away, they can't do that. Now, where have they put it?

The rest of the staff did not respond. What's the fuss about anyway, it was asked. Ach, just some poster advertising an exhibition in Edinburgh, sometime soon, next month. What's it about? An exhibition in Edinburgh, next month. No, I meant the exhibition, what's it about, what's the exhibition about! Em, let's see here, em, the Reformation, and, em, its impact on Scotland, em, population and a few other things, it says at the bottom. The Reformation? Aye, all the so-called advances over England and Europe that were made in Scottish education at the time!

Naw!

Aye! That's what it says here!

Naw!

Aye!

Is there another exhibition on how everybody's caught up with us, and overtaken us in all the years since the seventeenth century! Laughter. Did you say caught up or cock-up! More laughter.

Then again came Shakespeare's voice, they'd better not have taken that health and safety at work poster down, that's illegal, they can't do that.

A couple of people said something along the lines of shut up about the health and safety poster, what is it with you!

Shakespeare held his hands up, I'm just saying.

Well, now you've said, so you can just shut up then!

A few people were getting up to look at the poster, and as they did the crowd who had looked at it on the point of its discovery started to drift away from it back to their seats. A couple of people put their hand on the poster as they looked at it, sliding their hand down it, and maybe tapping it as their discussion was carried out, indicating a feature of the poster, a drawing, a diagram.

Scottish education!

Joke, know!

Then one guy would say, here, is that the time? It's halfway through the break already, Christ, I'll need to be getting my tea, gonni end up being late for my class, got fourth year next, wankers that they are.

…

Someone, some people, or a couple of nurses, had been in to talk to the whole of the fourth year group about sex, or contraception, and the Bin Brigade were talking about it, about the video they had seen, the

117

leaflets the nurse had gone over with them, and now leaflets were getting passed around everyone, the pupils were pointing out cartoon penises and vaginas to each other, aye mine's bigger than that, my god, that fanny's like a bucket, hey look at this one, there's a drawing on the boys' toilet walls just like it, hee hee!

The class talked amongst themselves about some of the things the nurses had said or had asked the pupils to talk about, aw sir, you want to have been there, ha ha! Anyone who had given an answer to the nurses' questions, or had asked the nurses a question, was mocked for not having known this fact or that.

Kelly looked at them, the boys, see yous, yous are all so immature, yous. The class looked at her, then one boy said aye Kelly, we know where you're coming from! Other boys laughed. Kelly turned on the boys who were mocking her, shut up yous, just because I chose to listen, get myself educated. The boys looked at each other and back at Kelly, aye Kelly, it's you who needs the education, we've heard, you're the one who's gonni need it more than most!

Kelly turned back to the front, you gonni let them speak to me like that sir?

The boys looked up, faced the front, and said no more

…

Scout spent much of his time in the staffroom standing by the window, an elbow on the sill, with his legs crossed below the knee. He looked out down on the playground if there was a game of football going on, it was the football that would be the thing that he looked at. Sometimes he lifted his elbow and used his hand to brush off the dust that had gathered on it from the sill, before putting it back on the sill.

Some of the boys in the school played football most breaks and lunchtimes, after they'd eaten. Scout stood and commentated on the game, or didn't commentate but instead commented, offering his thoughts on ball skills, the ability to run off the ball, passing accuracy, he would be speaking into the hand he held his head up with. Some but not all of his words could be made out, he wasn't addressing the staffroom, it was just a thing that if you were sitting in one place or another then you might hear him.

Most folk didn't say anything to Scout. He said things like aye, good ball that, or, no you shouldn't have done that, there, there, there's gonni be a whatsit now, see? Look what you've caused boy, and you canni even see it, blaming your team-mates now, look at you, ach, what a waste, what a waste! And he would point his arm with the palm facing out.

From time to time he turned round and addressed people in the staffroom, one at a time, not the group, just one person or maybe a couple of guys sitting together, asking had they seen this boy or that boy playing for the school, or saying see him, that kid's no all he's made out to be, thinks he's some kind of star eh! Well he'll no be one for much longer passing like that eh, should've seen him on Saturday morning, running away from the big defenders, like he does every week, scared of the big city boys, big softie!

Folk he said that to would look up at him and nod, and maybe nod once more, aye, sure.

Scout would then turn back towards the window. And the person who had nodded, and nodded again, and said aye sure, would then look at another teacher across the room and grin at him.

119

And Scout would turn to the window and be back commentating again in a minute.

…

Men in the staffroom took the piss out of Armpits on account of how the pupils often told other teachers about how Armpits would let them get away with things in lessons, not just slurping a Coke or munching away at a packet of crisps, but other things, this and that, talking about the rector, swearing even. His colleagues talked about how Armpits talked to pupils about any number of things that sometimes didn't have anything to do with the lesson, the news, school occasions, staff smiled and shook their heads as they recounted his classroom practice as described by the pupils, aye, no doubt he probably tries to get the kids to fill in application forms for the Labour Party, the bastard!

And the pupils themselves would speak about how they quite liked him, aw, Mister Whatshisname, I think he's magic, everyone does! People joked to him in the staffroom that the pupils got on so well with him on account of him having the same IQ as them, aye, he can relate to them better, they all share the same mental age!

And the staff who said that looked at each other and laughed, throwing their heads back, and then looked at him, Armpits. Armpits would be smiling and shaking his head at them, aye, go on, laugh, half-wits!

Armpits would just stand there and take it, laughing himself and saying aye, well yous are all just jealous bastards just 'cause the kids reckon I try and understand them a wee bit better than the average teacher like yous eh, and please note the pejorative use of the word average, I intend to insult and criticise!

Christjesus, eh, after the insensitivity of some of yous in your classrooms, fuck! The kids are bound to appreciate some, bloody, some bloody, aw for fuck sake I don't know, and he was smiling back at them, ya bastards!

Folk were laughing with him, aye, it's because the kids can talk to you about their spots and you can talk to them about your weight problem, heh heh!

Aye, fucking mutual angst, he said, keep talking boys, mutual angst, so it is, I'm glad I make you laugh, at least I realise I've got an existence in this place, some kind of definition, even though it's a shite one! Better to realise that, than be in total ignorance like you guys eh, fuck! Armpits still stood there grinning.

Then he turned and said remember son, who the role model is around here, eh! Folk were laughing. And as he departed, Armpits said, with further smiling, I canni take yous lot anymore, Christjesus, fucking murder so you are, fucking murder, you fucking kill me.

…

Sam sat and read his weapons magazine, it was on his desk and he was leaning back in his chair, sometimes lifting his legs up and pushing against the desk with his knees so that his chair tilted back. Then he released the pressure of his knees on the tabletop and tilted back towards the desk, before starting again, creating a kind of effect of a swing, the end of the chair legs made a half-parabola. As Sam did this, he flicked the corner of the pages of the magazine with his finger and thumb, the magazine was hanging over the edge of the desk a bit, and when he tilted backwards he had to stretch his arm just to reach it, and to do the corner-flicking thing .

Billy was wandering around the room and he stopped at Sam's desk, what you reading mate? Sam looked up and turned the magazine so the cover could be seen, then opened it again at the page he was reading, aw nothing, just. Naw, Billy insisted, what's in it! Sam didn't look up, och, nothing you'd be interested in Billy. Billy looked at the man on the cover with camouflage-clothing on and paint smeared on his face, hmmf, guns eh. Sam said aye, but it's more than that though, you canni just have a magazine that's only on guns.

Billy said what else is in it then, it looks like it's just a magazine on guns. Sam flicked through the pages, glancing up at Billy every half-second, then Billy tried to grab the magazine but Sam snatched it up and away from him, holding it out to the side, suspending his arm in mid-air. Billy grinned, so come on then mate, what else is in it?

Sam replied, saying that there was a bit of history in it, the magazine. Billy looked at people around him, aye, the history of guns! Sam said maybe, but also there's really history in it, proper history, 'cause there's information about warfare, and stuff about how countries get on with each other nowadays, articles on different countries, just. Billy said oh aye, do you need to know all that in order to learn how to fire a gun! Sam said no, but if I'm gonni be in the army, me, then I need to know a bit about how countries get on together today, or not, know?

Billy said okay, and wandered down to his chair.

Sam said aye, I dinni really read these history bits but, I think they just make it up so they can tell a story. He wasn't speaking to anyone, not looking at anyone, and nobody seemed to be listening.

In the middle of the room Billy popped some gum in his mouth and leaned back and whacked the palm of his hand off the back of William's head, hey fats, give us a sweetie. William said get lost, you've already got something in your mouth.

Sam looked round, then turned back and put his magazine in his bag.

…

One morning William said aw sir, Joseph's in today, sir, sir, know that boy we were telling you about! The Bin Brigade looked and smiled at each other as they walked into the playground and started on the litter, ha ha, Joseph! They began to pick up sweetie wrappers and bits of chewing gum, leftovers from lunchtime.

Ha ha, Joseph, hee hee, Billy grinned, then he was shouting, here's the ball guys, watch out! And then he was kicking a bottle about, jinking from side to side, saying Gemmill, Gemmill, Gemmill, still Gemmill, and still Gemmill! The other boys stood still and allowed Billy to move around them, dribbling about the place with the bottle at his feet, the plastic made a noise as it bounced off the cement in the area in front of the building. Billy booted the bottle against a wall, and he scores, star man! Gemmill scores a brilliant, fantastic goal to keep Scotland's World Cup chances alive! And he turned, raising one arm, making a fist in the air and pulling it down, spitting in front of him as he ran towards the other boys, the saliva forming a curve in the air.

Aw, that's disgusting Billy, the boys looked at him, anyway, shut up, and they told him they'd all get sent inside if they were caught making too much noise. Billy ran up to the bottle which had bounced back off the wall and was sitting on the ground, and went to kick it again, though this time he froze in mid-kick and turned his head to look back at the ones who'd spoken to him, ah, got you there!

He wobbled a bit on one foot and then bent down to pick up the bottle, and he held it over his bag, his hand hovering as he walked back, em, I'm not being rude, but you'll remember that Archie Gemmill goal sir eh? And the curvy spit afterwards, hee hee! Some of the other pupils said Archie Gemmill? Billy ignored them. Again, someone said, Archie who?

Billy carried on, my dad always says that was the greatest goal in the world ever, still is, Argentina, nineteen-seventy-eight, yeah? He said he was watching the game on the telly with his family and everybody leapt off the sofa and knocked over the table in front of them, beer, food and everything, everywhere, everybody's knees had banged into it, and they never cleared it up, well not straight away, they just danced about, shouting, Archie, Archie!

Billy dropped the bottle into his bag, started to look around, and then walked about, towards other pieces of rubbish, to get them into the bag, and as he crouched down he turned his head upwards and said but sir, the goal hadn't save Scotland's chances though eh!

He kept looking up, still sir, you hear Joseph was in school today sir, you met him yet? Then he walked away and towards William, ha ha, hey fatso, sir's gonni meet Joseph for the first time today! William poked his glasses up on his nose, frowning and shaking his head, I know Billy, it was me that told sir in the first place.

124

Billy said, I'm just saying, perfecto eh, hee hee! William stopped frowning and started smiling, and he also said, aye, Joseph, hee hee!

…

There was talk in the staffroom, some of the pupils had said to the rector, or somebody, that they hadn't liked the way a teacher had spoken to their class, they'd said it to somebody and the information had found its way to the rector, up to him. Some parents had phoned the school. There had also been a thing, like an incident it was, it was in the school office, when one dad had come in to complain, telling the office that the teacher had been out of order, he was shouting at the office staff, the parent, saying that guy's a bastard, the guy's a total bastard, he shouldn't be allowed inside a classroom, you tell that rector I want to see him, I want the guy sacked, bastard that he is, the guy's a total bastard.

Bastard Guy was the head of Modern Studies, and he was someone not many of the staff spoke to a lot, nor did they speak of him. He was a teacher, a colleague, no more than that, someone to be bumped into in a corridor.

If he spoke to Bicycle Clips, Bicycle Clips would listen to him and nod, and say tss, but say nothing else.

Mr Tambourine Man gave Bastard Guy the time of day, and sometimes Armpits would get into a conversation with him, though Mr Tambourine Man gave everyone the time of day, and Armpits would get into a conversation with anyone who spoke to him.

And if either of them did engage with Bastard Guy in time-giving or conversation, it would just be a thing between Bastard Guy and one of them, there

125

would never be a group, a huddle of three or four staff including Bastard Guy, all laughing or shaking their heads or nodding their heads about the thing. It would just be Bastard Guy and one other.

People would speak to him when spoken to, no-one would ignore him, though they didn't speak about him when he wasn't there.

This day a few people were mentioning the complaints, there was animation amongst them, a liveliness about the thing. It wasn't the first time, aye, know, not the first time. Aye I know, it's not the first time, he was bound to get caught one day, dare say it won't be the last.

Armpits would say listen to you lot, you don't know what you're talking about, it's all speculation, you're just gossiping for the sake of it, just leave it alone eh, bottom line, he's a colleague, eh, could happen to any of us.

And there would be much looking about from side to side. Checking of the staffroom door. Somebody jumped when the tannoy clicked on, and then the Phantom could be heard clearing his throat.

...

The Phantom had an interview coming up soon.

This was being reported by any number of people in the staffroom.

It was for a headteacher's post at a school nearby, not quite outside the town, but on the other side of the town. People were saying to him, when they saw him, aye good luck for the interview. When they couldn't avoid speaking about it, they said em, hope things go okay, eh, people that maybe spoke to him when he came into the staffroom would say this, plus

126

people whose eye the Phantom caught, oh, aye, em, good luck and that, know, em, just, the interview.

The Phantom said to them that the job he was going for, in its actuality, the thing the whole interview was about, well you see, it's not that important to me at all, you see, it's just that one of the chaps on the interview panel, well, it turns out that he's an old friend of mine, ex-colleague, you know, oh, from way back, old comrade-in-arms, you see?

People looked at each other, from one face to another, not looking at the Phantom.

There was the sound of newspapers being rustled, piles of jotters creaking on laps as people bent over and stretched round to look somewhere else.

The Phantom flicked his gown back over one of the shoulders, we've not seen each other in a long time and he called me up, here was this job he was interviewing for and, well there you are, you see, aah.

He continued on, about how the interview and all the stuff that goes on beforehand, the pre-interview visit and so on, would give the him and his friend a chance to talk about the history between them, reminisce on their days working together.

The Phantom said this to a few people in the days before the interview date.

Most folk knew it after a while.

…

You from Glasgow sir?

Billy waited for an answer. Then he said so sir, isn't it if you're from Glasgow you have to support Rangers or Celtic, even if you follow Partick Thistle, or Clyde or Queen's Park even, you still have to have a team that you want to win between Rangers and Celtic when they play each other. A few other pupils nodded.

127

Billy continued, my dad, he knows lots of folk from Glasgow and they all support one of they two, even if it's not their first team, isn't that right sir? If you're from Glasgow then you're bound to like one of them more than the other, have a soft spot, yeah?

Billy nodded at a couple of other pupils, see? I'm no from Glasgow but my dad is, know, born right next to Ibrox. Everyone he knows from Glasgow supports the 'Gers. Apart from the Celtic supporters.

A few of Billy's friends nodded, flicking bits of rubber across their desks, still nodding.

Billy continued again, what I mean is, they all support one or the other. If you ask them, that is.

From outside, some voices could be heard below in the playground.

The window had been half-opened and other noises could be heard.

Someone was whistling, a couple of pupils were singing something.

Billy looked around, that's how I'm a Rangers supporter, my dad being one and all, I still want the teams around here to do well but, I don't just want Rangers to win and everybody else to lose, know.

Billy smiled, think my dad does though!

…

Know what I think, see at this time of the year? Mr Tambourine Man was talking as he dealt the cards. He looked around and said em, it's alright, nobody listen to me. No-one in particular was giving him attention, he noticed this and said hmmf, but that's okay, that's just bloody alright. He looked up again, there were a few hmmfs and smiles from the others. He laughed, well it'll have to be effing alright then won't

128

it! He laughed again, continued dealing, and the others at the card table looked at their hands, laughing too.

Armpits was coming into the room, hanging his coat up. He looked over and smiled, you showing them your last year's exam results again, that what the laughter's about, eh! Mr Tambourine Man looked round, shut up man, I'm just saying, this time of year, know.

Armpits nudged him on his way past, what you boring everyone about today then, eh? Mr Tambourine Man mumbled, want in? Armpits shook his head, nah go on, I'll sit this one out, on you go guys, play, I'll just get a coffee, my breath's not stinking enough today yet, want to breathe caffeine fumes over these second years next period, see if they wake up for once. He looked at Mr Tambourine Man, sorry, you were saying something when I came in, were you not?

Mr Tambourine Man threw both hands back and said Christ, can a guy not make a point! Armpits pulled his head back a bit and raised his eyebrows, aye, aye, this time of year, this time of year, on you go, and he started to walk towards the urn, looking back at Mr Tambourine Man, spit it out then, man, let it all out, you'll feel better!

Hang on, you need to wait now, you've interrupted me that much, Mr Tambourine Man was into his game now. Armpits shook his head and poured his coffee and sat down on an armchair, he lifted up a newspaper and put it back down on the table again, ach, papers, nothing but rubbish and lies, rubbish and lies.

The game progressed and not a lot was said between the players, Mr Tambourine Man wasn't cracking the jokes the way he would, instead screwing his eyes up as he looked at his hand, shaking his head.

When it was over and the bell rang he walked across and sat down beside Armpits and said, nah, ach, I was just thinking, I was telling my wee first years as well, but I don't think they understood, that, well, just, well isn't there some songs, aren't there some songs that just make the winter seem the best time of the year to be listening to the radio, know, they make you feel you're glad it's winter, you're actually glad it's winter! Aren't there, eh?

Armpits said aye pal, you're no wrong.

Aye I'm no wrong, you're right! Mr Tambourine Man moved his arms as he spoke and raised his voice a bit, I mean Christmas songs are cheesy, I canni stand them personally, but I'm talking about, I mean, you know how you just get that odd one that's Christmassy without being Christmassy, it's just wintery, know, December Will Be Magic Again, a proper tragedy in the lyrics but there's just something about it, River, with Jingle Bells being played at the start, 2000 Miles, a wee guitar hook to die for, you know, I just love songs with winter references, know, cold, snow, December, frost, it's like the writers wanted to have a big Christmas hit but wanted the songs to be clever too, know? Artful.

Armpits said aye, but tell me this then, how come Walk Out To Winter wasn't a big hit then? Christ knows, Mr Tambourine Man shook his head, a truly ringing tune, don't know how he gets the guitars to sound the way they do, the backing vocals on the chorus where it goes, em, chill will wake you, and then again when it goes, chance is buried.

The two of them sat still, Mr Tambourine Man looked down towards the floor in front of Armpits, Armpits stared at Mr Tambourine Man's shoes.

Mr Tambourine Man then said his son was learning the drums just now, and he'd been playing them along to Walk Out To Winter last time he'd been visited by him, Mr Tambourine Man said he'd given him a copy of the song to practise along to.

He looked down at his shoes, isn't it funny.

Armpits then interrupted him, isn't it funny how the first half of the album is all songs with acoustic guitars, apart from Walk Out To Winter that is? And how the second side is practically all electric, or electric-based songs, apart from the last one? I mean couldn't they have swapped the two to make it an acoustic half and electric half? You know, you do get that sometimes eh.

Mr Tambourine Man said man, that's pretty insightful for you mate, melody-man that you are! Although there's actually two songs that are acoustic-based on the second half, but I suppose Lost Outside the Tunnel has lots of keyboards in the chorus which might make someone like you think they're electric guitars!

Armpits crossed his legs, are you patronising me again? Mr Tambourine Man shook his head and raised one arm up, and said no, no! Aye, just as well, said Armpits. Mr Tambourine Man smiled, I wouldn't patronise you, and then said, I just think you did really well to spot that!

Ah, fuck off man, Armpits laughed.

But you're right though mate, Mr Tambourine Man went on, I mean I realise now you point it out, that whole electric acoustic, acoustic electric thing, it's obvious now I think about it, but just, I never noticed it before.

He stood up, there you are then. He held the back of his chair, and was tapping his fingers on the back of the chair, anyway, I was just saying, this time of year, know, something about the songs.

Armpits nodded, you thinking about Christmas mate, how it'll be this year, after last year?

Aye, Mr Tambourine Man looked down, then up, ah well, got to get on. He looked at his watch, I was just saying, thinking, know? You know?

Armpits pursed his lips and nodded, yeah mate, I know, it'll be okay.

4. ABOUT TO SAY AMEN

Marie was back to coming in and sitting up in class, smiling again, and she smiled and answered questions and helped the others with their work. And the others smiled at her and said thanks Marie, and they looked her in the eye as they spoke to her, and she looked them in the eye aas she spoke back. And smiled

Kelly said you know, the place is happier when when you're here Marie, so it is. Marie smiled at her. Aw Marie, Kelly giggled, you know you always say that you just love thinking about something or other, well, I just love it when you're here and you're happy, the whole place just seems happier!

A boy looked at Kelly and asked how? She never says anything!

Kelly turned to look at the boy.

No other boy laughed.

The boy said aw, sorry Marie I was just making a joke 'cause you don't actually say a lot, sure you don't. And Marie smiled back at him. He nodded towards Kelly, I know I know, as Kelly scowled at him.

Marie laughed and said to Kelly och Kelly, it's alright, I know I'm not one for saying a lot.
…

Billy said he wouldn't be in the next Thursday, he would be going to Germany with his dad, aye I'm going to see the 'Gers again sir! Away to Cologne, know? Two-one up after the first leg, so we're bound to have a chance. He looked around, it's gonni be magic eh, come on the Billy Boys! And he started to punch the air, first with his right arm then with his left, chanting all the time, hullo, hullo!

133

Somebody asked how many times will that be that you've been to Germany, Billy, three is it? First time actually, Billy said, it was Holland he'd been to twice, and he faced the front again, it's great sir, you all go over and watch the match, leave about midday and come back the same night, aye, arrive in the wee small hours after a big sing-song on the bus, plus maybe a sip from a can of lager if my dad's mates spot that my dad's no looking, or he's asleep with a drink in him himself, ha ha! He was smiling, so were the others, at Billy.

Billy then said no, I won't be coming in the next day 'cause I'll probably no get much sleep on the coach like, and the school probably won't do anything much about me being absent, it never does, well, they might send a letter to my dad but he'll just tear it up, well!

Everyone laughed and Billy stuck his chest out and smiled looking around the room, if we get an away goal early on in the game then that's us, home and dry, perfecto!

…

One time Armpits was running to catch up, he was out of breath, look at me eh, fat bastard eh, ho'd on a minute, ho'd on, let's. And he leaned his arm against the wall and hung his head and took some breaths, Christjesus, ffew! He brought both arms down until his hands were at his knees, and moved his neck so his head went up and down, then stood up, that's better.

So, he began to get into walking again, speaking in between breathing, how you getting on eh? Avoiding pupils coming the other way, he said aye, you're doing alright, don't worry eh. He spoke about his own teaching practice, I never really liked it that much at first, actually used to think it would make me not fancy

134

teaching after all, but it became okay after a while, it was fine, and you'll be fine as well, eh.

Then he took a breath and asked so, do you stay up here then, at weekends, or go home to Glasgow? He nodded, aye it's much better here eh, all your mates here and that, aye. He picked something off the ground and put it in the bin, in the uni is it, halls of residence, aye, I remember, aye, Christjesus ho ho, shaking his head. He grinned, well, that's me just about caught my breath back now, so, em, so, what is it you students at the uni get up to nowadays eh, adding, know, when you're no all in your rooms studying!

He nodded, oh aye? And continued, I used to be in a band myself when I was at college, that's how I used to spend my spare hours. And the ones I should have been at lectures in! He held the folder he was carrying and strummed it, played rhythm guitar myself eh, aye, we were no bad, just a few of us, playing a few gigs on and off, never thought we'd do anything with it though, just played, know, for the fun of it, there were loads of folk like us. We were just in it for the fun of it. And for the free beer in pubs! Don't have the guitar anymore, think I gave it away, stupid thing to do.

He smiled and looked ahead and upwards, aye, played cover versions mostly, you know, Procol Harum, ELO, the Move, shit like that, plus stuff our dads made us listen to. Had the Jeff Lynne look, me, dark sunglasses and curly hair! And then Armpits was singing, forgetting the words, fuck how'd it go! She's crazy about Wagner! Or how about this one, we played the light fandango! And he pulled a ruler out of his folder and started to wave it about, conducting as he sang the organ solo to A Whiter Shade Of Pale, daaaa da-da-da-da-da-da-da daaaa da-da dee-dee-dee, da

135

daaaa da-da dee-dee-dee, da-da-da-da-da-da-da dee do-do-do-do da-da-da dee-dee-dee-dee daaaa, and the crowd called out for more, heh heh!

A couple of girls passing by had been looking at him as he was singing, and they walked on, laughing between themselves. Armpits held his arm up with his elbow pointing at them, raising his folder as if he was about to hit them, ach, though he was smiling, get lost yous two, dinni know a true melody when you hear it, or a great voice! The pupils giggled, aye, naw, you're a great singer sir! And they went away, still laughing, looking at each each other.

Armpits laughed after them, then put his ruler back and tucked his folder under his arm, those were the fucking times eh, and then he said the thing is though, I can't remember who I gave that guitar to either. And he kept walking on, singing the pizzicato played by the violins in the introduction to Livin' Thing.

...

If the Phantom made a visit to the Bin Brigade in class he would often talk to them about the Greeks, it would either be mythology, or democracy in Athens, or perhaps even the Romans, and he would enthuse, aah, Classics, aah, what I learned at school, if only they taught it everywhere nowadays, aah! The class always sat back and smiled while being told a story by the Phantom, and the Phantom was quite the one for telling them, so the lesson would pass this way, everyone would be smiling, the class, the Phantom.

Then one day he talked to them about art, since he had just been visiting an Art class about something, seeing a pupil, and he told the Bin Brigade he had been inspired by a print on the Art teacher's wall of Christ In

136

The House Of His Parents, aah, Christ In The House Of His Parents! And they stared at him without saying anything when he then quizzed them about the split between the realists and medievalists within the Pre-Raphaelite Brotherhood. He asked James, what do you think James, who are you for, Rossetti or Millais, Morris or Hunt, eh, whose camp is your foot in? And the class giggled as James shrugged his shoulders and spread his arms out, shaking his head. The Phantom continued, of course, Morris was never really a Pre-Raphaelite in the first place. Factions, factions, you see, factions. He shook his head and looked at Marie, although he didn't say anything to her, he just looked at her.

He'd asked Marie a couple of times, in other lessons, about some of the Classics she'd learned at the school she went to before this one, aah, Marie, a student of the Classics just like myself! But Marie had told him more than once that because she hadn't enjoyed the Classics in that school she hadn't paid attention in the lessons, I thought they were rubbish, sir. Marie smiled as she said this and the Phantom smiled back, nodding, but he never asked her about Classics again, he didn't pursue that line anymore.

Sometimes some of the others asked the Phantom why Classics was called Classics, or they would ask about aspects of Classics, myths and legends which the Phantom had already told them about and which they wanted to hear again, they showed an interest in names, personalities, stories, Daedalus and Icarus, Ariadne, the minotaur.

Billy sometimes made up names of characters to ask the Phantom about, tell us what Syphilis did sir, aw, star man, Syphilis was, eh, or he would scratch his head

137

and say sir, who was Clitoris and what did she get up to sir! The Phantom always took the joke, aah Billy, the old ones are the best, eh!

On this day, the Phantom was also telling the Bin Brigade that he'd been in Edinburgh at the weekend, and he'd passed by a statue of David Hume in the form of a thinker in Greece, an ancient, and the Phantom mentioned Aristotle and Plato. Billy asked if Plato was the one they named the planet after, but the Phantom ignored him and carried on, telling the class about the Treatise, and how Hume had been a Scottish thinker of some renown, and maybe one day one of the Bin Brigade would be a Scottish thinker of some renown, he looked around and saw William staring at the wall, like you are now William, a great thinker, aah. William jumped in his seat, eh, what?

The class laughed as the Phantom looked at William, smiling at him, holding his arm out towards him, aah, I can just imagine you William, dear boy, you, a great thinker of your time, sitting, naked to the world around you, your forehead resting on your fist, contemplating your navel and in it the great questions of the world, pontificating on the confluence of events, with a Rodin in the background, sculpting you in your torment!

William pushed his glasses back up the bridge of his nose, I wouldni sit naked! And he muttered under his breath to Billy that the Phantom must be a pervert. The rest hooted, ah William! Sitting naked! Yurgh, don't make me boak, Kelly laughed, and then she looked at William, sorry William, I'm just joking. Then she looked around at some of the others in the class and laughed again, again saying to William aw William, I am sorry, I didni mean it, and then she was giggling, hee hee!

The Phantom addressed the class, come come, now now, now, who knows which ones amongst you may one day be the leading thinker of his generation, or her, it could be a girl, you never know, one of you assembled amongst us here, in the future, breaking horizons with moral theories, incurring the wrath of the church, as Hume once did by declaring all miracles to be unbelievable!

Billy showed an interest at that point, is that right sir, did that guy Hume say he didni believe in miracles! Miracles out the Bible? Was he a brainy guy then? The Phantom said yes Billy, Hume was indeed brainy, and the Phantom then went on at length about the questioning of notions, em, aah, brainy people Billy, intellectuals, they are constantly questioning established notions. Billy blinked.

The Phantom continued, indeed Billy, em, aah, brainy people, they indicate, if necessary, when beliefs are irrational unless they are based on evidence, brainy people are aware of the conditioning which takes place around them, to them, the brainy people. As he said this, Billy blinked, and blinked once more.

And the Bin Brigade sat at their desks and looked at the Phantom, some nodding their heads when he looked at them as individuals. Then someone shouted, aw sir, tell us that one about the guy pushing the big stone up the hill again!

…

He pushed the door open with the palm of his hand and his foot at the same time, and marched through the doorway, first in to the classroom, looking around, alright sir how you doing. There were a few laughs from the line of pupils following in behind him, none of the pupils saying anything, just watching him.

Eh, I'm Joseph, alright? He looked around again, and I'll just sit here, right? And he pulled a chair out and sat down, aye, I was meant to be in at the end of last week but I dogged it, but I'm here now, right?

The rest of the class came in, looking from Joseph to the front of the room, from the front of the room back to Joseph and so on, not all at the same time, there would always be somebody looking at Joseph and there would always be somebody looking at the front of the room.

Joseph looked up, towards the front of the class, and asked what d'you mean sir, Kevin's seat. He scowled, Kevin's no here, is he, so this'll just be my seat now, okay, I'm staying right here, and he looked around at the class as he pulled the seat under him, then manipulated the desk a bit until it was right over his lap.

Joseph looked back at the front, well, he's no here today, sir. He looked round at the class again, you gonni do anything about it sir? It doesn't look like you're doing anything about it eh. Though you look like you want to do something about it. I'll tell you what I'm doing about it. Nothing. I'm staying right where I am, in my seat, not Kevin's, and he shook his head and folded his arms.

The class looked from Joseph to the front of the room and then at each other, some pupils just looked at the floor. There was a bit of a silence.

Eh sir? Joseph lifted himself up in his seat a bit, elbows resting on the table, cracking his knuckles. Aw hey Joseph, sir's alright, a boy said, there was no-one else speaking. Shut up you, Joseph turned round and back again, eh sir, what you gonni do about it, you

gonni keep this seat for poor wee milk-boy Kevin? And
he punched the palm of one hand with the fist of the
other, ha ha!

Aw hey Joseph, Marie intervened now, don't
speak about Kevin when he's not here.

Joseph turned and looked at Marie. She looked
at the front of the class. He turned back, saying nothing.

Billy then said to Marie, better leave it alone
Marie. But Marie spoke again, to Billy, saying well
Billy, there's no need to be having a go at Kevin behind
his back, that's all I'm saying, and Joseph knows that.

Joseph turned and said I wasni having a go at
Kevin, how, is that what you think I was doing 'cause I
wasn't, okay? I wouldni do that. Then Billy opened his
mouth for a second before saying, aw Joseph, she was
just.

Joseph looked at him and interrupted, you want
to make something of it Billy boy? And he stood up.
Billy said naw, naw Joseph, it's just. Joseph faced the
front again, then looked around the class. Billy talked to
Joseph again, maybe Kevin'll be arriving late this
morning, he sometimes does, know? Joseph shook his
head, poor wee milk boy Kevin, arriving late 'cause his
drunk mammy couldni wake him after after he came in
from delivering the milk.

He looked at Billy who was just staring at him
now, what's the matter with you Billy, you not got over
Rangers getting beaten the other night, ha ha!

Billy continued to stare at Joseph, Marie stared
at him as well, the class watched.

Marie said em, Joesph, Joseph?

Then Joseph looked at the front, ach, I can't be
bothered, I don't want to sit on this seat anyway sir, and
he got up and moved to another seat, nuttering och, this

141

is rubbish, and leaving Kevin's chair, half of it under the desk, half sticking out.

…

Sam was drawing a poster about the assassination of Franz Ferdinand, aw man, look at this, how do you spell Sarajevo sir, it's got a hundred different spellings on these maps here in the books, how's that, was the spelling for everything different in those days?

Then he looked up, aw sir, see if I'd been alive then, I'd have been right down the recruiting office and kidding on I was old enough so I could join up. I mean, only once those ten steps to war you told us about had happened but, not straight after the guy was killed. But see once Germany was in, that'd be me, signing up, there and then!

A few people in the class looked up from their drawings and charts and posters. Sam went on, good job for some of the guys, the young guys, that it never happened after all these other things that happened before nineteen-fourteen, all the crisises, naw, crises was it, crises. Crises and more crises, Morocco and Bosnia and everything. Bosnia!

That's still here today isn't it, Billy said, he was sitting next to Sam.

Sam replied that he knew that, then he said sir, this picture of the Czar, the cartoon in the book, with his head in his hands, when the other guy's telling him that the war's started, or it's been declared, it looks like he never wanted the war in the first place, the Czar, but you said Russia wanted a war so it could get to control the Balkans, how come he didn't want war then, if it was the only way to get that, to control the Balkans?

The rest of the class smiled. William said listen to Sam, he's trying to get answers so he does better at his next test to get into the army, listen to him asking about the Balkans man, the Balkans!

Sam said no I'm not, and then he said well, so what if I am, can't I do that?

Billy said okay, and looked at the class, wait for it, wait for it!

Then Sam said, I'm gonni join the army, me.

The class collapsed.

...

Armpits always said I'm telling you son, the Bin Brigade are the happiest pupils in the school, I love teaching them, me, happiest kids in the school. He sat up, naw, naw really, look at it, naw, if you look at it, you've got no pressure to get them high grades, you can just choose something interesting to talk about for the period and away you go! Kids take the discussion along, they stay relevant, and have some laughes, and then before you know it, it's thank-you very much, lesson over, finito. I mean, think about it, do you ever press them hard if you're doing something they find difficult that's gonni take you ages to explain? No? See what I mean then!

He sat forward, look, people think that these kids don't have a lot going for them, and maybe they don't, or at least they certainly appear that way, some of them present like the poorest kids on the planet. But I'm telling you, some of them are the brightest things we have in the school, the brightest pupils I've met in my career, in terms of awareness, sharpness, I'm telling you.

Around him a few people looked up and then looked back at what they were doing. Armpits sat on the edge of his chair, resting his elbows on his knees and clasping his hands, throwing his forearms outwards, continuing. And he scratched his head, and they're optimists. Someone sitting at the edge of the Joke Club chipped in that they'd have to be optimists, that lot, ha, things couldni get much worse for them, eh, ha, no-hopers stuck in a class that cleans up litter all day, and the Joke Club had a laugh about it.

Armpits said, well, they are optimists, the kids in the Bin Brigade, and it's precisely this property that makes them bigger people than the rest of the kids here, than the rest of us maybe! A couple of people said em, we'll have to go now, Armpits nodded at them as they left. And he continued, maybe they keep changing their minds about things, dropping subjects, and they do, all of them in the Bin Brigade, or they're told to and they just don't protest at it, but at least they're making choices all the time, probably because they're forced to make decisions. Look at us, adults though, or we're supposed to be adults eh! Look at us.

With only one or two people listening now, Armpits spoke about teachers, including him, letting events take over them, wash over them, and spending their lives reacting to stuff that was taking over or washing over them.

He looked at the guy in the Joke Club who had made the crack about things not getting any worse, but he had since stood up and was standing at the window with his hands in his pockets.

…

I mean, how could somebody as young as that produce writing like that, you think they could do that? Shakespeare was going on about how he reckoned a pupil, a girl, had got someone older to write an English

144

essay, he'd just been quoting from the essay in the staffroom, he was waving the pieces of paper in the air at whoever he was talking to over the course of the interval.

It was mooted by some of his colleagues that since the girl used to be at another school, aye, maybe she kept in touch with a teacher there, or older friends, or maybe she had friends whose big brothers and sisters went to uni now, and they could have done the essay, know?

There was disbelief, but surely the lassie wouldni do that! Aye, naw, you'd be bound to get caught, she'd never do that, no? Someone said naw, it wouldn't be right, so the girl wouldn't do it. Someone else said aye, naw, she's like any other pupil here, she wouldn't necessarily do what she thought was right, she'd just do what she thought was best for her, aye, she'll have copied it alright. Other staff nodded and said no. Or shook their heads and said aye.

Shakespeare went on, I can't believe these fifteen year olds, sixteen year olds, they think we could believe that they'd be good enough to write an English essay, or any subjects' work, like that, at that age eh?

Then Sandwich Toaster said, oh I don't know, you do get kids who're just dead good at something, know? It could be writing, but it could just as likely be drawing, or painting, maybe playing a musical instrument, cutting wood, speaking French, better than teachers even, there's no reason why they shouldn't be, know?

Better than teachers! Shakespeare looked at him, don't talk crap man, better than teachers! The other teachers looked at him. Sandwich Toaster turned and went through to the staff tuck shop.

145

Though from someone else it was, well I bet that pupil wouldn't write the words don't talk crap in an essay! There were laughs all round. People went to go about their staffroom business, marking, waiting for the urn, why isn't this ever filled and already boiling when we get here?

Armpits and Mr Tambourine Man looked at each other. Armpits asked how old Roddy Frame was when he started writing the songs that ended up on High Land, Hard Rain. He and Mr Tambourine Man raised their eyebrows, fifteen, sixteen? Fucking twelve, man! The pair hooted.

Imagine having the talent to write The Bugle Sounds Again at that age, fifteen, sixteen. Mr Tambourine Man raised his eyebrows and looked ahead, and where would you ever believe you could find someone so young to have acquired such experience that would allow him to express such melancholy in the lyrics!

Takes you aback, know, Christjesus, Armpits nodded as he spoke. Mr Tambourine Man nodded back, clever wee devil too, using clichés in the words, then saying that the clichés fit him like a glove, he knows he's using clichés, but now nobody can say he's taking the easy option with his lyrics, the cliché itself is a device.

A fucking device aye. Just as I'm about to say amen! Mmm. Armpits nodded.

They both nodded. Each time one spoke the other nodded. Mr Tambourine Man said, a bass solo too! A bass solo that's not boring!

Armpits shrugged his shoulders, mm, think you're gonni start to lose me mate, hey, what about that wee wobbly bugle bit right at the end eh! Just as you think he's avoided using a bugle in the whole song, there it is in the last few of lines, shaking away!

Mr Tambourine Man laughed, ha ha, aye. Anyway, kids of fifteen? Sixteen? I'm effing certain that girl can write a good English essay. Armpits grinned, aye, fucking certain!

…

The Germans always called British people Englanders in the Second World War, didn't they sir? Sam was flicking the pages over in some books, I mean the First World War sir, didn't they? Or both even, probably, kill ze Englanders!

The class had been looking at some cartoons from the time of the First World War, and some had commented on the language that was used, there was a kind of observation amongst them, the thing being that British cartoonists always indicated soldiers from Germany referring to soldiers from Britain as Englanders, and politicians from Britain as Englanders also. The class made all sorts of deductions, that's maybe just what cartoonists, the artists, from Britain said though, isn't it sir, maybe? The class expressed their puzzlement, maybe the Germans didn't say that at all, Englanders sir, and it was just what the cartoonists said they said, no?

Then Sam pointed out, it says here that the Prime Minister at the time of the First World War was Welsh as well even, so even he wasn't English sir! My mum says she hates it when foreign people think Scottish people are English, maybe the Welsh hate it too. I suppose it's because foreign people think that England rules Scotland that they think the Scottish and Welsh are English.

Someone else in the class said that her dad was Irish and he never got mistaken for being someone from England.

…

Bicycle Clips said he had these maps he'd just bought, aye, em, just got them delivered recently, look! They're new! He said the maps showed countries and the places in the countries that had links with events that were taught about in History, in schools and at universities, they're brilliant son, tss, know how you sometimes get these ones of Scotland, aye maybe in the Sunday papers, or the cheap bookshops? He looked around the staffroom, a few people were sitting up, they looked over their newspapers towards the classroom desk that Bicycle Clips was standing over, maps bundled together in his hands.

Some of the people around nodded, aye, I've seen them before, they show you things like where Bruce was crowned or where the Covenanters' hiding places were in different parts of the country, or, you know, this or that, Edinburgh Castle and such like. Aye, every wee town tries to say there's a cave just on its boundaries that William Wallace stopped for a bite to eat in, or took a piss in, when he was running away from the English eh! Stick a plaque at the side of the road, Wallace ate a ham sandwich and urinated here in the name of freedom, and suddenly it's history, binding local heritage with the destiny of a nation!

Bicycle Clips nodded back, aye, I suppose, well. In one hand he held one of his clips, he put one end of them in his mouth and moved his lips up and down on it, aye, these maps are just like that, but only they're for other countries, it's fantastic, I've never seen them before, tss!

148

He stood over the table in the staffroom and put the maps down on it, they were rolled up in scrolls, I think you'd probably be able to get them in the countries themselves, know, in the language of the country itself, just like we get these Scottish ones with the Wallace caves in them.

And he took a newspaper or magazine cutting out of his jacket pocket, but look here, I found this advert in one of the history monthlies I get, it said this was them in English, the maps, foreign ones, great eh!

Bicycle Clips said so then, when I'd sent for the pack I thought the maps were going to be all of European Union countries, aye, naw, but here you go, Switzerland, Peru, Argentina, note the use of Malvinas to describe you-know-where, Vietnam even, ergo I was evidently wrong, there are a few European Union ones, and a few odd ones from around the world that obviously aren't European Union, I think it must have been that the company making the maps, selling them, tried to push them as a thing schools could use to promote a European dimension, or a world view, know? That right, you think? A real odd collection of countries, tss!

And he rolled out some maps across the table and looked at Armpits, come and look, here's the maps I was showing you earlier, help me show them off to our young man here, eh. Armpits sighed and leaned forward in his seat, oh aye, I'll show you, here, what we've got, look, we've got Germany, France, Belgium, Austria, Switzerland, em, Italy. I think that's, oh Spain, aye Spain. Here you are, here's one opened out, Austria, look, Linz, where Hitler sang in the church choir, it says here, eh.

Someone across the staffroom said really? Armpits turned round, aye, though I don't know exactly if the Austrians want the rest of Europe to be constantly getting reminded of that, Armpits raised his eyebrows, ha ha, nor the people of Linz, I dare say, maps and everything!

Mr Tambourine Man stood up and came across, saying Linz? Does it say anything else about there, or that wee region? Must be loads of musical things on that map is there not, there's bound to be if it's a historical map of Austria, know, Salzburg, Vienna, eh?

Oh aye, come on round here, it's a veritable de facto history of classical music, or romantic anyway! Bicycle Clips sat down and spread the map of Austria out on his lap as Mr Tambourine Man leaned over to have a look. They were both pointing to different bits of Austria, their fingers banging into each other, sorry, oh sorry, oops, eh sorry, and both spotting things on the map and indicating them to each other, saying mm, mm aha, aye look here, oops sorry!

Mr Tambourine Man said to Bicycle Clips there you are, Linz! Bruckner, remember? Remember how you said Bruckner had numeromania yeah, well there you are that's the place where he played the organ, Linz, or practically that, just beside it, outside it actually.

Bicycle Clips looked up and asked, aye? And he asked again, is that right, Linz? Mr Tambourine Man said aye yeah, of course, it was Ansfelden I think, the specific place, Ansfelden or Anhelden, and he looked up, furrowing his brow, then nodding his head, aye, naw, Ansfelden, Ansfelden it was. Ansfelden he was born in, and grew up in too, but it's probably too small to put on the map, it wasn't too far from Linz, and there

150

was that church in a wee place called St. Florian, again not on the map, where he played an organ with over five thousand pipes.

Bicycle Clips opened his eyes, stretching them, five thousand!

Mr Tambourine Man laughed, aye, and he'll have had them all counted, down to the last one eh! Ha ha, oh aye, he'll have known exactly how many there were!

Bicycle Clips said aye he would have, old Bruckner, what with his numeromania and all!

Then Mr Tambourine Man said em, actually, maybe the two of us stand corrected, because actually wasn't it that the numeromania hadn't developed until later on in his life? With the depression and all that, the time in the sanitorium and all that stuff?

Bicycle Clips screwed his lip and said hmm.

Armpits, standing, put his drink down, he'd gone over to the other side of the staffroom by the time Mr Tambourine Man and Bicycle Clips had reached this point in their conversation, and he now shouted over, Eindhoven was it, Eindhoven where that Brooker guy was from? Mr Tambourine Man and Bicycle Clips looked at Armpits and then back at the map.

Armpits shook his head, oh aye, just cut me out of your intellectual discussion, I was just trying to show an interest eh, and he put his cup of coffee to his mouth, coughing as he took a sip, and then spilling the drink down on to his tie, looking at Mr Tambourine Man and Bicycle Clips, wiping the coffee off with the back of one hand, och, fuck sake.

…

The Dog-Catcher said bye darling, waved by holding her hand up and pulling her fingers up and down, and pulled away from the kerb, putting some chewing gum in her mouth as she did so.

Inside the station there were signs for trains that were heading for all over the place, all leaving in the next hour. There were only three platforms, but where the station was located, in relation to the development of the railways in Scotland in the eighteen-hundreds, meant that trains crossed through it going east to west, north to south. People stood in groups, twos, fours, a two and a one, a four and a one, sometimes an eight and a three, or just a five, or a five and a one. Maybe there was a four and a four, not standing together, but forming an eight anyway, it worked out like that, it worked out.

They all looked up at the screens, which were flashing information up, saying Inverness or Perth, Ullapool, St. Andrews and Wemyss Bay. Maybe Glasgow. Sometimes one or two individuals broke off from their groups to view the posters advertising trips to the islands, journeys which included the price of the boat, some kind of network collusion between the railway companies and ferries, it was a deal, sometimes there was a hotel thrown in.

The costs varied from thirty-two pounds to sixty-four, sometimes not a multiple of eight or even four.

…

The school's chaplain was in school for the morning, doing a couple of assemblies for the first years and second years, a prayer, a hymn, a talk on something in the news or relating to a school thing, Jesus might be mentioned. It was his habit to come in to the staffroom at some point to make smalltalk with a few teachers, he asked after them, how are you doing,

152

and he responded to their answers with of course, I see, ah, that's great, divine! Also, he would say do you know, the pupils sang magnificently this morning, it was absolutely divine! Plus he would maybe say em, is your mother okay, I didn't see her in church on Sunday. That sort of thing, it was the kind of thing he would say to the staff. Crossword Freak Number One was one for pulling Chaplain Divine to the side, having conversations with him, syllables with sh, ss, ts, all could be heard, Crossword Freak Number One punctuating everything he said with that is, that is. Crossword Freak Number Two threw a word or two in to the conversation. Crossword Freak Number Three said nothing.

Today, once Chaplain Divine had done with all the pleasantries, he then went over to Ex-Cop who was sitting on a chair at the classroom desk, he was marking jotters. Chaplain Divine and Ex-Cop had a conversation which, apart from Ex-Cop looking up at the start and saying me, you're asking me, nobody else could hear, sometimes one or both of them would look up and around the room if one of them had said something, a word or two, which was picked up by a few other people. The two of them weren't really whispering, it was more like they were talking in voices that couldn't be distinguished by anyone, what with the other conversations and noises going on in the staffroom, the water boiling in the urn, chocolate biscuits being unwrapped.

Ex-Cop wasn't looking in Chaplain Divine's eyes, he was still looking at his jotters, or the one on the top of the pile, but he was nodding and saying aye, thanks, yeah okay, and yeah, sure, and he smiled without opening his mouth, he was holding his pencil in it. Chaplain Divine said okay then, and put his hand on Ex-Cop's forearm which was resting on the table, and patted it a couple of times as he turned and went away, okay, I'll see you again then.

On his way out of the staffroom, Chaplain Divine nodded a cheerio to a few people. And a few people half-waved back at him, aye, see you another time, good sermon today, aye, all the best. Crossword Freak Number One said good day, that is, I hope you have one.

Ex-Cop carried on with his marking. He didn't look up at anyone and nobody tried to talk to him.
…

Some staff were talking about Social Education lessons and saying that they didn't like teaching them. One teacher had been given a Social Education class to do for a colleague who was not in today, aye, ach, man it was just last minute, just like that, no time to get something together to do while they worked, then when I got there, there was no work left other than a sheet of A4 on the desk saying litter, discuss! What's the point eh!

From some others there was agreement, you're right, I mean, it's a load of shite, the kids hate it, we hate it, what's the bloody point!

From the card table Mr Tambourine Man watched them and listened without saying anything, he shuffled the cards and played with the pack.

People spoke about the things they covered in the Social Education lessons they had to teach, health, sex, smoking, drugs, applying for jobs and such, and nobody could see the point in it, any of it, they said ach, the kids learn more off the television than they do in S.E. man! And they said god sake, we managed without

154

it! Nah, no point. This continued and at the end of break most of them left the staffroom, nodding to each other, no work set, it's a bloody disgrace.

See them all filtering away son, Mr Tambourine Man looked up now and nodded in their direction, saying there's no point to S.E., hmmf, as if there's an effing point to what we actually do want to teach them, what we've all gone to university for four years to learn to teach them, what's actually included in the curriculum, eh! You think about it, and.

Then there was another voice, aye aye, here we go again! Armpits got up, out of his seat, and as he put his jacket on he pointed his elbow towards Mr Tambourine Man and said em, better get your pen out son, he'll be expecting you to take notes eh!

Away and teach man, and Mr Tambourine Man hit Armpits with a sheet of paper as he passed by him, and said again, away and teach, eh, and how's the diet coming on and all eh!

Armpits laughed and said well, I've given up jogging! And Mr Tambourine Man laughed and said aye, round Sir John Clarke's estate eh, like the girl in the Lost Soul Band song! Armpits hooted, and said you can't win them all mum, and then left the staffroom, lifting his hands up and pretending to take notes, hee hee!

Mr Tambourine Man turned round, smiling, don't listen to that eejit, then said naw, I'm just saying son, I heard you saying to someone earlier you were doing an essay, thought you might want some pointers. I'm a secret intellectual me! And then he said aw aye, I like a good read and all, used to be doing a research paper for a PhD in Education Studies, gave it up but, job was too busy, makes you give everything up right enough. I suppose I could have stuck at it.

He leaned forward, anyway, Illich was my guy, Illich, know? Yup, that's the one, I'm a deschooler of society! Had to read all his stuff inside out, I was able to say it in my sleep, man! Aye, you've read it? All pupils are inmates, and then they become mindless citizens, yeah!

He sighed, these idiots there, and he indicated the door of the staffroom with his thumb, or a lot of them, not my fine fat friend of a union rep, he's okay on a good day! No, I mean those guys going on about Social Education, marching out of here putting the world to rights, I mean.

He sat back. I accept that it's not presented well, S.E. I mean, nobody enjoys trying to use the materials, and the kids do hate it, but it's actually the most essential stuff we could teach the kids. Naw, really! Compulsory too, aye, you're surprised, eh. It, P.E. and R.E., they're all compulsory by law, never mind English, or Maths, History, Music.

He went on. Why? Well, you think about it. We kid ourselves on that in our subjects, apart from the knowledge, historical facts, the notation, algebra, etcetera, etcetera, what we all like to think is that we teach so-called transferable skills, in our own subjects, skills that pupils can use in other subjects, or which they'll take into the big bad world outside of school when they leave, employment, college, training, uni and the like. You know, logical argument, constructive criticism, extended writing, independent research, problem-solving. But really, couldn't we, shouldn't we, have these as subjects in their own right? If they're that important? We could, couldn't we. We should, even!

He shook his head, seriously though son, think about it, if an alien came from outer space and observed how we lived our daily lives for a while, what skills we used, communication and so on, and then you got that alien to design an education curriculum that gave every child the potential to do well when they left school, what would they come up with? The stuff that's meant to be in the Social Education syllabus, or what should be in it, that's what, never mind the traditional subjects!

He shook his head again, it pains me to say it, but they certainly wouldn't come up with effing Music! They'd say, make it a hobby. History. Hobby. Maths, Geography. And then he said, leaning forward a bit in his chair, surely Social Education, surely if it was properly funded, structured, with a national syllabus, surely if it was taught by trained people who want to do it and would be enthusiastic about it, surely the kids would not only like it but really appreciate it, and start to place a value on what they're doing in school. But will it ever happen?

Naw, Mr Tambourine Man sat further forward, there's a hidden curriculum at work here. In Scotland. In most places. Think how times have changed in the last century, values, democracy, nationhood, technology, communication, and yet the subjects that are taught in schools are virtually the same as they were centuries ago, just a little bit of tweaking here and there, letting the kids sit in front of an effing computer for an hour or so a week, that's about all.

So, and he sat back again, pupils are still downtrodden by the system. Look at Social Education, they hate it, yet we still teach it. Illich, my guy, says we need to deschool society, and I'm not even sure that's the solution. Schools, education, should maybe be part

157

of the establishment, I don't know. Maybe it's the system that needs disestablished eh.

Anyway, that's about where I got to in my research. Probably going nowhere when I stopped. Let you have a copy if you want, I was nearly at final draft stage, aye!

He stood up, bring it in tomorrow? Aye I will. As he walked to the door he said, well I'll get off and go and prepare a lesson on Bach to repress my next class, heh heh. Lecture over, you can put your pen away!

…

Sir, what are associates, what does associates mean sir, the word associates? Billy said he had been chased away from hanging about at the bottom of a set of stairs in a building at breaktime, and the teacher who had chased him had told him not to bring his associates back there again, sir it was like, that teacher guy, he just looks at me and goes you boy, don't you think about coming down this corridor again, or bringing your associates round here again. And it wasni just me, there were hundreds of us, well five, four I think.

Marie told Billy that the teacher had just meant his friends, Billy's friends, aw Billy, it wasn't anything bad, you know, Billy, don't bring your friends round here again, that's all he was saying. Billy was turning to face Marie, she smiled at him, him shook his head, aw, well how come he didn't say that then! Associates! Making me feel stupid with his big words, man that's all teachers ever do.

He looked at the front of the class, how come he has to use fancy words like associates, who says that ever! Associates! He's only doing that 'cause he knows

I won't know what it means, thinks I'll have to ask him what he means, eh!

Marie said, well now you know what it means Billy, you won't have to ask next time. Aye, suppose, Billy sat, not saying anything for a second, then he said, people are always doing that sir, aren't they, using big words all the time just to make you feel like you're thick, 'cause you don't know what they mean, only what it is, it's that you've got half an idea, enough to get the message, but you don't want to ask them what they mean 'cause you know that's what they want they want you to ask so you look thick. Small.

Billy shook his head. Then William came into the classroom with James behind him, they went over to a desk and sat down. Billy saw them, ah William welcome! And I see you have your associate with you eh!

William looked at Billy and said associate? You better not be calling me a pervert, Billy! Billy hooted, ha ha William, associate doesni mean pervert, you think everything means pervert!

…

Did you go for that army interview again at the weekend Sam? Sam turned round towards Kelly, she had asked the question. He shook his head, then nodded, yeah but it wasn't really an interview, it was more a fitness test, and other things, it wasn't an interview, you just turn up and you just get a fitness test and then they ask you about school, and what you'd want to do if you got into the army, be a soldier or learn a trade like engineering or something.

That sounds like an interview, someone else said. Sam turned the other way to look at the pupil, aye well, they do interview you, sort of, but it's not an

159

interview. So, you do get interviewed, asked Kelly. Yeah, they ask you questions, Sam nodded, shrugging his shoulders. And Kelly asked, and that's not an interview?

The Bin Brigade were observing Kelly, who was looking at Sam, tilting her head a bit. She said again, it's not an interview? Sam looked back at her, aye, it's not! They were all grinning, the class. Kelly started to giggle, aye it's not an interview? Sam smiled, aye, naw! They were all laughing, aye, naw, aye, naw! Kelly laughed out loud, so it was just a fitness weekend then! Sam said aye!

The laughter died down. The lesson got underway. Later on someone asked Sam how he'd got on, how d'you actually get on then? Sam said he'd passed everything apart from the two-mile run, he always passed the other things whenever he went, geography, general knowledge, aye, I do well at them, so I do, and I'm getting better at the run each time.

But he'd failed it again this time, he nodded, he'd just need to keep on practising. He pursed his lips, in a few weeks time I'll get my last chance.

…

As the car passed alongside the canal, the Dog-Catcher looked at the water, then faced the road, then looked at the water again. She pointed out that she had grown up in another town which this canal passed through, the town was quite near to the town with the school in it. The school and her school were rivals over a number of things, sport, competitions, exam results, fights.

While she was growing up, she heard about people who had died in it, the canal, suicides, a lot of them from before when she was born, but a few that she was around at the time of. She said there were more attempts than successes, aye, people tended to be able to swim after all, or they got saved by someone else, or changed their minds once they hit the water and doggie-paddled to the side. She scratched her ear, em, there were deaths though, a small child as well even, a girl, she fell in and was later lifted out alive, but she'd suffered brain danage, too long without oxygen, and the machine got turned off eventually. She nodded, aye, most of all this was before my time, the canal's about a hundred and fifty years old, goodness darling, though I do remember some cases happening. But they've tightened up safety recently, footpaths and such like, still no fence however, going along by the canal, you could still try to drown yourself in it if you wanted.

The Dog-Catcher smiled, cheery conversationalist, me! Then laughing, so, since we're talking about suicide! She went on to say that in the time she'd been at the school she had been involved in three cases in which pupils had to deal with the suicides of parents, oh aye, deal with everything, me, though one was just an attempted one, never came off, but still, you put in the hours.

One mother had taken some pills and just walked out of the house and kept walking until the middle of the night, fell asleep in some woods and was found dead two mornings after, the Dog-Catcher had to spend the whole day the next day with the son and the daughters and the family, there was me and the boy and his wee sisters, I didn't know what to do, didn't want to be there, don't think they wanted me there either, and everybody was being too polite to say how we felt.

Then she spoke about another mother who had driven twenty miles away and then phoned her child, a daughter again, from the top of some cliffs over a gorge, they were heights of some sort darling, I don't know, and she then jumped off them still holding the phone. She made it though, with head injuries. The Dog-Catcher turned, em, aye, to go with the ones that were already there.

She sighed, then maybe a couple of years ago, was it three? Listen to me darling, I must be ageing even faster than I look like I am! Anyway, this case was when a father drowned in the canal, that one, back there, he had a daughter who was transferring from the local private school to this one, god knows why anyone would want to do that, though that was where the trouble lay I think, family tensions and all.

The Dog-Catcher changed the radio station in the car, oh don't you love this song darling, then she looked in the mirror, so, to continue, there had been all this domestic upheaval, the daughter had been top of the class since primary one more or less, but suddenly she'd become anti-everything, you know how the kids get at that age, there was a drama in the house every night according to the mum, the daughter wanted to leave the posh school to come to ours, she started wearing different clothes, choosing different friends, the wrong sort in her parents' eyes, just turned against everything the dad stood for, making some kind of a point at every turn, there'd been fights and arguments and things, and the whole thing ended up with the dad just killing himself just like that, couldn't take anymore. A walk to the canal, jumped in, and he couldn't swim, for definite. Police divers brought the body out.

She rummaged in the glove compartment and said bingo, I knew there was some left, you want a sweet darling? Anyway, the girl got transferred to our

162

place in the end after all, because she told her mum she'd do the same as her dad if she wasn't moved! What d'you say to a fourteen year old in that position? I just went round the house, tried to talk to her but she gave me the cold treatment, I don't need a social worker, don't call me darling, I want to be alone! She had the whole Garbo thing going on as well, lying on the sofa, back of the hand on the forehead. And the film star looks as well, lucky wee female.

The car came to a halt, the Dog-Catcher held the gearstick, she's still at the school actually, got put into that class of drop-outs eventually, I think, so some hope for her now, eh. One day when she's older she'll wake up and realise what she's caused, she still doesn't talk to anyone about it, I've still got her case-file open, got to ask her mum about her every so often, but the girl'll never see me.

The Dog-Catcher turned to the side, hands still on the wheel, education psychologist has tried too, there's all of us trying our hardest, oh well, other cases to deal with, haven't got time to spend on someone who doesn't even want the help, doesn't even acknowledge it to begin with.

She waved, aye, don't worry about the creaking, just slam the door, aye. Same time tomorrow morning then? Okay, bye darling, bye.

…

The Bin Brigade were laughing, aw sir, you should have seen what William did in French! William wasn't in class yet, the rest of them had come in by now, ahead of him, explaining the situation, aw sir, he's been kept behind sir, teacher's going mad with him for vandalising school property! Imagine, William, a

163

vandal, ha ha! As they took their seats they looked at each other, laughing together.

Ace was in today, there was an animation about him, he had been crying with laughter, I know I know, hee hee! Sir, sure William's not a vandal! He looked at the others as he rolled his sleeves up. Sam laughed, aw sir not yet, dinni make us get the books out yet, aw Christ, eh sorry for swearing sir, eh, but Christ man, you've got to hear what he did, eh, sorry again sir! Ace joined in again, yeah sir, listen to Sam! Naw wait, here he is, look, here's William!

At that point William walked in, followed by James who had been standing in the doorway. The Bin Brigade cheered William all the way to his seat. A few stood up even, William was patted on the back by a few people sitting near his desk, Billy shook his head as he smiled, aw, star man, William!

William had looked down at his feet when he came in, he wasn't looking at the pupils laughing at him, but by the time he was at his chair he was spreading his arms out and waving with both hands in two directions, smiling without opening his mouth, and as he did so the Bin Brigade cheered more, and he opened two fingers in each hand in the victory salute, speaking now, not shouting, saying fans, fans, no pictures please, no cameras!

When he sat down he looked up to the front of the classroom, not smiling anymore. Everyone looked at him, and his face didn't move, but then he burst into laughter and the class joined in with him. The class made comments, aw William, that was sheer class, hey William, did you really mean to do that! And Billy said aye, William, ya daftie! Then he said tell sir what you did William!

People wanted William to tell the story himself, but William declined, he didn't accept, though he still insisted that someone else speak.

Aw sir, Ace took over the conversation, we were all in French just there, last period, and we were given out those big jotters you get, know the ones, there wasn't any of the normal size left, and we were given them out one between two, and the teacher gave each desk a pair of scissors and told whoever had the scissors to cut the jotter in half so it could be used as two jotters, just for vocabulary lists and things. Ace looked at the rest of them, they were giggling as they listened, looking from Ace to each other.

William was looking at his desk shaking his head and smiling. Well sir, and Ace still had tears in his eyes as he spoke, it was obvious to everyone, well obviously not everyone, that you had to cut across the middle of both of the centre pages, left to right sir, but William had been given the scissors for the jotter him and James had been given, and he opened the jotter up at the centre pages like he was meant to, but then cut right down the centre of the double page, on the fold, past the staples and everything sir, Ace was crying again, aw sir, and William was left holding two piles of scrap paper with his arms stretched out, and he asked the teacher as he held them up in the air, is this what you're meant to have miss! Teacher had an epileptic fit sir!

The Bin Brigade hooted. James smiled and moved his head forward to turn and look William in the face.

And William grinned back at everyone, and looked around, and waved one hand again in the air, and announced, I thank you!

165

…

The rule, or it was a kind-of rule, was that student teachers didn't have anything to do with the rector, there had been one student from the uni who had gone to report to the rector's office on the first day of a placement one time, but the rector had been coming out of the office, the school office, not his office, and he'd spotted the student in the corridor and shouted on him, he thought he was a pupil, sixth year maybe, but not a member of staff, the student had black trousers and a black coat on and was facing the other way.

The rector had told him to turn round when he was speaking to him and started to lay into him about arriving at school on time, and not only that, but also about his being in a teachers-only part of the building, and all the time the rector was reading some piece of paper as he shouted, not looking up, and the student didn't put up any kind of protest, so when the rector had finished, the student just said sorry sir, and headed off.

The student had waited at the end of the corridor and watched the rector go into his own office two minutes later, and then went into see him, and the rector didn't recognise him from the corridor thing, but instead went ahead and told him that he shouldn't have reported to the rector's office at all, and said that there would be no need for the student and the rector to come into any kind of contact during the ten weeks that the teaching practice would last. The student departed his office and he never saw the rector again.

It was council procedure on placements for students to report to rectors and then maybe at least get told that the deputy rectors would be in charge of them, the deputy would be the student regent, but still, at least in most schools, it would be the rector who would inform students about that, and at least make the welcomes and introductions and so on, maybe shake hands and say good luck.

…

The Bin Brigade were all used to Kevin falling asleep in their lessons, not the same ones each day, it depended on a variety of factors, what was being taught, who Kevin was sitting beside, whether he had the inclination to fall asleep or not. He didn't start snoring at all, he'd just put his arms across his desk and leaned on them. Sometimes his eyes would be opened but maybe they'd close after a while.

If he was asked a question, whoever was sitting beside him, it might well be Billy, sometimes another pupil, rapped the back of his hand on Kevin's elbow or head and said hey, Kevin, Kev. Then Billy, or whoever, would look around laughing, em, Kevin's fallen asleep again sir!

Then Kevin would sit up, what was the question? Everyone giggled. He stretched his arms, no, I heard the last bit, just not the first bit. Then he spoke about not getting a lot of sleep last night, I kept waking up sir.

A few of the others in the class looked at each other smiling, and then they would look at Kevin. Kevin opened his eyes, still opening them for a couple of seconds, looking around as he did so, then he said what! He'd look at the others again, and then at the front, and then he said em, about half-ten sir, I went to bed round about then sir, aye.

…

Ace's name was Gabriel, the name his parents had given him. He had been giving some of the pupils a business card type thing he had brought in to school, look at this, it's supercool for cats, my agent's given me loads of these, he said. The business card gave his name as Gabriel, not Ace.

Ace wasn't in school in the afternoon, but he had been in during the morning, not at the start of school, but around the morning break, and then he was away again after lunch. The Bin Brigade were talking about his card, they all had one, yet they were still showing it to each other, pointing out the front, the picture of the masks, and talking about the fact that it said Gabriel, and not Ace. It doesn't say Ace anywhere does it? I never knew his name was Gabriel, the pupils said. They all looked at each other, shaking their heads, nope, I never knew at all.

No-one had been at his primary, apart from Marie in primary one and two, and she wasn't in today, and anyway, after primary two he'd moved away somewhere and later came back from wherever it was he had moved to. Marie would know his real name, but had never said, and she just called him Ace. So no-one knew his name, and no-one had ever asked, they had all guessed what it was beforehand, in lessons if he wasn't there and the subject of his name came up. I thought it was Gavin. Aye, or Gary, I heard. William said he'd thought it was Ken. Ken! The Bin Brigade hooted at William, aye, they all sound alike don't they, Gabriel, Gavin, Gary, Ken! You're a muppet William, what a numpty!

William half-laughed and told them to shut up. He looked at the card Ace had given him, he looked at the class and asked so then, how come Ace is never here?

That big Scottish film, someone said. Nah, it can't be, someone else said, that's not till summer.

William looked at the card again, rehearsals for it then maybe?

What's it to you William, the others laughed, you got a part in it!

William scowled at them.

Aye, Billy said, he plays an upholsterer!

…

The Phantom didn't get his job, people were saying that, and they were looking at him as he went up stairs and down corridors, walked past and passed by, or moved around the school. He came into the staffroom and said things, the things he said when he came into the staffroom. He used the tannoy five times in the one morning, someone mentioned, that's a bit unusual eh, thought he'd been told to cut down on the old big brother act, aye, naw?

Somebody said to the Phantom, more than one person said to him em, sorry to hear about, eh. But no-one ever got to finish that sentence before he waved his arm in the air, oh, aah, thank-you, thank-you, but really, absolutely no need, and then, shaking his head, he said gosh, I had no idea that people knew I was on an interview in the first place, here's me thinking one could keep a secret in this place, heh heh, I shall know better next time, heh heh, aah!

A couple of folk, whose habit was to wait to be spoken to by the Phantom before speaking to him, started conversations with him of their own accord, without his having said anything at all, they instigated the thing. Maybe it would be about a school issue, something that happened recently perhaps, or something that had happened on the day he had been away for his interview, they would give him all the details.

The Phantom replied but spoke in a tone that wasn't the same as his voice on days when he hadn't just failed an interview, he bowed his head a bit as he was talking too. Whoever he was talking to would say sorry, I didn't quite get that, gonni just speak up a wee bit, it's noisy in here today, and the person would lean his head towards the Phantom, squinting a bit as he did so, and looking at the wall and not into his eye.

The Phantom told folk about a colleague of his from way back that he'd bumped into recently, at the interview in fact, aah, an ex-colleague in fact, used to work here in fact, has done very well for himself, upwardly mobile as they say, headteacher now, and looking to move to another school, change of scenery and all that, aah! He smiled, inclined his head and shook it a bit at the same time. Then he straightened up, it was he who got the job, aah, does you good to see people you know getting on in their lives, aah.

Still! He clasped his hands together and looked around the staffroom and said aah, it's good, always heartening, to come in and see you're not plotting a uprising! Palace revolution eh! Then, from the Phantom, there was a movement and then he was out of the room, no-one had replied.

People who had been watching and listening to the scene waited a minute, watching the door before recommencing their conversations.

…

Not for the first time, someone was saying that there had never been anything brought in to replace the belt since it was made against the law in the eighties. Discussion, and then a lot of agreement followed, as was the case whenever such discipline matters were talked about. Teachers said of the pupils, some of the pupils, they've got no discipline, the kids in the school these days, you've got nothing to fall back on after you've given them a punishment or sent them to your head of department to give them a punishment, they all know their rights these days, cheeky bastards. Aye, cheeky, you're right, you should see the cheek of some of them telling you they know their rights, you canni do that to me sir, I know my rights!

Lots of nodding, and then yet more bemoaning took place again, and the teachers in the staffroom remembered how children who presented with behaviour difficulties in the past could be controlled, aye, you could teach them a lesson or two about self-control with one stroke of the belt across the hand, short sharp shock eh!

People looked at one another, aye, see even if you had a decent class, mostly good kids, just one bad bastard of a kid could still make life sheer hell for you unless you put him in his place, early on in the term was always a good time. Nowadays, Christ, you're totally stuck if the kid doesni respond to a punishment or telling off or whatever, they can virtually control the atmosphere of the lesson.

Although, not in some people's class eh, according to someone who spoke up upon hearing this, nodding in the direction of the door. A few people laughed, aye, it's already a frightening atmosphere in there, I mean, you-know-where, you-know-who's classroom eh! People looked at the door of the staffroom.

It was a reference to Bastard Guy, who was known amongst the staff as well as the pupils for being a bit of a disciplinarian, and someone said aye, you'd get a punishment for breathing in the wrong direction in there! Everybody agreed, strict? He's the definition of strict, man! Those teachers who spoke about him now, Bastard Guy, his reputation, they developed a line of thought, his strictness, and the effect it had on his classes and the school as a whole, other teachers, pupils' expectations in their lessons.

According to what had been said before, Bastard Guy was one of the three teachers in the school who the kids had to seek out, or go and see on an appointment basis, for advice about careers, training, post-school stuff and the like, he'd been on a course earlier in his time at the school and knew all the information, phone numbers and so on, contacts, but, again according to what was being said, the other two people had to do it all between the pair of them because no-one went to Bastard Guy, the pupils never went to see him, or they avoided him, and the other two had to do the lot.

There were a few sighs. Aye. Aye.

Aye, naw, but see when you had the belt though.

Aye, discipline wouldn't be an issue, it just wasn't an issue at all.

Job could be enjoyable.

…

James was giggling in the class, it was a half-giggle, he was putting his head down and putting his hand over his mouth, the effect was to suppress his giggles. What's up with him, a girl asked while she took her stuff from her bag and put it out on the desk. William looked at James and shook his head, can you not just shut up now, James? Another voice asked, what's up with him William?

Then William turned to the class and said aw, remember how we learned the German word for cinema last week, kino? Someone said aye, and someone else, a

172

group at the back, said that they'd done French not German. Another pupil said I did German William, aye, we did that, kino, it does mean cinema, yeah.

William moved about a bit on his chair, and he continued, kino, yeah, cinema. He looked at the front and then at the class, saying aye, and you know how people are talking about that new sex shop that's gonni open in the town, know? The one that people wanted banned? William looked at the front again, naw, sir, there is going to be one, honest!

There were a few sniggers from around the room. James sniggered too.

Billy sniggered, private shop, that's what my dad says they're called, those places, and he qualified what William had said. Aye, private shop, sex shop, same thing, William nodded and looked at James again.

James was still sniggering, spluttering, and did so more with every detail that William added to his explanation. William smiled at Billy, though he was addressing everyone in the room, well, at lunchtime we were passing the shop it's gonni be opened in, it's no opened yet but it's gonni open there, and all it was that set James off was that there was this sign, on the shop window, or the window on the door, that said opening soon sex kino, it's gonni be called a sex kino, as if it was in Germany or somehwere, I don't know!

At that point James spluttered even more, onto his right hand, dripping spit onto his fingers then having to reach across and into his right-hand trouser pocket with his left hand to get a handkerchief, and wiped his right hand on it, still laughing and salivating, looking at William.

The class looked at James.

Aw James, that's disgusting, how come you're laughing at that, asked Kelly. Billy said sex kino, what's so funny about that, it's just the name of the shop, James, what's so funny about that? Billy scratched his head and looked at William.

I know, said William, who slapped James's arm, look, there you are, no-one else finds it funny James! James continued to giggle. Then there was some silence as people were waiting for the lesson to start.

Billy looked at his desk and played with a pencil in his hands, then looked from side to side, catching the eye of some of the others, before looking at James and lowering his voice to growl, sex kino! James giggled more and the whole class laughed as well, except William.

Billy growled again, seeeeeex kiiiiiinoooooo. The class were hooting now, and some of them started to say sex kino in a variety of voices. They squeaked, sex kino! They whispered, sex kino! They said sex kino in a variety of accents, ooh la la sex kino! Billy stood up, clicked his heels together, and raised one arm in the Nazi salute into the air, and shouted ja ja nein, achtung sex kino!

The class continued laughing, James was half-off his seat, smiling at everybody else, half-giggling, his hand over his mouth. William stared at them all around him. Then Billy started moaning, oh sex kino, sex kino, oh ooooooh sex kino!

The class all hooted, James continued to half-giggle into his hand.

And William told them they were all perverts.

…

One time, Mr Tambourine Man brought a load of records into school in a box, he had to shove the staffroom door open with his knee, look everyone, here, guys, vinyl!

He held the box as he stood at the door and said a friend of his had just jacked in being a DJ and didn't need them anymore, the records, he'd given Mr Tambourine Man a lot of his stock because he knew he was a Music teacher. Mr Tambourine Man held the door open with his leg, aye, he gave me the remainder once he'd sorted the collection out, so who wants a look, here! He nodded down in the direction of the box as he entered the room, em, my mate just thought I might find them handy, it's all fantastic stuff as well man, come and look at it, vinyl! Can't believe he doesn't want to hang on to it all!

He banged the box down on the table, it was more of a crate, em, I've kept a lot of it for myself already, he was giving it to me after all, and this is the rest of the stuff, stuff I didn't want, or stuff I've already got copies of. I'm gonni keep them here at the school, might as well get some use out of them in the odd class when I'm bored of the syllabus, they're still in good nick like, and we've still got a half-decent record-player in the department, bought in the olden days, it's a real good quality one. Sounds great with the old vinyl on it, it's never got used much recently, so.

Mr Tambourine Man looked up, clapped his hands and said again, so! Here we are then. People were approaching the table, peering into the box, saying good for you man, great, good piece of luck eh! Everybody looked at what was there in the box. After a couple of seconds they started saying look, look at the amount of them! And, aw brilliant!

Aye, Mr Tambourine Man spread his arms as he stood at the table, sixties stuff in the main, things that

175

people'll dance to at discos, know, my pal was a DJ for
about twenty years right enough, so, he built up a big
collection, Motown was his favourite, that sort of thing,
but he covered everything 'cause of playing at old
folks' homes, kids' parties and so on. Here look, it's all
in sections, genres, he's a bit of an anal retentive, my
pal that is, anyway there we go, look, what have we got
here then, aye, there you go, the Supremes,
Temptations, Smokey Robinson, they're all there! And
here, country stuff, Gram Parsons, Emmylou Harris,
even Jim Reeves, that one about the ghost dog!

People were nodding and starting to sift through
the box themselves now. Mr Tambourine Man stood
back and looked on, aye, Beatles singles as well, see? I
think they go from around about the time of She Loves
You, practically all of them, through to I Feel Fine,
maybe a few of the later ones, some Stones too, aye,
Get Off My Cloud, Nineteenth Nervous Breakdown.
Amongst others as well, just take a look. Mr
Tambourine Man smiled, it's all there, look at the B
section alone of the sixties part of the box, there's the
Beach Boys, more Beatles, the Byrds, Buffalo
Springfield, remember them eh, Buffalo Springfield!
And he shut his eyes and lifted his head up, cupping
one hand round an ear and holding the other hand out,
stop children what's that sound!

Folk were handling the records now, looking at
the covers, turning them over in their hands, showing
them to each other. There must be about three hundred
of them! All in their covers too man! The Hollies,
Kinks! The Who, look, the Who! See, look at this one,
wouldni apply to our pupils eh, The Kids Are Alright!

A couple of people looked at Mr Tambourine
Man and enquired, does your friend not want to keep

them? Or sell them even? Mr Tambourine Man said no, he's got doubles of almost everything, it was just something he did every time he bought a new single for the business. Anyway, he'll have kept what he wanted, he couldn't be arsed selling them, and also anyway, he's a good guy and he thought I could use them, he's just a good guy. Mr Tambourine Man then smiled and added, plus he thought if I used them with my classes then maybe the kids would hear some decent music instead of the shite they walk around with in their ears!

His colleagues laughed, aye! Someone said look, all this seventies parties section, Wizzard, Roxy Music, Rod Stewart, Elton John, brilliant! The Osmonds, ha ha! Aye, party stuff eh! Aw man, Yellow River, I've not heard that in ages! And Edison Lighthouse! And they started singing, I'm a lucky fella, I just gotta tell her, na na na na endlesslee-ee-ee!

Mr Tambourine Man smiled and walked over to a chair and sat down, he laughed, aye, brings it all back eh! As long as you don't all start singing Hi Ho Silver Lining! Then he told people to take their pick of what they wanted, go ahead, take anything guys, I've got what I want so, on you go, yous can divide the rest between yourselves, it's fine, take what you want.

People looked at him, seriously?

Aye, he smiled. Don't not take the records, take them!

Everybody looked at each other, turning round to look at Mr Tambourine Man and say Christ! Thanks a lot man, this is brilliant! They looked at each other, isn't it!

Mr Tambourine Man said he'd play whatever was left in the box to the kids, oh aye, I'll take time out from the normal syllabus every so often and just let them sit back and listen to some decent pop music for once, see what they think of it eh.

Everybody laughed, aye, better than what they're used to listening to!

Mr Tambourine Man grinned back at everyone, think they'll like it though?

People were smiling and laughing, and everybody was agreeing, ha ha, the kids will at last hear some decent music, ha ha, and the kids will in fact not like it, ha ha, they'll bloody hate it!

…

Bicycle Clips was saying that the visit of politicians from England to the town for by-election campaigning was a disgrace. Some of them had been in the news, walking about the streets, canvassing opinions from the locals, appearing on TV at night. Bicycle Clips grimaced, ach, it's a disgrace, those London MPs coming up here, tss, what's an election up here got that's anything to do with them, tss! He pulled his trousers up and tugged at his socks, shaking his head.

A couple of people nodded.

He nodded back at them, I mean, everybody knows what they're up to eh, they're just here on the orders of party leaders, they'll hang around for a few days, suck up to anyone they can shake hands with, their minders'll get a feel for the place and then report back to HQ. Oh aye, the minders'll be here and all, don't you worry. And he raised his eyebrows, nodding his head, looking at his colleagues. There was a vigour about Bicycle Clips during this moment.

Aye the spinners, one of the teachers sitting next to him said, the spinners.

Bicycle Clips tugged at his jacket sleeve, pulling it past the end of his arm and over his fist, before doing the same with the other, sorting his watch around his wrist, fixing his ring of copper, making adjustments. Yes, he said, spinners, the whole lot of them, tss, listening in to what local people say to them, pretending to show an interest, passing the message back to Whitehall, or headquarters, Party Central you could say, aye, so then the big-shots can massage the way they word their policies, just so they can take everyone in! They don't care though, do they, they don't care.

His companion shook his head, tutting, aye, naw, then the big shots'll come up and say what they think the people want to hear. Aye, Bicycle Clips continued, tss, make people think their candidate's on the same wavelength as the local population, then it'll be vote vote vote for our guy, or woman, though it's unlikely to be a woman. Loudspeakers on the tops of cars, vote vote vote for our guy!

The bell went. Bicycle Clips stood up and pulled at his belt, oh aye, it's a well-oiled machine now, the whole by-election process, or a collection of well-oiled machines, they've all got plans, templates, they're all well prepared, then they just modify them according to whichever part of the country they implement the plan in, that's what they do now. He headed for the window and gazed out over the playground towards the parts of the town that could be seen, shaking his head again, I'm telling you, English MPs coming up here thinking they can tell Scottish people what they want, planting the seeds of hope that something might improve, it's a disgrace. He made for the door, putting his drink down on a table on his way, misplacing it, hitting the table-edge with the bottom of the mug,

179

before trying again and sitting it on a piece of paper that was lying there. He hadn't drunk it all and there was a spillage that he leaned down to mop up with the piece of paper.

The other man said em but, I thought that you were saying they were finding out what the locals wanted though, asking them, not telling them.

Bicycle Clips was on his way out the door by now and he looked back, nodded, then looked out the window again, hmmf, aye, I did, hmmf, but when you see them, asking, telling, it just seems like the same thing, eh!

...

It doesni matter if somebody says something about you, and you don't like it, what they're saying, it doesni matter does it? William was saying this, he was saying it to Marie, and speaking about how he knew himself better than anyone, and he said, you know, that means what I think, what I think about myself, it's the truth, isn't it. He turned, isn't it sir, it's the truth. For me anyway, eh?

You're right William, Marie nodded and smiled at him. He smiled back, aw, Marie! And then he turned to the others, see, I was right, wasn't I? He looked around, Marie says I'm right, so, and he looked up towards the front of the class, is that no right sir? And then he was smiling, see, I'm right, and also sir, my dad says to me sometimes, William you don't even know if you're alive sometimes! Don't know what he means when he says that though, my dad.

Your stepdad you mean? It was Billy who asked this question.

Nobody said anything.

Then William turned on Billy, snapping, naw, my dad Billy, my dad, can you not hear right? If I'd meant my stepdad I'd have said, my stepdad! And I said my dad, so I meant just that, my dad!

The others still said nothing, they looked from William to Billy, Billy to William.

Marie looked at Billy. When Billy caught her eye she leaned her neck towards him, Billy?

Billy looked around the class, and then he looked back at William, and said okay, okay, he looked at the others again, then back at William, it's just you don't mention your dad usually, and a lot of people call their stepdad dad. I just thought, I don't know, I didn't think. Sorry.

Not me, William scratched his desk with a pen, I've never mixed up my stepdad and my dad, okay? You've never heard me say that, not me.

After some silence, the rest of the class made a few remarks, just amongst themselves, about knowing if you were alive or not, as William had said his dad had talked about.

William looked up again, and said that he knew he himself was, alive, I know I'm alive, know. Everybody else laughed, there was a relief about them, listen to William, he just thinks he's alive!

William laughed along with them, then stopped, and he wasn't laughing anymore.

…

The Phantom was saying in the staffroom that some of the sixth year had been talking about how their applications for universities and colleges had been going, he was leafing through pieces of paper with things the students had written about what offers they'd received so far, summaries, aah, yes, interviews they

181

might have been to, it's something I do every year, I do like to keep a note of how things are going, aah. It was a kind of update he was talking about, though he said he only added information to it when he bumped into the sixth years in a corridor or wherever, there wasn't a system in operation, it wasn't a thing he applied in a method, a habit.

He said again aah, it's that time of year again, most of the students have heard back from universities and colleges already, but then again there's all the last minute changes going on, as usual, phone calls to be made, UCAS to be contacted, and so on and so on, panic stations if you will, aah! He held up the bundle of paper he was holding, a lot of them want to go to Glasgow or Edinburgh, but there's a few here who have been saying they would go further afield if they had to, or even by choice, Aberdeen, Dundee, Stirling and so on. He shook his head, they'll tell you it's a good course, of course, they get a degree, a job at the end of the day, but in my view they're not the same, you see dear boy, Stirling, Dundee, it's not Glasgow, it's not Edinburgh, but still. There's always St. Andrews.

Armpits looked up from where he was sitting across the room, and he turned from looking at the Phantom and grinned, aye, deputy, the St. Andrews applicants are all Oxford rejects, they've applied there and heard nothing, or failed the interview, or just bragged about applying but never did 'cause they knew they wouldn't get in! He laughed and then sighed, course, they only get called that though by those who didn't even apply to St. Andrews in case they become St. Andrews rejects! Wait and you see, these young bucks that come up from London to accompany their parties' candidates round the town for the by-election, you'll be able to tell by the suits which ones are Oxford graduates and which ones are Oxford rejects! Imagine, some of our pupils wanting to end up like that!

He sniffed, all except the socialist guy's minders that is, you'll be able to tell them alright, they'll stand out a mile, they'll be Oxfam graduates!

The Phantom smiled at Armpits and looked down at his papers, well, then there's the few who say they'd go to England, they somehow think it'll be better there, despite the fees. He bit his lower lip, mm, do you think they mean better as in better for jobs? Perhaps so, but education? I really don't think so, not one bit of it, oh, aah, I really don't know at all. I mean, think of it, the reputation of places like Edinburgh, Glasgow! He looked over at Armpits again, and St. Andrews for that matter! And the others, even the new ones. I mean, you tell these students, as they make their decisions, do they even realise that many of the Scottish universities have been well-established since the time of the Enlightenment, aah, the Enlightenment! You see?

Armpits laughed, ha ha, Scotland! Providing world-class education since the 1700s! Vote socialist next month and see it start to happen though, I wish!

The Phantom smiled, well, it has, Scotland, my dear man, you know? Armpits folded his arms and nodded, aye I know, I know. The Phantom nodded back, yes, I know, aah. Know, Armpits smiled, still, you do sound like some publicity guy for the Scottish education system!

The Phantom looked around, well, maybe, someone should be allowed to do that job eh, aah, I'm sure I could do it very well! Armpits nodded again, canni argue with you there, deputy, but all the same though, some of our kids, know, think England's the place to be, just, 'cause, it's not Scotland. I don't know.

The Phantom shrugged his shoulders, then pushed his gown back and away from hanging over his chest, well, a lot of Americans do come here to study, it is very popular, that at least must say something, and with that he started to leave, moving as he spoke.

Aye I know, Armpits got out of his chair, I know, usually it's just an exchange job but, yeah, a term or two's enough for them, one year of Consider The Lilies and Sunset Song, hike up the bottom bit of Ben Nevis, then it's back home to the United States of Have a Nice Day!

From the staffroom door the Phantom agreed, you may be right, dear friend, you may indeed be right. Then he turned, aah, goodbye, and he was gone, aah!
...

You play the beautiful game yourself son? Scout came away from the window, the bell had gone two minutes beforehand, and everybody else had all gone off to their classrooms, maybe smiling at Scout without opening their mouths, or giving him a kind of nod upwards in recognition. Scout continued, aye, that right? And said that he himself had played, oh, way back in the seventies, aye, aye, I know I look older than that, and I bet folk have said to you I'm about to draw my pension and all! Aye, I was a pro for a wee while, not for any big clubs or anything, but I remember playing a few games against some of the bigger teams.

He looked across the staffroom, aye, I played against some right good players, even in the lower leagues, in those days you didni have to be famous to be good, they were all good, aye. But I did play against some of the bigger names, Pettigrew was one, could hit the ball as hard as anyone in the game, who was that other one, something Murray, aye, Murray, a teacher now and all, could hold the ball up better than anyone I knew, McLean, he was a player too, turned on a whatsit, and Hay, and the rest. You didni have to be famous but. Now who was that wee guy I couldni keep up with when I played in the juniors? I could never keep up with him, and he was another one who ended up teaching as well! McVake, I think, canni mind his first name, did a lot better in the juniors if I recall correctly, aye. Great players, all of them.

He grinned, ach, not me though.

Waste. He paused, standing beside a chair. Aye, I moved around a few of the lower division and non-league sides, all in the central belt, or up this way, nobody hung on to me for too long, mind. He looked towards the window and then back to the centre of the room.

Training, that's what got me, he said, aye, or it was the lack of training, more like, and he continued with his explanation, since I could never be bothered, with the trainng that is, I thought that playing was all that mattered, doing the business on the pitch, I thought all I had to do was turn up on match-day, I never made it properly, no preparation. Nope, I wasni a huge fan of George Best, me, more a Baxter man, eh, you'll have heard of him boy eh, Slim Jim! He sat down and smiled, no, they could keep Best, and Greaves if they wanted, it was Slim Jim for me, there was never any other, eh. He was, you know, the, whatsit.

There was no-one else around in the staffroom. Scout spoke more about Jim Baxter, calling him Jim, just his name, aw, see the way he played boy, Jim, ach, you won't know. Hee hee, taking the piss out the

185

English at Wembley in sixty-seven eh! Bloody well put on a show all his own, and that being the first time the English had been beaten since the World Cup, cocky swines, it just made it all the sweeter! He laughed again, aye, but Jim showed them, aye, so he did! And not for the first time either, he'd scored two against them four years earlier and all.

Scout looked up again. Jim never liked going to training much either, or so they said. Never really became the world star he could have been. Wasted talent. Nothing worse.

…

The class was silent, watching.

I'm not upset, I'm just, Kelly shook her head, it's just that, it's just, okay okay, and she held both hands up. Marie put her hand on Kelly's arm. Kelly smiled, aye okay, I am upset.

Everyone looked at her.

She blew her nose and held her tissue out, the back of her hand rested on the desk, it really is only important what you think about yourself isn't it sir? I mean, what your opinion is about yourself. What we were talking about the other day, know? Not what everybody else thinks about you, know? She had been telling everybody this at the end of the lesson, it had been a discussion about being yourself, and she said that she just enjoyed herself in her life and enjoyed making the most of what she had, you've just got to enjoy every minute eh, haven't you not sir? You never know if you're gonni be knocked down by a bus tomorrow, or the day after or the day after that even, do you?

The others didn't say much, and were just packing away their things in their bags to go off for the

186

morning interval, sometimes looking up at Kelly as they left the room, starting to hold their bags to their chest and run a bit as they got nearer the door of the classroom, sometimes there was a race between two people over the two metres between the front of the desks and the door.

So, without too many pupils listening to her, except for Marie who was standing waiting for her, Kelly continued, saying that people could call her what they wanted to, it wouldn't bother her at all, she sniffed, it really wouldn't bother me one little bit sir, see? Nobody who was still in the room said anything, they didn't have a response. Kelly looked around, well, that's what my mum's always taught me to think.

There were no pupils from the Bin Brigade in the classroom now, Marie had said to Kelly that she would give her a few seconds and then see her outside, some pupils in the class that was coming in after the interval were dumping their bags at their desks.

They were third years, and a couple of girls made remarks between themselves.

They looked at Kelly and then muttered something more between themselves.

Kelly walked out of the room, looking back at the girls, and saying that they could call her what they want.

5. WE CAN CALL IT STRESS

The Joke Club were hooting at break time, one
of them had driven in that morning and there had been a
sign he passed by, aye, just driving along I was,
thinking about how I could get away with giving my
period one class reading so I could get my feet up for an
hour, and then there was this huge sign, more of a
banner on the outside of that church, know the one just
as you get past that new roundabout, well it's not really
a church, but more a kind of worshipping hall, don't
know who it's for, there'll be an evangelist thing of
some kind going on anyway.

Another of the Joke Club got up out of his chair
and started preaching, using his diary as a Bible,
making the sign of the cross in the air as he stood over
the rest of them. The others were falling back in their
chairs, ha ha, aw, we shouldn't! Aye, naw, bless me
father for I have sinned!

Sandwich Toaster looked across at them all, but
when he'd poured his drink he went and sat somewhere
else, he had been with them before the church banner
story started to be told, but now he went elsewhere.

The first one then went on about this banner,
aye, bloody enormous it was, and he said, gesticulating,
spreading his arms, there it was, huge, capital letters for
the start of every word, in red too, know, for emphasis,
Jesus Is Alive Today! And he repeated, this time using
his hands to indicate each word in its entirety, Jesus.

Is.

Alive.

Today.

There were a few sniggers before he said what
the banner had read, he had told some of them when he

188

had come in at the start of the morning about it. The Joke Club were looking around themselves now and up at the rest of the staffroom, people standing up, talking.

The storyteller went on, you know, I mean, that's some pretty big story, I couldn't help thinking to myself, Jesus, alive? You'd think it'd have been in the papers, know! As the Joke Club laughed again, he talked through their noise, you know what I mean, I watched the news last night and it wasn't on any of the channels! More hoots, and the rest of the Joke Club started joining in, ha ha, and here's our correspondent interviewing people from outside the church, and he has with him Judas Iscariot, who's pretty damn surprised! Ha ha! Judas, your reaction? Well yes, I was taken aback, and the thing is, I've spent the pieces of silver already!

And the storyteller looked over towards Ex-Cop sitting at the classroom desk, hey, you not telling the kids about that, Jesus being alive now, eh!

The Joke Club turned and looked at Ex-Cop. Ex-Cop had been watching them all, on and off for a few minutes, now he looked up again, pardon, you're asking me?

I'm saying, the Joke Club guy waved his arms in the air, Jesus Is Alive Today, know, get it into the syllabus quickly, bet you'll have to rewrite a few tests now eh! He looked, blinked, waiting for Ex-Cop to reply.

Ex-Cop looked at the Joke Club, all of them smiling, but he didn't smile, just looked, and a few of them stopped laughing. Ex-Cop looked back down at his work.

The guy who'd seen the sign sat down, lowered his voice and then looked over again and said to Ex-

189

Cop, aye, I'm just having a laugh, you'll be telling the kids that news eh, I was just saying here eh.

A couple of the Joke Club looked at him, one of them whispered something to him and smacked his knee with the back of his hand.

The guy furrowed his brow and shook his head, what, eh, what?

…

From the other side of the staffroom, Scout looked around. He looked around, and down at the seats, up at the classroom desk, across to the card table, over towards the urn and beyond to the door with the sign that said Mixed Staffrooom. He nodded, and nodded again, aye.

Nobody had said anything in reply to a question he had asked. A couple of folk did look up at him, though avoided catching his eye, and then they looked round the room themselves, and then back down again, to newspapers, diaries, marking.

Scout looked back out the window. He turned again, staring into the centre of the room, it's a bit whatsit today eh? This weather!

Somebody coughed.

And Scout turned, coughing too, and looked out the window again.

…

On the bus from the town centre to the school, one out of the two pupils sitting together towards the front turned round and leaned over the seat, and he asked, hey, hi there sir, did you have a good weekend away from the school sir? What d'you do sir, go and see your girlfriend, have you got a girlfriend sir, eh? The boy laughed and looked down at his companion.

190

The other boy popped his head over the seat as well, hanging his hands off the metal with his fingers. The two hung over the back of their seat and looked at each other, then began a conversation amongst themselves, speaking about someone buying cider for them out of the off-licence on Friday night. They waited a bit. Then they looked at each other again.

The one beside the window faced the back of the bus, he peeled at a sticker on the glass and said em, sir, know that Kelly girl in your class sir, well she got shagged on Saturday sir! Then he ducked down below the level of the top of the seat and turned round to face the front. He and his friend were laughing, his friend hit him, ya daftie, saying that!

A few other passengers now looked in their direction, a couple of people in front of them, pensioners, turned round to glance at them and turned back to face the front again. Someone tutted.

The boys lowered their heads a bit. Then the one who had spoken about Kelly turned round again and said aw no, sir, I was only kidding sir, about Kelly, don't tell her we said anything sir. He turned back.

After a while, several stops down the road, they looked over again before standing up and heading for the door as the bus pulled up.

The boy said again, sir, it wasn't true sir, what I said about Kelly sir, it's just a joke, dinni tell anybody, or Kelly sir, gonni?

…

Nobody called Walks In Snow by a name when they bought their morning snack or post-lunch confectionery from her. They usually didn't give her a name at all when they talked to her, or just said something else at the start or end of sentences, the orders they made, the thanks on the occasions that thanks were made when exchanges came to a halt, maybe love, or just dear. Most didn't attach a name of any sort. There was one member of staff, a woman, who called Walks In Snow sweetie, though that teacher called everybody sweetie.

Staff did always say please after everything they said to Walks In Snow, when they were asking for a cold drink out the fridge and not off the counter, or crisps out of a box that hadn't been opened yet, or whatever it was they wanted, aye, I'll have one of those this morning please. And sometimes they said thank-you as well, after they had finished their transaction. Walks In Snow would always say everybody's name, each individual was named, she would call them Mister so-and-so or Missus so-and-so, Miss, and so on. She addressed the Phantom as sir though, she would always call him sir, and he wouldn't correct her.

In the staffroom the Joke Club referred to her as the tea lady, in actuality others did too, the fact of it was she was talked about as the tea-lady.

…

The tannoy was used in the school a few times when something had to be said to everyone, if there was information for everyone that had to be imparted. It was the nature of the thing about such information, in the normality of a day, that a note would come round the school, perhaps one of the Bin Brigade would get told to carry it from classroom to classroom, and teachers would read it out to their classes.

But sometimes there was not enough time left in the day to get the note out, because the office would have to make the note up and then maybe photocopy it

192

too, so the tannoy would be used, it was the only thing that was left that could be done, the tannoy.

It was a communications system that had been fitted in the school many years beforehand, when a lot of schools all of a sudden had the idea to have one. As the system wore down over time in the places it was implemented, and technology didn't meet the needs of the times, or the school of thought changed to saying that maybe tannoys weren't the thing they had been made out to be, they were another thing, they got in the way of teaching, had something of totalitarianism about them, then it never really got repaired, the system, no-one ensured that maintenance was carried out.

The only microphone that still functioned in the system in the school was the one in the Phantom's office, so it was he who operated the system now, on his own.

Maybe he would use it to say something about a revision of the arrangements for a couple of the school buses at the end of the day, perhaps a football team would have to be read out, or a school disco would be getting cancelled. When it was snowing there would be a warning not to throw snowballs. Only a few times did the Phantom use the tannoy to summon someone to his office, it would have to be a thing that needed dealt with in the immediacy.

Before you heard an announcement over the tannoy, there would be a few crackles of electricity as the Phantom switched it on and held his hand down on the button on his desk while he leaned over to the microphone.

He cleared his throat with some coughs. The number of crackles was rarely the same as the number of coughs, sometimes it was three or four crackles, two or three coughs, sometimes it was just one crackle that lasted over a second and a few coughs. Three then one, two then two, six then two, the thing came to eight and it worked out. The Phantom's last cough would usually make a mm hmm sound, usually one mm and one hmm, sometimes a second hmm before the intake of breath which would precede what he had to say.

…

There was bit of a commotion in the playground, a commotion that was being observed from the staffroom window. The staff looked out of the window, aw look there, ha ha, there's that freak in fourth year who won't speak! Ha ha, he never speaks, that one, ha ha! Freak! Someone said it looked like there had been a fight, one of the boys had run away, but the other was still there.

James and William were at the centre of what was being observed.

Then came the Phantom, pacing over the ground, he was walking from the building entrance towards a group of boys, they looked at him, about six or seven of them, he was shouting. A couple of boys were walking behind the Phantom, with their jackets draped over their shoulders, they were flapping their arms up and down behind him, he didn't see the thing that was going on.

The Phantom turned round and looked at them, the boys. The boys stopped. The Phantom headed in the direction of James and William, who were standing with four or five other boys in the group, William was talking to the other boys, James didn't say anything, he was looking at the ground, sometimes looking up at William.

The Phantom gesticulated towards James with his hand, and then gesticulated again, this time with his finger, pointing at the entrance to the building, and then walked away towards the entrance himself, heading with a purpose at the building. Then he looked back and saw that James was still standing, standing still, where he had been when the Phantom first gesticulated to him, James wasn't moving.

And so the Phantom gesticulated to him again, signalling to James.

James still stood where he was.

The Phantom could then be seen to be saying something, and he pointed at his feet, and then he pointed at James, and then at the ground in front of his feet again. James was still standing where he was. The Phantom shouted something at James, and pointed down again.

James then started to head towards the Phantom by moving one foot at a time, keeping his feet side by side, moving each one by what looked like about a centimetre at a time, keeping his hands by his sides all the while.

The Joke Club were all at the window by now, they had been alerted to the fact that something was going on, some of them were hooting, look at him, ha ha! Freak!

In the playground the Phantom shouted at James, the staffroom window was shut but some of the words he was saying could be heard through the glass, you, here, now, boy, here, now! James continued to move his feet towards the Phantom one centimetre at a time. William stood and watched him, smiling and covering his mouth with his hand and looking away when the Phantom looked at him.

The Phantom continued to shout, at James, and William, and the group they had been with, in fact he continued to shout at James for what seemed like another minute, perhaps less.

And in that time, James was continuing to make some progress in getting from the bit of the playground where he had been, to the other bit where the Phantom was, a distance in totality of about five metres, the first metre of which James had travelled already.

More teachers were now congregated at the window. Ha ha, look at that scene out there, eh! Look, I bet he's gonni walk up to the boy and smack him, I swear! Nah nah, the boy's gonni speed up, eh, he surely canni sustain that, it'll take him another five minutes to get there, freak that he is! Who d'you think's gonni blink first!

In the playground, William was picking up James's bag and following him, walking beside him but looking ahead and talking to the Phantom. The Phantom then started to inch his way back, heading towards James, looking around him.

The Joke Club spotted it. Look! He's doing the same thing! He's going even slower than the boy! He's thinking nobody will notice. Aye, well we see you, you old fart! He doesn't even know anyone's looking at him!

Then, when James and the Phantom were a metre apart, maybe another two minutes later, the Phantom stood still and leaned towards James, one foot stepping out to balance himself, and shouted something at James's face for about thirty seconds, and then he turned and marched away. The pupils surrounding the incident all cheered.

As did some of the staff at the window, ha ha, he's given up! The boy beat him into submission, wee idiot! One member of the Joke Club banged once on the window, then they all dived back to their seats.

As the Phantom turned and looked up, James took his bag from William and the two walked into another part of the building, a couple of pupils threw things at them as they did so.

…

She actually took me on about Freud, she actually took me on!

Shakespeare was talking about Marie, he was displaying exasperation in his manner towards his colleagues, standing around him, I mean, she told me I was wrong about something in that last lesson there, the girl actually told me I was wrong, you're wrong sir, she says! Sir, as well! Wrong, me, the teacher!

He gathered his breath, then spoke again, not finishing any of the sentences or questions he tried to say, I mean, where does she think, what gives her the, where does she get the! He looked up, and said again, me, wrong!

The men around Shakespeare laughed as he told them about how he had been explaining Freud to his English class, it was something he did every year, aye, I do it every year, if it's a good class, it would fly over the head of anything but a top set, so anyway it fits in with something in the syllabus, and the classes I teach have always told me they liked the Freud lesson when I've done it, I can crack a few jokes about dreams and things.

But Marie had taken him on this year.

The other teachers smiled amongst themselves, exchanging glances, oh aye! Ha ha! Your Freud lesson not go down well with the ladies this year then! Surprised you get away with that every year anyway! Ah, it was bound to happen, a complaint, sooner or later! Nobody volunteered to be psychoanalysed this year? Hee hee!

Shakespeare looked at his colleagues, aye right, shut up. Know what? I'm hurt that you say that, I'd never do that, psychoanalysis! Then he said and anyway, the girls in general always like the Freud lesson, they do but.

And he then went on to speak about how Marie had taken him on.

He'd told the class they were going to learn about Freud, it was a preparation for reading some poetry about dreams, some background. So, he related, in my build-up to bringing Freud in to the lesson, I'd told them about a few other revolutionary thinkers and writers, you know, just to get some background. I started by saying that the traditional way that everyone had read the scriptures for two thousand years, or interpreted them, it always led them to believe that one of the Bible's purposes was to encourage people to perceive themselves, or more to the point, perceive themselves within the human race, as being at the centre of life, life and all living things, etcetera etcetera, the whole cosmos itself, and I said that this perception had changed completely after Copernicus proved that the earth wasn't the centre of the universe, and the sun didn't revolve around the earth, and so on and so on and so on.

Someone interrupted Shakespeare, man, the kids must love coming to your lesson, do they no have a sore head when they leave! The others grinned.

But Shakespeare continued, naw, the pupils love listening to that stuff, and then about Galileo and the fury of the Church and all that, and I always get some humour into the lessons when we do it, just having a joke about excommunication and such.

Jesus, the other teachers looked at each other, it's a right barrel of laughs in your lesson eh!

Shakespeare smiled and shook his head, ah, it's a heady atmosphere right enough, I'll not deny it! Anyway, then I'd moved on to telling the class about Darwin, he's always someone the pupils have heard of but don't really know too much about, I've always asked them do you not do that in Biology? As he spoke, he made a glance to the side and said to the two Biology teachers listening to him, do you not teach them that in Biology?

One of the Biology teachers grinned, course we do ya eejit, and he walked away from the group, sorry, I'm gonni have to excuse myself, got a lab to set up. He stopped and turned, though I don't know that there's much point in me doing any teaching at all, am I not just surplus to educational needs now, since our colleague here has inserted the theory of evolution into his English lessons!

Shakespeare laughed, aye, see you later! Anyway, and he turned to the others, I gave out the usual stuff I give out, a booklet I made up, spent ages updating it this year too, and the pupils got to look at some wildlife photographs, and I told them about giant tortoises floating along in the ocean, and then eventually getting carried by currents to the Galapagos, with the fur seals swimming in the same currents to the same destination every year, then the good ship H.M.S. Beagle turning up, and Darwin getting off with his bottles and tins and things to put things in, and having the idea that man wasn't in fact the sole object of all creation, he wasn't the whole aim of the process.

The other teachers stared at him.

Shakespeare continued, the pupils really feel they're learning something when I do this lesson, I'm telling you, they're alert to their education, they stay awake!

One more teacher walked away, blinking, heading to the urn.

Shakespeare said I love doing this lesson, really. So anyway, then I moved on to Freud, oh, I'd given them wee hints last week about what Freud was all about, some of them had done some research themselves over the weekend, asked their parents and such, ha ha!

The remaining teachers listened, you'll get into trouble one of these days!

Anyway, he continued, so I told them that Freud had said all that stuff about your consciousness, I don't know the exact scientific language, if it's a science at all, actually it isn't really, but you know, all that stuff about how your consciousness isn't the main force that controls what you do and say, it's not the key thing, and then I finished off by saying to them that all those interpretations I'd been telling them about, discoveries as well, that was how people came to understand themselves in the world today, the Bible, and then the revolutions, created by Copernicus, Galileo, Darwin, Freud, and that was it, that was bloody it.

His colleagues looked at their feet, aye! That was it, aye! Bloody it, bloody!

Shakespeare nodded back at that them, I mean, I didn't say that I necessarily agreed with the Bible, or

Darwin or anything, or that I believed all the mumbo-jumbo that Freud said, I was just reporting how people thought of themselves.

His colleagues nodded, saying nothing.

But Marie had taken him on.

So this Marie character, and Shakespeare shook his head, she hadn't been happy, I could see her shaking her head and scribbling things down, I had told them all to take notes, but she was writing her own stuff, she was only half-listening when I was doing the teaching.

Someone said half, how dare she!

So Shakespeare said aye, and then she challenged me, it was like the wee madam wasn't interested in anything I'd said before! He shook his head, course, she hadn't been listening properly.

The staff laughed, not interested in what you were saying? God forbid! They offered a variety of opinions, agreeing with each other on the point of whether Marie would have been interested, and someone grabbed Shakespeare's book off him and looked at the cover, I mean, who wouldn't be interested in coming into school to have On The Origin Of Species By Means Of Natural Selection rammed in your face when all you want to do is pass your wee English exam!

Some of the group who had gone away then came back across the staffroom holding cups, biscuits, other things. And the Shakespeare was still going on, not giving up, he was now on the subject of how Marie had said that all he'd talked about in the lesson was men, aye, men she said! And that the way people see women was evolving as well, as well as the way people see the world or humans' place in the world, evolving she said! And that the way people see the human race

201

wasn't finished yet, and how neither it would be until women were equal to men, equal she said! Shakespeare shook his head again, I don't think she knows what the word perception means, cheeky wee madam.

He was greeted by responses, ah, the achievement of equality, his colleagues smiled, aye! Equality!

He nodded, that's what she said! How people a hundred years from now would see the world differently once women get equality, and how people today who think they know how people see themselves, think they can sum it up, they still don't really know what they're talking about, it was me she was talking about, I'm bloody positive, it was me she was meaning! Jesus!

As Shakespeare spoke, his colleagues around him were laughing, ha ha, looking at each other, starting to split up and head to different parts of the staffroom, some to the door and out.

Some of the men, who were in the Joke Club and had been listening in, made comments about Shakespeare having been challenged by a female, aye, proved wrong by a woman you were, survival of the fittest eh, just a pretty wee lassie as well, ha ha, you might as well have been talking about The Descent Of Man, think of the imagery!

…

Ace was crying in the corridor. It was daytime, but the corridor was in darkness, the only light there was came from the doors of some of the offices, the corridor lights themselves weren't working. Ace's face could be seen in the shaft of light that came from one doorway.

The silhouettes of a few members of staff could be seen around Ace, heads facing down towards him, then up and across at each other. A couple walked away from the scene, shaking their heads, not saying anything to each other, and now there were two teachers left with Ace. One was Shakespeare.

They had been asking him what the matter was, what's the matter Ace? Ace said nothing, nothing's the matter, but then the words that came from him were just, just, just fucking leave me, and he shouted, there's nothing the matter, just fucking leave me alone! And he took a step past one of them and reached over to the corridor wall and banged it with his fist. Then he stood back in the place he had been standing in when the teachers had been asking him what the matter was.

Shakespeare and his colleague, a woman, looked at the wall, then at each other, then at Ace, then at each other again. Shakespeare shrugged his shoulders, the woman shook her head. Shakespeare flicked his head in the direction of the end of the corridor, and the two of them started to move away from Ace.

Then Shakespeare stopped, and turned, tapping Ace on the shoulder, and said it's okay Ace, it'll be okay, you can go home if you want, I'll tell the office. Ace looked up, and the man repeated, it's okay, I'll sort it with the office.

Ace kept looking at Shakespeare, yeah, maybe sir, em, I'm, sorry. For swearing sir. I shouldn't have. He looked at the woman who was waiting a couple of metres away, Miss, I'm sorry for swearing.

And the two of them watched Ace walk down the corridor and turn to go out of the building.

…

The girl from England that some of the staff had been talking about, she had arrived at the school just after Christmas, she had been getting bullied for being from England by some of the pupils, not a lot, not all of the pupils, just a group of five or six others, other girls.

Some staff said it was a state of affairs that could not be tolerated in the school, this is shocking, in this day and age, see some of our kids! Bloody nutters so they are. Some teachers said the thing was an outrage, aye, nothing but racism so it is. Naw it isni, it's no racist against the English, how can it be, they're the same as us man! This discussion didn't last.

Anyway, someone said, it's not been in school, or at least not on the school site, eh, it's always been on the way home or in the town at lunchtime, so. Someone else said, so what, so it's not the school's responsibility, is that what you're saying, we just sit back and, knowing that it's going on, we just do nothing? Someone else said no, no, no, surely it's the school's responsibility to tell the kids not to be racist, in or out of school, towards English people, or anyone, yea?

Another teacher said yeah, and went on, I mean, I lived in England for six years, straight after I finished uni up here, and I never experienced racism ever, not even once, when I taught in schools down there, not once.

Everybody looked at him, saying mm.

It's true, he said, not even once.

People nodded, agreeing.

…

In which Smith takes economics and history, and puts them together with morals and logic to, em, em, and with that Scout stopped talking about football, and now was talking about The Wealth Of Nations, but

204

somehow relating it to the transfer system, well boy, do you not see how it's all linked together, the professional game and big finance eh, it's all just one big whatsit, no? Can you no see?

Someone spoke from across the room, that was the bell just there, it's no been working in this building today, not all the time, but it just rang in the rest of the school just there, I heard it out the window. And with that, a few staff got out of their chairs and headed for the door, Jeso, bloody computerised bells now, and still you canni get anything to work properly in this place!

Scout looked out the window, ach, look at that, no-one's in a hurry to get anywhere, look, the kids are taking their time, so, so will I.

Then he said, again, do you see boy? Smith was right, look, think about it, they tried to restrict the number of foreign, well non-British players in Scottish and English teams, remember? And remember it led to Leeds playing Rangers in the European Cup, or whatever it is that they call it now, know, mind how Leeds got through by default or something, after that other team was disqualified for falling foul of the foreign players rule, they'd been playing too many in the previous round when they'd beaten Leeds, remember?

Scout started to move his arms around, laughing, aye, and then there was that McCoist goal at Elland Road, what a build-up and all, that guy on the telly called it a sweeping parabola of a cross! Scout stood up, commentating, a sweeping parabola, and there was the diving head of a talisman meeting it in the area, au revoir Cantona! Scout sat down, and said this my boy, this proves that Smith had been right all along, correct boy, and furthermore boy, he was proved right in his theory of economics by a McCoist goal, I'm telling you boy, it proved it!

And then he turned to talking about the time Smith was writing, and I mean boy, the time when he produced his best work, back then, back then when pneumatology was what they called philosophy boy, pneumatology they said! Oh aye, I know these things.

A few people still in the staffroom looked at Scout. He glanced back at them, then at the teachers leaving the room, all of us today, we get a degree and we think we're all clever dicks, but isn't it the case that everybody gets a degree nowadays eh, in anything, a B.A. in Disney Studies maybe! Or a B.Sc. in, I don't know, Vegetarianology!

He looked back at the door when all the staff had gone, nope, Scottish philosophy, that was it! Optics! Jurisprudence! You couldn't get a degree then without studying philosophy boy, at least in Scotland you couldn't! Ach!

He went back to speaking about Smith again and how Smith would have found it funny, the football transfer system in Europe, and its changes and anomalies, aye, especially given how he worked for the customs and the whatsit and everything, oh aye, especially being as how he was actually a commissioner for the customs in Edinburgh, hee hee! Ach!

Scout said that he taught about free trade, mercantilism, protectionism and such like in Modern Studies, aye, well, I do my best to relay the finer points, but it's not so interesting for the kids I don't think, and to be honest it's not that interesting teaching it, unless you get into the philosophy of economics, and you need four years with decent students to do that properly boy, and who's going to give you that in a bloody comprehensive education system eh, eh?

Scout looked around, and then out of the window, ach well, there's no-one left in the playground, so, and he looked at his feet, so I suppose half the school's climbing the walls in my classroom by now.

He stood up and headed off to teach, shaking his head and making mutterings about Adam Smith and telling himself what a talisman McCoist was, aye, that's all he was, McCoist, a bloody talisman and no doubt about it, eh.

…

Ace said he thought the Bin Brigade, the lot of them, were heroes, and he included himself in the description, aye we all are, we're heroes!

The class looked at him and laughed, heroes, us! A couple of people caught each other's eyes and smiled and wobbled their heads about, heroes!

Ace laughed himself, and then said aye, I know, I know, but you know what I mean, eh? And then he stopped speaking, he didn't say anything for a bit.

You no fancy being a film hero, a movie hero Ace! It was Sam that enquired, eh, you no fancy being a hero in one of they films you're gonni be in, or you'll be in when you're older, know?

Ace shook his head and said no, he said he didn't want to be a movie hero, he said he would prefer acting roles where, well, he said, sitting forwards in his chair, I suppose I would want to be the kind of hero who isn't the all-action kind of guy, know, jumping off burning buildings, saving a baby, nah, more the kind of person who just does good things for people, rather than heroic things.

Billy said, maybe if there's a guy who does things like that, things that are good, maybe you can still say he's a hero, if you want, some people might think he's a hero, the person he does the good things for, no?

Aye, said Ace, looking over, as long as the guy, the character in the film, as long as what he did was good, the things he did were good, and he always worked the things out as well, and did what he thought was right, and he always committed himself to doing what he thought was right too.

Sam said, aye, I know what you mean, you mean a guy who's commited to being good. Aye, said Ace, supercool for cats, that.

Billy smiled and stood up, one arm was outstretched. He started narrating, and suddenly, from nowhere, came a somebody, a man! A man who doesn't waver from his cause, a man committed to being a good guy!

The class laughed, Ace was laughing too, aye, aye Billy, something like that, aw, never mind! And he smiled again.

But Billy continued, both arms out now, a somebody, a man who doesn't just do things that people just think are heroic like jumping down ropes or rescuing damsels in distress, a man who does, what, he, thinks, is, right! Coming to a cinema near you!

The laughter died after a few seconds.

Then William said aye, but that type of hero, the one that jumps down ropes, he gets all the best money to be in films, know, the actor, yeah?

Ace said aye.

…

208

There was no-one playing cards. Mr Tambourine Man looked across the staffroom and then turned to Armpits. He leaned over towards him, making his chair balance on two legs. Armpits looked at him, and raised his eyebrows, looked to one side, and then the other, and then back at Mr Tambourine Man who was still leaning his body towards him. And Armpits asked him hey, you gonni ask me out? 'Cause I like to get chatted up first, and I'm not cheap either, hee hee!

Mr Tambourine Man looked across the staffroom again, he saw that there were a few other conversations taking place, then spoke, only to Armpits, glancing up every now and then in between what he said, sometimes looking behind himself, or stopping what he was saying if someone brushed by where he was sitting.

Eventually it could be distinguished what Mr Tambourine Man said, it's enough to make you want to get out of this bloody job eh, or this bloody place well, I mean, eh? And he nodded to Armpits as he said this. Armpits said something back to Mr Tambourine Man, you're not really able to get out anyway, even if you wanted to, or even if you felt forced to, just because of, know, your situation.

Mr Tambourine Man leaned his chair back on all four legs, saying what d'you mean, I could get out any effing time I wanted, I could, you trying to say I don't control my own situation, well I'm telling you I do, I could get out anytime I wanted, I know I could.

Armpits didn't reply.

A few seconds went by.

Mr Tambourine Man started tapping a finger on the card table beside him as he spoke now, saying listen, I wouldn't stick around here if I didn't want to, okay?

Armpits nodded.

Right? Mr Tambourine Man moved his neck so his face was further towards Armpits.

Aye okay right, Armpits said, I was only saying, and he put his hands up in the air.

Mr Tambourine Man sat back in his chair and slid his arm across the table as he did so, aye, well.

…

Billy shouted out, sir, before I got chucked out of the History exam class, I was learning about how people said Scotland was only half-educated in the nineteen-hundreds, or that's what the teacher said anyway, the nineteen-hun, eh, aye, em, naw, the ninetenth century. Half-educated, how d'you get like that! Is that still it?

Billy looked around the room after he asked the question. The others looked at him. Then from William came the question eh, what did you mean, the nineteenth century or nineteen-hundreds Billy? This led to an exchange between the two.

Or did you just mean the nineteenth century Billy?

Naw, aye.

The nineteenth century?

Aye, naw.

The nineteen-hundreds?

Aye, wait a minute, I'll ask sir.

Billy then faced the front and asked what is the nineteenth century anyway sir? Is it not the years that start with eighteen?

William interrupted, saying ah, em, naw, you mean the eighteenth century? Eighteen-something, yeah Billy?

Em, aye, so the nineteenth century is years that start with nineteen then? Billy squinted his eyes to one side and skewed his lip to the other side, a year that starts with nineteen? Naw, what I was learning about was years that started with eighteen.

William pushed his glasses up the bridge of his nose, eighteen?

Aye, Billy was nodding now, eighteen. You were talking about the twentieth century, I think, years that start with nineteen.

William looked at his hands spread out, palm upwards, on his desk, I wasni talking about any years! I was just asking you what you meant!

Billy smiled, aye, you're right. Well, I think I meant years that start with eighteen, that was when Scotland was half-educated, according to the teacher I had.

William shook his head, so, years that start with nineteen are the nineteenth century, aye?

Billy laughed, naw! I mean aye, naw! You're a daftie William, star man though!

Marie then looked up and said sir, what do you think, do you think we're still half-educated now! The class around all laughed.

Billy laughed too, aye sir, I mean, I don't know, sir! That's what I was saying, asking, what does that mean, half-educated? It was just something somebody once said I think, I don't know if it was someone at the time or someone later in a history book.

Sam then said aye, they all just make it up in history books anyway Billy. Someone at one of the army career days I went to, one of the officers, said that they knew someone whose brother or cousin wrote history books and he just made up the names of the people in the past, for a laugh, named them after their relations, or their favourite singers and actors, they toffed up their names to make them sound more important, called them Sir this or Lord that, so they did, just made the whole thing up.

Billy waited for Sam to finish, then raised his eyebrows, was it all about schools for the rich, was it sir? That's what I thought the teacher said, but surely the rich didn't make up half of Scotland in the nineteenth century!

…

Sandwich Toaster asked if anyone had heard the stuff on the radio about the by-election.

What stuff, was one reply. Then, a counter-reply from someone else was Jesus, what do you mean what stuff, you can't get away from the bloody by-election on the radio or the TV! Nobody's going to care who wins by the time the whole thing's over! All the guys are saying the same thing, just blending into the one candidate, what is it the kids say nowadays with the computer graphics and everything, morphing!

Armpits looked over his shoulder and interjected with aye maybe, but not the socialist one.

Aye not the socialist one, people would say, okay not the socialist one, but he's the one no-one'll be voting for, and no-one but you wants to win, it's just you who'll be voting for him! And Armpits said he wouldn't, aye, naw, see, I won't because I can't, I won't be voting at all, 'cause I live in the next constituency, so I can't vote for anyone.

Well, how come you've been banging on about who should win then, people would ask him. Armpits said, have you heard me?

Sandwich Toaster then said he was going to vote for the socialist. A couple of people turned to him. One said, what do you know about socialism son? The other said, how come you're voting socialist, someone as young as you shouldn't be voting socialist! What's wrong with you!

Armpits told them to leave Sandwich Toaster alone and looked at him, saying good on you, son. Sandwich Toaster said aye, heard it, and then when he left the room a minute later and the conversation had changed by then, Armpits did say to the others that he didn't have a clue as to why someone like Sandwich Toaster would be voting socialist, Christjesus, why would he say that eh, socialist! When I think of myself at that age!

He's just trying to ingratiate himself with you ya fat bastard, someone would say. And Armpits smiled back and said, he's just trying to show me he could be a bigger person if he wanted to, and to be fair, the boy could do worse than try to impress me, he could do worse!

...

Hey sir do you know any French! Ace was asking what nouvelle vague meant and said that he knew, it's just a wee test sir! He looked round the room as well as towards the front, anyone know?

Sam looked across and said naw, what does it mean then Ace? Ace said it meant new wave. Sam said right, oh, right then, is that French? Ace said yeah, it's French.

213

Sam then asked okay then, what's it about? And Ace said what's what about?

Sam said that film, New Wave, what's it about, is it a surfing thing, are there French girls in it on the beach? Whoa! Ace, you've brought a decent film in at last! The class laughed.

Ace laughed, aw Sam you're funny! Sam smiled, how? You just are, supercool eh, and Ace continued, so, sir, you seen any new wave films, you must have done at uni, all your mates round the telly, you students always watch arthouse stuff yeah?

Sam looked at Ace and said em, so Ace, you just gonni ignore me then, think I won't understand your New Wave film, only sir'll know anything about it?

Ace said aw mate, I was just talking to sir about it, it's not a film called New Wave, it's a set of films called new wave, and anyway, new wave film isn't something you have to understand, anybody can get it. Ace reached into his bag, like look, I've got this with me today, it's called Tirer Sur Le Pianiste, it's French, you'll see when we put it on later. He looked at the front, Charles Aznavour's in it, you'll have heard of him sir eh, my dad remembers him! Know the words? And he sang, one hand on his heart, the other held out in front of him, his face smiling, his voice quivering, she-ee-ee-ee-ee-ee, may be the face I can't forge-e-e-e-e-et!

Marie looked at Ace, who're you singing about Ace, anyone in here! Ace shook his head, aw, shoosh Marie. A few people in the class looked at each other.

Sam shook his head, then nodded up the way, pointing his head towards Ace's hand, and said so, new wave isn't a film then, I was wrong about that, eh. How

come you were laughing at me though, and saying I
was funny then?

Ace said I wasn't laughing at you, I was just, I
dunno, laughing, sorry. There was a pause. Ace then
said to Sam, Sam, nouvelle vague's the name given to
French films that broke through the traditions of cinema
around the nineteen-fifties and sixties.

Kelly interrupted and said Ace, you sound like
you're reading from a book again, one of your dad's!

Ace said, shut up Kelly.

Kelly smiled and shrugged her shoulders, at
least I know who's face you can't forget! And she
looked at Marie who smiled and waved Kelly away.

Ace turned back towards Sam, aye Sam, new
wave films had different narrative forms and camera
techniques, know? They used music as an artistic
device, jazz, and stuff like that, the new wave directors
and writers established themselves as an influential
force in cinema.

Sam said, so there were no girls in bikinis?

The class laughed.

Ace said aye, naw, no girls in bikinis, that's
right Sam, no girls in bikinis!

…

Sandwich Toaster sat on his chair, staring into
his coffee mug, blowing on the surface of the coffee,
looking to the side, looking back at the coffee, blowing
on it, staring at it, his eyes following the circles made
by the water when he stirred it, blowing it, blowing it
again, looking to the side.

He turned his head and looked at someone who
just came in. Sandwich Toaster asked the guy what he
had said to him as he'd entered the staffroom. The guy
said that he hadn't said anything to him, he'd been

singing to himself or maybe he was talking to someone in the corridor when he was at the door, he'd not said anything to Sandwich Toaster. Sandwich Toaster said aye, okay, sorry, heard it, understood.

The guy went over to someone else and said hi, how you doing?

Sandwich Toaster followed the guy with his eyes and then looked down, put both hands round his mug, blew on the surface of the coffee again and continued to look at it. Eventually he took a sip.

…

First thing in the morning and the class were talking about drink, the drink. What people had had at the weekend. What they said they'd had. How much they had before they got drunk. How much they had and how long between when they stopped and when they went home, eating the mints and stuff so their mum wouldn't smell it on their breath, or at least walking around the neighbourhood until they'd sobered up by the time they got in the house.

Then someone mentioned Kevin's mum and the drink, together in one sentence, eh, how much would she have to have to get blootered! Nobody spoke then, after the mention of Kevin's mum, and they all looked around the room.

It was five minutes into the day and Kevin hadn't arrived yet. When the class saw that he wasn't in, there were a few sighs. The pupils looked at each other and then quickly down at the ground.

The pupil who'd mentioned Kevin's mum looked up and half-whispered sorry to the rest of the class, only the first letter and a bit of the first syllable of the word could be heard, then he looked down.

…

216

You ever think about why you're becoming a teacher, why you're actually becoming one, Bicycle Clips was wondering, and he said tss, you have to think about it seriously, well, at some point anyway, it's all very well enjoying the study of something and even thinking that you'd be good at teaching it, but you've got to consider if you can get children to enjoy the subject, it's not just a matter of getting them to pass exams, oh that's important, tss, but it's more than that, you want to inspire some of them to want to learn more, you know?

Bicycle Clips said that he felt a sense of achievement, aye, really I do, a tremendous sense of achievement, if just one pupil each year leaves school and goes to study History at uni, you just think, wow! He smiled, and pulled one knee up, holding it clasping his hands around it. So, you have to look at all the options, so, tell me now if you can, go on then, we'll have a bit of fun eh, tell me, have you ever thought about why you want to become a teacher, it's not just because you think you can't do anything else? Have you thought about the options?

He waited and laughed, oh, I'm not trying to put you off, far from it, ha ha, tss!

He leaned down and scratched his leg, I'm just saying, if you've thought about it, and you've then made the conscious decision that it's something you want to do, then you're doing the right thing, ergo, the right thing by yourself.

Bicycle Clips said that some teachers in the place would try and put any student off trying to become a teacher, aye, the ones who don't like it'll try that with you, but in reality they're the ones who should be giving it up, getting out, I mean, trying to put young

217

and enthusiastic people off going into a job where they can inspire children, it's a disgrace.

He held one knee with two hands again, children today, what choices do they have eh, so-called sexy jobs, jobs with money, sexy jobs they say nowadays, don't they, money, finance, a fast buck. Teaching? Kids today, the careers advice they get, it channels them towards the so-called sexy careers, and there's nowhere near enough of them for them, all coming out of university or college with qualifications in forensic science or computer software or games design or whatever, a hundred people a year from one uni, fifty from another, and there's only twenty or so jobs in the country!

Bicycle Clips sighed, I'm just saying, think about it. Once you're in, it's hard to get out. I mean look at some of the people in here, it's like they're trapped but won't say it.

I'm, just saying, think about it.

…

A teacher was talking about a pupil he had to write a reference for, aye, I'm more than happy to do it, aye, good kid, great lad.

Someone else said that he had been sent a reference to do for Sam, it was for the army, look here, at last they're agreeing to let him in! A few people laughed, that right, they're letting guys like that in the army now!

The Joke Club cracked jokes about Sam, aye, we can all sleep soundly now, the country can breathe easy, Sam's patrolling the coast making sure the enemy doesn't get in, defending the shores eh, nothing to fear, ha ha!

Well, I think it's actually true, the guy said, it looks like Sam'll be getting in, I think there's still a few formalities and such, he's probably not even been told yet himself, just, the way the army does things, I think, but see these army references these days, sounds like they'd let anybody in, they hardly ask you for anything, exam results, what extra stuff he did, you get a tiny space to write in, they'd probably prefer it if you said nothing! I'm telling you, anyone can get in these days if they can run for more than twenty minutes without fainting!

…

When the Bin Brigade came in, they were talking about the lesson they'd just come out of, Kevin had been half-asleep in it, and wasn't really paying attention, it was Social Education, S.E. sir, it's usually crap, but last week it was sex education, and we'd been told about all the different methods of contraception, but Kevin hadn't been there though, but he was there today but.

The class couldn't wait to say what had happened, they reported it in bits and pieces, anyway sir, the S.E. teacher asked who could remember the different methods of contraception that we'd been taught last week. Aye, Kevin didn't really hear what was asked, he was falling asleep again and never heard her properly! Yeah, and so she raised her voice to get him to, em, focus she said, and then she said to him to tell the class as many different methods of contraception as he could think of, go on Kevin she said, she must have forgotten how he wasni there last week, sir!

Billy laughed, and raised his fist, shaking it in the air, aye, go on Kev, star man!

219

The rest of the class giggled, aye sir, Kevin told the teacher that she wasn't allowed to ask pupils questions like that sir! Ha ha, but what it really was sir was that even though he was only half-concentrating on the lesson and half-falling asleep, he still knew it was a sex education lesson, and when he'd been asked about contraception he'd already been thinking about sex, know, different positions!

Kevin interrupted the story-tellers and said naw, I hadni been! Aye you had, William replied, that's what you said in the lesson Kevin, you pervert!

William continued the story himself, saying right enough, Kevin did explain to everyone at the end of the lesson that he'd had sexual intercourse on his mind because they were in S.E. and talking about sex. So sir, Kevin thought the teacher was asking him to tell the class different methods of intercourse, but she didn't know that, and she insisted that he gave her an answer, sir!

The class giggled. Sir, d'you know what he said after she insisted that he give her an answer? He never even asked her to say what the question was, like he usually does when he wakes up, he just said missionary and blow-job!

The Bin Brigade fell about laughing.

Billy put his hand on Kevin's hair and ruffled it, aw Kev, perfecto!

Kevin smiled.

…

Billy said he had been in trouble in Music. All the Music teachers had been out at some meeting in another school. All Billy's class got to do in Music when their teacher was in was play the instruments, it was a non-certificate class Billy was in, and they didn't complain, they thought that playing instruments wasn't work. But since the teacher wasn't there, Billy's class had to go in with the other class, he explained, know, the exam class sir, we got told to just go in there and just sit and be quiet, sit at the back, keep quiet, the exam class had a supply teacher in to teach them sir, 'cause obviously their teacher was out of school too.

What, you just had to sit at the back and do nothing? William looked back at him, I hate getting told to do that when we sit in with the exam classes sometimes, it's like, we canni do anything except sit and do nothing. I understand some of the stuff they do, I understand it.

Aye, Billy continued, just sitting at the back we were, and then the other class started listening to this music, I thought it was rubbish at first but actually it wasni, it was alright, a bit mad, but alright. He looked around, but anyway, this supply teacher told the exam class, after the music finished, that it was by this guy who was a great man, the teacher said he was a great man, he kept saying he was a great man, and he'd started life in a choir when he was a kid in Austria, and I heard him say this, and then all I said was so did Hitler, he sang in a choir, it doesni mean you're gonni be a great man, actually I didn't say it, I shouted it out from the back, I was supposed to be looking at some crap book.

The Bin Brigade laughed around Billy as he told the story, can't keep your mouth shut, Billy! And he went on, I told him we did it in second year History sir, honestly, we did sir, and he looked around the class, didn't we, Hitler was in a choir and that's where he got the design for the swastika, know, it was on the wall of

221

the church or in the window or something, I canni remember.

Window, William said.

Anyway, Billy carried on, I got a punishment exercise 'cause the teacher got angry and started asking me more questions about Hitler and the church, and I couldni remember anything apart from the stuff about the swastika, and he kept saying how he knew more about history than me, and did I even know what part of Austria it was that Hitler had grown up in, and did I think that he knew nothing about Hitler, or history, he was going off his nut sir! And in the end he gave me a punishment, just 'cause I'd talked in the class when he'd told us all to sit and be quiet, that's what it said at the top of the punishment, talking in class, talking, that's all.

The Bin Brigade were hooting, from what they were saying, it was kind of less at Billy and more at the thought of Hitler singing in a choir. William put his finger across the top of his mouth and said look at me I'm Hitler in the choir, singing to all the other choirboys, and he sang tra la la tra la la, you vill sing in ze same time as me, sing in ze choir! William then started to whistle, and shouted, vistle, vistle in ze choir! The Bin Brigade hooted again.

Billy laughed too, aye, hee hee William, perfecto! Then he pulled a piece of paper from his pocket, naw but look! I've got all this stuff to write out about the music he was playing to his class, it's the same exercise he gave his class to do, except it's a punishment for me and normal homework for them! I'll never be able to do it, writing about what the music I heard meant to me, how am I gonni do that, I don't understand about symphonies and things!

222

Marie said, but you said you thought the music was okay Billy, you were in the class for a while before you got into trouble, he played the music before you got into trouble, yeah? You must remember it, a bit.

Billy said, aye, suppose so. He scratched at the desk, I'm just gonni write about what he told the class the music was, it was meant to sound like a fox hunt, or hunting or something like that. Whatever it was, you were meant to hear all the horses' hooves and the horns of the hunters in the music.

Sounds crap, William was interjecting, and he put his finger across his face, under his nose again, and made the salute of the Nazis, you vill listen to zis music and hear ze fox hunters and zeir horses' hooves or you vill get ze punishment exercise!

Billy laughed, and then turned to the front and said actually, the music was alright sir, you could hear the horses actually. Aw shut up Billy, William was laughing, hear the horses, naw you couldni! Billy said shut up yourself William, it was drums and things, it was meant to sound like horses hooves, know? It was an exam class remember, the music they listen to, it's all meant to sound like something that isn't music!
…

The Phantom had this theory that the Bin Brigade were like some kind of a sub-culture, aah, yes, aah, he would say, if he was in a discussion with the likes of Crossword Freak Number One, you see the pupils in the, aah, Bin Brigade came to this school wanting to be part of it, you see, part of the school, expecting to be part of it like anybody else, all the other pupils, and indeed, why wouldn't they?

Indeed, replied Crossword Freak Number One, rolling his pen around in his hand. Crossword Freak

223

Number Two and Crossword Freak Number Three looked on.

The Phantom continued, and, aah, you see, yes, they just wanted to be just like everybody else, and the thing is for the first two years, perhaps three years even, they would have felt that they were being successful, making friends, learning a bit about this and that, getting on, they would be obeying the school rules, for the most part, and conforming, or at least not rebelling, participating in the dominant behaviour patterns of the body academic, as I like to call the student population, the broad church. They would see themselves as succeeding.

Yes, yes, and Crossword Freak Number One would reply that he had read about this in his Open University notes, yes, its what can be termed as an internalisation of, em, that is, an internalisation of something, yes, no?

The Phantom nodded and half-closed his eyes as he looked at Crossword Freak Number One and finished his sentence off for him, yes, aah, yes, tradition.

Crossword Freak Number Two repeated the word, tradition. Crossword Freak Number Three didn't say anything.

Crossword Freak Number One then repeated the word himself, tradition, that's it, that is, an in-school cultural custom.

The Phantom nodded, yes.

…

Ex-Cop had brought in a book on Kant into school and he had given it to Bicycle Clips, explaining em, it's just a small volume but, sorry, you'll find it interesting I think though, em, and he handed it over.

Bicycle Clips turned round in his seat and smiled and said oh thanks, thanks a lot, no, don't worry, thanks a lot, it's fine, oh aye, I'll definitely have a look at this, and he put it beside his briefcase, patting it, smiling, that'll be me for the evening after my tea, a de facto great thinker in my own house, and he rubbed his hands together, fantastic, tss!

Teaching the kids philosophy now mate? Armpits tapped Ex-Cop on the shoulder from behind him. Ex-Cop didn't turn round, and instead faced forwards, you asking me about what I teach?

Armpits nodded and then shook his head, and then pursed his lips behind Ex-Cop. Ex-Cop got a book out to put on the desk in front of him, and as he did so he said that everyone called his subject Religious Education but the reality was that it was named Religious and Moral Education, and he started to scribble something down on a pupil's work as he said aye, it's just easier to call it R.E. though, and not R.M.E..

He turned round and looked up at Armpits, Armpits nodded down at him, didn't know that.

Ex-Cop faced his work again, aye, and actually the law states that it's morals, moral education, that has to be taught in Scottish schools, and not specifically religious. He carried on looking at his work, a book and some writing of a pupil, as he was talking, aye, so Kant fits in just fine with the syllabus.

Armpits nodded, stuck a bit of his tongue out over his lip, and raised his eyebrows at the same time, oh aye, now I think about it, aye, I think I did know about that. Bicycle Clips looked from Armpits to Ex-Cop, so how do you teach Kant to the kids then, you can't just get them to understand, what, the fundamental

225

principles of the metaphysics of morals in the one period a week that's allocated to R.E., sorry R.M.E., stuck in the middle of the timetable between between Maths and Geography, tss! Or can you?

Ex-Cop said well, we teach about broad moral issues in the syllabus, and maybe we might tell the kids, if it was relevant, that thinkers like Kant would also have considered broad moral issues, and written about them, for example such questions as whether the consequence of actions made the actions moral or not, simple stuff like that. Then the kids might write a wee piece of work with their own thoughts.

Armpits interjected with oh aye, you mean whether the end justifies the means, is that what you mean, Machiavelli and all that? Ex-Cop looked round again, and said yes. Armpits nodded again. Bicycle Clips shifted his chair over and clapped his hands together, Machiavelli, now we're getting somewhere!

Armpits sat down at the desk alongside Ex-Cop and listened in.

Bicycle Clips then asked Ex-Cop about the worth of actions, as quantified by morals, and gave answers to his own questions himself, with Ex-Cop nodding. Armpits folded his arms and looked from one side of the staffroom to the other.

Bicycle Clips then said okay then, what about about de facto categorical and hypothetical imperatives eh, what would Kant have to say about them, tss!

At which point Armpits raised his eyebrows, stood up and started to leave, shaking his head, Christjesus, time for a sharp exit eh!

…

Billy said that one school lesson that he would regard as a favourite if he ever looked back on his school life, had been in second year, aye it was in here sir, in History sir, or was it Geography, maybe the two departments did it together? Well it wasn't even in a classroom actually.

Ah, I know what you're talking about, Geography it was, said William. History, said Ace. History day trip, but a Geography teacher was on it as well, and she took our group, said Kelly. William and Ace both agreed with her, History and Geography!

Billy said they'd gone to just outside the town where there was a site of where there used to be markets, it was in the olden days sir, medieval times I think it was, the eleven-hundreds I think, doesn't matter. It was a great day, and there were all these actors acting out what it was like in those days, no cars, no electricity, you got to act along with them, dressing up, know! And pretending! Billy was nodding, and you got to ask the actors questions and they answered them like they were really from the olden days, we learned loads of stuff for the local environment project we were doing back in the school, and I remember I got a really good mark for mine! Better than some of the brainy ones in the class too!

Billy looked round at the class, and nodded his head and said it was a brilliant day, absolute perfecto, and that's what school should be about, sir. The others nodded.

…

The Phantom appeared to be walking past the staffroom door, there was some noise as he tripped and said ahem, aah, and then he looked in as he was passing. Nobody looked up. He paused and stepped in, looking down at his feet, he stopped just inside the doorway, looking around the place. Nobody was looking up.

The Phantom sighed, paused again for a moment, then turned and walked out of the door again, bumping into a teacher who was just coming in. Oh, eh, sorry the teacher said, lifting both forearms up, palms outwards. The Phantom said no, no, aah, it's fine, fine, smiling, I was just leaving, and he backed off a bit and stood still, holding his arm out towards the centre of the room, indicating something in relation to the bumping into each other that had just taken place, something of his view of the thing and the notion that it had been his own fault, the Phantom's, and he smiled, after you good sir!

The teacher walked past him, em, thanks, looking at whatever papers were in his hand.

The Phantom smiled without opening his mouth, and strode out of the room.

…

One dinnertime, Armpits was speaking about the secret of success in this business, aye, if you want to make it in this business, the business, that is, of career advancement within education and the pursuit of it thereof, then you have to be seen at all times to be keeping a folder under your arm, look at me for example! Folk sitting around looked at each other and laughed, and said em, we'd rather not if you don't mind, thanks all the same, and they said aw man, do we have to look at you? It'll be bad enough smelling you at the end of the day, after you've built up a sweat, fat boy!

Yeah, yeah, no, listen, Armpits insisted on making his point, I'm just saying, it's important to be seen to be always doing something, know, or being

228

seen to be on the way to do something, give folk the right impression eh? Always keep a folder with you when you're on the move, son! And he continued on, saying aye, it's a shame, it's not enough just to be a good teacher these days, the fuckers want blood nowadays, so they do, and he turned, you just listen to me boy, I'll give you all the advice you need eh. And he looked at everyone else, Christjesus, I'm the only suitable role model in here for a young teacher, look at the rest of you sitting about, blank looks on your faces!

Everybody laughed. Somebody asked hey, how come if you're such a role model then, if you're such an example, how come you've got nowhere in teaching in, what, twenty years then eh! The guy who said it was laughing and looking round at everyone as he spoke. Just as he finished there was the sound of someone, maybe two people, starting to laugh and then stopping, suppressing the noise, coughing.

Armpits turned and faced his colleague and asked what he'd meant by that, em, what do you mean, got nowhere in teaching, I'm still here, am I not?

The teacher looked at the others and then back at Armpits, well, you're still a bloody ordinary teacher aren't you, just like the rest of us, the teacher looked round again, then, I'm just saying, know, no harm, we're all ordinary teachers, most of us, no harm.

Armpits put his folder on the table and leaned against the table with one hand and put his other on his waist, he said he'd only been having a laugh with the folder-under-the-arm thing, Christjesus, I hadn't meant anything deep. He looked at the window and back at the other teacher, Christjesus, there was no need to attach any depth to it.

He paused and put one hand in his pocket, and if you're counting, it's twenty-one years anyway, twenty-one years teaching and yes, getting nowhere.

…

Marie was in the newspaper because she had won a writing competition, the school had entered one of her compositions for it, Shakespeare it was, something she'd done in his class and taken home and finished, or changed, for homework, and she had won.

Shakespeare was talking about it in the staffroom, showing off the article in the paper, and telling everyone about how she'd handed her work in to him, the original, and he'd read it and then helped her re-draft it, well, I made some comments in the margin on the original short story, and she had to take them into consideration when she re-wrote it, it was a class exercise, just something we do regularly.

People congratulated Shakespeare, aw, well done mate, well done man! Someone said to him, you're entitled to be a bit excited by the thing eh! Someone else said aye he should be, not every day one of your pupils gets in the papers eh! There was an agreement, aye man, you should take every bit of credit that's coming your way out of this!

Someone else in the staffroom said, was that not the wee lassie whose father killed himself before she came here on a free transfer from the private school?

People looked up.

Someone asked, that right? There was an answer, so they say, aye.

And the thing was discussed, some people knew all about it, others didn't, they'd heard rumours, there was conjecture about the thing, questions about how they had found the body in the canal, and the issue of

230

nobody ever having been done for it, aye, naw, police never arrested anyone, aye, suspicious circumstances they said, aye but most likely suicide though, or so it was thought, that's what the police thought anyway.

Shakespeare shook his head and said, well, I kind of knew there was something of a history to the girl but I never asked, and no-one said, so, I didn't know. He looked back at the newspaper he was holding, the story's nothing about death or anything, in fact there's not much a of a storyline to it all, nothing in the way of a plot you might say, it's just a wee piece of writing about a young girl playing in the park during the summer holidays, pretty innocuous really, it was the descriptions she used that I liked, places, thoughts and so on, spot on so they were, spot on, intuitive, and you don't get many pupils like that these days, do you?

One of the guys in the Joke Club brought the subject of Marie's father up again, em, don't you think that if the girl's dad really did commit suicide, then, you know, it wasn't very original, know, throwing yourself in the canal, I mean, know, it's hardly the most original way to top yourself eh!

Another Joke Club member joined in, aye! You'd think with having such a creative daughter, know, and that sort of thing very often being in the genes like, you would have thought he would think of something a bit better than that eh, throwing himself in the canal!

His Joke Club colleague came back with yeah, it's not gonni win any awards for originality eh, know what I mean, and he lifted a piece of paper off a desk and held it in his hand, looking down at it as he announced, ladies and gentleman this year's Suicide of the Year is, well, we don't have any winners because

231

everybody threw themselves in the canal! There was a real hoot amongst the Joke Club, one other of their number said, even if there was a winner, you'd have to say, well, he can't be with us tonight! The Joke Club laughed again, one man lifting his feet off the ground and slamming them back down again.

When their noise had subsided, from elsewhere there was speculation from a couple of teachers, actually I bet she doesni turn up for the writing award, aye, she's a real moody one that lassie, I taught her last year.

Someone else clicked his fingers and said ah, that's what the thing on Monday was all about, the thing in the office corridor! And, as the rest of the staffroom looked at him, the teacher continued, well, there was meant to be a picture getting taken in the rector's office, in school, on Monday, one of the office ladies told me, a guy from the paper was in. I didn't know what it was about, I just assumed it was just something about, I don't know, the new science wing getting confirmed or something, and they'd grabbed the nearest pupil around who was well-dressed with a nice smile to be in a photograph with the rector. But anyway, the girl who was meant to be in the picture, it must have been this Marie person, she'd come up to the office and then told the camera guy she wouldni be seen in the same photo as the rector!

Everybody laughed. She did that? She must have made him look bloody stupid in front of the photographer eh! The laughter died down. Someone said, she'll be nicer in a couple of years eh, that lassie, once she's got over everything, she's okay I suppose, just been dealt a bad one recently.

232

Shakespeare said aye, I've maybe been a bit unfair to her in the past, now I think about it.

Then a voice from the Joke Club said aye, but was it no a bloody funny thing about her dad though eh! ...

Crossword Freak Number Two was shaking his head, what commotions we have going on today. Commotions, commotions, commotions, look at that out there, is that how all children behave nowadays? Crossword Freak Number One said yes, yes, looking up, em, yes, and Crossword Freak Number Three nodded.

The Crossword Freaks and the Joke Club were all standing by the window to drink their coffee and do their crosswords, looking out into the playground. They weren't sitting down, any of them, sometimes they looked back at the staffroom seats they sat on at breaks, observing their occupants, then they would look at each other but not comment on the situation.

There were about eight people in visiting the school this day, people from the council, looking at all the buildings for health and safety purposes, wandering about in and out of classrooms, interrupting lessons to ask teachers about light bulbs, ceiling tiles, sockets and so forth. The health and safety guys were in having a coffee in the staffroom, sitting in the two areas where the Crossword Freaks and Joke Club sat if there were no visitors in.

One of the health and safety guys was a woman. She was chatting away to her colleagues, and had lifted a packet of digestives from the urn table and brought them over to where she was sitting. When one of the Joke Club had approached the table, she offered him a

233

biscuit and he had refused, em, no thanks, I'll just, and he moved to the window.

Crossword Freak Number One looked at the council visitors, his gaze passing from speaker to speaker, stopping at the woman, and then he would look around the whole staffroom, exchanging raised eyebrows with other teachers, this was in between writing in his crossword solutions whilst he stood at the window, placing the palm of one hand under the part of the newspaper that he was writing on.

The visitors sat in a group of three and a group of five. Once during morning break, one person from each group got up at the same time to refill their cups from the urn, creating a group of two and a group of four for a minute. A balance was then achieved when the two went back and sat down beside each other, meaning there were two groups of four, the eight was there, it worked out.

At the window, Crossword Freak Number Two continued to comment on the commotions going on in the playground, what a commotion, look there, are we allowing that now, kissing in the playground, full-blown kissing! Look at that, right in front of everyone, look at that pair, that hand's got a firm clasp on her bottom, it's explicit! Can no-one get them a classroom for some privacy! And then he moved his line of focus, and look, see that group of third year boys over there eh, was there ever a more evil collection of pupils than that lot, what's their leader's name again? Can't remember, but he's a real evil so and so, eh.

Then, from someone in the Joke Club, there's that whatshername, that new woman in Home Economics, can't remember her name, bit of a battleaxe I think though. Woops! She'll need to watch out walking by that game of football, she's gonni get, whoa!

The Joke Club smiled and looked on, ha ha, thought she was gonni get hit by the ball there! Oops! Taking the short cut over the grass to avoid them, wise. Oops, nearly, again! She's gonni try and kick it back to the lads now, watch out for this! Oh! Ha ha! He ha! And she's over! Ha ha!

The rest of the Joke Club roared.

The Crossword Freaks looked out of the window at the Home Economics teacher who had fallen over the football she was trying to kick back to the boys she was passing in the playground. Then they looked back at their newspapers and across at the council visitors, and the woman. The Joke Club were still hooting, classic!

You can't write on these things standing up, Crossword Freak Number One said.

…

I'll just tuck this under here, sorry about the state of the car again darling, so, how'd your day go then darling, okay? The Dog Catcher switched the ignition on. Then came the words, as she drove out the gates, had a quiet one myself, appointments with kids in school in the morning, always set aside an hour for each one, and they only take up twenty minutes apiece, so you can catch up on some paperwork when they've pissed off back to class, the darlings. Then a couple of home visits this afternoon, no difficulties there. Though, there was this one visit, the mother's a real drinker, big style I mean, nice and all, like, really nice in fact, offers you a cup of tea and everything, keeps the house tidy too, could do with her round mine once a week in fact, I suppose it's an actual genuine medical condition she's got, she doesn't fake it, and you don't get many of them nowadays, though I wouldn't call her a wino or anythng, I've never seen her drunk, like, not live, in the flesh like, but wow, you can smell it off her, for definite! I've met her a couple of times before, just when she was needing help with her boys while she was moving house, something like that.

The Dog-Catcher drove out the gates and away from the school, anyway, I got asked to make the visit after the headteacher was told that another teacher in the school had heard that the boy, think he's third or fourth year, was being made to do a milk round or a paper round or something, though it's definitely a milk round, I've since established that, and that he was being made to do it by the mum, just so she could get his pay off him and buy drink with it. Wouldn't be the first time for something like that, I can tell you.

The Dog-Catcher looked in her rear-view mirror, well, I couldn't just go into the house and ask that straight away, know, the thing about her son doing the milk-round just to give her the money for drink, know, but you have to get the question out somehow, it's your job, know. She checked her blind-spot at a junction, so, we were talking about this and that, me and the mother, and she knew fine why I was round, you can always tell, if they don't ask why you're round then they know, nobody just has the social services drop in on them without any notice without asking them why they're there, so she knew alright, darling, she knew alright!

So, and the Dog-Catcher continued, she's pouring the tea, the milk-boy's mum, and handing out the biscuits, and I just told her what the headteacher had told me, the stuff about the son giving her his hard-earned wages, but the only thing is she's going crazy that she doesn't get to know who the teacher was that had heard the thing about the milk-round and the drink, headteacher didn't even tell me, so I couldn't tell her.

The Dog-Catcher sniffed, so, then she just came right out with it, aye he does do a milk round, and aye he does give me some of his money, you get paid a lot on the milk, it's no like a paper round. Digs money it was like, she called it. And the Dog-Catcher pulled in to the side of the road. She put her hands on her lap and said so, I said, look darling, it's not for me to pry into your personal habits, but I'm telling you, just to tell you, it's my job, to tell you, that underage employment is illegal, or it is if it gets in the way of full-time education, I said to her that it was my job, to tell her it was my job

Anyway, the moment was over, that particular hurdle jumped over, though I do think the mum does actually send the boy to school when she can, though she said he was ill today, stuck in bed all day. But she seemed really nice when I met her, and by all accounts the boy's decent enough, mum tips up occasionally at Parents' Evenings, so. Can't be all bad. Not much for me to do other than monitor the situation. I like results like that. Don't need to tell my boss anything, just go in and say to my boss, not much paperwork needed on this one!

The Dog-Catcher took her hands off the wheel and held one palm up facing herself and made a writing action on it with her other hand, action required, nil!

…

Armpits insisted, now I'm not romantic at all, not romantic at all, me, but maybe a romantic, singular noun, A, A romantic, a romantic, the noun maybe, but

237

romantic adjective, no. Then, in the immediacy, Mr Tambourine Man said that Armpits was just denying he was romantic as a precursor to confessing that he got all wishy-washy and misty-eyed when he listened to We Could Send Letters, the song the two of them had been listening to and talking about for ten minutes.

Dinni take a rise out of me, Armpits started to say this, but was talked down, interrupted. Mr Tambourine Man then came back at Armpits, accusing him of getting on the defence, and Mr Tambourine Man then leaned over to tickle Armpits under the chin, going kootchy kootchy koo, and making kissing noises, hoo hoo, go on son!

Armpits sat back and sighed and said ah well, maybe I am romantic, it's just that, and he looked around before continuing, the song is a great love song, purely about the being away thing, being away from someone, people, a family, and the epic nature of being distances apart, the pressure you're under, and Roddy sings the words so if we weaken we can call it stress, just the sound of it, man, and the sound of the male backing vocals as well, Christjesus, I'm no a weeping man but I could bubble any minute!

Mr Tambourine Man sat back now, aw, mate you should come and talk to my classes sometime, you're being transformed into a poet in response to great music, and I keep telling my students, that that's what it's meant to do to us eh, great music, isn't it! Armpits looked at him, don't start patronising me again. I'm not, I swear I'm not, Mr Tambourine Man swore he wasn't.

Then Mr Tambourine Man said och, know what I really wish? I wish I could find the same depth of meaning in the music I play to my senior classes

238

without having had to study it, deconstruct it, over and over, know, listened to it again and again, just so that maybe my responses to it would just come naturally to me, I'd stray from established thought for once, question established notions, eh, an effing revolutionary, me, I don't think!

…

Billy held a fruit juice carton up and tossed it through the air. Joseph, who had turned up for the day, lifted up his rubbish bag into the air as well and the carton went into it without touching the sides. He punched the air, aw, again man! Billy looked around and said there weren't any more juice cartons, then he said hang on but, Joseph, there's one in my bin bag, hang on a second, and he reached into the sack to get the juice carton, looking up and squinting his face, god it smells awful in here! Then Billy twisted his neck to stop his head from going into the sack, and he stretched his arm into it, squinting his mouth again, looking at the sky as he did so, hang on Joseph mate, nearly got it!

Aw, you're disgusting Billy, a couple of girls were laughing at him from a few yards away. Billy smiled, aye, but watch this though girls, and he pulled the carton out and squeezed the leftover juice out of the hole that was there for the straw, here you are Joseph! And threw the carton towards Joseph. Joseph jumped up and let the carton hit his chest and drop towards the ground, then he kept it up off the ground, using his feet to keep it up, kicking it into the air, once, twice, and he started counting, three, four.

Aw, keepie-uppie with an orange carton man, perfecto! Billy was shouting, clapping, and pointing Joseph out to the others, heh heh, star man! Joseph was still counting, thirteen, fourteen, fifteen, aw, shit! He

239

picked up the carton and put in into his own bag now, fifteen though, no bad, eh.

Billy stopped looking at the girls who were watching Joseph, and he asked Joseph when his next trial with the football club in the town was going to be.

Joseph said ach, it's the week after next, if I decide to go, I mean, I mean all they ever want from you at these things is for you to run around the pitch a million times, I can do that anytime I want, man I'm sixteen I don't need the fitness training that these guys in their twenties need, how come they never want you to show them what you can do with a ball? It's all running, pace, running round the pitch!

Billy raised his eyebrows, Joseph man, see you, you've had the chances to play for any number of teams in the last year, and you just waste it man, refusing to run round the pitch, how can't you just do as you're told! And he stared at Joseph, and stretched both arms out, eh?

Joseph looked around, look Billy, nobody tells me what to do, right, nobody, alright? I'll still make it in football, I'm just waiting for the right team to come along. Anyway, the manager at this club says you canni have a drink the night before a game, Christ, no have a drink on a Friday? He laughed, they can piss off if they want me to turn up for a trial just to be told that I canni drink on a Friday, eh!

Billy looked at him, mm, hmmf.

…

You see, that is, because, basically the function of schooling is to integrate society through an education-economy relationship, Crossword Freak Number One clasped his hands and went on to make a point about what he thought the point of education was,

240

that is, the whole point in my opinion being to establish an order, you see, an ordered society in which adults can thrive as a result of their achievements and experiences in education, and in which the position which they attain, that is, within their place of employment, is secured through skills acquired at school, and later articulated in training and further and higher education, and eventually advanced through professional development carried out whilst at work.

Armpits looked up from what he was reading and then looked across at the Crossword Freaks, and he shut his book, what? Then he repeated, what? What shite is it that you're spouting now, man!

Crossword Freak Number One lowered his glasses down his nose and looked upwards towards Armpits, excuse me, could I possibly conduct an intellectual discussion with a colleague? Please?

Armpits nodded, saying aye, and excuse me, could I scratch my arse please? And Armpits lifted up his arse so that Crossword Freak Number One could see the back of his trousers and observe what he was doing, and Armpits scratched his arse, looking and smiling at Crossword Freak Number One as he did so.

...

A girl in the class replied aye, your dad would know about that, Billy! Billy, who was fidgeting with something on his desk, asked em, what d'you mean, he would know about that, know about what? He looked up with deliberation, and turned round towards the girl, he kept opening his mouth after he spoke, the class looked at him.

Crime and that, the girl said, smiling, and she continued on, talking about the fact that Billy's dad would know so much about crime because he must be involved in it, she nodded, know what I mean Billy, seeing as he's down the police station enough of the time!

Billy said back to the girl that his dad had never been at the police station, he turned away from her, muttering see, you don't know what you're talking about. Then the girl said ah, but how come I've seen a police car outside your house about a million times then!

Aye well, that's no the same thing as going down the station though is it, eh, Billy was looking right at the girl as he replied, aha!

…

At the end of a Friday, people were getting their things together in the staffroom and saying things to each other, like enjoy the weekend, or maybe they were asking a group of people if anyone was doing anything at the weekend, something with their families and so on, making goodbyes and see yous, before wandering out the door with their car keys dangling from their hands.

Mr Tambourine Man, as always, was waiting until most people had gone before he left himself. He said to three or four men that were standing around that he could do without the tutoring sessions he had to give that night, ach, going to two different pupils' houses this evening, got to take a bloody bassoon in the car with me to one of them, effing hassle I can tell you, other nights of the week, they come to me, know, the other pupils, but not Fridays.

Somebody said I don't know why you can be bothered doing it, on Friday nights too, eh, and the speaker looked at the others in the group, a couple of people nodded, coats were being put on. Mr

Tambourine Man sighed, and he said well, it all pays for the divorce, know, I need every penny I can get these days, know.

Most folk looked at him and said things like aye, and nodding, suppose. Except Shakespeare, who said Jesus, I didn't know you were getting divorced, when did that happen, or when's it happening, or whatever happens! And he stopped and looked around at everybody else.

They all looked at Shakespeare and then looked back at Mr Tambourine Man.

Shakespeare said sorry, none of my, em, sorry, I shouldn't. And he picked up his briefcase, I just didn't know, sorry mate, and he lifted an arm and patted Mr Tambourine Man on the arm.

Mr Tambourine Man said aye, it's okay mate, don't worry, I actually thought you did know eh, he smiled and said actually, I thought that everybody knew everything about each other in this bloody place, eh, schools eh! Shakespeare said no, I never, and, em, I'm really sorry to hear about that mate, so I am, really, em, sorry.

Mr Tambourine Man then raised a laugh from the others in the group by saying something about himself, ach, don't worry, I'm not really sorry, doesni bother me eh, worth the money, worth every penny, know!

Folk looked around, there was silence for a minute as scarves were put on, briefcases zipped up.

Right then, Mr Tambourine Man mentioned the names of the two pupils he was going to tutor that night, here I come! He stood back as people all said see you to each other and then went out the door.

Mr Tambourine Man picked up a carrier bag, his briefcase and then the bassoon case that had been standing in the corner of the staffroom during the afternoon. He balanced all three in one arm before grabbing a sandwich that had been sitting on the table since lunchtime. He turned as he left, this is me eating for the first effing time today, heh heh, see you son, have a good weekend, see you Monday!

And he squeezed through the door with everything he was carrying, nodding goodnight to a cleaner as he headed down the corridor.

6. I DON'T CROSS MY FINGERS

The Dog-Catcher said she was going to be seeing this boy today, her boss had contacted her at home to say to come in at nine o'clock, yeah, that's how I was able to pick you up and take you in this morning, I wasn't meant to be coming in till later, but this boy, a pupil, he was in trouble with the police last night, apparently there was some kind of serious domestic at his house yesterday morning too, violence, blood and everything, police called to the scene, so I've got to go and see the boy today, no-one from the office has seen him yet, I don't think, I don't even know what it was that happened last night yet.

That's all the Dog-Catcher knew anyway, there was no more detail than that, she said she hadn't had any involvement before with the boy, though she thought knew of the family, aye, one of the older brothers, he'd maybe been in trouble at school, it was a wee bit before I started here, but he's sorted himself out now, was doing an apprenticeship, furniture, upholstery, something like that, anyway, he's earning money now, my supervisor seemed to remember something about it, I think there was a case opened on him but no-one was ever assigned to the boy, and the office managed to close the case pretty quick, it was only the Children's Panel that got hold of him, so.

She wondered what it would be all about today, it's all a bit of excitement eh, lucky this incident's taken place darling, otherwise it would have been the bus for you this morning!

…

There was truth in what had been said, truth, about Sam joining the army, Sam was leaving, the guy

245

in the staff room said so, aye, apparently Sam did better in the run than he told me he thought he'd done. Others in the staffroom laughed, Jesus, really, who're they letting in these days eh!

The Bin Brigade said that Sam had gone away at the weekend, he had to report to some barracks. He's gone, that's him away, sir. In the army now sir. Cap, uniform, gun! Someone said that Sam would just be away for a week at the moment, some work experience thing, it's not the actual thing now, being a soldier, it's just an introduction thing. They all agreed with this point, aye, then he'll be back and he'll have to stay on at school until the summer, do his exams, the ones his name's down to do anyway. Then he'll be leaving, we'll only see him whenever he comes back on leave, know.

Marie said no, it won't be like that, the thing is, you just don't see people anymore once they leave school, isn't that true sir? Marie said she knew, I know sir, 'cause some of my big sister's friends just say that, that that's the way it is, people leave and you don't see them anymore, it's like they go away and they change, or they come back and it's you that's changed, or the way they remember things is different to how they really were, so.

She paused, they can't come home again, it's almost impossible, you know? To return, it's impossible.

…

William wasn't in school. But some of the class said they'd seen him on their way to school, he was in the street sir, aye he'd been buying sweets sir, aye I saw him as well sir, with the sweets. He saw me as well, someone else said. Aye, he was hanging around the

246

school main gates later on, or just outside them, ten minutes before the bell.

Somebody else suggested that William would be dogging it. An argument ensued, William, a truant? No! He never dogs it! Imagine what his mum would say! A couple of others spoke up, aye, you're no wrong, ever seen his mum go for him? Pure mental so she is. And imagine if the truancy woman went round the house as well, his mum would go crazy with him, and that's only after she'd gone crazy with the truancy woman!

The class all looked around the room, at the door, at the window, nobody was speaking.

Then one voice said, wasn't James here earlier? Someone replied, aye, he was, but he was sent to the office for something though.

They continued to look about the room, so, where's William gone then, if he's not dogging it, he must be somewhere, yeah? Some of them started smiling, and, looking at each other, they were sniggering.

They started to laugh, ah, ha ha, William, dogging it!

…

Kevin sat up and wiped one of his eyes with his wrist, he screwed his face up to one side, and his lips curled upwards underneath his other eye which he was closing as he did so. Some of the class laughed. He caught a couple of people's eyes and spluttered a laugh, then he looked at Billy sitting next to him, before facing the front, em, what did you say sir, eh? He half-grinned, eh, I didni sleep much last night sir, he smiled but it was still only half a grin, he was only half-grinning.

The others laughed a bit with him. Then Billy said em, maybe you should just leave him, sir, let him catch up on his sleep eh, looks like he needs it, eh, looks like you could do with a wee snooze Kev! The class laughed again.

Kevin told them all to shut up, I'm alright, okay, and I can look after myself, you don't need to say anything to the teacher, alright? And then he laughed again, and then the laugh turned into a yawn. He turned to face the front and said sorry sir, it's just that I got up early that's all, em, and em, well, that's how I fall asleep during the day sometimes and, well I don't really fall asleep during the day, I'm just.

The pupils looked at Kevin.

And he smiled, I'm just dead tired sometimes and it's better with my head down, I'm not really sleeping, I'm still listening in class. I just get up early, that's all. He looked around the class, what?

There was a bit of a silence, then Billy spoke, he does a milk round sir, Kevin does.

Billy looked at Kevin as he spoke.

Kevin looked at Billy as soon as Billy had spoken and shouted at him, aw Billy, god sake, shut up! Then he shouted again, this time facing the front of the room, no, no I don't! His chest rose and fell a couple of times and he shook his head, I don't do a milk round sir, Billy's lying. What were we learning about, I'm listening now.

Billy said it's alright, you can tell sir, eh Kev, he's not gonni tell anyone. Will you no sir?

Kevin asked, will you no? He won't, Billy said, tell him Kevin.

Kevin wiped his eye again, thing is, I'm too young, I mean, in the law, the law says I can't do it 'cause I'm too young, I'm not supposed to do it. It's just that, well, my mum, my mum knows this person who works at the milk depot, and he was able to get me the job.

The class were not saying anything, a few of them looked at the wall or the door or the window.

Kevin looked at Billy, then at the front, aye, he looked down for half a second, the pay's okay.

After a bit more silence, Billy said see Kev, it's okay, sir's not gonni say anything.

…

In the staffroom, folk were talking about William having thrown a brick through the windscreen of a school bus the day before, just on its way into the town after school. They were discussing both the incident and the character of William, they called him Willie though, aye, happened yesterday right at quarter to four, my next door neighbour saw it from his car too, said the boy Willie had just walked into the road just at a set of traffic lights, stood there, and lobbed a brick right at the bus facing him, he hasn't come into school this morning either, the wee bastard!

William was being talked about most of the time, a lot of teachers didn't know him, hadn't taught him, and they checked what they thought was William's identity with each other, em, Willie, fat little bugger in the fourth year, isn't he, that right? Someone in the Joke Club said aye, Bin Brigade and all, say no more!

People in the staffroom were saying that there had been no injuries as a result of the incident, the driver had put the brakes on and William had just stood there waiting for the police to come, aye, lucky no-one was hurt, good job. And on account of this aspect of the story, there being no injuries, the Joke Club were laughing at the thing, aye, hee hee, shame he never

249

came up to the school with his ammo, there's a few people's windscreens in the car park I wish he'd thrown a brick through as well eh, the rector for one!

Bicycle Clips shook his head, tss, walked across the staffroom and looked out the window. The Joke Club continued, och, it's only a jest eh, aw, nobody was injured, it's okay to see the funny side of the affair eh?

Armpits smiled at them, and then walked over and stood with Bicycle Clips at the window.

Although a lot of other staff raised their eyebrows and didn't say much, though in the end most of them were laughing, bloody mad little bastard!
…

Scout said he felt he had never pursued a teaching career, aye, naw, somehow I got pushed into teaching. He looked down. It was once he realised he'd never make it in football. He'd played a bit, then coached a bit, never really made a success of any of it though, aye, naw, I'd got the coaching badges and everything, did the S.F.A. course, it's considered one of the best you know, but afterwards, I wasn't getting decent jobs, know. He laughed, and then somehow I got pushed into teaching.

He looked up, and stopped smiling, and the funny thing was I'd always thought I'd be a teacher, a P.E. teacher but, right from when I was at school, but it just didn't happen. I mean, I'd gone to uni after school, at the same time as I got a few gigs playing football with minor teams in the league, mostly reserve games, but a then I hit a few first-team starts, regular appearances eventually and all boy, and, well, just after I quit uni to go full-time professional, suddenly I was back in the reserves, and after a getting transferred a few times it was obvious I was going nowhere, so I

250

went back to uni to finish my dgree, just to have something to do to fill in the time for a couple of years after leaving football, I did Politics and Economics, with a bit of Philosophy too. Don't even know why I chose them either, came out with a general degree, not that I deserved anything more than that. So.

He rubbed his hands together and clapped, so, when I considered teaching, or other people suggested it to me, friends, family, it was just easier to put in for Modern Studies, it would've taken a year or so longer to train as a P.E. teacher, so. There I was. Maybe no-one who knew me thought I could do anything other than teach.

He stared at his mug, plus it was easy to see what the job entails, I mean, know, everyone thinks they know what teaching involves, a classroom, kids, the odd bit of hassle but that's just part of the job yeah. He took a drink, so, I was kind of pushed into teaching.

He laughed again, and so I ended up teaching something I didn't want to! It was okay though, especially at first, you think you're serving society and everything, on some kind of whatsit, or crusade thing, but it's always frustrated me when I see pupils not making the most of their talent, underachievers, know, ones who've got brains, ideas, but just fart around, they just fart around. Some of them, know, kids here, they fart around, end up in no-good dead-end jobs, or underachieve and end up following a career they've got no passion for, like me.

He said ach me, school? I could have tried harder at school I suppose, put in more whatsit, I could have been better at things, could have been a better footballer than I was too, hid behind wee injuries all the time, colds, never pushing myself. He sighed, fear of failure, rejection.

And he sighed again, so, I ended up with other people pushing me, pushing me into teaching.
…

One week, some of the fifth and sixth year pupils in the school who were in bands were putting on concerts at lunchtimes, and Mr Tambourine Man had taught them to play songs from Scottish pop bands, they'd chosen them from a list he'd drawn up. It was part of a Scottish thing, a Scottish week, organised by some organisation with government funding, to get schools a Scottish Promoting School Award for promoting Scottish achievements in the arts and culture. Not all schools were doing it, it was something you bought into or not, there were forms to fill in, boxes to tick, and after some time there were Bronze, Silver and Gold certificates to be won by schools, depending on how much work they did. Haggis in Home Economics, Logie Baird and others in Physics, The Dear Green Place in English, Sorley MacLean for some schools. Learning and teaching in schools didn't change, it was affected, it was more a thing for publicity than for the education of pupils in the actuality, classroom teachers didn't get into it in a way, unless they were the sort that said they wanted promotion.

Mr Tambourine Man had been allowed to go on the tannoy to announce who would be playing each lunchtime, which pupils and what kind of songs they would be playing. He had to ask the Phantom for permission for this, and the Phantom introduced Mr Tambourine Man each time he appeared. On the first day he had played some music as well as giving the announcement, and everybody could hear the Phantom whispering to him to turn it off.

Some of the Bin Brigade had been to see a couple of the music shows in the first couple of days of the week, the pupils had to pay fifty pence to get in and the money went to charity, Mr Tambourine Man had chosen causes which related to children in Scotland or Fair Trade issues. If you bought your ticket in advance you could get out of class five minutes before lunch to get to the canteen before everyone else, so.

The Bin Brigade reported in the afternoon that in general it wasn't an event they had taken enjoyment from, they knew some of the songs that had been played, if they were from a band they knew, or if their parents played them around the house or in the car, but most of them they didn't know, so they couldn't take enjoyment from the event.

Billy said och sir, you want to have heard it, the songs are rubbish, and the bands are crap anyway sir, they canni play in tune. A few people in the class laughed, nodding, aye, it was crap sir!

At least they're trying man, Ace defended the bands, and said come on Billy, at least they were trying, they'd learned their stuff. But Billy continued to dismiss the efforts of all of the bands, aye, they're trying, that's about all you can say man, you can definitely say that, they're pretty trying on the ear!

Apart from Ace, most of the Bin Brigade asked why they had to pay fifty pence to hear songs they'd never heard of by bands they'd never heard of played by pupils who couldn't play their instruments.

Marie interrupted and said she'd taken something from the shows, I really liked the song, I think it was called Some Candy Talking, you know, the

one that the sixth year boys sung, you know, the boys
with the Jesus and Mary Chain t-shirts, they were so
cool, aw, wow, I just love thinking about it now, they
were brilliant!

Jesus Mary Joseph more like, Billy replied,
looking at Marie and shaking his head, what a racket!
Everyone was laughing, including Marie, and she
smiled, aw, you're funny Billy, Jesus Mary Joseph!

Naw, Kelly now said, the best act was the boy
who sang that song about Venice, funny name for a
song though, eh, wasn't it? I never really understood it.

The guy with the guitar? Singing on his own?
That was called Vienna, not Venice, said Ace.

Aye, Vienna, that's what I said, Kelly nodded,
anyway I was never any good at Geography, me! Aye,
that fifth year boy with the guitar, she smiled and
laughed, but I fancy him so that's why I liked it!

Some of the other girls laughed. Ace said, aye,
he was okay, that guy, even though song was meant to
be done with keyboards, the way it was written, but he
made a pretty good attempt, the guy.

And from Billy came the judgement, listen to
you Ace man, the way it was written! Ace smiled and
said to Billy, I'm just saying, my dad's got that at
home, Vienna, and you know what, I'll tell you what.
Okay, who's heard of Bob Geldof? Bob Geldof, Band
Aid, Live Aid and stuff?

They all had.

Well, Ace continued, Midge Ure, the guy that
wrote that song, Vienna, he put just as much work into
Band Aid and Live Aid as Bob Geldof, and he helped
set up those Prince's Trust concerts that are on the TV
as well, and nobody's heard of him now. My dad's got
a book that tells you stuff about him.

Midge what? Other pupils looked at Ace.

Ure, Ace said. He played in Ultravox, Thin Lizzy, Visage, practically all at the same time at one point, he was some guy, supercool for cats! And he wrote most of Do They Know It's Christmas, as well as organising a lot of the Band Aid stuff to go out to Africa, the goods, checking it on to the planes, making sure it got to where it was meant to go.

Wasn't that Bob Geldof that did all that Band Aid stuff, pupils asked.

Ace laughed, aye, Bob Geldof did it all.

…

Pupils would sometimes talk a bit more on the bus than when they were in school.

Some staff who came to work on a bus, or who had travelled to or from school by bus sometimes if their car broke down, or they'd had to stay on after school and missed their lift, or their husband or wife had the car for the day, said this about pupils, aye, the kids feel they're on their own territory as soon as you're out of the school, see when you meet a kid out of school they act differently, especially if there's a crowd of them, or even just one or two, and especially on public transport, it's like a wee safety zone for them, you canni send them to the deputy rector's office or run for help from the head of department.

Pupils would indeed turn round on the bus and say alright, or talk amongst themselves about something to do with school, perhaps name a teacher or two, and look round, they would be looking to see who had heard them.

This had been observed by teachers, aye, they'll try to get a reaction from you son, but just ignore them, they'll stop eventually, oh aye, it might seem tempting to get into a bit of banter with them, even direct the conversation, but once you're talking to them they can say anything, and you can't take them on for swearing or saying something they wouldn't say in school, because you're on their patch now, so suddenly they're telling you they don't like this teacher or that, or asking you if you like this teacher or that, and what can you do, you're just gonni look stupid if you suddenly back out the conversation. Then you're weakened the next time you see them in school, aye, naw, best to stay out of it, don't talk to them. A wee smile, maybe a nod, then look out the window!

…

The Bin Brigade were learning that in the trenches of the First World War the soldiers sang songs they had learned in Britain, or at least songs they had learned in Britain and then changed the words to when they got to the trenches, it was such songs that the Bin Brigade were learning about.

Why did they do that sir? Some of the pupils said that some of the songs, It's A Long Way To Tipperary, Pack Up Your Troubles In Your Old Kit Bag, others, had this thing about them, aye sir, they all seem like happy songs and sad songs at the same time, sir, don't they? Aye, naw, songs to sing on the way into battle and then sing again coming away from it, collecting guns and knives from your dead enemies eh! Aye, songs to sing when you attack the enemy sir! Aye, run at the Germans and sing the words at the top of your voice, is that what they were meant to do! They all laughed at the image.

Songs for killing to, Ace said, seems strange.

The class looked at him.

256

Then as he looked at a piece of paper that was on his desk, and he traced a line across it, he asked em sir, could I draw an aerial view of a group of soldiers singing a song with someone conducting them, know, like a choirmaster sir? The choirmaster would be a general. What d'you think, supercool, eh?

The class laughed and someone asked hey Ace, how could anyone get an aerial view of the soldiers? Ace spoke about observation balloons, that right sir, they were cheaper than planes eh?

Someone else said that you'd never get a group of soldiers singing together in a choir in the trenches of the First World War, wouldn't you sir eh, what about the bombs and everything, I mean, imagine it, it'd be crazy!

Aye, suppose, Ace said, but everything else we've learned about what happened in the First World War so far's crazy anyway, so, suppose, eh, it's just my imagination, so, I suppose.

…

A poster was on the staffroom wall and the poster showed, or was meant to show, the progress of Scottish football teams in European competitions as the season went on. Someone had got it out a newspaper, or a football magazine or something, it was to be filled in with the names of opponents, results, scorers and such, who was substituted for who and so on, there was kind of an idea that what you had to do was keep filling it in as teams got in to rounds beyond the first stages, assuming they did so, and it could be filled in the day after games took place.

It was said that a couple of guys, students, had attached seriousness to the thing at the start of the term back in August when all the teams were still in the competitions and there had been a couple of results that gave everybody hope, but as time wore on the teams fell away, and the students had finished their placements and moved on somewhere else anyway, and by October-November most had been knocked out, and by Christmas, they all were.

Sometimes people would remark as they passed the wall and glanced at the poster, aye, naw, no like back whenever it was, when we had four or five teams in Europe, and more than a couple in with a chance eh, people would say, Aberdeen winning a trophy, Dundee United in a final, Celtic and Rangers at least showing promise until after Christmas!

The poster on the wall was falling off on account of one of the corner drawing pins at the top having dropped out of the wall. As each day passed, shoulders rubbing against the poster pulled it further and further off the wall until one day someone walked past it on the floor and picked it up and held it up with an outstreched arm, em, anybody wanting this? This was a question to which there was no reply. The poster was binned.

…

Joseph had been for a trial with Rangers, or he was meant to go for one, one of the P.E. teachers had arranged it, or he'd asked Scout about how to go about it, what the way forward was for sorting a trial these days, and Scout had spoken to someone he knew and found out more. Anyway, the thing about the trial was that Joseph hadn't turned up for it.

The P.E. teacher mentioned Scout's involvement in the thing, ach, he doesn't have the big connections anymore, the P.E. teacher had said, but I suppose he was helpful in moving things on initially, I was only half-thinking about the possibility of a trial but he seemed really keen to move things on, like he wanted Rangers to think he'd discovered Joseph or something!

Scout had been telling people in the staffroom beforehand that he had sorted things for Joseph, once the trial date had been set. Though some staff said that they doubted Scout's word on the matter, hear him claiming all the glory? Some of them said ach, he just found out a name, aye, naw, he never spoke to anyone important. Also when they spoke about it to each other after Scout had been in the room and had then gone elsewhere, they said listen to him, you'd think he'd been on the phone to the manager himself! The Joke Club spent ten minutes on it while Scout was out of the room.

Not many staff said they liked Joseph, on account of him being a pupil with behaviour issues, he was spoken of in the staffroom as being a difficulty for most staff, aye, nothing but a hooligan if you ask me, definitely not one of the good kids, I send him out the room if he breathes in the wrong direction, me, and so on.

So, people had been talking about the trial, since Joseph was a pupil at the school and it wasn't every day someone at the school got a trial with Rangers or Celtic anymore, or anyone, it used to happen a lot, but now, not now. However, whilst speaking about it, staff voiced concern about not wanting to appear like they would be congratulating Joseph next time they saw him in class, it was just observations they were making, in the context of a school pupil having an opportunity to advance himself.

Someone might say, I suppose its big news but actually it's not big news, he might be a big star and all, but he's still a gobby wee shite in my book.

Then, after what happened, with Joseph not turning up, people in the staffroom smiled and said that they knew all along what a let-down the boy was.

So, the thing was, Joseph never went to the trial, and he never told anybody he wasn't going to go, he just didn't turn up at the venue, and it was Scout, who'd made the effort to go and watch, who'd ended up phoning Joseph's dad from the venue to ask why he hadn't turned up, and asking why it was in fact the case that Joseph wasn't getting allowed to go, it wasn't the P.E. guy who'd phoned Joseph's dad up, the P.E. guy didn't hear about it until the Monday. It was Scout as well who had to do the explaining to the people from Rangers.

The Bin Brigade knew about the affair, Joseph's dad was a Celtic supporter, aye, sir, his dad wouldni let him go for the Rangers trial, no way! Imagine that, the chance to play for Rangers and you turn it down, bloody daft, eh sorry sir, but it is daft but! His dad told him he wasn't going to allow it, I don't know why Joseph ever agreed to it in the first place!

Joseph wasn't in the day after the trial date. Billy said Joseph told me last night sir, I saw him around the streets, he told me that the old Modern Studies teacher, I canni mind his name sir, but Joseph said the teacher told him beforehand that he'd practically had to beg a friend to arrange the trial and he was going to look stupid if Joseph didn't go, so Joseph had just gone along with it, the idea of going, it was easier than saying no and upsetting the guy. Billy

260

shrugged his shoulders, of course, now sir, the old guy'll be mad with Joseph!

Anyway, that's how it went, Joseph didn't go.

At the end of the day a couple of the class said Joseph had come into school about lunchtime, apparently he'd told Scout he hadn't really wanted a trial with any team anyway, he was getting a bit sick of football.

Scout had just sent him away without saying anything to him.

…

In the staffroom more than one teacher was saying hey, did you see that thing last night, they're making a new movie about Culloden? Aye, I saw it on the BBC! I saw it on one of the other channels and all! Isn't the big thing about it that it's being made by the English, or it's got an English director anyway, and it's being filmed in Wales, Wales!

Bicycle Clips listened to what was being said, and shook his head, I don't understand, such an important piece of Scottish history, a major event like that, Culloden! And it's the English who get to make a movie about it, och I know it'll be funded by Hollywood in some way, but it's a de facto English film, tss! He shook his head again and almost took a drink of his tea, instead blowing on the surface of the drink and shutting his eyes when the steam waved about and rose into his face.

He was standing up, and now he lifted one leg up and rested his foot on the chair, he scratched at his ankle, then up to his calf and then round the front of his leg and up to his knee, then scratched his thigh and eventually his groin before putting his leg back down and lifting the other one onto the chair, still shaking his head, aye, Culloden, I ask you, an English film. Oh, like I said, it'll be Hollywood hokum alright, it's bound to be, well you just had to see the way it looked last night on the telly, the way it was going to look, all swashbuckling and fancy white shirts and kilts and spotless redcoats, never a drop of mud or anything!

The person Bicycle Clips was talking to had been nodding his head all the way through what Bicycle Clips was saying, nodding his head when Bicycle Clips talked about the television programme about movies, nodding his head when Bicycle Clips talked about the English making the movie, nodding his head when Bicycle Clips was shaking his head, nodding his head when Bicycle Clips passed his scratching hand all the way up from ankle to groin, nodding his head and looking at the scratching hand, nodding his head and tracing the movements of the hand with his eyes.

This was what people did with Bicycle Clips, nodded their head along with what he said and what he did.

Bicycle Clips continued, aye, I mean, if you ask me, and he looked up, and I'm not saying you would ask me!

The listener nodded.

Bicycle Clips smiled and nodded back, I'm just saying, if you ask me, I'd put Culloden up as one of the most defining events in Scottish history, for definite, it sealed the Act of Union for good, if it wasn't already sealed, mind you, tss! He paused, and it's the English who get to make a movie about it!

The other teacher then said aye but, but, if Culloden's such an important date, it being a defining part of history, like you say, sealing England and Scotland forever and all that, maybe it's an important

262

date for the English too, and that's maybe why they want to make a film about it.

Bicycle Clips looked up.

The other teacher continued, and it's not as if Scottish people don't know how to make films, eh? Bicycle Clips kept looking up, stopped shaking his head and now nodded it instead, his own head, raising his eyebrows, aye I never thought of that.

The other teacher nodded, well?

Then Bicycle Clips said ah, but they'll not be thinking of it like that, the English though, and he started shaking his head again.

The other person smiled and nodded and laughed and shook his own head, aye, naw.

…

Billy was remembering when there had been a History lesson taken by a student when the Bin Brigade were at the start of third year, em, we weren't the Bin Brigade at that point sir, or were we? But anyway, about half of us were in the same class, and this student had been doing something to do with Mussolini, know, the Italian guy, it wasn't a whole thing on Italian, what is it, fascistism, facism? It wasn't that or anything, but Mussolini had been getting mentioned, it was maybe the causes of the Second World War, and this student had been explaining why the Italians called him Il Duce, I'll always remember that, Il Duce, the student told us to remember the nickname, and he'd test us again in another lesson.

Billy continued, well the next day, or whenever the next lesson was, a guy from the uni was in to watch the student teach us, and the student started by asking if anyone could remember Mussoilini's nickname, and Kevin ended up getting given a punishment for saying

263

Mussolini's nickname was Moosy Baby, although he said that only Mussolini's friends got to call him that!

Aye, someone else said, you told him to say that Billy, didn't you!

Billy turned and scowled, naw I didni!

He faced the front and smiled. He turned round again, aye you're right, I did so, perfecto!

...

Apparently the Phantom had been a writer, well, folk said, of sorts. Meaning that he had done a bit of writing in his time, people would say oh aye, ordinary writing, although some poetry as well and that, he was meant to be pretty good, our deputy, aye! Was he not published once? Yeah, well, aye, naw, well he had something put into a wee book of stuff once, to celebrate a big anniversary of the town, it's in a drawer in his office, shows it to the sixth years sometimes, reckons they'll think he's the top man 'cause of it, poor guy!

People had mentioned a few times before about the deputy rector having written something, aye, an actual book of poetry, a real book, know, oh this was when he was younger son, oh much much younger they said, in his twenties, maybe hadn't even started teaching, but it wasn't published was it, it never ever got published, or maybe it did, but it didn't sell, something like that.

People nodded, aye, he was an English teacher before all the big promotion started, before he got into, know, management, head of department at another school for a while too, one of the big Glasgow posh schools too, fee-paying!

Folk said he was always going on about loving the teaching part of the job these days, loving it, teaching aye! But, no, it must have got to him, being passed over these last couple times for the rector's job. Plus, the further on in education he's got, the less actual teaching he's done, know? He only does a couple of periods a week now. So maybe he loves it 'cause it's the only part of coming to work he likes anymore!

This was the school of thought amongst those who had known the Phantom and remembered him from before he got into management, or knew a bit about him from the time before he got into management, the thing being, how he went on about loving the teaching part of the job.

And they would say, aye, but don't we all love the job too, eh!

…

Hey son, join the police, you should become a police officer eh, join the police! Don't not join the police, join the police!

A variety of members of the Joke Club had the same opinion on the matter of the police force versus education as a career. There was an agreement amongst them that the police force was an option, some of the Joke Club were saying man, the police force is a better option, it's a far better option son, better than this eh, I mean to say as well, think of the pension, you canni beat it, a policeman's pension!

Ex-Cop looked up from his desk.

Aye, think of the pension son, someone in the Joke Club continued, your pension's everything eh. Some of them said as well look, son, the only reason I'm still in teaching is for the pension, any number of us would consider leaving, aye, this is too much bloody hard work if you're trying to do it well, and the kids are just wee bastards! Others said the thing is but, I've

265

never been able to get out because nothing else would give me the same pension, apart from the police of course, and once you're thirty that's no an option anymore. I'm telling you son, think of your pension, join the police before you're thirty, you'll no get a pension like it. Aye, someone else would say, you're still young enough, son, get out while you can, you'll be well out of it. Into the police man!

One of them looked round to see Ex-Cop, then they all looked round, one of them asked him hey, sure the police force would be a better option for the kid here, surely you enjoyed the job with the police as well as the money eh, that right?

Ex-Cop just looked up. The Joke Club all looked at each other, one of them spoke again, em, I was just saying, the pension and everything, you think the boy should join the police rather than teach?

Ex-Cop put his pencil down and moved a couple of jotters around on the desk, and looked up again, you're asking me? He lifted his hands up to his glasses and touched them and then removed his hand without taking his glasses off, no, don't son. Ex-Cop said not to join the police, nothing more, just not to join the police.

One of the Joke Club asked why Ex-Cop had said that. Ex-Cop just said, well, you asked me and that's what I'm saying, the young man'll know what he wants to be. He looked back at the jotters he was marking, picked the pencil up and twiddled it about in his hand.

…

That was brilliant, Kelly smiled, brilliant, so it was Marie!

Marie had just read her story, the prize-winner, out to the class. She'd said she didn't mind them

266

listening to it, no, not at all, though I got a telling off from my English teacher for not reading it out in front of everyone else in English, and not letting him read it out either, he was angry a bit, I could tell when he spoke to me after the lesson.

The Bin Brigade told her they had enjoyed the story, aw, never mind what he says, it was really good anyway, what you wrote Marie! You could be be a writer if you wanted when you leave school, you're that good, you'd be famous and everything, seriously! Rich and famous!

Marie laughed at this, saying hee hee, I didn't really try to write it the way it came out, it just, I don't know, ended up that way.

How come it's called Pure, someone asked her, that was the title of the story, Pure. Another pupil joined in, yeah, Pure, what's that all about! How come not, A Day In The Park or something like that? They said they couldn't understand why it was called Pure, how's the story called Pure, Marie? I mean should it not have been called something else?

They didn't have many other suggestions, one boy said em, just, something else other than Pure, Marie! Kelly told the boy to shut up, what do you know about writing! What class are you in for English! And everyone was laughing.

Marie laughed too, well I thought it was just something to do with the story, she said, you know it being just a simple story. I was going to call it My Xanadu, you know, like the place, just 'cause of it being about happiness, I just love thinking about somewhere like that, and that's what the thoughts of the girl in the park were all about, and why I nearly called it Xanadu. But I didn't, in the end. And she didn't say anymore.

The class expressed a satisfaction with what she said, her explanation. One boy did suggest that she should have called the story Simple, could you not have called it Simple then? But he was told off by the others, it's you that's simple, what class are you in for English and all! And the hooting started again, the boy shook his head. And smiled..

Marie smiled at the rest of the class, the friends that were around her, all laughing and yet quietening down when they looked at her.

…

After an issue had been talked about in the staffroom, concerning a pupil who had been excluded five times had been allowed back into school after some people had predicted he would be expelled elsewhere, a few staff started to speak about what they could remember about the day that the belt was banned, or the last day of the belt before it was banned. Some of them had belted a lot of pupils, aye, we really went for it, didn't we! In front of the class, out in the corridor, didn't give a monkey's, just totally belted the shit out of some of them, course, a few pupils knew it would happen and stayed away, or left at lunchtime with sore hands!

Someone else said aye, there was this young French teacher and all, a daftie so he was, or he was a nice guy with some daft ideas more like, can't remember his name, anyway, he was just out of uni a couple of years, and he used to think he was the cool guy, though right enough the kids did like him mind, anyway he arrived at the school during the last year of the belt, and he used to tell all of his new classes that he

268

didn't believe in corporal punishment, and he wouldn't be using it on them, so they just ran all over him, they liked him mind, so there was just a wee bit of nonsense, though it must have been gradually getting to him, 'cause see that last day of the belt he must have belted twenty pupils if he belted one eh, was that no right!

A few others laughed, aye, canni mind his name either. Nice guy, poor bastard!

Aye, we all had a go that day! Aye we did, we all had a go didn't we!

Though the story was that Bastard Guy just belted the same number as always. The staff recalled this, aye, didn't he no! And the bastard still ended the day having hit more pupils than anyone else!
…

There had been talk on the news about raising the school-leaving age, an education proposal from someone in the government, and Shakespeare asked in the staffroom if anyone knew when education became compulsory in Britain, what the date of it was.

Shakespeare shook his head and went on, I mean, some of these kids today, not all of them but some of them, some of them could do with just dropping out of the system altogether and just going straight into a job. Employment! Training! What's the use in us trying to teach these kids Geography, History, Maths?

One teacher replied by asking what's the use teaching any kids Geography! Shut it, came a couple of responses from elsewhere in the staffroom.

Someone else said they didn't know the date for Britain, em, I don't know what it is exactly for the whole of Britain, but was it not in eighteen-seventy-two

269

that the Scottish Education Act was passed? Eighteen-seventy-two, aye?

Shakespeare, and a few people looked up, Christ that's a bit early, is it not, or sounds early anyway! And so the discussion developed, think that's before it became compulsory in most countries, before the date for compulsory education elsewhere? Before England anyway, for definite, someone said. Then, but was it not the same date in England too? Eighteen-seventy-two? Aye, Eighteen-seventy-two. Don't know. Eighteen-seventy-two then, so that's the particular piece of legislation to blame for our older charges today!

Naw, someone else said, it was when they stopped National Service, that was the particular piece of legislation to blame. Aye! The conversation changed. People were talking about National Service, how it would do some of these kids a bit of good. Not everyone agreed. Only some said it would do them good.

Some didn't, and they said what, you mean take some of these bad wee bastards and turn them into fighting machines! Train them in hand-to-hand combat! Jesus! It's not like that, would be the reply. Well what would it be like then! The conversation continued, I'm just saying, maybe if education wasni compulsory, or kids had to do National Service instead of it, I don't know, I'm just saying.

At that point, Sandwich Toaster, who hadn't said anything up until that point, then said he'd read about this place in South America, Peru it was, I think, or was it, aye, naw, Peru, for definite, when I was studying to be a teacher, where they decided to make secondary education totally optional for a while, it was a wee village somehwere, well, small town more like, it was an experiment.

A few heads turned to look at Sandwich Toaster, he observed everyone looking at him.

Anyway, he went on, there was a few schools taking part, and at the start practically all the kids stayed away from school, hardly anybody turned up.

People were listening to Sandwich Toaster's story and throwing in their thoughts, hey, could you choose which kids came and which ones stayed away eh! What did the teachers do, they get a holiday too?

Sandwich Toaster said, well, they came into school as normal.

With nothing to do? Shakespeare was smiling, bloody hell, brilliant! And they got paid?

Sandwich Toaster looked around at all the people listening to him, aye, I know, heard it! Understood! He smiled, yeah, they got paid as normal. Anyway, eventually the kids started to drift back into school, slowly at first but then wham! Virtually all of them came back, apart from the ones that probably never came even when they had to. Sandwich Toaster leaned back on the counter behind him, both hands propping up his hips that bounced off the counter's edge as he nodded his head and said mm hmm.

Christ, Shakespeare said, you mean they all actually wanted to go to school!

Teachers stared at each other, turned their heads and stared at each other again.

Sandwich Toaster said well, I don't know if they necessarily wanted to come back, but the guy who conducted the experiment and wrote the book about it said he reckoned they all worked out that they needed to come back, they wouldn't get ahead without an education, they'd not get a job.

Folk looked at each other, needed to? Needed to? They shook their heads, so, the teachers had to start teaching again after all that, the experiment?

When the kids came back, yeah, Sandwich Toaster spoke as he observed people drifting away from him.

People drifted away, muttering amongst themselves, too bad, eh. Think our kids would do that, come back? Probably. Wee shites!

…

The class were full of the thing in the news, that guy the other day sir, know, the one that got a pickaxe through his head, it was William's stepdad sir! Aye, and it was William's dad that done it sir!

The class had heard about it, read about it, discussed it. First thing in the morning sir, he went straight round the house and done it, smashed it straight into him, the whole family was there and seen it, granny and all. Did you no see it on the news, sir? Domestics, eh.

William had been on telly, or his picture had. The incident, the domestic, it had happened the morning of the day that he'd thrown the brick through the bus window when it was leaving school just before four o'clock.

A lot of the pupils were saying things to each other about it, what they knew, what they'd heard, what they imagined, guessed, hey, hadn't William's dad taken the axe with him when he was doing the bins? Aye, and then jumped out the lorry and broke into the house when the other binmen were emptying the

272

rubbish? Aye, naw, one of the binmen was interviewed on the news and said he hadn't seen any axe.

They speculated on William's stepdad's condition, he's in the Intensive Care Unit at the infirmary now, and he's only got a week to live, or, if he lives, then he'll be in a wheelchair, or, if he lives, he's gonni be brain dead.

Some of the pupils said that's rubbish, how do you know? You shouldn't make things up, you don't know anything about it. Tell them sir! Sure he's not got a week to live eh sir, sure he's not gonni be brain dead or in a wheelchair sir, is he, eh?

Marie then said, maybe if it's William's dad we're talking about, and it's got something to do with William, then maybe we shouldn't be talking about it at all, he's our friend after all, and maybe we shouldn't be talking about it at all.

The Bin Brigade stopped saying anything.
…

The England football team had just qualified for the World Cup, and Scotland hadn't, and in the staffroom the conversation was all about whether you wanted England to do well or not, in the World Cup.

From someone came the judgement, see me, see whenever I see England go into the World Cup or European Championship, or even the bloody Olympic hockey team does well and it's full of Englishmen, part of me is really pleased, proud even!

Everybody said they knew what was coming next, what the guy would say he was bothered about.

And what came next was, but it's the bloody London media, aye!

There was a chorus of agreement, aye! I canni stand the way they go on as if the entire fate of the

273

world depends upon the English football team's success or failure! TV programmes dedicated to them! TV programmes about past successes and so on! Past success singular you mean! Jesus Christ! And there was was much nodding of heads.

Then someone asked, are we jealous?

And again a chorus of voices replied to the question saying, aye, you're right! This was followed by laughter and much shaking of heads.

…

Teachers did tend to do a thing, talking about pupils, and they tended to do it a lot as well, and they would describe them in the same two ways. He's a good kid, that one, she's a good kid. Or, see her, she's not a good kid. One opinion might be aye, that girl, I know she might have got into trouble about a few things in the past, but basically she's a good kid. Or, oh him? No good, no good.

Sometimes three or four pupils might come to the staffroom looking for a teacher, or with a message or something, and when they went away someone would say something about not liking one of them maybe, perhaps not liking two of them, but that one on the left, he's a good kid.

A pupil might have a friend, the two might be seen with each other often around school, and a teacher would say, I don't know how the two of them hang about together so much, because she's quite a good kid but that other one, no good at all, used to be good though.

Armpits once said, it's a binary state, isn't it, being a good kid, you either are one or you aren't, much like an adult being a good guy or not, know, the history of the world being a history of people divided into good guys and bad guys, know? Though sometimes in history it's not so much that a man or a woman was a bad guy, he or she just wasn't a good guy, know?

For teachers, it was the same with pupils.

…

Pupils were talking about the dumptruck that worked on the slagheap not having been operating in the last few days, this had been observed by a number of them.

Even some teachers mentioned it, saying that this was on account of their having heard the pupils talk about it, Christ can those kids not get more animated about learning, or raising themselves up in the world, and not be so excited about a bloody dumptruck!

Then another teacher said mind you, the truck has been getting close to the fifty second mark recently, fifty-two, fifty-one, she'll be getting pushed too hard, she's bound to break down sometime.

Some heads nodded, aye, good point, good point.

…

Armpits came in and said he wouldn't be at school one day next week because he was on interview. Folk looked up and said what, another one? After all this time? And, how many is that now? You going for the record eh!

Shut up fuckers, Armpits waved his hand in the air. It was for an assistant head of department's job at another school, Armpits stood up and stuck his chest out, Assistant Principal of History to give it its proper title actually! The job was not in another school in the town, he looked out the window, but it's close by at least, well, it wouldn't be too far away, it's in the same authority at least.

Armpits said he reckoned he was in with a chance, they've decided just to see four of us, on a leet, kind of. This was the ninth time he'd been involved in such a procedure, aye, ninth time, despite for the fact that the eighth time was a wee while ago, I've applied for a few posts since then, and been overlooked, Christjesus, the region must know my name by now, eh!

Armpits got a calculator out of his pocket, and on the spot he tapped out the buttons, punched them, saying he was working out the pay rise he'd get if he was given the job. He rubbed his hands together and looked at everybody, I'm an ambitious bastard for a socialist am I not!

Folk spoke about him sacrificing his principles, and he replied well, you may say that, but under the Conservative government such a fucking thing as principles became extinct, did they not!

People were making as if not to listen, but he insisted, hey, no, listen, is no-one listening to me! Aye, look at you all, you remind me of that one about being able to tell E.T. votes Tory because he looks like he fucking does! Aye, never a truer word was spoken, look at you all now, all getting ready to phone home any minute eh!

Folk laughed and said aye, very good, but said to each other, look at him all the same, rubbing his hands together and everything! Armpits opened his arms out and said aye, aye, I'm simply, simply, then he laughed and said aw, Christjesus, can a man not be allowed to have a bit more money if he wants to work for it, fuck!

...

According to some of the pupils, Ace was getting taken on by another agent who had got acting parts in films and television for other actors Ace's age. So it was said. Ace had told the Bin Brigade in the past that this was going to happen, and he had used the word stablemates to describe him and the other child actors whom the agent was representing, aye, some of my stablemates have made a lot of money already, they're getting wee gigs on stage for a few pounds and all, as well as making TV money.

The Bin Brigade said they thought the word stablemates was a hoot, and they made jokes about horses acting in films, does that mean you're going to have meetings with Black Beauty, Ace! Ace smiled as his classmates extended the horse theme to jokes about film scenes with cavalry charges or farmyard-based children's TV programmes.

At morning break, a few people in the staffroom were talking about Ace and his agent as well, Ace was talked about quite a bit in the staffroom, from time to time, aye, did you no read it, it's in the school section of the local paper this week, this guy's just taken Ace onto his books, apparently the agent's been in the papers a few times, just photographs really. Nobody in the staffroom had heard the names of any of the actors whose names were associated with the agent in the paper's feature on Ace, aye, naw, I've never heard of any his new stablemates, someone said, shaking his head.

Ha ha, stablemates! The Joke Club laughed at the term too. Sandwich Toaster asked what stablemates were. Armpits looked across and said, all it means son, is people who share the same management, or controlling organisations, actors or footballers even, with the same agent, pop stars with the same manager, or record company too, yeah? Sandwich Toaster nodded, okay, heard it, aye, understood.

Armpits turned to Mr Tambourine Man and said it would be the same in music as it was in films, that right?

Aye, Mr Tambourine Man replied to Armpits as interest from the other staff turned to other matters, the Beatles, Gerry and the Pacemakers in the sixties, same manager, Brian Epstein. Armpits pointed his finger, the Eagles and Jackson Browne in the seventies! Mr Tambourine Man said correct, Aztec Camera and Orange Juice for a wee spell in the early eighties.

Armpits looked at him, raised his eyebrows and spread his hands wide, palms facing upward, nineties, give up!

Mr Tambourine Man continued, Teenage Fanclub and the BMX Bandits for a period in the nineties, if I'm not mistaken. Armpits sat up, that right? Mr Tambourine Man said actually, I'm not that sure, but they wrote similar songs, and they were all from around Bellshill, or that part of the world anyway. Aye, Armpits agreed, though it was Teenage Fanclub who emerged as Big Star, the Beach Boys, Byrds and Nirvana rolled into one, didn't Kurt Cobain even say that Bandwagonesque was the best album of the year the same year Nevermind came out? Go the Fannies, unlucky the Bandits! Mr Tambourine Man smiled and nodded at Armpits.

Aw, Armpits grinned, Roddy Frame and Edwyn Collins in the same meeting, and he folded his arms and smiled, imagine being a fly on the wall in there, eh!

Mr Tambourine Man looked up and furrowed his brow, well, they made great music mate, but I'm not sure I'd want to watch them chew their effing biros!

…

I may as well not exist in here eh! Scout knocked on the window sill, and when folk glanced up he laughed and smiled, eh, so some of yous are alive eh! He said, I'm a virtual whatsit in here, eh. A few people laughed with him, and maybe a couple of words were said, exchanged even, before other conversations continued.

Scout began watching the football out the window again, and after a minute or so he turned round and looked at the people in the staffroom. Then, he walked through the room and out into the corridor, knocking twice on the door as he passed it.

…

Kelly sat in the class and announced that she wasn't going to speak to anyone. The girl sitting in the chair beside her told the others to leave her, she's alright, just leave her, she's upset about something I think, that's all.

The others didn't say anything.

Nobody said anything.

Kelly then shouted, I'm not upset! I'm just. She rested her head on one hand, okay I am, I am, sir can I go out the room please, I wanni go to the toilet, please! And she ran out, pursued by her friend and another girl.

A boy sitting at the back said hey, maybe Kelly's pregnant again eh! A couple of the other pupils told him to shut up. A few boys laughed amongst themselves, but soon stopped, then looked towards the front.

Nobody was talking when Kelly came back in and sat down. She looked and said well? What yous lot staring at? You want me to do tricks or something?

Someone said, did you really go to the toilet Kelly, or were you just standing at the door when we were speaking?

And Kelly looked at the class and then faced the front, speaking, so sir, we doing any work today then?
…

The Phantom was in the staffroom talking about Durkheim. People sitting beside where he was standing were looking between him and each other. Aah, the question is, at least this is how it appears to me, the Phantom would say, and, but I have to ask myself this, he continued.

Crossword Freak Number One entered the room. He saw the Phantom and stood listening to him. As the Phantom talked more about Durkheim, Crossword Freak Number One went to sit down. Armpits leaned down and whispered in Crossword Freak Number One's ear and smiled as he walked away. Crossword Freak Number One turned round to say something to Armpits, but by now Armpits had gone to put his headphones on, and was grinning at his cup of tea.

The Phantom said to the people who were still beside him that self and society could be linked through history, and that values could be transmitted from one era to another, and amended according to belief systems, and this was what he thought Durkheim had meant.

He went on, aah, of course is society more important than individuals? And can individuals be taught to co-operate within the rules of the society they exist in? People said em, and eh, aye, maybe, don't know the answer to that one, it's a tricky question. The Phantom looked directly at Crossword Freak Number One, and when Crossword Freak Number One looked up the Phantom asked him, mm?

Crossword Freak Number One said, em, well, that is, I think Durkheim just meant that we should consider the relationship between the individual and society. The Phantom was still looking at him, just meant? Just meant? Everybody looked at Crossword Freak Number One. He said, em, but he said no more than that.

People looked back at the Phantom, who looked around the room, and Crossword Freak Number One started looking at his paper.

Indeed, said the Phantom, smiling, holding the side of his gown, so as a school it becomes our duty to facilitate the role and many functions of education within society, that is, to encourage the duty of the individual towards society, and also to encourage restraint. Restraint, you see, eh!

He looked around, but I have to, indeed I must, offer this cautionary qualification of such a theory. And it is this, are those values of duty and restraint, which Durkheim espouses, the real values of society? Or are they the values of society's ruling elite? And with that he lifted one side of his gown up and flapped it in the air once, saying good day colleagues! And he turned and left the room.

After about a minute, people talked to each other again. Armpits still had his headphones on, and, still listening to them, laughed and shouted to Crossword Freak Number One, drawing the attention of everyone in the staffroom, aye, ha ha, you've not done that in your fucking Open Uni course yet have you!

…

One of the pupils in the class said to Billy, well then Billy, how come you live where you do but your dad's always got loads of money, eh?

Billy replied, no he hasni, he hasni always got loads of money. He said his dad didn't have a job, see, he's unemployed, so how could he always have loads of money, eh?

Aye, the other pupil said, but he's always doing something else on the side isn't he, a thing to make money, one thing or another, he'll be doing something, the other boy said, smiling at Billy.

Billy smiled back, and said I don't know, what, och, dinni ask me questions like that!

…

Here, listen to this, listen to the instrumental in this, Mr Tambourine Man stood up to pass his headphones to Armpits. Armpits laughed across the table and sat up, I was just gonni fill in my travel expenses, but, och man, the form can wait till later, hee hee, give us them then, the headphones.

Mr Tambourine Man stretched across to give the headphones to Armpits, as Armpits raised his hands up to his ears, Mr Tambourine Man shook the wires as they dangled down and put them in his hands. Armpits took them, aw great, what is it again, Pillar To Post? Aw, Pillar To Post!

Aye, just the instrumental though, Mr Tambourine Man had some paper on his lap, I'm scribbling down the concepts from it for my fifth years, trying to get them to listen closely to music for more

282

than just, well, and he paused and smiled. Armpits smiled back, melody you mean, ya bastard!

Mr Tambourine Man laughed, aye, melody, aye, well, we don't want them leaving school with the same limited critical skills as you! And the conversation developed a bit over the next two minutes as Mr Tambourine Man explained some stuff to Armpits, listen carefully to this bit, the instrumental, and you'll see how a small understanding of the finer points of music appreciation can go a long way towards you enjoying your music even more, and he continued on about cadences, grace notes and other things Armpits should look for.

Armpits made a shape with his mouth and lifted his head in a half-nod a few times.

Mr Tambourine Man manhandled the headphones on the head of his friend, lifting one earpiece off, can I just hear what bit it's at? Right, take this instrumental, naw, hang on don't play it from the start, I'll put it forward to the bit, hang on, hang on, I'm no gonni press play yet, okay, pause. Now, listen to me, and listen to how the guitar and drums play the same rhythm, driving the music on, the instruments are singing man, it's a wee song in the middle of the song!

Armpits shook his head, and said aye, and he looked round the room.

Mr Tambourine Man looked at him, okay, then the whole thing changes key for the instrumental, then the backing vocals come in, humming the main tune of the chorus, still in the higher key, and when the chorus comes back in, its in the original key, okay? You'll see, aw, it's just.

Armpits nodded, and said aye okay, can I just play it now, I know what I'm listening for.

Mr Tambourine Man pressed play and watched Armpits sit back. As the music played Armpits shut his eyes, tapped his fingers on his lap and start to hum along with the music. Mr Tambourine Man shook his head, touching Armpits on the hand, aw man, listen to the music, listen to what I was telling you about man, stop singing along!

Armpits looked up and, half-lifting one earpiece off, shouted eh, what did you say? Mr Tambourine Man started to speak, but Armpits took the headphones off and said, that's the end of the instrumental now, not sure if I got what you were saying about, totally, that is. It is a good instrumental though, what a tune!

Mr Tambourine Man sighed, put his elbow on the table and rested his head on his hand, looking down at the notes he had been writing beforehand. Armpits smiled, so, you thinking that if I can't get it then the kids won't?

Mr Tambourine Man hooted, aye sure, I can really use you as a benchmark for the intelligence of sixteen-year olds! Then he stopped laughing, smiled, and looked at Armpits. And said nothing.

Armpits asked Mr Tambourine Man how he thought next Christmas would go, this year.

Mr Tambourine Man said he had tried not to think about it, I don't know, just, I don't cross my fingers anymore.

…

Chaplain Divine was in the staffroom again, it was a time when the Phantom was also making a visit, aah, Chaplain! So good to see you again, and isn't it a fine late winter morning to be visiting us, cool and crisp and even, aah! To what do we owe the honour, how are you! And he headed to where Chaplain Divine was sitting and talking to some staff.

Chaplain Divine shook the Phantom's hand and said I am fine thanks, sir, just divine! Just in for a quick cup of tea with the staff, I've been at a meeting with some of other chaplains of the school and the primaries, talking about the Easter service, assemblies, the contributions the chaplains would be making over the coming session, planning, that sort of thing, you know?

The Phantom stamped his feet, jolly good, jolly good, and then he lifted a finger and pointed it at the ceiling, question! Chaplain Divine put his cup on his saucer, looked at the teachers he had sat down beside, and smiled, okay, fire away sir.

Well, aah, I was reading at the weekend something in one of the Sundays that said there was a debate at the moment about whether Christians, or the Christian church, can accept such a thing as human nature, or if this, and I mean our nature, is something just given to us by God.

Chaplain Divine lifted his eyebrows, a debate? At the moment? That debate has been going on for two thousand years sir! There was laughter from around the staffroom. The Phantom waited until it had subsided and said aah, well, I think a book has just been written on the subject.

Ah, books, books, books, Chaplain Divine shook his head, smiling, everyone is writing a book nowadays, aren't they? Sometimes I think it would be easier to be a Christian if no-one had written the Bible at all, and instead we just spoke about what we believed to be the right thing, or did what we believed to be good, and nobody measured our words and actions against some interpretation of the scriptures or other, eh.

A few people nodded, aye, would be. The Phantom said good god, no Bible? Then, raising his own eyebrows, so what do you think then, are you going to risk religious controversy in the staffroom? Aah!

Chaplain Divine said that he knew of the book that had been written and was being written about, but that reading it would not alter his opinion that it didn't matter where somebody's nature originated, he clasped his hands, as long as you do good work sir, that is what I would say. I'm sure every book on the subject makes good sense on its own, and I'm sure that it's very nice and gratifying for the authors to know that people read their work, but that's about all I can offer, I'm afraid, without, as you say, risking religious controversy. That's all I can offer.

People smiled when he answered.

The Phantom smiled too, aah!

The bell went and people filed past, saying it's good to see you again Chaplain, and then there were just a few people left, including the Phantom.

Chaplain Divine put his cup down and smiled at the Phantom, it's always nice to come into the staffroom for a cup of tea with one's friends, even when one is busy, one has to find time to be the bigger person, and he walked out the door. The Phantom looked at the people left, clapped his hands and said, you can't beat a bit of stimulating theological debate at break, what! Aah! And he left.

Then from Armpits came the comment, I love the smell of bullshit in the morning!

…

286

In the staffroom they were speaking about Ex-Cop, who was not in school.

Someone had said his cancer had come back, aye, one of my neighbours knows his family. That's how he's off work today, five years he's been free of it and all.

There was silence.

Someone else said what?

Others questioned this too, cancer?

I don't think that's right, cancer?

There was further silence.

Another teacher said aye, naw, he's at his dad's funeral, his dad died last week did he not, he'll be back in a few days, maybe a week, I think.

The person who had mentioned the cancer apologised, he said he hadn't realised about Ex-Cop's father.

There was more silence in the room.

And with silence in the room, he looked at a colleague sitting beside him, how was I to know, I didn't know about his dad, how was I to know? It's just that my wife had talked to one of the neighbours and, well, maybe she got it wrong, you know how things get mixed up sometimes, sorry, sorry everyone.

Then another voice said well, it could still be true about the cancer though, no?

Some people said cancer, really, did he have it?

A few other faces looked across the room, yeah.

7. THE FORCE OF LOVE

Kelly was talking about children's names, names for babies, her cousin was having a baby in the next week or so, aw sir, she's gonni call it Parris, you know, like Paris with an extra R in the middle, isn't that nice, I think it's lovely!

Someone asked why Kelly's cousin was putting an extra R in the middle. Kelly furrowed her brow and said well, em, it's to make it more original, know, everybody's calling their children after place names these days, but with the different spelling it'll be, you know.

At which point Billy asked, how is it original then, if everyone's doing it? Kelly said she didn't know, it just was, do you know anybody called Parris, Billy? Naw, and he shook his head. She said aye, naw, back to him and nodded.

Someone else then asked if Parris was a boy's name or a girl's name, and what was Kelly's cousin going to call the baby if it turned out she couldn't call it Parris? Kelly laughed and said Parris was a girl's name, and her cousin knew it was going to be a girl, she'd asked the doctors to tell her.

Billy shook his head, oh no, I wouldn't want to know that, I wouldn't want to know if it was a boy or a girl. Kelly agreed, aye, you'd just want it to be healthy, eh. Billy nodded, and said he supposed if a woman wanted to know, know, a mother or a future mother I mean, then she could ask and just not tell her husband, yeah? Kelly said yeah, but it's prospective Billy, not future, my cousin says she's a prospective mother, not future mother, and anyway, she's not married and the

288

father doesn't show an interest so that doesni matter. It's not an issue Billy.

Billy stared at the wall.

Marie then said she if she ever had a child and it was a girl she would call it Penelope, I saw this film, a cartoon it was, in my old school when I did Classical Studies, and this film, it was practically the only thing I paid attention to in the Classics lesson, and it told the story of Odysseus, you know that guy the deputy rector keeps telling us about?

The class looked at her, Billy said oh aye, the Odyssey, and he lifted his jacket off the back of his chair and draped it over his shoulders, standing up, I'm the deputy rector, aah, aah, aah, dear boys! The class giggled and Billy sat down, sorry sir.

Marie looked at the front and continued, so, his wife, Odysseus, his wife in the story was called Penelope.

Kelly asked why that meant that Marie wanted to call her daughter Penelope, is it just that you like the name Marie?

Marie smiled, well I do now, but it's really because she just seemed dead clever, Penelope, I'd want my daughter to be like that. Penelope didn't go about telling everyone she was dead clever, she just, I don't know, seemed that way. All the time Odysseus was away from home fighting wars and mucking about with other women, she sat at home and all she would do would be weaving, she would just weave and weave and weave, and we got taught by our teacher that she was weaving the story of her own life. The story in the cartoon was all about Odysseus, it was Odysseus who was in it most of the time, but all the time while all that was going on, Penelope, well she didn't exactly know everything that was going on, but she just kept in control, and it was like, she had her own story to tell and it was an even better story than the one about Odysseus. I liked the bits with Penelope more than the rest of the film, especially after the teacher told us she was weaving the story of her life, maybe weaving it on a tapestry, I just loved thinking about the idea of that!

Marie stopped talking and the class kept looking at her.

Then Billy interjected with, so, you gonni call your kid Odysseus if you have a son then Marie? Marie smiled and laughed, aw Billy, and Billy looked at his desk.

Don't be stupid Billy, Kelly shook her head at him, and then she looked at Marie, Marie, you're not, are you?

…

Jesus, another Parents' Evening, how many's that this term, can they no organise it better! Folk were bemoaning the fact that there would be a Parents' Evening that night, it's gonni be a long enough day as it is, I mean, this term, with the run-up to the exams and everything, Christ, plus the parents you most want to see are the most likely to never turn up!

There was a kind of agreement in those parts of the staffroom where conversations were being held, that the majority of parents who would come up to the school for Parents' Evening wouldn't require a lot of talking to, aye, Mr and Mrs Shortplank, your son did actually receive a bloody straightforward report from me, you'll have seen that for yourselves, so what more do you want me to say, can you no read! The teachers laughed amongst themselves, and said aye, we'll all end up telling the parents how pleasant their children are, aye, that's if we can get a word in, some of the parents just want to be your pal for the evening, you end up nodding and saying ah yup, yup, no problems at all, doing really well, just keep up the good work eh. Or maybe some kid's mum or dad would be a teacher, in another school, aye, and they'll ask smart-arse questions all evening and piss you off. Or there'll be some parent who thinks it's impressive to say they've got a degree, as if we haveni! Or maybe the parents of some of the horrors would turn up! Aye, they'll walk about the school complaining about the deal their kids are getting, you're picking on my son, and so are six other teachers in this place, it's about time something was done about it!

A guy then said he never much looked forward to Parents' Evenings, I always know I'm gonni get a sore throat the next day, but I suppose it's okay once it starts, quite pleasant actually.

A couple of other teachers nodded back at him, aye, you'll no be saying that tomorrow when you've got to shout at your third years period one with a burning larynx but!

…

Just at the wall of the staffroom, the notice showing who was in the paper club was lying on the floor. A few people stood on it as they squeezed between a chair and the wall to get past and head to the door.

Mr Tambourine Man watched people walk over it, the notice, sometimes their shoes scraped over it. Sometimes a guy would actually stand on part of the paper and another teacher would come along and scrape a bit off with his heel as he passed by, not noticing, and in a few minutes it had been torn into several pieces.

291

Mr Tambourine Man got up at the end of break when most people had gone, and said em, I'll just pick this up then, shall I? As he spoke, the tannoy came on and the Phantom said something about a meeting at lunchtime for pupils who had said they wanted to go on a school trip to see a musical in Edinburgh, so no-one heard what Mr Tambourine Man was saying as he tried to finish his sentence.

He sat down and copied the list of people out onto another piece of paper which he then pinned to the wall again, beside the noticeboard headed Male Staff Social Activities, which had information about a snooker night he was organising the next month.

…

As they entered the classroom, some pupils reported that Ace was leaving. He's left school, sir. Aye, he's going to some big stage-school in England, well, not big, but famous, well, not famous exactly, but, just a stage-school that's meant to be good, know, his new agent got him into it, sir. One of the class said hey, did you hear, that big Scottish film isn't happening anymore. Aye it is! Aye, the film's happening, but it's no happening for Ace, it's being made but Ace isni gonni be in it! Aye, I heard.

There was a dispute though. Naw, that's just something he's telling people, the stage-school thing, what it is, naw listen, it's that his mum's leaving his dad and going back to live in London where she lived before she married Ace's dad. Yeah, that's what I heard, he's going to go to school there, but it's not a stage-school.

No, no, no, that's not true at all, he's going to stage-school in London, and his mum's moving down

292

to London with him, just to be with him, his dad's still working up here, but she's no leaving him.

Once people had run out of variations on the possibilities for Ace, they looked at each other and sat down.

Someone looked at Marie and asked em, Marie, didn't Ace tell you what he was doing, that he was leaving?

Marie just shrugged her shoulders and half-smiled, no, why would he? She laughed, we're just friends, not even good ones, I don't think.

…

Bastard Guy was in the staffroom, he emptied the pigeon-hole with his name on it and started talking, joining in a conversation two other teachers were having about discipline in the days of the belt. He smiled at them, oh aye, I remember getting belted a few times myself at school!

A few people looked at him, Bastard Guy never talked but he was talking now.

He didn't look at the other staff, just continued talking, aye, this one bad bugger of a woodwork teacher, he kept his belt in a drawer, and made the boys unlock the drawer before he belted them. Well, did he not have the biggest damn set of keys that you ever saw!

All the men in the staffroom looked round at him. A couple of people smiled at each other.

Bastard Guy gesticulated, and this teacher, he was really a bad bugger, he'd tell whichever boy was in trouble to unlock the drawer himself and get the belt out for him, and he'd say that however many goes it took for the boy to open the drawer, that was the number of times he'd get belted. Aye, five attempts, five strokes!

293

A lot of people put down what they were doing. Some leaned on the back of their chairs as they turned round to listen to Bastard Guy.

He clenched his fists, aye, you'd get the hardest boys in the school sweating beads, grappling with this set of keys, holding them up, trying to estimate if they'd fit in the lock or not, trying to keep a check on which ones they'd gone through already, so as not to use the same one twice, and all the time this woodwork teacher would be standing, arms folded, no a smile on his face, watching and counting out loud. Slowly as well, one-ah, two-ah, three-ah!

Someone laughed.

Bastard Guy smiled.

A few other people laughed.

Bastard Guy laughed, and laughed again, at first it would be funny seeing a lad use the wrong key two, maybe three times, but Jesus, it became damn tense once he was on the fifth or sixth go, frightening even, especially watching it happen to one of your pals.

By this time everyone in the staffroom was looking at Bastard Guy. He laughed, I'm just saying, it's funny, it's just something funny I remember!

A couple of people grinned, looked at each other and smiled back at Bastard Guy, someone else said aye, I had a teacher like that too!

Then the whole staffroom was reminiscing about bastard teachers, someone else said, aye, there was this teacher at my school, aye, woodwork he was too! He used to hit us with saws, angled the serrated edge, so he did, just so the notches bit into your arse!

Bastard Guy slapped his knee and laughed, people around him did too, they laughed with him.

294

Then from Bastard Guy again came a story, our P.E. teacher once got a boy's wrist bleeding, he hit him that hard with the belt, the tawse he still called it, eh, giving it its proper Scots name, old bastard, and the boy was greeting his eyes out. And the thing was, the boy was getting the belt because the P.E. teacher thought he'd sworn at him, but he actually hadn't. The teacher had been shouting the register at the start of the lesson and taking names for the school swimming gala at the same time, and this boy never wanted to do the swimming gala, he didn't like swimming, but he knew he'd have to do it anyway, so he signed up when his name was shouted out. But the P.E. guy knew the boy didn't like swimming, so when he shouted his name from the register and asked what event the boy wanted to go in for, and the boy half-shouted front crawl, the P.E. teacher thought he'd said fuck all! It was in the P.E. changing rooms, and with two whole classes getting dressed, and football boots clicking on the floor and everything, the teacher must have misheard him! Bastard Guy hooted as he told this story, the P.E. guy just thought he was doing what was right in punishing him!

Those beside him and behind him laughed at the thing too. Men around the staffroom looked on and smiled, many eyebrows were raised.

When Bastard Guy got up to go, people said cheerio, and he half-waved and said aye, see you later.
…

Sam was back in school after all, the rest of the class said to him that they thought he'd joined the army and wouldn't be back at all. He shook his head, smiling, aye, I'm joining the army now, me! I've joined up and everything, went down Army Careers with my mum and signed the papers, the thing is though, I need to stay at school.

You don't get to leave school then? Billy enquired, I thought you'd be able to get the rest of the term off and no do your exams?

Nah, Sam tapped the desk with his knuckles, I thought I'd be able to leave but, somebody at the school careers office told me, well, I don't know, anyway, I think I picked them up wrong. The army say I've got to finish off school, sit Maths and English and all.

Nae luck Sam! Billy laughed.

Ah well, they still might say I don't have to do my exams at least. You don't need them to be in the army. A guy said they might contact me yet and say I can just leave, so here's hoping for that, eh!

Marie said, Sam, do you not think that now you know you've got into the army you can enjoy being here, knowing that you've got somewhere to go to after you leave? Know how you've said a few times how you don't like some things, education just being made up to, I don't know. I think you'll enjoy your last few weeks now, I really do.

Sam smiled at Marie, aw, you're always right Marie, aye! I suppose I will! Imagine that, me actually enjoying school, hee hee!

…

The Phantom said on more than one occasion that he couldn't stop addressing the rector as sir. It was simply that he had always just called the rectors he'd served under sir when he had met them for the first time, and it became, well, like a habit, you see, and I've done it ever since.

He looked at a photograph on his desk, lifted it up, placed it back down again.

296

It's not something I really like to do, but it's expected of me now. The rest of the staff certainly don't call him sir, and there's absolutely no reason why I should have to!

But I do.

And he did.

…

If the pupils on the bus said hi sir, or alright sir, or when they got into a conversation and they said sir at the end of everything they said, then sometimes other passengers, adults, would turn around and stare, listening in, hearing the pupils saying sir and drawing attention in this way.

One pupil once said excuse me sir, do you get embarrassed at people knowing you're a teacher, do you sir?

Aye he's a teacher, one pupil once said to another passenger, a woman, a pensioner.

The pupils laughed and looked at her.

Oh aye? The woman turned and smiled, oh is that right, my son's a teacher as well, perhaps you'll know him, oh, he doesn't teach around here, not around these parts, he's up in the Orkney Islands, used to be in Shetland, then it was Wick, then another school on Orkney before the one he's at now, and she said his name and then agreed that it would mean nothing if he'd never taught around these parts, she said och, listen to me going on, old biddy, eh!

The pupils who had talked to her were grinning and half-laughing.

Then she looked at the pupils and asked them, em boys, what subject is it your teacher teaches, the pupils, who were now leaning over the back of their seats said History miss, sir'll teach a bit about Skara

Brae to first years, sure that's in Orkney eh, the stone age settlement place, and other things like that miss, sure it is!

They called her miss.

Oh very polite you are, she said to them, and turned, very polite young men you teach, young man!

When the woman was getting off the bus, she said I've just had a wonderful journey, it was so nice to meet another teacher, and meet his pupils, who are obviously so polite and respectful, not like some young people nowadays. She alighted and walked along the street, and then the bus pulled away from the stop.

The pupils looked out the window and one of them smiled and waved, said through the window hey, wave if you're an old fanny, and the woman waved from the road.

The pupils hooted and said ah, you laughed sir! Och, you've got to admit sir, that was funny! Ha ha!

…

Sandwich Toaster came in the staffroom door. He stood looking at a chair, and then he was looking over to the table with the urn on it. He put his hands in his pockets and took them out again. He sighed.

A couple of people who were laughing came in the door behind him and one of them bumped into his shoulder on the way past, sorry son, and continued laughing. Sandwich Toaster looked up and half-waved, oh aye, heard it, it's okay, sorry, my fault, but the other person didn't turn around.

Sandwich Toaster walked over to the urn.

Just before he got to it another teacher rushed up to it also, getting there in front of him, excuse me son, I'll just, and he put a mug under the tap and poured in

298

some boiling water. Sandwich Toaster stood back a bit and smiled.

Then he picked up a mug, looked inside it, found a spoon, turned it over, scooped some coffee into the mug and held it under the tap of the urn. When he had finished pouring, he started stirring his drink and walked away to sit down, then stopped halfway to his seat and finished stirring and walked back to the urn to put the spoon down beside it.

When he returned to his seat he looked at his coffee mug but didn't drink from it. He blew on it a couple of times but still didn't drink.

One guy sat beside him and said hi, but quickly got up again to sit beside another teacher after he saw the other teacher sit in another part of the room.

Sandwich Toaster sighed, glanced at his diary, snapped it shut, and continued to stare into his coffee mug.

…

Sickens me. It just sickens me. Bloody, just, effing, just, sickens me.

He sat still for a second, Mr Tambourine Man, saying it sickened him, just, when I see other staff no caring, no trying, know? He looked from one side to the other. He stood up. And sat back down again. I'm not pretending I've read it start to finish, but you know in that book Nausea when the guy's sitting in the café and he thinks he's gonni throw up 'cause he's so detached from the world, alienated from everything around him? That's how I'm getting now in this place, seriously, I think I'm gonni effing throw up sometimes, in fact some of these guys I'd like to vomit over. Just.

He shook his head.

299

My brother's doing this course, Open Uni and all, aye don't tell you know who! The fat bastard! Or that boring, anally retentive eejit of a Geography teacher doing the crosswords! Anyway, he lent me this book, or booklet, my brother, with stuff in it, about Heidegger, you know, one of these guys you hear about but you never really know about, yeah? Or, more like, he left it in my house when he was round one day, just been at a tutorial or lecture or something, some class, and when I phoned, him he said to have a whisk through it, just, not so much out of interest but so he could have someone to discuss it with. Anyway, I don't understand eighty percent of it, ninety! That is, of the introduction and the first ten pages of the first chapter! But just this wee bit made sheer sense to me, where it says Heidegger didn't like using words that had been used so often that they became meaningless, or at least their meaning became blurred, know? I think consciousness was one of the words. So he never said it, just didn't use it, or other words like that.

Mr Tambourine Man stopped talking, then started again, God knows what his philosophy was, Heidegger, but, just. I think he would have been a guy who would throw up every time he heard another philosopher say consciousness or morals!

He stood up and stretched, och, I need to head to the department to set up the classroom for practical prelims for my Highers, and he yawned.

So, and he walked towards the door, looking back, anyway, all the time in here, you hear the people in here use words like kids, or good kids, or education even, you hear people say that kids come to school to learn to read and write, eh, ach, and he sighed, ach, Heidegger. I don't even know if he's the guy in the booklet, maybe it was someone else. Is he the one who said I think therefore I am? Or I am therefore I think!

Mr Tambourine Man paused for a second, he tucked his shirt inside his trousers, and shook his head and ruffled his hair on either side of his head with the fingers of both hands, then looked up, what the eff kind of rubbish was I talking about there, forget everything I said!

…

A few of the staff were talking about Kelly, and they were saying that she was away from school for another abortion, Christ, is that the girl's second one, what age is she! Not sixteen yet, no? She can't leave till Easter? Aye, naw, she'll be sixteen by then eh, but god sake anyway!

Someone said, see some of these kids? What are they like eh? She's no a bad lassie, but still, look what she's done eh, look what she's become, eh? More staff joined in, aye, they don't realise what this place, the school, does for them, it's a safe environment, the world it creates around them, protecting them, know? Teaching them, teaching them stuff that'll prevent things like two abortions before your sixteenth birthday, eh! Aye, and after they do leave they soon bloody realise but, they soon look back and regret not listening in bloody S.E., eh!

That one, Kelly whatshername, she'll have three or four kids by the time she's twenty-one, with no house to keep them in either I bet. Aye, and we'll all be teaching them all before we retire!

…

Armpits said that even if he kept going for jobs and didn't get them, at least he could look at himself in the mirror and accept that where he was now, the position in his life, was something he could accept responsibility for, know mate, my first principle is that I am now the person who I make myself, or who I try to be, know, if I can be pompous for a moment, if that's okay with you, momentary pomposity, I mean.

Mr Tambourine Man stared ahead and said aye. Armpits looked at him, you know? Mr Tambourine Man stopped staring ahead and turned to look at Armpits, aye, mate, aye, you're absolutely right mate, I was listening, you said the way you see yourself is more important than what other people think of you, yeah?

Armpits was still looking at him, that's what I'm saying is it?

Mr Tambourine Man shook his head and grinned and poked Armpits in the stomach, aye, I mean, if you think your diet's going well, then who am I to puncture your self-confidence by telling you it's not working!

Cheeky bastard, Armpits smiled at him, naw, but I don't really mean self-confidence, or the way I see myself. It's just, if I go for a job and end up not getting it, then I'm not gonni have a perception of myself as being in that job, the one I went for and didn't get, am I?

Mr Tambourine Man looked up, you're losing me man, what d'you mean, how could you perceive yourself being in the job? You wouldn't have got it! You'll get it though mate, you'll walk it!

Ach, Armpits shook his head, obviously I mean I'd never have fucking got it, Christjesus! But if I can keep going for jobs, is what I'm saying, then at least I'm willing myself on towards getting them, or one of them, know?

Getting a bit deep for me this time of day mate, Mr Tambourine Man sipped at his coffee, ach, this is too hot. Need to go and put some cold water in it, hang on, I'll just, and he headed towards the urn, keep my seat for me, mate!

Armpits nodded upwards after Mr Tambourine Man, aye, no bother mate.

…

A few of the Bin Brigade were tidying up the doors and the area in front of them, where the Main Entrance sign was hanging by one hook, they'd been told to come towards the end of the afternoon when there would be less visitors coming and going. Just inside the foyer there were photographs of pupils doing activities, certificates that had been given to the school or to pupils in the school for winning competitions, or in recognition of achieving levels of attainment, excellence in sport, or charity-collecting. Some were framed, some were pinned or stuck to the wall, and the corners of these ones had curled outwards into the corridor.

Billy stepped out of the way of another pupil who rubbed her shoulder along the wall as she passed him before he could take his rubbish bag towards the office. In doing so, the girl tore a corner of a poster off the wall with the strap of her schoolbag, though she didn't notice. Billy picked up the piece of paper and put it in his bag on his way into the office. The office door was half-opened as always, and a few secretaries were sitting at computers, one of them was standing at a counter with a sliding window on top of it, talking to a pupil.

Can I empty the bins please, Billy walked in as he was asking, nobody looked up, and he emptied the bins and said thanks, and then he walked away again, turning once to look at the heads of the secretaries, facing down towards their desks.

When he went through the door, one of the women in the office then looked up and asked somebody else if she could borrow a sharpener.

…

He didn't get the job he was going for, Armpits, and he was saying that he couldn't understand, I thought I had it, know, it was right there, for me I mean, mine for the taking, you know eh? Eh? And he held his hand out in front of everybody, his eyes kept opening, a twenty-seven year old, they gave it to. I mean, I was the fucking man for the job and they gave it to somebody fucking just out of school! I mean okay, so he's been working there for a couple of years, but Christjesus, know what I mean eh, twenty-seven!

Somebody asked Armpits if he thought the rector hadn't given him the references required to impress the panel, maybe that was it, no? But Armpits said no, it couldni have been that, the deputy always does my references, apparently he asks to do them, always has done, I know that, I was told at my last interview, Armpits was still staring ahead, his hand was back by his side by now.

Well, him then, the deputy, somebody else said, maybe he's been holding you back all this time eh! Two or three other people spoke at once saying no, it couldni be, man! The two of them have known each other for years, didn't he teach you, no? Then the teacher who had made the reference to the Phantom holding Armpits back looked at Armpits, and said aye, naw, I was just joking.

304

Armpits nodded, looking down, and said aye, aye, and then he looked at the colleague he was addressing, aye, naw, it couldni be that.

And then Armpits was nodding his head again and still staring ahead, smiling, repeating the words years, years, for years, so we have, so we have, then pausing, then saying again, for years we've known each other, so we have, and he was still smiling, Armpits.

It was at this point that the Phantom came into the staffroom. People didn't say anything, and the Phantom looked around a bit, saw Armpits and said oh, aah.

Armpits smiled and said hi.

The Phantom wiped the hair from his brow, aah, well, the chap I'm looking for isn't here, must be in his classroom, cheerio all, and he left.

After the Phantom went out the staffroom, Armpits looked at the door, still smiling. When he stopped smiling, his mouth was still opened a bit and his teeth were still together.

Aye, ya bastard, he said to himself, nodding. Nobody said anything and there was a silence that lasted two seconds before a conversation started, one teacher saying to another, that visit wasn't as long as usual eh, he usually stops in for a bit of a blether eh.

…

Crossword Freak Number One was asking Crossword Freak Number Two if he felt that Scottishness was defined by Scotland's relationship to England. Crossword Freak Number Two said he didn't know, em, I don't know, is that one in this paper? Which clue is it, are you doing the same paper as me, I've not seen that one, have I?

Crossword Freak Number Three kept a silence and carried on with his own newspaper.

Crossword Freak Number One said it wasn't anything to do with a crossword clue, it was just something he'd thought about, he'd read a few short stories in Dubliners the night before, it was part of an introduction to the arts module he was doing along with the Open Uni sociology course, and he'd started to wonder about Irishness, and Irishness being defined by the relationship between Ireland and England, or Britain even, that is, more probability though that it would be England, given the time that Joyce had been writing.

Armpits was standing over them, behind them, having a drink, he didn't say anything. Crossword Freak Number One saw Armpits and told Crossword Freak Number Two it didn't matter. Aw naw, you're alright mate, Armpits said, don't mind me, seriously, I'm just listening.

People looked at Armpits.

Crossword Freak Number Two furrowed his brow and didn't say anything for a few seconds, not looking at his crossword for the duration. Then he said em, I suppose if you think an awful lot about England and Britain, or if the idea of Britain is all around you, in your life or what you do or, I don't know, in the words people say, and then someone asks you if you're Scottish, or if you're filling in a form, and you maybe start to think, well, I'm not English, you might write Scottish just so nobody thinks you're English, even though you wouldn't mind people thinking you're British.

Crossword Freak Number One was looking up at Crossword Freak Number Two and down again to his own crossword, and up and down again as Crossword

Freak Number Two was speaking, and he replied uh-huh, uh-huh, uh-huh, at the same time looking at Armpits who smiled at the pair of them.

When he had finished expressing his thoughts on the matter, Crossword Freak Number Two asked, is that what you meant? Crossword Freak Number One said yes, I suppose so.

Armpits nodded, aye, suppose you're right, and walked away.

Crossword Freak Number One said again, yes, yes, I suppose so.

…

Some of the Bin Brigade had seen Ace on television the night before, and there was an excitement around the room, they asked each other did you see it, aye, were you watching, did you see Ace on the telly! Aye, Ace was on the telly! What about those clothes he was wearing eh! Aye, the cap too!

Marie said that she'd seen Ace too, aw didn't he look great! She said she remembered him telling her the term before about making the programme that they'd all seen, and telling her he'd take her on the bus to where the filming had taken place, aw sir, he said we could go for a walk up the Falls of Clyde during the Christmas holidays, hand in hand, he said we would be, aye in his dreams! And he would have taken a photo of me he said, with the Corra Linn waterfall pouring over the rocks behind me. She smiled, he never did though, he was all talk, that boy!

Others smiled.

Staff had already mentioned the programme, it had been a drama-documentary about children working in the mills of New Lanark at the time when Robert Owen had taken over the factory management. Bicycle

307

Clips had told all of his classes the day before to watch it, and told the department to tell all their classes about it, Armpits had told his classes to watch it if they didn't have anything else to do. Bicycle Clips insisted that his pupils watch it, aye they should watch more stuff like that, lots of good information about Owen starting the whole social experiment thing. The day after the programme he was saying aye, I'd told them it would be useful for the industrial revolution part of their exams in third and fourth year, though I never knew that boy Ace would be in it, if I'd told them that, then maybe more of them would have turned it on eh, tss!

According to the staff who'd watched it, Ace had played a boy who gets patted on the head by Robert Owen as Robert Owen talks to the TV camera, och, it was a bit arty-farty like that, the programme, know, but still.

Armpits had said he'd seen it, aye, actually I thought it was surprisingly quite good, eh, I should have sounded a bit less unenthusiastic when I talked to the kids in my classes about it yesterday, it was all about how Owen tried to run a business as well as make life better for his workers, know? Decent conditions, fair wage, food and clothes at cost price from the shop he owned, reduced child labour too, ye canni whack it! And there was wee Ace looking as cute as he could for the ladies watching, and saying how he got paid even when there was no cotton to work with, eh! And looking up at Robert Owen and saying thanks Mr Owen!

At that moment Ace had run out of shot.

In the class someone asked, so, does that mean Ace is still in Scotland after all?

Marie said no, I said he made the programme last year, remember? He's gone. We've seen the last of him.

…

Brando.

De Niro.

Brando.

De Niro! I'm telling you, de Niro!

Armpits and Mr Tambourine Man couldn't agree about the two actors' performances in the Godfather films. Mr Tambourine Man told Armpits that the reason Armpits liked Marlon Brando was because he could relate to him on the size issue.

Armpits told Mr Tambourine Man, well, someone like you would like de Niro, because he just sticks his chin out and screws his mouth and face up, and does that thing where he puts his head from left to right and left again and it's meant to mean a hundred different things, when in actual fact he's just saying nothing, nothing. And then a film critic says aw, de Niro, de Niro, he's so expressive, the most brilliant exponent of his generation. Brilliant exponent bollocks and my fucking arse!

Mr Tambourine Man hooted, you get it off your chest mate, your Brandoesque chest!

Sandwich Toaster now walked into the room, and he smiled, hey guys, and attempted to join in the conversation, asking hey, what are you two arguing about now, eh! Armpits and Mr Tambourine Man kept arguing, talking over what Sandwich Toaster was saying, before Armpits said shut up a minute to Mr Tambourine Man and turned to Sandwich Toaster, em, eh, sorry, what was it son, sorry?

Sandwich Toaster asked again, how come the two of you are arguing again, what's it all about this time!

Armpits said to him okay, listen, and don't be looking at him now, indicating Mr Tambourine Man to Sandwich Toaster, and then he looked at Mr Tambourine Man, and don't you be giving him the nods and winks, you ya, and then he stopped talking to him for a second, staring at him all the while, raising his eyebrows, mm?

Mr Tambourine Man shrugged his shoulders and stretched his palms upwards, sticking his chin out, and screwing his mouth and face up, and putting his head from left to right and left again, and said, don't look at me. He looked at Armpits, then looked at Sandwich Toaster and said are you looking at me, you talking to me? 'Cause I don't see anyone else here!

Armpits asked Mr Tambourine Man if he was finished, then he asked Sandwich Toaster, okay, now, no looking now, okay, now, who's the best actor, de Niro or Brando? Don't think about it, just say.

Sandwich Toaster blinked.

Armpits sighed, don't not answer, answer!

Sandwich Toaster blinked again, and said actually, I've always thought Al Pacino was better than either of, or both of de Niro and Brando.

Mr Tambourine Man and Armpits looked at each other, what? Aw, get out of here you! Armpits waved Sandwich Toaster away, and he did go away, laughing. Mr Tambourine Man was starting to grin. Armpits followed Sandwich Toaster, hey come back here you, hey, Al Pacino!

Sandwich Toaster came back, yeah?

Armpits looked at Mr Tambourine Man who was still grinning, and then said to Sandwich Toaster, hey son, I know you're just a young buck, but you've seen the Godfather films, haven't you, yeah? Sandwich Toaster paused for a second and said, well, the first two, aye.

Okay, Armpits nodded, so nobody gives a toss about the third one anyway, and on that I think we are agreed. He looked at Mr Tambourine Man who was nodding, we are indeed agreed, my man. So, Armpits put his hand on Sandwich Toaster's shoulder, who, just in your opinion, and without looking at this pretentious idiot behind me, who gave the best performance in any of the Godfather films?

Sandwich Toaster looked straight at Armpits and said, it would have to be Johnny Depp, and then paused, and then repeated his answer, nodding, aye, it would definitely have to be Johnny Depp.

Armpits took his hand from Sandwich Toaster's shoulder, right then! And he went back to his seat, picked up his folder and tucked it under his arm and headed for the staffroom door. Mr Tambourine Man hooted from his chair, asking Sandwich Toaster, Johnny Depp? Aren't you getting him mixed up with the guy in that film, What's Eating Vito Corleone? Ha ha!

As Armpits passed Sandwich Toaster he looked at him, looked away, then looked at him again, and said Johnny fucking Depp.

As Armpits exited the room to the sound of Mr Tambourine Man's giggles, Sandwich Toaster blinked again as he stared after him, what?

…

The Joke Club were having a discussion because of something Walks In Snow had done, one of them had said see her, she bloody gave me the wrong change when I paid for my bloody shortbread just there!

While they continued to speak about the matter, the teacher who'd been short-changed referred to her as that bloody tea lady, that bloody tea lady tried to say I'd given her a fiver when I'd given her a tenner!

What, she actually said that?

Well not exactly, but I handed the note over and when she gave me the change back I had to bloody point it out, that was a tenner and not a fiver I gave you, she gave me the extra money quick enough, old twister.

Aye, old robber so she is.

Bloody tea lady.

...

The Bin Brigade were commenting on having seen a politician who had been visiting the school. Billy had told everyone the man in question was a politician, and he hadn't been the first one to set foot in the place since the announcement of the by-election. Some disagreed, or voiced a doubt, how do you know he's a politician Billy? Because I've seen him on the telly once and my dad said he was a wanker, that's how, and 'cause my dad says all politicians are wankers, well, I just figured, Billy nodded to the others to confirm this view, they nodded back at him, and then he looked at the front and said woops, sorry sir, forgot I was in school. But you'll know what I mean, yeah, sorry, sorry.

No-one in the class said they knew why a politician would be in the school, they shook their heads, so how come he was actually here sir, did you

312

meet him, is he famous? The pupils asked if the guy was English or Scottish. Scottish I think, Billy told them, but he'll live in England now, I bet you. That makes him English then, the others concluded, yeah? And Billy shrugged his shoulders, aye maybe, I don't care.

…

Since the last time William had been in school, James hadn't appeared much. James had been in school sometimes, this was for definite, but not all the time, and not as much as he did when William was in. He still didn't say anything in lessons, and pupils didn't really invite him to, Billy would say alright James, Marie smiled at him and asked are you okay James, and she would nod in a way that indicated that James didn't need to answer her, so he just grinned back.

People didn't really speak much about William when James was in the room. Once when James wasn't there, Marie said did you ever notice sir, William always looked after James in school sir, in and out of school I think actually, I don't know why, they've just always been close pals since primary school, haven't they, I mean, I didn't know them then, I've just heard peole saying, did their families not live together at one time when one of the families was going to be moving house? And she looked at the rest of the class, a few people shrugged their shoulders. So Marie continued, I think if William's not here, not in school I mean, then James doesn't really think he has any friends. I mean, we all like him, we'd be his friends if he needed us, for definite, it's just. I suppose it's just a habit he's got into. Depending on William, James depends on him, I suppose.

313

Sometimes if James was in school, a pupil, a boy, might look at James and shrug his shoulders, have you heard from William at all? And James always shrugged his shoulders too and shook his head, and the boy would say okay.

…

People were discussing a decision made by the council about all the schools in the area, a decision which centred around the question of how the schools would operate if there was a strike by workers like janitors and cleaners, there had been a thing in the news about the possibility of such an event. Canteen staff would be involved too, maybe some of the women in the office, nobody in the staffroom really knew. It was an issue about conditions at work across the country, and there was talk about the possibility of a strike, there could be several strikes, that threatened the operation of schools and hospitals and other places. Armpits, plus some other staff at the school from the unions with only a few members, had heard that, in the event of strike action, school buildings would be opened by the rectors, headteachers, or council people, and would still manage to operate, although only with teachers working in them, not with any pupils attending. There would be enough non-union workers to maintain health and safety standards for the employees on the premises, heaters would get brought in and such like, and it was reported that the Phantom had told people that everyone would be told to bring in sandwiches, aah, just get up fifteen minutes earlier than usual, you see, have a packed lunch like you used to when you were at school yourself, aah!

Sandwiches? Hmmf! Armpits raised his voice when he spoke about it in the staffroom, this is the response to a national strike! Sandwiches! He said for fuck sake, all the authority's concerned about is keeping teachers in schools, and not actually addressing the needs of those on strike. Following the national lead, that's all the council's doing, that's all, Christjesus, I ask you! What's the point in having local authorities if they're just gonni follow the national lead, it's all just bloody absolutist centralisation, a supreme beady eye being kept on town and city councils, the divine right of Holyrood, or Whitehall more likely if you ask me, aye, one and the same!

People agreed with him, aye, so even if the kids don't have to come in, we still have to! Whoever thought of local control over education! Man! Can't the local authority make one decent decision for once!

Bicycle Clips spoke for the first time in the staffroom conversation, saying I think, em, it was nineteen-eighteen that local education authorities were set up, know? Right at the end of the First World War it was, that's how long ago it was, you'd think that one of them would have had a good idea by now, but they're just led by de facto messenger boys for the government, or some of them are!

People were looking at him.

Bicycle Clips repeated, aye, nineteen-eighteen it was, that was the date, nearly a century ago, tss!

People kept looking at Bicycle Clips, and then they looked at each other again, continuing. Bicycle Clips got some marking out and put it on his knee.

Then someone said that mediation was taking place over the next couple of days, aye, so the government'll probably beat the unions into submission anyway, maybe it won't be an issue in the end, yeah?

…

315

Ex-Cop had been away from school for over a week now, it was cancer he had, it had been confirmed.

And people were talking about him, lowering their voices as they did so, aye, I've heard that he's very ill now, it's terrible. Some people thought that one member of staff, someone who didn't come into the staffroom, he was a Mixed Staffroom guy, had been to visit Ex-Cop, but whoever it was hadn't told anyone about it, so it was said. People speculated, was it at home he visited him? Hospital? Hospice, I heard. Hospice? No! That's the end then, that'll be it, eh. Och, maybe no-one's been to visit, maybe it's not true!

One person said perhaps it's just the strain of his father dying that's caused him to be ill, maybe it's not actually the, I mean, not. Cancer. You know? Some people nodded, others looked at their feet and shook their heads, but we know it's cancer now.

This was a case where the pupils had been asking some teachers if Ex-Cop had died, boys and girls in their own way were asking, is he dead miss, is it true that he's dead sir? Folk in the staffroom said god, this whole thing is sickening, how long can it go on, it's bloody terrible.

The Phantom wasn't making as many visits to the staffroom as he would be expected to make, and it was said that he had also been to see Ex-Cop, but didn't want to be asked anything, he said he didn't want anything to be made of it. It was said in the staffroom that the Phantom had actually been made to visit Ex-Cop, told to, because the rector didn't want to do it himself, aye, the old bastard couldni bring himself to go himself, it's him that's sick so he is, unfeeling old bastard.

There was a mood about the place. The Joke Club had started making a collection in the staffroom for flowers, one of them had the idea and the others agreed, it was just a tin with a label sellotaped to it. People argued about that, do you no think it's a wee bit premature? Well, we're just thinking ahead, know, I mean, em, and maybe it would be a nice wee gesture to send something at the moment, know? To his wife, or to him really. Just to let him know we're thinking about him in the staffroom, eh?

Staff accused each other of a variety of attitudes, that's just insensitive man, you're so patronising, I don't know how you can be as uncaring and cold as that.

When arguments ended, Bicycle Clips said, can we not just behave normally eh? Let's try and get on with each other, get on with the job, our jobs.

People looked and nodded.

Bicycle Clips finished by saying and lastly, friends, can we understand that however we talk to each other, someone we know could be dying, a human being, a colleague!

…

Mr Tambourine Man was talking about how he used to enjoy the job, know, for what it was, yeah, it was just a good job to have, just a good job, a great job even! When I'd been rejected any number of times by orchestras after finishing uni, aye, I thought I might head in that direction for a while, and then I ended up in schools, I quickly thought, man, I've landed effing upright here, in schools, know?

He tapped his pencil on his lap, but now, Christ! And he spoke about how it had become his life, taken over, I bloody live it now, there's nothing else but it.

317

Christ! Christ, he said, and of course my divorce bothers me, of course it effing bothers me! It bloody well drives me, I don't know, crazy, stupid, mad sometimes, god sake man! I actually go wild sometimes, at the house, at home, on my own.

He paused. And sighed. One time, I knew it all, man, knew where I was going, my life had that bit of direction, know? Now though, man.

…

Bicycle Clips said he was teaching Education, the subject of Education, to his exam class, aye, I am in actual fact teaching them Education, tss! You see, part of the course covers the causes of the French Revolution, and the students have to learn about the influence of the philosophers. Ergo, in class we have to look at how the pamphlets the philosophers wrote, and the books they'd published in France, affected the thinking of the educated bourgeoisie, who in turn then diluted the philosophers' ideas into slogans for the urban workers and the discontented peasantry, who all made up the Paris mob, so that there were slogans and ideas for the mob to grab hold of, ergo creating a revolutionary atmosphere. Ergo, I have to teach about Rousseau! Amongst others, that is. Oh yes, Rousseau was dead by 1789, long gone, although actually I don't remember when he died, or is it just that I've never known? Tss! I actually think that I've never known! Must look that up sometimes, make a memo to myself, find out date of Rousseau's death!

Bicycle Clips smiled and scratched at his ankles under the socks which still had the trousers tucked into them from the morning's ride to school, I'll find out again by the time you come and watch me teach it. And no, Rousseau wasn't in my opinion the key

318

philosophical influence, by no means. No, that would be Montesquieu, with his advocation of limited powers for the king, a de facto constitutional monarchy based on the post-sixteen-eighty-eight-eighty-nine British model, but then Louis XVI totally ignored this advice at the abortive Estates-General and, well, that was it, burn the Bastille, march to Versailles, end of.

In the chair behind where Bicycle Clips was sitting, Armpits yawned.

Bicycle Clips pulled at a nostril hair, of course, we cover Voltaire and Diderot as well, briefly, but they offered no solutions, merely critiques of the Church and nobility. Then he looked at Armpits, that right?

Aye, Armpits sat up a bit and rested his chin on his hand, Voltaire's satirical plays and Diderot's Encyclopedia, the kids learn about it all, hmmf, aye you'll see in the lesson son, he looked at Bicycle Clips, em, I'll have to go now.

Bicycle Clips laughed, aye, on you go! Then he went on, though, to go back to my teaching the pupils about Education, I do always tell the pupils about Emile, Rousseau's son, whom he educated at home and wrote a book about, it's interesting to note that some of Rousseau's thinking is still taught in institutions, universities, aye, outside France too. You learning about it yourself too? Hee hee!

He stopped laughing, and he smiled, well there you are. Makes you wonder if some of the brightest pupils are best served by the school system at all, or if they'd be better off elsewhere, of course there wouldn't be the social benefits of state education, mm, tss.

Bicycle Clips reached into one sock and pulled the trouser leg a bit out of it just as the bell rang, and then tucked it back in again and headed for his class.

…

Was that not forty-nine seconds? Aw man, this is brilliant! The boys were shouting and hooting. The girls smiled at each other and then across at the boys, shaking their heads when they looked at each other, what are you like? You boys!

The boys were standing up and clapping, the dumptruck's got up the slagheap in record time! The watch that had been timing it was being shown to everyone, still on the wrist of its owner.

Sir, forty-nine seconds, not just under the minute but under fifty seconds! It came back this week, and broke the record, just there! Must have a new engine or something!

The girls laughed, one of them said, aren't the boys immature sir? So they are sir!

…

In one lesson when Marie wasn't in school, someone said her dad had killed himself when Marie dropped doing Latin at the other school, know sir?

Someone else explained, sir, know how some pupils here have got to go on the bus to the posh school some lunchtimes, for Latin lessons? 'Cause they don't do Latin here, know. But they do it there, they teach it at the private school, so they do.

Then the class returned to the subject of Marie, and Marie's dad, what was the other one she dropped, Classical Studies, was it? That one the deputy rector's always on about, Classics, the old fart! Aye, she got chucked out of Latin and dropped Classical Studies. Or the other way round, wasn't it? She stopped doing them both anyway. She'd never wanted to do these subjects but her dad made her take them, sir.

The others listened while the story was told, looking between each other and the front of the classroom and showing an interest in the thing.

Marie never did any of the work then, she just stopped doing it, all the homework and that, so they'd have to chuck her out, off the courses. Then she was gonni be chucked out the school, so her family took her out of it, put her in here.

A few pupils looked at each other, two girls were biting their nails.

Then one boy looked at the front and said, that's when her dad killed himself sir. He turned to the class, isn't it, when she was coming here?

One pupil said there must have been other things as well, know, to make her dad go and commit suicide, he wouldni do it just for that eh, Marie wanting to transfer from the private school to here, eh! You just don't know, none of us know, they never tell you about these things.

The class looked about.

Nobody spoke.

Then one pupil said, maybe Marie doesn't even know.

…

So what is a major-seventh then?

A couple of people were talking to Mr Tambourine Man, there had been something on television the night before about musicians who were from Scotland or who were influenced by living in Scotland, and Roddy Frame had been mentioned in it. The teacher who'd seen the thing said aye, just after eleven o'clock it was, it was a bit arty-farty the programme, know, but the guy presenting it had been talking up Aztec Camera a fair bit, and one of the

321

people he inteviewed had said more than once that Roddy Frame used major-sevenths effectively, they went into a couple of his songs in a lot of detail.

God sake, wish I'd seen it, he sounds like me, Mr Tambourine Man laughed, a pretentious tit like me, eh! And he looked at Armpits who raised his eyebrows, smiled and nodded.

The other teacher said it was one song called Release they were talking about, mainly, and a song called Backwards And Forwards too, ach they were good songs, but the whole programme, the analysis thing, it was too much detail for me, and they never let you hear either of the whole songs, just wee excerpts, know? Maybe they played them at the end, I never stayed up. School night!

Armpits sat up, Backwards and Forwards? He stood up, putting his folder down on his chair, aw, I wish I'd seen that too, aw, magnificent, Backwards and Forwards, that wee instrumental bit at the end, and he held his arms up and pretended to pick out a melody on a guitar, and that wee bit in the middle too, goes up a key there, he nodded to Mr Tambourine Man, see I've been listening to you!

Mr Tambourine Man nodded back at Armpits and said aye, he had been listening, very good, so what's a major-seventh then! Armpits sat back down smiling, em, must have dozed off when you did that bit, hee hee!

Mr Tambourine Man then explained to the teachers who had seen the programme what a major-seventh was, you see, Roddy Frame not only used it effectively, know, it sounds good when you hear it, but he moved from the major-seventh through the seventh as part of a progression, know, C-major-seventh to C-

322

seven and into the F-chord, or E-major-seventh to E-seven and into the A-chord, you know?

When the others asked why this was such a thing, Mr Tambourine Man shrugged and said em, just, well, when you hear it and you know what it is, I suppose, I don't know, it just, it works out, know? Mr Tambourine Man turned and looked at Armpits, in Release, when he sings, em, you laughed and turned and fled, just before the chorus, you know, yeah?

Armpits closed his eyes a bit, where he sings the force of love could kill, there as well?

Mr Tambourine Man shook his head, naw, before the chorus, it doesn't matter what the words are, just, I mean, before the chorus comes in. And he looked at the two people who had seen the television programme.

One of them said, oh aye, and then turned to his friend, if you missed the end then you'll not have seen the film on after it? Spaghetti westerns, you canni beat a bit of Clint to wind down when you've marking for three hours, eh!

Mr Tambourine Man looked up and watched the two men walk away, then looked across at Armpits who was filling in his travelling expenses form. Armpits looked back across, what? If I don't get this done before the end of the day today, they willni pay it!

Mr Tambourine Man got up and walked away. Armpits stood up, approached him and tugged a bit on his sleeve, everything not good, eh?

Mr Tambourine Man said out loud to himself, without looking at Armpits, no, the force of love can kill, mate.

…

323

There were two voices that could be heard from inside the cubicle, the men were at the urinals, one of them was Shakespeare, and he said aw Jesus, I'm needing this!

The other voice said aye, ha ha, you got a class next?

Aye.

Aw Christ.

A third person was in the toilet too, at the taps, at the sink, switching, turning the taps on, turning them off, taking a paper towel, scrunching it up and dropping it in the bin.

Then he said, see you two later, eh? The others said aye, see you, yeah, see you later.

Shakespeare and his colleague continued, it was a kind of conversation about another teacher, and they said, see him! Then talking about the football match on telly last night, aye, I saw the second half, was marking till nine. Aye I listened to most of it on the radio, had to do reports, saw the highlights later on, fell asleep, same story as always eh! Then a pupil was discussed, yeah, he's a good kid, but I couldni have thirty of him in the class, never shuts up. Aye, naw! Good kid though. Aye, good kid.

Then Shakespeare said that's me, catch you later pal, and there would be more running of water and scrunching of paper towels before the door would be opened twice and it was silent again.

…

Fifteen years ago I worked closer to the club, but these days I just do the odd bit of work, know?

Scout then spoke about how the pupils used to ask him to get autographs for them, oh, this was way back when boy, we're talking twenty years, on account of me knowing a lot of the top folk in football at that time, aye, me, I did, aye! Bumped into a lot of them, and not just on the Saturdays either, got invited to training sessions, behind closed doors they were sometimes, aye, internationals as well I went to and all, seat in the south stand at Hampden, sat beside Rod Stewart once too! There he was, coat collar up, wide-brimmed hat pulled down, I recognised him though, he signed my ticket, gave it to the wife when I got home, she's got it framed now!

Scout said he had been able to get a few big names' signatures at games, aye, though they didni want to be bothered that much during a game, it was just at half-time you could ask them, know. Celebrity in the school I was, aye, and not just with the kids, the staff too and all! If folk wanted something special, a ball or something for their kids, it was me they asked!

He smiled and nodded his head, saying that nobody ignored him then, naw, and they were practically begging me on a Friday to say who I was going for on the pools, wanted my inside whatsit, know!

And he laughed again.

And then he stopped laughing.

…

Someone shouted to Billy, looking at the front of the room, tell sir about the weekend, Billy! Billy laughed, aye okay, and said d'you want to hear sir? And then he said aye, right then, but promise you'll no tell any of the real teachers though, yeah?

He began, well, somebody from the social security came round the house on Saturday, and my dad saw the guy out the window coming up the driveway, and he told us not to go to the door or shout or anything, it was the social security guy, so we all kept quiet, but we wereni hiding or nothing, so the guy could see us, through the curtains or something.

People around were laughing as they were listening to Billy. He said shut up, I'm trying to tell sir! Then he went on, anyway, this guy was trying to put something through the post box, a letter or something, for my dad, and he held the flap up and shouted in, but then all of a sudden the dog ran into the hallway and up to the door and bit his hand, the social security guy's hand!

The class continued laughing, and someone asked, what kind is the dog, Billy? Someone else hadn't heard the story yet, and asked, so, Billy, what happened to the man from the social security? Billy said, the dog's a cross between an alsatian and labrador, and the guy was howling on the doorstep, yelping like a puppy, and my dad wanted to help him but he didn't want to appear like he'd seen the guy, officially, it would mean he'd get money taken off him or something, so he put some bandages and a plaster back through the letter box to the guy in case it was bad, his hand, know, he never said anything, my dad, not a word, and the guy went away and never came back or anything. He was alright, Billy said, or he would have been, 'cause he took the bandages.

After the laughter died down, Billy said it's totally true, so it is. He would have been alright though, the guy.

…

The Bin Brigade had been doing anti-smoking posters in an S.E. class earlier in the day. Some still had them with them when they came into the room. Billy was getting teased for smoking a few times now and

326

then, ah Billy, you don't want sir to know! Billy screwed his eyes up and looked at whoever teased him and shook his head, curling his lip.

Sam looked towards the front of the room, hey, what does that mean on the board sir? A red flag equals revolution sir, on the board?

The attention of the class was now drawn to the writing on the board indicated by Sam, and they looked at the booklets that were on their desk too. The booklets had the title The General Strike on them.

Sam half-lifted his off the desk, what's the General Strike sir?

Some of the class opened their booklets, Sam still wanted to know what the writing on the board meant, how can a flag, or a red flag, mean revolution sir?

Soon a few of them were arguing with each other again, about the smoking. Billy said he didn't smoke, then he said okay, well I used to smoke, then he said aye alright, well I gave up and then started again, or he said I've given up now anyway, I just have the odd one, you know, socially.

Sam threw a rubber at Billy, ha ha, socially! What d'you mean Billy, socially, ha ha! Billy just shook his head, you know what I mean, just when I'm having a wee smoke when I'm with someone else, a smoker, know?

The lesson eventually started, and soon the class were looking at photographs of miners and factory workers, railway and shipyard workers. Billy found a picture of James Maxton in hospital, and he had to read out the caption which said that the stress of all the speeches he had been giving on the Independent Labout Party platform in support of the strikers had seen him end up with, Billy read out, a, a, dued, a dudna, dud, d-duednal, duedenal ulcer? A duedenal ulcer, whatever that means sir.

Nobody in the room knew what it meant.

Someone asked why the article under the caption said Maxton criticised the Labour Party for deserting the miners and not supporting the strike, I mean, sir, if he was in the party and was giving speeches supporting the strike. Then they worked out from its name that the Independent Labour Party wasn't the same as the Labour Party, and a few pupils looked at each other and nodded, ah. There was some writing underneath the Maxton source on the role of Ramsay MacDonald at the time but the conversation about MacDonald dwindled out.

Then someone noticed that Maxton was smoking in the photograph, look sir, he's smoking! In the actual hospital bed! And the whole class were in animation about the thing, imagine that, being allowed to actually smoke in hospital! There was a discussion on whether Maxton was allowed to smoke in hospital because of who he was, he was an important guy sir, wasn't he? Then there was an agreement that the authorities probably didn't care much for Maxton, perhaps he's getting special treatment 'cause they want him to become ill from the smoking and die sir!

Billy said maybe though, that was just the way of it in those days, people were allowed just to smoke in hospital, yeah?

Then Sam said hey Billy, maybe you can't see it in the photograph but Maxton's probably talking to Ramsay MacDonald who's come to visit him, and he's just smoking socially!

Billy blinked at Sam, eh?

328

Sam laughed and waved Billy's attention away, och, never mind!

…

A boy was saying that Kevin had been away from his home, he's been missing for twenty-four hours sir, and his mum hasn't even called the police. The boy had told his own mum, but she'd said to him not to get involved, it was Kevin's mum's business. The class was talking about this after Kevin had been off school for the second day running.

Other pupils said that it was Kevin's mum who made him go out to work on the milk round. And she makes him give the money to her, sir! All of it and all sir, the pupils looked at each other and nodded, aye, Kevin's mum's an alky, or she drinks a lot anyway, they said.

One girl said her sister was in Kevin's brother's class at primary school and her mum had found out from the other parents. All the time pupils of the Bin Brigade were speaking, they were looking each other in the eyes, everybody watching whoever it was that was saying something.

Billy then said he used to go round to Kevin's house quite a lot and, you know, and he paused, you see things, well.

The class looked at Billy and he scratched his desk with a finger.

He looked up and said that Kevin kept talking about running away, aye, he does, or he's said it a few times, but really it's as if he doesn't really want to, like he doesn't want to run away at all, he just says it jokingly, like he's just imagining, like we all do, imagining what it would be like, know, what it would be like to run away, but really he doesn't want to go away and leave his brother with his mum, the two of them on their own, it's like he really wants to stay, or he feels he he needs to, or has to, or something.

Someone else said ach, he'll turn up sir, won't he eh?

They all looked at the front.

I mean, it's only been two days sir, eh?

8. UNTIL IT GOT TOO DARK

Whenever a woman teacher was coming to the staffroom, she would knock on the door that separated it from the Mixed Staffroom and wait to be spoken to. She wouldn't come in, the thing would be that a guy just would just go and speak to her, he would usually hurry to the door, aye, aye, it's okay love, hang on there love, and he would hold his hand out to say stop, and he would say aye, I'll come to you, hang on. The woman might just have a piece of paper to sign or something to be checked, or just something, a message, something to be passed on.

Then the guy would deal with her, get the thing signed, pass the note on, whatever was required, and the woman would go back into the Mixed Staffroom.

Whichever man it had been, or whoever it was that the woman had wanted to see, would always explain to the others when he sat down the reason why the woman had come to see him, the others would be looking at him as he sat down, and he would explain, saying oh, she just wanted me to sign a letter, it couldn't really wait, the thing has to be posted before tomorrow. Or he might say aye, I just had to change a couple of things on a pupil's report, apparently you can't write that a boy's worse than his father anymore! There would always be replies from some of the others, which might be oh aye, okay, or just aye.

Or someone might say Christ man, could she not have waited the five minutes to see you in the bloody department, eh, it had to be dealt with now?

It might be the case that if a woman came to the staffroom that a man might leave the staffroom to go into the Mixed Staffroom to have a conversation with a

331

woman, if it looked like there would be a conversation about the thing. Sometimes they would even have to go into the Female Staffroom for the woman to get something out her bag, another report, something to check, and the man would go in with her. He wouldn't knock or anything, and if he had wanted to see her about something and had travelled on his own from the staffroom through the Mixed Staffroom to the Female Staffroom, he would just have gone in, not knocking, it was only the women who knocked on the staffroom door, the men would not announce themselves if they were tipping up at the Female Staffroom.

It didn't happen every day, it maybe happened a couple of times a week, maybe none at all, the thing with women coming to the staffroom. Sometimes a week would go by and in the staffroom there wouldn't be any women seen at all at the staffroom door.

The women would always look about when they came to the door, they would see that a few men would be looking up, and the women would always say sorry, sorry, this would be before they announced why it was that they were standing at the staffroom door at all.

…

Somebody said to somebody else, they were talking about Scout, how come he seems to hate kids so much, especially any of the boys he teaches? According to some voices, Scout had said the words I hate kids, or he'd said them, these words, at the end of the day, the day before. One of the two or three people talking about him said och, we all hate kids at some point, I've had days like that, bloody infuriating so they are, or they can be. The others looked at each other and nodded, mm.

Somebody else sat down with the group of people who were talking, and the conversation drifted off Scout in the specific, he was no longer the subject of the conversation, and the three or four teachers discussed the rationality of hating children on occasions, and how this feeling, the rationality of hatred, could be reconciled with wanting to educate them, to make a difference to their lives.

There was a logic to it, at least, they said there was a kind of resolution, and what one teacher said was em, isn't it that sometimes it seems that you hate children if they stop you trying to help them, or they make it difficult for you to help other children, know?

Someone else might say aye, you just want them to make them respect or like you, know, the kids.
…

It was raining and the Bin Brigade were not picking up the litter.

Sam had discovered something, look, the litter-picker-uppers are hollow! He had chanced upon the fact that if he took off the clamp at the bottom of his litter-picker-upper, and then kept his thumb over one end of the litter-picker-upper and dipped the other end at an angle in and out of the puddles that had gathered at the edging-stones between the playground and the grass, and then in and out again, then some water would be sucked up inside it, look, these things are hollow, and he smiled at the others, he laughed, and then he showed that if he lifted up the litter-picker-upper after it had sucked in water, and manipulated his thumb in a way, it would scoosh water at another person, whoever he was aiming at, and he turned, watch out sir, I'm gonni get you! Aw, just kidding, hee hee! If he put his hand over the thumb-end of it just as it emerged from the water

333

then he could save it inside the litter-picker-upper and it would really only spray out when he released his hand, he could aim it at one of the others, ah, ha ha, there you go!

They had all emptied the bins, but now they had observed Sam's demonstrations, they were just firing water at each other, laughing, taking sides, maybe ganging up on one person at a time, boys against girls, variations of that sort of thing. Sam looked at the sky, at the rain, look at the weather, man, this is never gonni stop man!

Then the Phantom came out of one of the buildings, they all saw him, and someone said aw look, the deputy rector! Gonni scoosh him! And they all ran towards the Phantom with their litter-picker-uppers held out in front of them, hands over the tops of them.

The Phantom stood with his hands on his hips as the Bin Brigade ran towards him, then they started walking and looking at each other, Sam looked around himself, at the others, and said well? And they looked at each other again, then at the Phantom, then at each other, aw, aye, naw, we're not gonni get you sir, dinni worry sir!

The Phantom observed them disperse and carry on with their litter duties, picking up the amount of litter that was left. He shook his head and smiled, aah, what a fine team you have there, and he looked around him, to the left and to the right, the so-called Bin Brigade, eh! Waterbabies, today, aah, waterboys and watergirls, and, as he turned and went inside, and heaven knows what tomorrow, eh?

...

At the school assembly in the morning, or at the school assemblies, because yeargroups had them at

334

their own times of the day, people got invited in, guest speakers, this week they'd been talking to the pupils about conserving energy, and talking about types of energy that would provide an alternative to types of energy that were used at present, renewables and so on, it was a thing to tie in with something going on worldwide, a United Nations thing, the school had signed up for it, to get another certificate or award.

The speakers during the morning were taking an approach with each age group that they thought would make sense to their audience, they knew that each time they might be talking to twelve year-olds, or maybe thirteen year-olds, or even sixteen year-olds.

It was the kind of thing, an assembly, that staff usually said was a waste of teaching time, och, the speakers always patronise the kids, don't they? Aye, on account of misjudging their age, they think the fourth years are ten years old! Yeah! The staff thought that at assemblies the speakers usually underestimated the kids' intelligence, aye, they do, they try too hard, don't they, to be entertaining, know?

The talk of the staffroom was of Armpits causing a stir at the sixth year assembly in the morning, he had been standing at the back of the hall, and during the question and answer session he had been whispering questions into the ear of a sixth year boy who had been firing them at the speakers, you could see Armpits whispering, well, all the staff could, they were all standing up. The speakers had thought the boy was showing an interest in what they were saying.

One of the speakers had kept saying to the students, I represent a company that deals in nuclear power, kids, yes, nuclear power! Or, he would say, my company is preparing to establish nuclear power

335

facilities, kids, yes, nuclear power! And he informed them, we will establish these facilities in different parts of Europe, including Scotland kids! He kept addressing the kids as kids, to their faces, right in their faces.

Armpits had got this boy to ask the speaker about the Faslane peace camp, and the way the Thatcher government, which his company had supported in public, had treated the women there, and the guy had said something along the lines of well, the protesters at Faslane lost the argument about nuclear weapons, kids, and the point of proof of this is the fact that they went away and called off the protest, point of proof, kids! And he had looked around the hall, catching the eye of teachers who were there with their classes.

Armpits had then interrupted the guy, the speaker, Armpits interrupted him himself, teachers who were there said he'd just started firing questions at the guy himself, aye, never mind the sixth year lad! Armpits had shouted out that there were still women at the Faslane camp, and it turned into a thing where the pupils were egging Armpits on and booing the speaker, the teachers laughed about it, man you had to be there, best assembly I've been at since I came to the school!

The speaker ended up having to shout the students down and saying kids, kids, I'm here not to talk about nuclear weapons but about nuclear power, kids, kids! By that time disorder had broken out and the teacher organising the thing, one of the deputies that sometimes got called assistants, he had to stop the assembly earlier than planned.

And also by then, Armpits had sloped away during the melee, with some of the pupils at the back of the hall applauding him as he did, and him telling them

336

not to, and the students getting confused about the thing. The teachers who were there laughed as they reported events, hee hee, the whole thing was a hoot!

When Armpits came into the staffroom during the lunchtime he was quizzed on what had happened afterwards, after the assembly, and he had said not much, meaning not much had happened, he'd spoken to the Phantom afterwards about it and the Phantom had brokered an agreement between him and the speaker guy, Armpits smiled, know, the nuclear wanker?

A couple of people in the staffroom shook their heads, ha ha! An agreement? Armpits smiled. The teachers laughed, an agreement! Not like that time when that ex-pupil, the young guy, the motivational speaker, came to talk to the upper school about how to be an entrepreneur and run your own business, and when he asked the kids what should people do when they fail in business, you shouted out, become a motivational speaker, hee hee!

Armpits looked about, and smiled and said aw, I didni say that, did I? And then from the others came the words aw, hey, aye you did ya liar! And also, anybody but you would have been floored for that, man, good job you and the deputy go way back, eh, lucky bastard!
…

When Kevin walked into the room everyone looked at him. There was a bandage over one of his eyes. His other eye was blinking a bit, and watering. He rubbed the bandage over his eye, and stuck his finger underneath it, moving it around whilst holding the bandage on with his other hand.

Billy was the only one who wasn't looking at him. He looked down at his desk, and wrote something on a scrap of paper and then scored it out, scrunched up the paper and threw it at the bin, the paper bounced off the rim of the bin, hit the wall behind it and fell into the bin. Ah, in off the backboard, eh! Billy laughed, and then he looked up at Kevin and grinned, alright Kev, I knew you'd turn up.

Then Marie said aw, Kevin, are you okay?

Kevin sat down and said he was okay, and in response to questions some of the class asked him, he said there were some elements of truth in what they had all heard, he had stayed out overnight a couple of nights ago, but nothing had happened to him, he'd just left the house about half-past nine to go to the shop before it shut, he had to get something for his mum because she said she was tired, and kept falling asleep and couldn't go herself, he had intended to go back home, but he'd ended up walking around a bit, aye, just walking around, thinking about stuff.

Kevin looked around the class and sniffed a bit as he spoke to them, aye, so then I thought it would be too late to go home, I thought my mum would be fast asleep downstairs by then, and I'd just wake her up, and then she might make a noise going up the stairs, and then my wee brother would wake up. So I went to the milk delivery office at the depot and slept in the security guard's shed, it was a while before the guard saw I was there 'cause he was doing his rounds with the dog, and he just aked if I was okay and gave me something to eat, and I was starting work at five in the morning anyway, so I just started an hour early when the milk arrived, that was all.

A few pupils shook their heads, man Kevin, out all night, would your mum not have woken up and got worried?

Kevin said he'd tried to phone his mum from the delivery office when he finished work but couldn't speak to her because she'd gone out to her work by then, and then he'd just gone home and slept it off. He'd seen her when she got home from her work, just for a minute because then she had gone out again, herself, and hadn't come back until just before bedtime.

The class looked at him.

Billy said, he wasn't really missing then, was he, I told you all!

Kevin nodded, aye, naw, I hadn't really been missing, know, I was just, I don't know, out of touch.

Pupils were nodding and saying aye, aye, still though, eh, aye.

Then someone asked, so how'd you get the black eye then Kevin?

…

Bicycle Clips stood at the urn table and picked up a coffee mug. He turned and spoke about there being truth in what he'd read in the paper one day, aye, or was it a Sunday magazine? Tss, anyway it was recently, and this article had said that we, all of us, people in general, we all accept lower standards of hygiene in the workplace than in the home, even though we, or they, spend more waking hours there than in the home, aye, at work, we do, what do you think about that then, eh, think about it, lower standards of hygiene, tss.

A couple of heads turned towards him. He continued, I mean, look at these cups, I know they've been washed and they probably get washed every day, maybe more than once even, but come on, you wouldn't still have these stains on them if you were washing them at home, you'd make the effort to clean them properly, yes? Or you'd have throw them out by now, know, it's all bacteria, tss!

Someone walked passed Bicycle Clips up to the urn table and took a cup up, put it down, and lifted another one up off the draining board, ran it under the tap, swished the water around in it over the sink, and then spooned some coffee into it, poured in boiling water from the urn, stirred it and took the drink away, leaving the spoon on the table shaking from side to side, with a little bit of water and coffee swirling about in it till the spoon came still.

Bicyle Clips watched and sighed, and lifted the spoon and examined its concavity, observing the drip of liquid left there. Then he put a tea bag in the mug he had been holding, and poured boiling water and milk into it before stirring it round with the spoon and then using the spoon to squeeze the tea-bag onto the inside of the mug before lifting it out and dropping it in the bin.

He picked a dish-towel up from amongst the cups and cutlery, and wiped the spoon with it, before replacing it on the table and went to his seat, shaking his head.

…

Some of the class said they had seen William from the school bus again. Sir, I know I saw him sir, he was standing in the street with a policeman and policewoman plus another woman. Social worker, one girl said, that would be his social worker. It wasni a social worker, another pupil replied, how would it be a social worker! How would it no be? Just! Well it would be! It wasni, it was the dogger-woman, the truancy officer! She's no the dogger-woman! Aye, she is, she's both at the moment!

340

Then there was a conversation in the classroom about how it might have been a social worker and how it might not have been. There were silences between bits of the conversation.

At one point someone asked if they should even be talking about William again, with him not being there, remember, aren't we his friends?

The pupils looked at each other, then agreed, yeah, we are, but that's what makes it okay, because we are his friends, we're not slagging him or anything. They all nodded.

Then one of them said, but still, eh?

...

With Ex-Cop not having been in school for a while, a variety of teachers were standing in for him, to take his classes, and the Bin Brigade had just been taught their R.E. lesson by Crossword Freak Number Two, and he was just saying in the staffroom, I just gave them the first video I could find lying around, it looked like it would be about Easter, I just thought, it would make sense, know, with Easter coming up in a few weeks, or next month or whenever it is, at the end of this term, but it was actually about Christmas, this video, and I just let them watch it, I had marking to do. I figured, it doesn't matter what you give the Bin Brigade just now anyway, they'll all have left school before the summer. But the thing was though, in the class, they liked it, the video, they actually liked it, that was the thing!

And Crossword Freak Number Two developed what he was saying by pointing out how the Bin Brigade had asked for paper to draw on, or play puzzles on, when the video was over, and he had thought they would be playing hangman or noughts and crosses, or

341

just doodling, but no, some of them had drawn angels, pictures of Jesus even, aye, and religious symbols, there I was, thinking they just wanted to sit and idle their time away, and maybe they did, but they actually wanted to idle their time away drawing religious objects, stuff that was relevant to the lesson, such as it was, the video I'd put on, what a thing eh!

Someone else said aye, the last time I had the Bin Brigade, it was in January, or the start of February even, they asked for Christmassy things to do, and it was a Maths lesson! I just told them to do what was written on the bloody board. When the bell went and they left the room I discovered that a few of them who'd been sitting together had actually drawn Christmas decorations round the pages of the jotters they'd been doing their work in! They live in totally another world!

From across the staffroom Scout said there they go now, the Bin Brigade, jackets off in this weather, Christ look at them! Must be some kind of stupid game or a dare or something, eejits, bloody whatsits, no?

Outside, it was raining, and the wind was blowing the trees in the gardens neighbouring the school so much that they were bending with the force. School pupils were running through the playground to the shelters, or towards the bits of buildings they were allowed to go in at breaks and lunchtimes, dashing into entrances and foyers, holding their schoolbags over their heads with both hands.

Some of the Bin Brigade were walking in the other direction, with their school shirts on, billowing in the wind because the Bin Brigade had untucked them from their trousers and skirts. They stretched their arms out to the side, laughing, sometimes leaning forwards into the wind and having to put one foot out, forwards or to the side, to avoid falling over. They looked up at the staffroom and waved at Scout. Their voices were lost in the wind, but their faces mouthed the words hi sir, and they waved again.

Scout banged on the window and indicated with his thumb for them to move on and not to look up at the window and wave at him. They stopped waving and moved on, running after each other, a couple were skipping.

…

During a discussion about all the reading that has to be done during the time it takes to study for an exam or a degree, the Dog Catcher spoke about books she'd had to read in sixth year at school, oh, and I don't mind telling you I hated reading, and our English teacher, kept giving us this rubbish stuff, de Beauvoir it was, mostly, and the thing for me was I could never understand if the books were meant to be novels or something else. It's like, oh, woe is me, the blood of all the people I know is on my hands darling! I've lived for centuries and I know everything darling! Am I not the cleverest bitch ever darling! As well as the ugliest! I still don't know what our teacher thought we were to make of de Beauvoir, what we were meant to think.

She said she didn't really understand the books in the way her teacher explained them to her, although she liked the stories in a few of them, yes, darling, there was one about the French Resistance in the Second World War, it was quite exciting. It's meaning? Och, don't ask me, she laughed, I'd just talk rubbish, I just thought it was the only one with a proper story, a plot!

She continued once the car had made another turn, now, what was the name of that other writer I had

343

to read as part of my studies, to get into Social Work it was, now what was she called, em, em, yeah! Warnock! Warnock she was called, you know, I can't remember her first name, I think she was actually some kind of Lady or Duchess or something, had a seat in the House of Lords anyway, and it was her stuff I had to look at when I was training, aye, I bought the book but really just read the photocopied extracts we got given as part of the course. God, you're going to think that this sounds terrible darling, but, and I know I'm a woman, but I hate clever women, you know what I mean? The ones that can't get by just being clever, they've got to be known as a clever woman?

She halted the car and switched the engine off, I mean I know this Warnock, she was into things well beyond the realms of my understanding, and that's perfectly fine, stuff like special education and embryo fertilisation and other such lofty things, all totally beyond me, but the funny thing is, honestly, I do still try and think about it sometimes, honestly. Even if I felt that I didn't understand Warnock, I still felt that it was something I should. Understand, I mean. That it was a good thing, what she wrote. I did actually try to remember bits of it when I talked to that girl's mum, you know, the one I told you about, about her daughter having to have an abortion, mm, hmm. But the only bit I could remember was something I'd read in an article or something, I can't even remember if it was this Warnock who mentioned it or not, or maybe it was a piece of writing about Warnock that my tutor gave me, some critique, I don't know, but it was something about, and I'm not kidding, and these were the words, obfuscating red herrings! Seriously! Obfuscating. Red herrings! I couldn't say that to the poor girl darling, I mean I don't even know what it means myself!

She leaned forward and turned the key in the ignition, I think it's something about people having rights, or people not having rights, and then whatever it is that gives people, women, control over their body, the right to own their body, oh I don't know. Christ, abortion.

So, tomorrow then eh?

…

The boy who stood at the entrance to the school, the boy who sometimes got hit by other boys when they walked past him, was making the shape of an arc with his bag again, there was no radius, no radius that was fixed anyway. Right left, left right, left right, right left. Four four, two two, two two, four four. It always worked out.

Some boys walked past him, most of them ignoring him.

He continued to swing his bag in the arc, first forwards, and then backwards, then backwards again, and then forwards again. Forwards. Forwards backwards and backwards forwards, a four each time, forwards for four and backwards for four, all balancing up.

Sometimes he moved his head at the neck, right front left front left front right front, then left front right front right front left front, then again left front right front right front left front, and to finish right front left front left front right front. The right and left balanced.

If he went back to swinging his briefcase, no longer moving his head at the neck, it would be no parabola, an arc would be made, then no parabola again, and then a parabola. Anytime he did something

345

to the right, it was then to the left next, then maybe to the left again, but always to the right after that, balancing.

Everything matched up, everything balanced.

…

Then, the Phantom and Crossword Freak Number One had again picked up their debate on sub-cultures, and they were speculating on the issue of whether the pupils of the Bin Brigade, by misbehaving in classes, or at least not working, or working but not achieving anything, would in some way be rebelling against the tradition they had been fighting to be a part of. This was the Phantom's theory, aah, in my own amateur socio-psychological manner I propose my theory, aah! Crossword Freak Number One went along with it, agreeing, yes, that is, an informed socio-psychological manner!

They both agreed that the Bin Brigade's rebellion, or the series of rebellions, the collection of rebellions that had been perpetrated by individuals within the Bin Brigade, were manifestations of what the Phantom said was a desire to protest against the majority, aah, yes indeed, their desperation to stand up for the minority, their willingness to begin advocating values, aah! Values!

Crossword Freak Number One nodded, squinted his mouth a bit, and nodded again.

The Phantom shook his head, smiling, aah, and with that, values, suddenly the Bin Brigade are starting to become aware of rights. Aah.

…

The Bin Brigade had just come from R.E. again, it was someone other than Ex-Cop who had taken them, and they'd been taught about God by the teacher replacing Ex-Cop, yeah sir, it was about the Christian one sir, it's crap when you get told about the Christian God, whoever tells you about it is always trying to force you to believe the same as them, and we just have to sit there, and we never try and get them to not believe in God, but they want to force us to believe in one!

Ex-Cop had always told them it was no wonder some people don't believe in God, Sam said Ex-Cop had always told the class that he never believed in God, but then there was this one day sir, he said that he believed in Jesus, or was it just that he believed that Jesus existed, it's the same thing actually, and it was just that he didn't think he was the son of God, Jesus that is, isn't that weird sir? Jesus being the son of God, he said that was one of the myths that people got told on Sundays!

The class remembered, and Sam continued, explaining that Ex-Cop had said he didn't even believe in the disciples in the Bible, aye, naw, actually he told us he thought they were just creeps, crawling all over Jesus who was a good guy, or trying to be a good guy, and the disciples just tried to make him into something he wasn't, just so they could say that they were the disciples of the son of God, I don't really know, I can't really remember what he said, anyway he didn't exactly say they were creeps, it was just that, oh, I can't remember, and, another thing he said was, to look at the world and the state it's in, you know, you just know it must have been created by humans, eh, so there couldn't be, em, a connection between Jesus and the disciples and God.

Sam smiled, and that proves that the whole Jesus thing's just made-up, sir, more made-up history to

make people believe, I don't know what, believe,
worship or do things that make it easier to control them
eh. More made-up history!

Marie nodded, and said she didn't know about
history being made-up, but this was what she believed,
she believed that everyone was the son of a woman and
a man, you know what I mean sir, son as in child, but
anyway born with human parents, yeah?

Sam said yeah, see the Bible sir, it's just history
really, isn't it, history that's been made up, to get
people to believe in God, that's what I think anyway.

Someone else then asked, how did we get to
talking about this, my head's hurting!

They all laughed together, and Marie asked if
any of them could remember the name of the guy Ex-
Cop had been talking about whenever they did morality
in class, em, Kant was it he was called? Then there
were a few jokes from the others, like no I Kant say, or
I Kant remember, or I Kant believe anything the Bible
says.

Marie smiled at those making the jokes, then
said sir, I think everyone should learn about that guy,
just to learn that you should always try to do something
good, good things, like good deeds, and if it doesn't
work out, or it works out bad, then it was still a good
thing to do in the first place, you know?

The class didn't say anything while Marie
spoke, though they all looked at her.

…

Sand? Sand! Ah, ha ha! The Bin Brigade were
laughing at the idea of sand being used as an ingredient
in some recipes and foods consumed by people living in
Germany during the First World War, the sand being in
the recipes because of the food supply shortages

348

brought about by the Royal Navy's blockade of German ports and the failure of the German government to introduce rationing to any effect.

Someone said, hey isn't ersatz the word sir? I read it in one of these books we've been looking through. Doesn't ersatz mean substitute? Some of us learned the word ersatz when we did a topic on sport when we did German in first or second year, in the German class, I don't know if they did it in French, it would be a different word anyway.

Sam then said aw sir, my grandad had to eat funny food during the war too, I don't know if it was the First or Second World War, must have been the Second. Kelly shoved his elbow, aw sir, tell him about the cannibal boy, that thing you said your grandad told you!

Sam said aw, I shouldn't tell, but Kelly said aw, don't not tell, tell!

Aye, Sam grinned, okay then, aw sir, listen to this! Sam then mentioned what he had been told by his dad one time, about a boy in his grandad's class at school, sir, he got called Cannibal because he ate the ashes of his mum's American aunt who'd died of old age during the war, the ashes got sent to Britain because she never had any relations left in America, and when the thing the ashes were put in, aye, the urn, was sent over from America, it had cracked a bit on the plane or the boat or whatever it came on, so the ashes ended up getting put in another container when it was delivered to the family, a box or something, while the family waited to buy a new one.

Kelly snorted, wait and hear, sir, he he!

Anyway, Sam said, this wee boy, he was in my grandad's class at school, he was left one time in the house on his own, and he found the container with the ashes in it, but he thought it was powdered egg, the stuff they used to eat all the time during the war, and he mixed it with water or milk or whatever it was that they used, and he ate it in a sandwich, and then his family came home and found out what he'd done and went mad with him for what he'd done, and they had to call the school the next morning to say that the wee boy might be ill, 'cause of what he'd eaten, and the teacher had told the class and called him a wee cannibal, aye, the teacher actually called him a cannibal in front of the class! And then the boy got called Cannibal for the rest of his time at school!

The Bin Brigade hooted, imagine that, ha ha! Billy leaned back on his chair, imagine being a cannibal, aw, perfecto! The class looked at each other, they all had a smile for each other, looking at each other.

Sam then said, I wish Ace and William were here. And James, Ace and William and James.

The class looked at him.

He repeated, doesn't anybody else wish that Ace and William and James were here?

…

Mr Tambourine Man tapped Armpits on the elbow, hey, I was reading this book about Bruckner last night, remember, Bruckner? Armpits said who? Mr Tambourine Man shook his head, doesn't matter, a composer, that composer, the guy that was born in Ansfelden, we saw the place it was near, Linz, on those historical maps you brought in here once, yeah, the Austrian one, Ansfelden, you thought it was Eindhoven, there was a pupil's drawing outside the entrance to the building, yeah?

Armpits looked up at the ceiling, eh?

Mr Tambourine Man smiled, hmmf, anyway, this guy, the guy writing this book, said Bruckner always said that the diminished-seventh chord was like a musical Orient Express, eh, a musical Orient Express, isn't that a brilliant description, eh! He said it because of how the chord could, what was it, take you on fantastic journeys to the most the fantastic places you could imagine going to, Mr Tambourine Man sat back and put his arm over the back of his chair and smiled, just like that eh. I think that's fantastic, eh?

Armpits pursed his lips.

Mr Tambourine Man continued to speak, talking about how melody was what Armpits liked in music, and he looked at Armpits, that's probably the most important thing mate, I know I bang on about lots of other things, and you think I'm patronising you, but melody is, in actual fact, the thing, it's what the listener hears. And actually, I do think that too, and in the book, this guy, the writer, he was saying as well, that if Bruckner had been more concerned with melody, and perhaps encouraged a bit of free composition amongst his students, and he maybe allowed himself to be inspired by them, well then maybe what he wrote would have been less, I don't know, Wagnerian, and it would have been more appreciated at the time, and maybe he wouldn't have gone mental either, though whether it was being mental that caused him to be so precise in his composition or whether it was the precision in his composition that drove the critics to pan him and therefore caused him to become mental, who bloody knows eh, who the eff has a clue about such things as these.

Armpits now blinked.

351

Mr Tambourine Man went on still, telling
Armpits that he would like listening to Schubert, with
your ear for melody and everything mate, because
Schubert, know, he was never particularly adept at any
instrument, he wasn't an expert on anything, so he
couldn't really sit down and play anyone the stuff he'd
written, or, he didn't have the opportunities to put
orchestras together and show people what he could do,
but he was just brilliant at taking other people's words,
poetry and stuff, and putting music to them, he was a
craftsman, an actual tunesmith, a songsmith! A melody
man. Think of all those guys you like nowadays,
Difford, Tilbrook, Frame, Duffy, Dando, Murdoch,
Hannon, I'm telling you, descendants of Schubert all!

Armpits shrugged his shoulders and said maybe
he would listen to Schubert some time.

And Mr Tambourine Man smiled and laughed,
hmmf, saying did you know Schubert had been a
student of Salieri's? Know? The guy who wanted to be
Mozart, or at least as famous as Mozart, or at least as
renowned as Mozart, you must have seen the film, eh?

Armpits shook his head.

There was a pause. Then Mr Tambourine Man
said hey, you'll know this, you know how people say
the thing about Van Gogh was that he only sold a
couple of paintings in his life? And even they were only
to family members? Armpits nodded now, Christjesus
mate, I haveni had a fucking clue about anything
you've said so far, but I do know about Van Gogh
selling just a couple of paintings in his life, and no
fucking wonder eh, fucking sunflowers, every bugger
paints them!

Mr Tambourine Man carried on, well, did you
know that Schubert never had any of his music

published until over fifty years after he died? Aye, fifty years!

Armpits raised his eyebrows, is that right, Schubert? How come I've heard of him then?

Mr Tambourine Man laughed, because, people eventually liked his tunes! They'd been written down, and people liked going to hear them, the tunes, in concerts. Like you say, the melody's the thing!

Armpits sat up and laughed himself, wait a minute, I think I can see a parallel here! No, listen, so, you're telling me that Schubert was taught by a guy who never attained the success he felt he deserved, and he wasni brilliant at anything, but he liked melody, and he was never recognised, for his talent or whatever, in his own lifetime? Undiscovered?

Mr Tambourine Man laughed, aye, undiscovered, ha ha!

Armpits nodded and said, well that makes me the fucking Schubert of the education world, undiscovered, eh!

…

The pupils were talking about a thing that had happened the night before on the television, they had seen it on the news, it had been a by-election thing, when one of the guys standing for Parliament had poured water over one of the others and he'd been caught on camera.

Hee hee! It was just at the side of a stage sir, or a room, somewhere they'd all been talking to the TV people, the cameras, and the papers too, there was all the guys who're wanting to be voted in, the candidates, aye, and after the thing was over these two guys had got into an argument about something, and you can see one of them saying something and pointing, and his finger hits the other guy's tie and the second guy just throws the glass of water he's got over the first guy's tie, hee hee, big babies, politicians, so they are, big babies!

No-one in the class, nobody, they hadn't really noted the names of the politicians or their parties or anything, nah, we just thought the thing with the water was funny sir, it'd been on the news and everything. They said they didn't expect that kind of behaviour from politicians, aye, naw, and them supposed to be running the country as well, sir!

And the pupils had all seen another thing on the news, a feature about an agriculture exhibition, a show outdoors, where there was a guy whose job it was to go round the cows and clean their bottoms before they were judged, shit patrol, that's what he said he was on sir, shit patrol! The pupils laughed, the guy had said the words shit patrol but it had been bleeped out, but you still knew what he'd said!

The class then said the two guys with the water had appeared on telly at the end of the evening saying they were pals again and it was just a misunderstanding, but sir, that's just so folk'll still vote for them!

…

He sat down, the Phantom and leaned his head on one hand, now then, aah, your review, I, em, I haven't yet had the time to put together a summary of your progress, in writing, as it were. I've just, it's just I've, em. Aah, aah.

He looked out of his office door, towards the corridor and the door of the rector's office, I know that some people think I'm just an old, well, an old tosser, that's what they say, don't they, is that what they say? That's how they speak about me, isn't it? It isn't? Aah, you're too kind, dear boy, too kind.

354

He moved on to speaking about his still wearing his graduation gown, there wasn't any link, no relevance of it to either context, the progress review or what he was called by the staff, and he spoke about how he knew other people, other teachers of his generation even, didn't do it anymore, aah, I am aware that it's such an old-fashioned thing to do nowadays, but still, aah, I enjoy so much putting it on, you know. He sighed and said that it used to mean so much. He sighed and said that back when he started teaching it used to mean so much, it had status. He sighed and said nothing.

Then he said well, you're doing just fine, just fine, I'ill finish the review at home tonight.

He sighed again, and then he changed the hand he was leaning his head on.

…

Armpits talked about a union action in the past, when only a few teachers in the school had declared their support or even shown an interest, it had been a thing to support janitors and cleaners and people in another union, Armpits said he had just been a teacher just out of teacher training college, and couldn't really do much to motivate his colleagues, he didn't have the position, it wasn't within possibility that he could persuade them to take action, he had no position in the union and he didn't think he had enough presence in the staffroom for his opinion to have weight.

Nowadays though, ach, it causes me a bit more anguish, still, 'cause sometimes I still don't feel that if there was a similar situation again that I could be able to bring people out with me, there's been times, it wasn't so long ago we even held the council to ransom, it was in the days of the old rector, aye, but we held the council to ransom over the way a cleaner who was about to retire was getting treated. Her hours were getting cut to avoid her earnings going over a certain amount that would have given her a better pension, and the staff, almost to a man, and woman, said they'd do no marking at home, or any extra-curricular activities, beyond anything contractual, unless the council fixed the situation, and after just three days the council caved in, whoa, I felt so, so, proud isn't the word, but just. Now though, it's just that you can't rely on people anymore. Plain and simple. Och, I know that I couldn't force people to do something they didn't want to do in a situation, I wouldni want to, but what frustrates me is just that they just don't think about it, teachers, now, they don't even make a choice, it's easier not to choose, know? Fatalists, fatalists, it's as if they're not even a member of the union.

He lifted his pen off the paper he had been scribbling on since he had started to speak, aye, they fucking live without hope, so they do, they live in fucking quietism, you know. They probably think that if they were ever in any bother then someone else will come along and bail them out, though not if everyone's like them they won't, em, ach, I suppose it's just human nature, no hope, quietism, ach.

…

The bus stopped at the side of the road, not at a bus-stop. The driver turned the engine off and came back down the aisle, to the middle of the bus, and he pointed, hey, you're a teacher aren't you, yeah, well are you no gonni tell these wee bastards at the back to calm down eh, I'm trying to drive a bastard bus here, never mind control a bunch of bastards, I'm having to try and think about health and safety on the bus as well as drive the bastard thing!

Other passengers, adults, turned round to look at the two pupils he was talking about, they were fifth years. The pupils looked up the bus from the seat at the back and then stood up and lifted down the first year boy they had put in the baggage rack overhead. The first year boy dusted his jacket down and laughed, then turned to face the fifth years and shouted give us my fucking schoolbag too! The fifth years pointed up the bus, laughing, hey, you watch your language wee man, there's a teacher up there can you no see!

The first year boy looked up the aisle and then looked back at the fifth years, I said, just give us it, give us my fucking bag! As the passengers looked to the middle of the bus, one of the fifth years said, aye alright you, ya wee fucking bastard, and he pulled the schoolbag out from under a seat and gave it to the first year.

All three pupils looked up the bus, the other fifth year boy said it's okay sir, it was just a bit of messing around eh, we were only having a bit of fun, eh.

The driver looked, tutted, and said thanks a bundle, and then he went back to the front of the bus, bloody health and safety, man, he was shaking his head, health and safety, Jesus. He jumped into his seat, and as he switched the engine on and pulled away again he kept his eyes on the mirror, aye, don't think I'm not looking at you, he spoke towards the reflection of the three boys in the mirror.

Aye, well just keep your eyes on the road mate, the first year boy said, fucking health and safety!

...

Ex-Cop was still not back in school. Pupils had been allowed to write get-well-soon cards to him and

357

hand them in at the school office, there was a box, and the Phantom was taking the cards to Ex-Cop's house, it would be the hospital some days if Ex-Cop had been in overnight, there were tests he had to get, to see if the cancer was spreading or if the treatment was causing further problems. The staff had sent a card and flowers to him twice, there was a thank-you note from his wife on the noticeboard.

Sandwich Toaster went up to the noticeboard, and took the wedding-gift thank-you note from his wife down, and put it in the bin.

Nobody was talking about Ex-Cop in the staffroom, people just went to the note from his wife as individuals, and read it to themselves, then left the room.

…

In the queue for home-baking, two or three people were commenting that Walks In Snow didn't look herself, and hadn't done so for a few days now. They were whispering, I think someone had been ill in her family, is it her mother, or her father, is it? Aye, I think it was someone quite old, wasn't there a note going round the teachers of her grandson last week, or a couple of weeks ago, no? The usual stuff if a pupil's relation's not well, or dying, know, just saying to apply a bit of sensitivity in his classes, as if we wouldn't, eh. Anyway, hasn't the person died? The relation, has she? Was it a woman? People continued to whisper about it as they looked up to see where they were in relation to the front of the queue and also in relation to where Walks In Snow was standing, serving, behind the tuck-shop table.

At the tuck-shop table, a couple of guys from the Joke Club cracked a joke between themselves, and one of them reached out for change before they walked away. As they got to the door going into the Male Staffroom, Walks In Snow shouted after them, my name's not dearie!

The two Joke Club men turned round, and they both stared at her, one of them taking the biscuit he had half-bitten into out of his mouth.

People in the queue stopped talking.

Walks In Snow stared at the two men in silence, she was pausing now, after having shouted. She could see that everybody in the room, the Mixed Staffroom, not just the queue, had stopped speaking, and they were all staring at her, some people turning round in the armchairs to look at the scene.

There was another pause.

Then Walks In Snow said, and she was speaking now, not shouting anymore, it's Jenny, Jenny is my name, not Dearie, or Dear. Jenny. One of the Joke Club men swallowed and kept staring, holding his biscuit in mid-air.

Walks In Snow continued to look at the two men, my name is Jenny.

The men spoke now, both of them, saying alright, and nodding too, alright, sorry. Then they didn't say anymore, they just looked at her.

And Walks In Snow said to them, but you can call me Mrs Malcolm, do you hear me? Mrs Malcolm! The two men looked at her for a few seconds and then turned and went into the Male Staffroom, not saying anything.

Mrs Malcolm looked at the next person in the queue, wiped her hands on her apron, took a breath, smiled and said right now hen, what can I get for you, and within a minute people were talking to each other

359

again as she asked her next customer, well did your daughter pass her dancing exam then? Aw, that's good hen!

…

The talk amongst two of the staff in the staffroom was about the dumptruck, it had just set another record for getting up the slagheap. The men looked at the watch they had laid on the window sill, one of them was holding it up so they could both see the face, Christ, she raced up man! One of them turned to someone else in the staffroom who was sitting down, forty-seven seconds, just there! Aye? Aye! I timed it on the stopwatch, forty-seven seconds just at the end of break, forty-seven point zero nine and all, cruised the record yet again, no sweat!

The other teacher at the window said aye, I witnessed it and all, good job we decided to wait to time it one more time, good job and all that we came down to the staffroom at all today, aye, I had an inkling this was gonni be a fast one, she's been getting faster these last few days. The two of them agreed on this point, the dumptruck, it, her, she, had been establishing a trend over the week, aye, she's been managing speedier climbs up the slagheap with every passing day this week, in fact, since earlier last week even.

They continued speaking. A colleague who was sitting down started to look up at them, he had closed the book he was reading, and they spoke to him, aye, normally we've been timing it just twice in a breaktime, but we managed a third this morning because we came down to the staffroom earlier than normal, lucky eh!

…

During the war it was, aye.

Bicycle Clips had been mentioning schoolkids in Scotland during the Second World War, just some of them, and talking about what they did in wartime for schooling, to get an education, with the bombs and everything. He nodded as he spoke, of course, children of school age, at that time, remember, they wouldn't understand anything about Hitler or the Holocaust, or the Nazis, or anything other than what the government told them about the enemy, there was nothing based on a depth of understanding, nothing ideological. He smiled, tss, neither did most adults too, tss! Aye, the government knew more than it was prepared to let on to the people, I'll tell you that!

People were listening, watching Bicycle Clips, they smiled and nodded.

He continued, the Second World War just meant a bit of excitement, and as for schools, if you got evacuated away from the towns to the countryside, sometimes there might not even be a school big enough to take you! He looked ahead, or maybe the family you lived with didn't force you to go to school, eh, they might not even send their own children.

Bit like that Peruvian experiment, someone said. There was laughter from around the room, and after it was over, people went back to having the conversations they had been holding with each other before Bicycle Clips started talking.

Bicycle Clips raised his eyebrows, rubbed his shin and sat back and looked around.

…

Billy was telling the class that he'd decided to leave school at Easter, or the school had decided he had to leave at Easter, or I think it was more my dad actually, the school phoned him the other day, don't know who it was, my dad says it was the rector but it wouldn't have been him, probably the deputy. Billy sniffed, anyway, my dad said to me it didni matter about me leaving school before the exams, I mean, what do I need exams for anyway?

Wish my dad would let me leave school like yours, said someone else.

Aye, naw, it's not that he's letting me, Billy looked back, I mean, I know he's letting me, but it's not something I'm demanding off him, like, or something he's just going along with, or anything like that. He looked to the front of the class, sir, I know you're a teacher, well you're gonni be one, eventually, but still, you must know that there's not always a point in everyone doing exams, I mean, no disrespect, but I'm no gonni actually need History when I leave school am I? Or any other of the qualifications I could get, eh?

Someone shouted aye, not to rob houses!

Nobody laughed.

…

What is a meritocracy anyway! Mr Tambourine Man was complaining about the jargon in some education authority literature that had been issued to everyone in the staff, he waved the leaflet in the air, and how much has it cost to produce all these effing glossy leaflets, eh? Then he breathed in, and he repeated himself, how much, eh, local authority, they expect us to believe that, eh, actually it's the bloody government at work here, you mark my words!

Crossword Freak Number Two nodded at Crossword Freak Number One and said, you'll know about that won't you, meritocracy, from your Open Uni, no? That not in your Open Uni course?

362

Mr Tambourine Man didn't notice Crossword Freak Number Two talking, nor Crossword Freak Number Three nodding in agreement, nor Crossword Freak Number One whispering to Crossword Freak Number Two, look I don't want involved in this, look at him, you can see the mood he's in. Leave me out of it!

Mr Tambourine Man looked down at Crossword Freak Number One, and said hey, what you hissing in his ear? No secrets in here, eh! Aye, meritocracy, you'll know about that won't you, that course you're doing, meritocracy's a pile of pish isn't it!

A few people turned and looked at Mr Tambourine Man as his voice raised.

Crossword Freak Number One looked at Crossword Freak Number Two, and then looked up at Mr Tambourine Man, em, well, I'm not sure.

Crossword Freak Number Two put down his education authority leaflet and picked up his newspaper, feeling for a pencil on the coffee table.

Mr Tambourine Man laughed at Crossword Freak Number One, ha ha, you're not sure eh! Go on then, tell us, who's the world's leading authority on meritocracy that you're reading this week! Crossword Freak Number One looked over the room and out of the window and said, em, we're reading something by Parsons this week. Mr Tambourine Man spread his arms out, oh, Parsons? Parsons? And what does Parsons say?

Armpits came in, and looked over to where Mr Tambourine Man and Crossword Freak Number One were holding their conversation. He kept looking as he picked up a glass, ran it under the tap and went to the corner of the room to drink it, saying to Mr Tambourine Man hey mate, everything okay?

363

Mr Tambourine Man didn't acknowledge Armpits, and instead, he looked down at Crossword Freak Number One, well, eh, well?

Crossword Freak Number One looked down at his lap, well em, well, Parsons says that the gap between family and society can be bridged, but only if education is meritocratic and applies level standards to all, to everybody, preparing children for adulthood, em, and assuring their future role in the meritocratic society, that is, within the meritocractic society, in a meritocracy, that is.

Mr Tambourine Man looked back at him, interrupting him, that is? That is? Aw, away and raffle yourself man, that is, get yourself into in a raffle! You understand? I bet it was you that wrote this piece of pish the government's giving us eh! They send someone to the Open Uni tutorials and ask for volunteers to write a piece of pish to give out to teachers, eh?

Armpits hooted from the corner of the room.

Crossword Freak Number One said well, you asked me, and then he was interrupted, Crossword Freak Number One, he was distracted by Armpits waving his arm at him and shaking his head, from behind Mr Tambourine Man. Crossword Freak Number One looked from Armpits to Mr Tambourine Man.

Mr Tambourine Man said ach, and walked away and sat down at the card table alone, meritocracy, Jesus.

Crossword Freak Number One looked down and went back to his newspaper.

…

Bastard Guy had given up teaching.

He had just walked out of school, a couple of days after the day he had been exchanging stories with colleagues in the staffroom about teachers from their own schooldays, ones who gave the belt, the saw and so forth.

The rector had looked into the allegations about Bastard Guy having a go at that class, some of whose parents had made the complaints about him going over the top. People talked about the class in question, aye, difficult buggers to teach, that lot, even the good ones in it don't mind being a bit lazy, laughing at the arseholes whenever they play up, not just getting their heads down, they might as well join in, you canni win with them, teach them, let them laze about, it's always difficult to do what you think is right.

It had emerged that in the meeting with the pupils and their parents, the three or four pupils had told the rector they'd just made up a lot of what they'd said about Bastard Guy, just because they hadn't liked him. One boy had cried in the meeting, saying he didn't realise it was going to end up in a meeting. The thing had then been dropped, the parents had made the pupils write an apology to Bastard Guy, and the parents gave a letter of apology to the rector.

Bastard Guy had asked not to be at the meeting.

A week or so after the meeting, he had been all smiles in the staffroom, laughing, getting the thing going about teachers and the belt, joking about the thing..

Then he had just left, got out of the job, walked out the school, gone home and phoned the office to say where he was and ask if someone could be found to take the first years that would be in his classroom.

In the staffroom, some people said Christ, it's a kind of surprise, him just leaving, just like that, but also it's kind of not a surprise either, given the way the

365

whole thing's been handled by the rector, I mean, allowing the parents to demand a meeting and everything, before the pupils had even been spoken to! People said aye, what a shame it is, aye, shame, and him having turned out to be a good guy after all as well!

One man said that someone he knew, or someone his wife knew, was a mate of Bastard Guy's, or one of his wife's friend's husbands knew Bastard Guy's brother, and they'd been to dinner with Bastard Guy and his wife a few times, aye, says you couldn't meet a nicer couple.

…

There was a silence.

It was a minute or so before it was broken.

Someone asked the question, em sir, will Kelly be away for a fortnight like last time, it was a fortnight last time, will she be a fortnight again, is that how long it takes to, you know, get over it? They all knew about it, her pregnancy, everything. A girl turned round and snapped at the boys, no smart comments or anything, right?

The boys protested, aw Christ! We wouldni say anything, alright? Alright eh! Eh?

The girl had turned round, facing the front, but she turned back to look at the boys again, aye alright, sorry, still looking at them as she spoke. A couple of the boys smiled at her, looking in her eyes as they did so, and she smiled back.

And then there was half a minute or so of silence again, a boy unzipped and zipped up his pencil case..

Then someone said, I heard that she's keeping it this time, is that no right?

…

Armpits entered the staffroom, and started talking as he came through the doorway, talking about some folk just not having a clue, I'm telling you, not a fucking clue, away with the bastard fairies sometimes, I think, eh! He shook his head and put his hand on the back of a chair, no-one else in? Just gonni have a coffee, you want one? No? Health kick is it, you never have a coffee!

He walked across the room, aye, I'm telling you, some people, not a fucking clue! He turned, listen son, I'll tell you, guess how much savings I have, eh? Go on, seriously, know how much money I've got saved after twelve years of teaching, me and my wife both? Go on, work it out, twenty-one years, both of us teachers, she's been head of a department for the last three, and how much savings do we have? Nothing. Nothing!

He stood in silence for a few seconds, then he said again, nothing, that's how much! He laughed, I shouldn't laugh, it's not funny. It's a fucking joke isn't it, two of us working eh, and nothing, not a bean to show for it. A house with a bloody mortgage attached to it that we'll not pay off 'til after we're sixty! Ach, some folk don't know a thing, just about.

He put some water into his mug, then spooned some coffee into it, that's the fucking climate of it now though, eh. Isn't it.

…

Mr Tambourine Man walked into the staffroom and over to the urn table. He picked up a cup and looked inside it then put it down again. He picked another cup up and looked inside it, then slammed it down. He walked away, then he walked back. He picked up the first cup he had looked at, and he placed it on the table, and he scooped some coffee into it before filling it with boiling water.

A few people looked up at him and then down again.

Mr Tambourine Man looked across at them but didn't catch anybody's eye, he said oh aye, milk left out of the fridge again, and he poured his milk and then put the carton into the fridge. He looked around at a few people as he walked to the card table, smiling quickly and asking them, aye, lost my sense of humour today, is that allowed?

Nobody else was sitting at the card table.

Armpits had been watching Mr Tambourine Man, and was sitting behind the card table, looking now at the back of Mr Tambourine Man's head. He leaned over and tapped him on the shoulder, alright mate?

Mr Tambourine Man said hmmf, aye, suppose.

…

Scout was sitting down in the centre of the staffroom, where most folk sat, or at least had to pass to get to their seats. He was smiling and saying aye, cheers, and cheers, aye, to people passing by him, people who were saying well done to him, aw, you did really well, good man!

Scout looked at people as they approached him, and when he caught their eyes they would say well done, well done man, and he smiled, ha, thanks!

Joseph had been suspended from the school after swearing at Scout.

Many of the teachers in the staffroom spoke more now about not liking Joseph that much, in fact not liking him at all, aye, naw, nothing but a hooligan so he is, how the rector can keep him here in the school at all

368

I don't know, surely he should be asking the council to put him to another school!

One man spoke at length about Joseph being the pupil he would like most to have seen getting kicked out the school altogether, aye, never mind a two-week suspension, get rid of him competely, I mean, let's face it, no-one would miss him, the school can manage fine without pupils like that, d'you not think!

Also, staff said that Joseph had always managed to avoid getting into trouble that would lead to suspension, someone said aye, that boy usually stops himself taking that extra wee step, eh, something to push him over the edge, know, sly wee bastard, isn't he? Or it's just that he just never gets caught, someone else said.

But now Joseph had sworn at Scout, and folk were singing Scout's praises, what a man eh, getting the wee bastard suspended, give us all a break for a fortnight!

Scout smiled and shook his head, sitting in the centre of the staffroom, taking everybody's praise, smiling, not standing and looking out of the window at the football being played during the lunchtime.

Aye, and you having got him a trial with the Rangers as well man, someone said, and him no turning up for it, ungrateful wee shite, so he is.

Scout looked up at this remark, he opened his mouth, and then shut it, not saying anything.

Then he clasped his hands and rested them on his lap, and stopped smiling, although he still said cheers to people, and he got pats on the back through the rest of lunchtime. He looked ahead, and sometimes up at the window, and he didn't look anybody in the eye.

369

...

I know what you're saying sir, but sometimes it doesn't matter what other people think about you, you know, or what they think when you're going to do something, if, if you're going to do that something, I mean, when you want to choose to do something and you know they won't like it, it doesn't matter, does it sir. And after saying all of this, Marie was looking down at her desk, and she was lifting up the end of a book and dropping it, before lifting it and doing the same thing again, it made a noise.

It shouldn't matter at all sir, should it, she said she knew it didn't matter at all, it doesn't matter sir, I know how we have to think about other people sometimes, don't we sir, we have to be unselfish and that, but sometimes, we're not trying, not wanting, we don't want to hurt other people like that, but, I don't know, it's like you'd be hurting yourself more if you didn't do something just because somebody else doesn't want you to, when it's going to be your final choice anyway.

Marie looked around, and then looked to the front of the classroom, you have to be, I don't know, bigger than that, yeah? Do you not? Or am I not making any sense at all! She smiled, I'm going to shut up!

Marie looked around at the others who were staring at her, she laughed, and laughed again, and asked if someone else was not going to say something, anything, eh, nobody going to speak but me, ha ha! And she stopped talking.

The others still stared.

And still smiling, Marie asked, are we going to talk about something else now sir? Sir?

...

I was listening to some music that you like, Sandwich Toaster was saying, a friend played me that High Land, Hard Rain album you're always going on about, I thought it was pretty good. I had a drink in me, mind, so anything eighties sounds good though, eh, heard it, eh! He was telling this to Mr Tambourine Man, Sandwich Toaster was telling Mr Tambourine Man that he'd heard him talk about the album the week before, and other times before that, with Armpits, and he had been round a friend's house at the weekend, and his friend had a copy of it, plus some other Aztec Camera stuff, so Sandwich Toaster had asked to hear it.

Oh aye, Mr Tambourine Man used both hands to reach and scratch both sides of his head above his ears.

Sandwich Toaster went on, Lost Outside The Tunnel, that was my favourite song, at least, I've only heard them all once, know, the rest of them, just once, and some of them just the introductions, if I didn't like them I just wound through to the next one, know, but, em, Lost Outside The Tunnel, that was really good, yeah, funny first line though, I laughed until it got too down!

Dark, Mr Tambourine Man exhaled and looked at Sandwich Toaster, I laughed until it got too dark. I laughed. Until it got too dark, I mean, that's the line.

Sandwich Toaster squinted and asked, was it not down? He said he'd had a laugh about it with his friends, aye, I thought it didn't make sense, becoming too, down, it becoming too down, whatever that meant and whatever it was.

Mr Tambourine Man waited until Sandwich Toaster had said this, and then said well, no, it's dark, it rhymes with bark at the end of the second line, yeah?

Sandwich Toaster raised his eyebrows, really? Then he said maybe, aye maybe, and Sandwich Toaster shrugged his shoulders, anyway, em, it was a good song. He paused.

Mr Tambourine Man said nothing.

Then Sandwich Toaster picked it up again, the conversation about Lost Outside The Tunnel, that bit in the middle of the song, it's major-sevenths on the guitar, and then the keyboards playing the same tune after the guitars, yeah?

Mr Tambourine Man looked up.

Sandwich Toaster said, see, I've been listening to you too! He smiled and headed for the door, saying cheerio, I was right about the major-sevenths thing, heard it, eh!

Mr Tambourine Man put his arms on the desk, turned round and called after Sandwich Toaster, ninths!

Sandwich Toaster turned round, looked back at Mr Tambourine Man, and said what? Mr Tambourine Man said you were wrong, that bit in the middle you were talking about, in the middle of the song, the guitar followed by keyboards, it's ninths they're playing, not major-sevenths. You're right about the keyboards following the guitars though, and even playing the same tune as the guitars, but it's ninths they're actually playing. Not major-sevenths.

Sandwich Toaster said oh aye, whatever, em, see you later. And he left the room, waving behind him.

When he was gone, Mr Tambourine Man looked at Armpits, who had been watching the discussion, and said to him it was ninths, but, em, whatever!

Aye, Armpits said, aye mate.

…

372

The bus pulled away. After it had gone down the road and was just approaching a corner it stopped, the brakes could be heard.

The driver could be seen jumping out of the bus door, he jumped down and he turned and stood on the pavement waving his arms about and shouting something. The engine was still whirring.

The bus started to bounce up and down a bit, and the figures of children standing up at the back of the bus, inside, they could be made out through the emergency exit windscreen. They were jumping and singing.

Some passengers followed the bus driver off the bus and walked away with their shopping or bags or pushchairs. The bus driver watched them all leave, and then he climbed back up onto the bus. It stopped bouncing. Nothing could be seen for a few seconds.

Then the driver re-emerged, pulling a schoolboy out of the bus with him. On the pavement he stood the boy up and held his shoulder with one hand and pointed in his face with the other. From the distance, it could be seen that he was shouting at him, and then the boy waved at the other pupils on the bus, he was punching the air as well.

The driver looked back at the bus, before kicking the boy in the shins. The boy cried out, hopped about, holding his leg with both hands, and then the driver kicked his other shin. The boy lurched forward and bent over towards the driver, and then the driver kneed him in the face and the boy fell backwards and onto the ground.

The driver walked away from the boy who was lying down now and then walked back towards him. A couple of ex-passengers, who had been walking away and had turned round when the boy cried out, ran back towards the scene as the driver leaned over the boy and screamed at him, and then kicked him in the stomach before the passengers reached him and apprehended him. The driver threw his hands up in the air and then stretched them out the way either side of him.

One of the passengers got a phone out of his pocket and the other went onto the bus and came out with the pupils following him.

A few pupils went over to the boy on the ground while the others went across the road, or walked this way and that.

After five minutes, the boy was sitting up on the ground, with the two passengers, the driver and one boy standing beside him, the boy holding two schoolbags.

A police car pulled up to the scene. Two officers got out and one of them pointed to the bus.

The driver got into the bus while the officers and the passengers stood together, the boy stood up.

The engine stopped whirring.

…

Ace walked into the room.

Ace!

Ace, you're back!

The Bin Brigade jumped up, some of them jumped down from the desks they had been sitting on, and some of them went towards him, hey, Ace, how you doing!

Ace laughed and said I'm okay, I'm okay, really, I'm okay, honest, I'm okay! He said he'd just needed time to go away and think about stuff, he and his mum did. But they were back now, I know you know about my mum and dad, but they're working things out. He said he was going to stay on at school.

The Bin Brigade cheered, yeah!

Ace put his hands up in the air, then put them down again. He laughed, yeah, gonni sit some of my exams too, my mum's seen the rector. Got to be positive, don't not do it, do it, that's me from now on! I'm getting some tutors for the subjects I'm still doing, and I've got to go back into a few more of my normal classes, the exam ones.

A few of the class looked down, what, does that mean you'll not come in here again? With us, the Bin Brigade?

Ace smiled, aw, don't worry, I'll still dog two or three lessons now and then and come in here though, he said this to the class, and they cheered again.

Marie got out of her seat.

She approached Ace.

And then she looked at the class, and then looked at Ace and leaned into him and hugged him, looking at the class as she held him, and then she kissed him on the lips, aw, Ace, I've just loved thinking about the time you'd come back, I knew you would, aw, it's great to have you back Ace!

Ace backed away from Marie, smiling, saying aw, I'll definitely be coming back to this classroom every now and then, if that's the reception I get, eh! From the place he had walked back to, he was still holding his hands out and holding onto Marie's hands.

Marie smiled at Ace and looked him in the eyes as she let go of his hands.

Aye, Billy nodded, and smiled, but just keep your distance Ace, eh, you'll no get a kiss off us all but!

They all laughed, and there were smiles all around the class, until Ace said he had to go to Maths now, I'll be back though, afterwards, you can tell me everything that's been going on, hey, where's Kelly? William?

They all stopped laughing or speaking amongst themselves.

Ace raised his eyebrows, oh well, you can tell me when I've finished Maths, yeah? And he walked out the room, I'll see you all later, for definite, yeah?

Marie sat down, smiling to herself.

The Bin Brigade looked at each other.

They cheered again, yeah!

…

Ex-Cop had died.

People were speaking about how they couldn't believe it.

How it was hard to perceive of him being dead.

Of him not being alive.

Anymore.

Ex-Cop.

Ex-Cop had died.

He had died.

He was dead.

The news was being spread all around the school.

The news about Ex-Cop.

It was being greeted all around the school.

Pupils were crying.

Teachers were crying.

9. PULL ME UP WITH GRACE

At the memorial for Ex-Cop's, Chaplain Divine said Ex-Cop had been a person who respected other people, and other speakers said he commanded the respect of people who knew him. Everyone said things that made people who were sitting in the church look at each other after the service and say aw, aw, that was nice, aye, or, aw, that was nice what the chaplain said. As they met in the aisle before they even left the church, they said aw, his wife was awfully nice, I thought the service was really nice, it was just right for him, he was such a nice man.

A pupil and an ex-pupil spoke. Some of the pupils in the pews were sobbing into tissues, holding each other round the shoulders. It wasn't one of those memorial services where someone participating, a speaker, might treat it as an occasion when he or she could say things which drew laughter from the people in attendance, even though people might not expect to be laughing, it wasn't a service like that.

Ex-Cop had only been teaching for a few years, as he'd been in the police force for some time, but people said he'd nevertheless made an impact in the time he was at the school, he'd transformed the way R.E. was taught, or at least the way it was learned, he got the pupils to ask questions, find things out for themselves under his direction in the classroom, he even got some of them, the sixth years, wanting to take exams in it.

The police force was represented at the service by two officers, it was the police that had organised the funeral a few days beforehand. The officers talked to some teachers and pupils and parents afterwards, talking to them about Ex-Cop. Ex-Cop had retired from being an officer when he'd got the cancer, he wouldn't take a desk job, he wanted to go to uni and train in something else, learn another skill, he thought he would live for another ten years, and in the end it was nine. People, teachers, said they felt an admiration for the two police officers who attended the service, aye, they were very nice, weren't they, and nobody commented on the fact that the Phantom had introduced them as a policeman and lady policeman.

After the service, as the day wore on in school, staff had commented on the fact that school had been made to continue for the day, och, how can you go to something like that and then teach straight after it, eh, how can you do it! It was noted that it had been an authority decision, though teachers told each other that they thought the rector should have stood up to the authority, aye, I bet that bleeding arse of a man is just sitting in his office right now, or he's gone home or to the golf course, and probably no-one's gonni notice, or he's said to the office that he's going to a meeting and he's really just pissed off home, the bleeding arse that he is.

There was an anger.

…

Ach, you can't get the promotions these days, son.

Armpits continued, saying teaching, the actual job I mean though, it's something that you can feel good about doing, you can have a shitty day and you can still go home and look yourself up and down in the mirror and say to yourself that you've done some good, know, at least for someone else if not for yourself, and for that alone it's an acceptable job. I mean, you've got

378

a definite career path, you can come in, do the job, get better at it, maybe get a wee bit of promotion, departmental, pastoral, maybe even higher, join the ranks of the senior management, you'd turn into someone everybody hates though, hee hee!

When Armpits had started he had discovered some things about a variety of aspects of the job, well, I found the unexpected aspects of the job initially welcome, something I could brag about in the pub, difficult pupils and how I handled them, eh! Oh aye, you sit there with a beer, and your pals are saying how they could never be a teacher, don't know how you do it and everything, you're quite the hero, a kind of respect you got, know? You feel important, energised, you feel vital, there's a vitality that comes with coping with the pressure, telling people about it, you become a champion in your own life, aye that's it, a fucking champion.

He looked at the papers he was holding under his arm.

Ach, then you realise you're just on a treadmill, and you can't get off it, you just, you can't get off it, ach, you can't get off. The lack of promotion gets to you, the way you used to feel like you were the best teacher in the world, the sense of that, it just disappears soon enough, when you realise everybody can do it. You used to think you could teach anything, Geography, Physics! Just as long as you kept, I don't know, a week ahead of the kids. But then.

He swapped the papers from under one arm to the other, did you know that in England you can teach any subject as long as you've got a qualification to teach one subject? I've got a mate who teaches in the Midlands, he says the P.E. guys get farmed out to departments with staff shortages once they get over the hill, too old to do one lap of the football pitch with the kids, I'm telling you! One minute your third years are holding you aloft when you win the city cup, then you hit forty, and suddenly you're up in front of the headteacher and it's, what other subjects did you like at school, Geography? That's handy, 'cause there's someone retiring at the end of term, you can trade in your tracksuit for a plastic globe and set of fucking coloured pencils!

Ach, you just can't get the promotions these days, Christjesus. Interviews now, it's like they're exams, you need to study, you need to bloody study for them! It's no longer enough to be able to say why you think you're the best guy for the job. You need to have read all the recent documents, the theories of the day, the currently accepted bullshit, and you can't be bothered with the application forms.

He sighed, ach, but you can't get the promotions.

Still, got to look up son!

And he shook his head and smiled.

…

A few of the staff were talking about Kelly, saying that she was away from school for another abortion, that'll be her away for a week or so now, once again, Christ another one! What? That's her second one, her second! Second? What age is she! Not even sixteen yet? Aye, naw, so she can't leave till Easter, she'll be sixteen by then, but god sake anyway, eh! The faces all looked at each other.

Then someone said to the others, I heard she was keeping it this time. The staff looked up, keeping it!

380

A variety of opinions were offered, some of these kids, what are they like eh? They just don't realise what the school does for them, protecting them, know. People agreed, aye, if Social Education serves any half-decent purpose, is it not to teach them how not to get pregnant twice before the age of sixteen man! That's how we protect them, but do they listen? Not a bit of it.

Aye, naw, but when they leave they soon bloody realise it but, don't they always tell you if they come back in for something, or you bump into one of them at the weekend, oh sir, I wish I'd worked harder at school, or it's, I wish I'd listened more at school, eh! Aye, and you smile and tell them that they did their best.

The conversation drifted back to Kelly, aye, that one'll have three or four kids by the time she's twenty-one, and there'll be no house to keep them in I bet!
…

It's all a pretence isn't it. Mr Tambourine Man bowed his head and looked up again, this living, this place eh. The whole living thing, a whole pretence, so it is. We're all just keeping it up, an appearance. The appearance of it all. Total pretence. I'll tell you. Some of us are further up the road than others, but don't you worry, the rest will catch up.

He was looking at the table again and saying, looking down, that none of them were what they used to be, know, you know, we can't be, not anymore, we can't go back. What we've become, eh. And look what I've become, what we've become, where we were, where we've been, but where we are now, attached to this place, the school. The attachment to the thing, the school. Jesus, the school. You can't remember. What was home, before this, and you certainly can't go back there again, this is where you are now, you're stuck here.

Someone came in the staffroom, looked around, went out again, Mr Tambourine Man looked up at the guy, and went on, it's not teaching is it, it's just, us eh, teachers, it's just us, isn't it. Here's, och, nah, listen to me, clever boy now, eh, am I not.

He said that when it began for him, teaching, a career, there was an ease to everything, know, aye, it was easy, a breeze, almost too easy, but, but. But then I got promoted, and it was kind of a trap for me, I couldn't get out. The whole thing's been a process, everything seems okay for a while and then you get pissed off again, things giving you grief all over the place.

He looked at the table, aye, grief, and gradually the job turns into life and then it turns into a life, it is the life your living, the thing your living. And nothing's different, it's all the same and this is the way it's going to be. And then you think that you could have had a different life, the orchestra would have accepted you, and you would have held things together.

And then Mr Tambourine Man said but then, you still might die of cancer anyway.

And he was still looking at the table.

…

During the lunch hour, Sandwich Toaster came back into the staffroom and sat back down again with the Joke Club, after having left the room at the start of lunch, and he was then teased about having been at the toilet for longer than normal, good shite was it, boy!

Sandwich Toaster didn't say much in response to this teasing, he smiled and then didn't smile, smiled and then didn't smile, and just said shut up, or he said

382

get lost yous, heard it, yeah, he managed to be half-smiling as he spoke.

The Joke Club were hooting at the images they created of him sitting down in the toilet, trying to start, but continually being interrupted by folk he heard coming into the toilets, so he couldn't actually get going, were you having to keep holding it in, boy! Ha ha! Must have been agony! Or ecstasy ha ha!

Sandwich Toaster stood up and then sat down again. The Joke Club kept at it, and then Sandwich Toaster asked them to stop, and they quietened down a bit until one of them said they shouldn't have cracked jokes about it and they started hooting again, it's just toilet humour mate!

Eventually Mr Tambourine Man looked over to them and said come on guys, some of us are still bloody eating eh, as he put the lid on his sandwich box. The Joke Club looked over at him, and he said, just, some people are still having their effing lunch, keep it down eh?

The Joke Club stopped talking for a second, then the tannoy came on and when it had finished people in the staffroom started talking again, and from within the Joke Club there were a few whispers and giggles, and then some comments about Mr Tambourine Man's mood these days.

Sandwich Toaster got up and left.

…

Ha ha! But sir, that's not even the stupidest answer someone in here's ever given! The Bin Brigade were telling of how in a History class in the morning that was getting taken by another teacher, Billy had been asked to read out what he'd put in response to a question about when the Battle of Britain had reached its height. The class had been taught that the answer to this would be the late summer of 1940 sir, but Billy had read out from his jotter the answer ten thousand feet, he had memorised how high the planes had been flying over London, sir! A couple of pupils smiled.

The class had giggled, then they gave other examples, one of them had been in a class in second year which was asked to name to countries that mid-nineteenth century immigrants to the USA came from, and Kevin had given the answer Liverpool and Ethiopia, he did sir! One pupil laughed.

Also sir, Billy wrote in a test, when the question was to say what jobs slaves did on cotton plantations, apart from working in the fields, shooting squirrels and other wildlife! Billy grinned, nobody laughed.

Then a pupil said but sir, the peach was when William answered in Geography after the teacher had been talking about when they'd decide to build houses in a town or which part of the town they'd actually plan to build the houses in, William had tried to say it depended on the circumstances that people were in, only he'd said circumcise instead of circumstances sir, go knows why!

Some pupils laughed, they said they weren't laughing at William, with him not being around anymore. They looked at the seat where James usually sat too, James had been in the day before, but hadn't come in today.

Someone said just, it was funny what he said, William, just getting the words mixed up.

Anyone heard anything more about William yet?

…

A radio was on in the staffroom, there was a speech being made, talk of the by-election meant people were showing an interest in the speech. Some of the student teachers, or probationers at the school, made comments about the government trying its best in the circumstances, the circumstances being the present condition of things, economics, society and other categories.

The government? Anybody in the staffroom at the time who had served more than two or three years in the school, in education, said to the students and probationers, listen, best in the circumstances? Can you no see that it's pointless trying to tell the difference between who's in power now and who was in power then, or who's trying to get into power! Circumstances!

The students and probationers looked at each other.

Teachers then went on, taking it in turns to speak, it's pointless trying to tell the difference between what they all say about what they'd do for education if they did get into power! They all seem to kind of half-carry on what the last lot's done, and then when it goes tits-up they actually blame the last lot! The lot who were probably continuing the work of the lot before! Government! Government?

The students and probationers looked out the window, or at the floor.

Someone else said, it seems that whoever is, or whoever was in the government just stumbles from one half-solved crisis to another, creating a crisis that's actually greater than the sum of its parts! Teachers were all looking at each other now, not looking at the students or probationers. I mean, do we ever have an Education Minister for any longer than a year or two these days, it's the new Northern Ireland, that bloody job!

Nobody could think of more than one, aye, naw, now they just change about so bloody frequently it's unbelievable, and they all bloody look like each other as well, or bloody sound like each other on the telly too, em, just call me Mr Blah-de-blah-de-blah!

The students and probationers listened to the staff talk about education and politics and nodded their heads if they established eye-contact with a speaker, and didn't open their mouths.

…

The Phantom explained that for the Bin Brigade, another stage in their development as a group would have been the process of finding out that they were called the Bin Brigade, called this by other people, discovering that they had a name, and now had something of a status, a status given to them by their having a name, the Phantom started to nod as he spoke, aah, they would have a standing, aah, of some sort, aah, well, a standing, aah, apart from the, em, madding crowd as it were, you see, and he would continue to nod as he said these words, the Phantom.

As he nodded, Crossword Freak Number One nodded himself, indicating something of an agreement. Crossword Freak Number Two scratched his head. Crossword Freak Number Three said nothing.

The discovery of themselves as a group led the Bin Brigade to adopt, aah, and the Phantom nodded again, an insular stance against the school, aah, according to my theory, and this turning inwards made them, and still makes them, less dependent upon the body of the kirk as it were, as I like to say, so they then claim the name of, the actual words, the Bin Brigade, for themselves, as a title, and the more they call themselves the Bin Brigade the less other pupils, teachers even, will call them the Bin Brigade, they embrace the whole thing as their own.

Yes, I see, an ownership of the label, that is, said Crossword Freak Number One.

Ah! Like black people saying nigger, or women singer-songwriters saying bitch, Crossword Freak Number Two interjected.

Crossword Freak Number One turned and stared at Crossword Freak Number Two, excuse me, did you just say nigger? Crossword Freak Number Two said yes, but.

The Phantom smiled and clapped his hands together once, and laughed, ha ha, at the very least it is like that, aah, nigger!

That was the Phantom's theory and he said he liked to stick to it.

…

Bicycle Clips had brought in the family tree that he was working on, it's actually very interesting, aye, well, not my family tree exactly, that's just interesting to me, and maybe my family I suppose, tss! But the process, the research, the whole process, you find out loads of fascinating stuff when you're looking up things, aye, how they used to keep records, I don't know, tss!

People around Bicycle Clips looked at him, holding the half-turned pages of their newspapers, and he kept talking, aye, I went with my son to this church in Perthshire a couple of weekends ago, I've been involving him since he dropped out of university, know, just to keep him occupied. Anyway, it was just to have a look through its records, the church, I thought there

387

might be records of marriages there, involving at least two great-great-uncles on my wife's side, but there weren't, but anyway I got talking to the minister there, we were talking for ages, and it ended up with him showing me the church organ, the one they used today, aye, the one actually in the church, and then it turned out that there was some connection between the man who had fitted it, the organ, and someone in my mother's family after all! Oh, only a couple of generations ago, but still, it was something that affected my research, more information, a route to more clues if nothing else, aye!

A couple of people looking at Bicycle Clips blinked and swallowed as he went on, and he said aye, I was fair excited to hear of that connection!

People listened to him as he told of the minister sitting down, so, he wasn't the organist of the church, obviously, but he said he'd had piano lessons when he was younger, a boy, and he sat down and played Abide With Me right in front of us, me and my son, now, I'm no religious, but that tune, there's just something about it, eh, and when he finished, the minister, I asked if my son could have a go, he'd received piano lessons himself, when he was younger, and Bicycle Clips mimed playing a keyboard as he told the story, aye, he was really keen to have a go on that old church organ! So what had happened then was that Son Of Bicycle Clips had sat down and played You Can't Always Get What You Want, and the minister said oh that's lovely, it's got a nice tune, but he, the minister, hadn't known it was by the Rolling Stones, he'd said this when Son of Bicycle Clips had told him it was by the Rolling Stones, the minister had thought it was a John Lennon song, or it sounded like one.

The folk who had been listening to Bicycle Clips nodded as they carried on doing what they were doing.

Bicycle Clips smiled at the story he was telling, oh, ha ha, my son just laughed and said that although it wasn't a John Lennon song, Lennon might have actually used the words, know, you can't always get what you want, eh!

Bicycle Clips sighed, and said aye, it was the first time during the whole trip that my son had showed an interest in anything I was doing, first time in fact since he'd applied to do History at uni before he left school that he'd shown any interest in anything to do with the past at all, aye, tss!

…

A pupil was dressed up as a panda for the day and walking around school in the panda outfit to raise money for charity. Staff supported it, aye, he's a good kid that boy, he's no letting it get in the way of lessons either, it's just him, no-one else is involved, he's a nice lad as well, what charity is it he's collecting for anyway, anyone know? No? Aye, well, he's a good kid anyway. Aye, good kid.

Someone else said aye, but what's it like when he comes into your classroom to ask for money, and it's bloody mayhem for a few minutes eh! Then the few minutes after he's gone as well, when you're getting the excitement to die down so you can get back to Kes or Cal, or whatever book your pretending to read with the kids after you've shown them the film, eh!

People laughed, and someone else said aye, is it not in Gregory's Girl that a wee lad wanders about in an animal outfit too, is it a panda?

The staff discussed this point. Somebody else said aye, naw, was it no Local Hero? The reply from somewhere else in the staffroom was naw, aye, Gregory's Girl. The one with Sean Connery? Somebody else asked, Sean Connery? And everybody else said no, Sean Connery wasn't in Gregory's Girl.

The guy who had said Sean Connery then said no, he had meant to say Sean Connery was in Local Hero, didn't he play the guy who lived on the beach, aye, I realise the panda was in Gregory's Girl, but Sean Connery was the guy who lived in the hut on the beach in Local Hero. Everybody else said naw, that was Fulton Mackay, the guy who lives on the beach. The man who had said it was Sean Connery said yeah, Fulton Mackay. Fletcher!

Someone else then said aw aye, Inspector Mackay! And then asked, was it actually a panda in Gregory's Girl at all? Then, from someone outside the conversation, now coming into the conversation, came the words hey, are you starting a bloody Bill Forsyth appreciation society in here!

Ha ha, folk laughed, naw, but what animal was it again, was it a furry animal? It was. The staff went through several of the possibilities, ostrich, kangaroo, aye, the kind of animals you could get costumes for, one of those Donald Duck ones Elton John wore in the seventies, when was it, was it in Central Park? Eventually someone said penguin. And the teachers all said together, penguin! It was a penguin outfit the wee guy was in! Aye, and every time he bumped into different teachers they would send him to another part of the building, a different room, aye! Though a penguin's not furry, but still. A penguin!

At that point the staffroom door was knocked. It would be a pupil then, given the knocking, it was only pupils that knocked, so no-one shouted come in. Someone went to the door and opened it, hey look, it's the panda! The men cheered, it's the panda!

The panda walked into the staffroom and three or four different people shouted, room sixteen! Room four! Room twenty-eight A!

The panda looked up, what?

Nobody said much, they were just laughing, just, och dinni worry son, how can we help you!

Em, I'm collecting money for cancer sir, my grandad died a couple of months ago, would anybody like to give something?

The place stopped, the people in the place, the staffroom, they stopped what they were doing, nobody spoke for a second or two.

Someone standing beside the noticeboard fidgeted with the card on it from Ex-Cop's wife thanking the staff for the flowers, adjusting how the card hang on the wall, straightening it, then checking it and straightening it again.

No-one laughed anymore, at the penguin thing.

Staff looked at each other, at their feet.

Then teachers dipped their hands in their pockets and came over to the panda who was standing with his tin hanging from his paw, and they all had a word with him as they put money in the tin.

Aye sure, sure son. Woops, here you are there, that's all the coins I've got in my pocket. Aw, good cause son, good choice, here you are. Aye, here you are and all, you collected a lot yet, you think?

And the panda said thanks, then turned and left.

Nobody said anything.

391

…

What about Set The Killing Free, or Haywire, or Mattress Of Wire? Queen's Tattoo? Just Like Gold, or Orchid Girl, all the stuff he recorded around the time of The Boy Wonders, or before it even, the stuff that no-one's ever heard, bloody child genius stuff as well eh, just as much as the stuff that ended up on the album, eh? Mr Tambourine Man raised his eyebrows as he finished the question.

Armpits continued to nod as Mr Tambourine Man spoke about the discordancy of Haywire, aye, and you can't help but detect the rockabilly origins of Queen's Tattoo, and the rest, you know what? Undiscovered gems mate, undiscovered gems.

Gems, aye, Armpits nodded again, undiscovered gems.

Mr Tambourine Man sighed, and he talked more about the nature of being such a gem, and being something that, if found, would then be a discovery, although perhaps if to be known by too many, or even just to be known at all, then could not be a gem anymore.

…

The Bin Brigade walked from one classroom to another, the bell had just gone for the change of period. They had to go from one end of the school to another, going out the building one door, and then walking through the playground, before going in another door, there was a thing in the school about going along corridors inside the building.

As the pupils passed the block where woodwork classes were taught, a few first year pupils who were part of a class lining up waiting to go into the woodwork block shouted at them, there's the Bin Brigade, ah, thickos! Aye, ah, thickos!

The first year class laughed and didn't stop, even when the teacher came out, he called them to order and they got into a line, still looking at the Bin Brigade. One of them shouted aw, see them, you can just take mickey out them, they'll just take it, they won't say anything back! The teacher just waited for the first years to stop.

The first years continued to laugh though, and the Bin Brigade walked on, looking over and back at the first years, not saying anything back, just taking it. When they got to where they were going, in another part of the playground, they talked about some of the first year pupils, speaking about how they hated them.

Sam pointed out one boy and said to Billy, see that one, he's gonni get it from me one day.

Billy nodded, rubbed a finger back and forth across his face between his mouth and his nose and put his hands in his pockets.

...

The by-election was going to be taking place in the next week. And Billy was telling the class that when his dad had been in the school a couple of years before, when it was being used as a polling station, he'd played a trick on one of the people helping with the voting, it was his dad who had played the trick. Billy asked, what do you call them sir, know, the guys, and the women too, that help with the voting, I don't know what they're called, is it officers, aye? Something officers?

Billy said his dad thought the polling station officers thought they were better than everybody else. Sure they do sir? And all they are is just bloody, sorry sir, they're just workers hired from the banks or council offices or whatever.

Someone threw a rolled up ball of paper across the classroom, it bounced on a desk and ended up on the floor. Billy watched it land.

Anyway, he continued, my dad thought he'd ask a dead stupid question just to see if they were so stuck up that they'd actually believe someone was so stupid. He went into the wee bit where you fill in the voting form and when he came out there was this huge black box with a sign on it saying put your votes here, or place votes here, or something like that, and there was a thick white arrow pointing at the slot you put the vote paper in. So my dad finished voting and went right up to the wee women helping and coughed loudly, and said, em where do you put the votes?

The class giggled. A couple of pupils looked at each other and shrugged their shoulders, what's he getting at, where do you put the votes?

And Billy said that one of the women pointed at the slot in the box and said to his dad, you place it in here sir. Just where the arrow's pointing sir. Sir! Haha!

Billy leaned back on his chair, my dad could hear them laughing at him as he walked away, and all the time he's laughing at them eh!

But Billy, someone said, would they not just think your dad was dead stupid?

Aye, Billy said, but that was the point eh! He looked around, aw, you don't understand!

...

The children here just imagine I work at the school simply to see them when they're in trouble, and I wish it were not so true, but those are the circumstances now. The Phantom had his hands

394

clasped, squeezing his knuckles down and moving them a bit to the left, a bit to the right. Every so often he chewed his lip at a corner.

It's over for me, nobody has to tell me that, promotion, now. He said, when I think about sitting in here for the first time all those years ago, imagining how it would go on, that it could go on, and look, now, I ask myself, others, what have I achieved? Tell me that! How have I progressed! I'll never get a head's post now, I know it, nobody has to tell me that. Aah. Passed over, that last time, at interview, and how many times before that? All this time.

He paused, and then he said aah, perhaps I should have been happy with what I had, I should be happy with what I have, accept the circumstances, but I had to fight them didn't I. Oh! Aah. Now, oh dear. I must have sounded so absurd, I have been, so absurd!

If I died, would the people here cry for my passing? At a memorial service? Feel that they couldn't work for the day? I think not, indeed!

He looked up, speaking, you don't know, you don't know. All I am is what everybody here thinks I am, I'm not who I think I am, not anymore, not who I thought I was. Not anymore. Who I should have been. This place has chained me, and when it first did, for a while I was happy, content, not to be, aah, free, free from the place, this place.

Eventually though, you see, I realised I couldn't get away, I was here, this was where I could be found. The Phantom raised his fist to his face and then lowered it.

He sighed again, I know, this week is your last week, aah, next week is your last week, Wednesday. I must try and talk to you before then. You've done well.

He looked to the side, I know so much!

…

Sometimes, when Ace was mentioned by some staff, or at least a couple of times when he had been mentioned by a teacher in the staffroom, it had been discussed as to whether he was a homosexual, or not, Ace.

Shakespeare had said a few times that Ace raised the issue of homosexuality and the law in the English class, or homophobia in schools, homophobia in the workplace, and when pupils in the class expressed views about it, Ace chastised them, he said to them that their attitudes were stereotypes, the same as the attitudes of teenagers today in general, and that they, their attitudes, would change as they became adults.

Shakespeare said that Ace had also shouted once in the lesson, in an outburst of his during a class debate, teenagers are homophobic, even me! Whatever that meant, Shakespeare said. Then Ace had said that the teenagers would change, aye, he was saying stuff that I think his trendy dad would have taught him, about how teenagers would become more liberal, or at least more tolerant, as they entered adulthood, and then they would become homophobic again once they had kids of their own, and the Shakespeare sighed, it was too deep for me, homophobic, liberal, tolerant then homophobic again, too deep, man!

Another English teacher, in his first year of teaching, said aye, I took Ace's class once, Jesus, that boy does indeed have pretty fey mannerisms, like Morrissey, or that guy out of Belle and Sebastian. Shakespeare came back, saying aye but, I reckon the boy's heterosexual, but actually wants people to think he's either gay or bisexual, or even wants people to think that he's confused about his sexuality, but that Ace is most definitely not confused about his sexuality, though he's definitely confused about something, that boy seems to have a lot going on in his head at the moment.

The rest of the staff looked at each other, someone said aye, naw, nah, he's just gay.
…

When I was at school, no listen, when I was at school, Armpits held his arm up to the people laughing at him, no listen, I'm telling you, just listen, and he bowed his head and angled it, and looked around at his colleagues, I'm just saying, when I was at school we had to just bloody toe the line, do as we were told even if we thought a teacher was wrong or unfair, or just stupid.

Two or three others laughed at him, aye, and where did you go to school!

It doesni matter where I went! Armpits was protesting, saying look, I know I went to a fee-paying school, but all it means is I didn't have to follow pointless rules and suffer from a bad education, like some of those, all of you, who went to state schools and couldn't do anything about it, I shouldni have to apologise for it!

Mr Tambourine Man, who had been looking down at the card table, then turned to Armpits and said to him, look, for once, can't you see? He shouted, can't you see! Can't you see! You can enjoy your position of being the bloody union rep, and you can play the oppressed citizen all you want, nobody in here's going to see you as anything other than someone who's choosing to be working class, rather than it being your condition, they perceive your condition as being a choice. Stop playing your wee game of politics and just accept you can't do anything about anything. Eh? Just stop it eh!

Everybody in the staffroom looked at Mr Tambourine Man. Mr Tambourine Man looked around.

Armpits looked at Mr Tambourine Man, fuck man, what's the fuck's up with you these days? All you want to do is put a fucking downer on everything!

Mr Tambourine Man turned his head to look away from Armpits, then turned back to look at him again.

Bicycle Clips stood up to stand beside Armpits, and put his hand on his shoulder before saying come on son, come on pal, let's sit down.

Aye, Armpits sat down, looking up at people around the scene. He looked at Mr Tambourine Man, aye ya.

Mr Tambourine Man was looking at the wall again, saying nothing.

Someone said to him em, you look like you're about to say something.

Mr Tambourine Man shook his head before Bicycle Clips wlked across the staffroom and took him by the elbow and walked with him out of the door, with Armpits sitting down, watching the pair of them leaving.

…

A teacher was talking about someone who'd been speaking at the by-election hustings during the week, quite impressive I thought, he was a candidate for one of the smaller parties, I don't know which one it was.

Anyway somebody, one of the candidates there, and the teacher scratched his head as he spoke, somebody, one of the big parties' candidates I think it was, don't know which, they're all the same, anyway, the other candidates were talking about the difficulties faced by some people today, the usual stuff they all go on about, and someone said that circumstances are just against everyone, and everyone applauded and said hear hear, or whatever it is people shout, and all the candidates, or most of them, they all agreed too that misery could just be waiting for people, anyone, just around the corner, it was like some people would just know that they were destined to never lift themselves out of where they were, so Christ knows what it was that kept them going. And whenever a candidate said something like this, the people there cheered or nodded, like it was, I don't know, a truth, and a universal one too. And then this fellow had just stood up and said no, no, no, you're wrong, it wasn't even his turn to speak, but he just said no, you're wrong, to the whole meeting, everyone who'd been clapping, he told them they were all wrong, well, there was just this silence, and so he had to go on speaking. Everyone was looking at him, this guy, and he just said that, that if you think that everything's against you from the start, then you might as well pack it in, and never fight to get your mother's name further up the waiting list for a hip replacement, never make any effort at all, never try to get that next promoted post in the organisation you work for, it wasn't really politics the guy was talking, more a philosophy, a mode of thinking, he said you're better to sustain yourself, those were the words he used, sustain yourself, those were the actual words! Sustain yourself, by taking opportunities, actually creating them, he was

399

bloody impressive, got a round of applause himself, aye, and the other candidates all agreed with him, whatever party they were from. They were like nodding dogs, once they saw that everyone in the audience was clapping!

There was a kind of nodding of heads from those listening in the staffroom, and then someone else asked the teacher, so, you voting for him then?

And the teacher said naw, I'd never vote for someone like that, he doesn't stand a chance!

…

The class were talking about something, amongst themselves, lowering their voices every now and then, and then from among their voices it was Kevin who spoke, saying that he gave some of his money to his mum, know, a fiver or something off my pay from the milk round.

The rest of the class looked at each other, and a few of them looked down, maybe a couple actually looked at Kevin. He looked back at them, what is it? He had a bit of a frown on his face. No-one replied to his question, and he said so what, so what, he gave his money to his mum, and so would they if they worked as well, he said, I mean, she pays for all my clothes and food and that.

Some pupils were looking at him and then looking away, not looking at each other.

Kevin turned to face the front, the conversation between the pupils had been getting held amidst chairs all facing towards each other around a couple of desks, but now Kevin was opening the conversation up, isn't that normal sir, wouldn't you give your mum money if you were working and living at home eh? Loads of people will do that, eh, kids, know, and then he looked at everyone else, see?

Billy turned his chair to sit facing his desk and picked a pencil up, aye okay Kev, okay.

Kevin continued, and I'd still give her a bit of money once I've left school and all, and he continued to talk about how even when he wasn't living at home his mum would still need a bit of money, it would be to look after my wee brother, and I'd give it to her, money, so I would, yous just don't understand, you don't understand anything, and Kevin then said that was just how life was, just, just that's how it is, and yous'll just have to accept it when the time comes for you too, whenever.

He looked back at them all, and lowered his voice, just, just, whenever, eh.

…

Armpits had been asked by Sandwich Toaster if he thought there were still the same promotion chances in teaching now as there had been when he came in.

Not a fucking chance mate, Armpits said there were two reasons, one being son that there are less promoted posts about since local governments started trying to save money and cut the number of people getting given extra paid responsibilities, and the other being son that in order to get promoted, god knows what it is that you have to do, it doesn't seem to be about being good at your job anymore, Christjesus, god forbid that you'd get promoted for actually doing a decent day's work! Naw, you've got to go on this fucking course or that fucking course, get this qualification or that, and they tell you that you've actually got to pay to get some of these fucking qualifications just so you're qualified to get promoted, even though there's still no guarantee that you'll even get promoted, I mean, how many other professions make you pay actual money to develop your skills!

Sandwich Toaster looked at some of the papers that he had in his hand, they were articles and press cuttings, and he shuffled them about, em.

Armpits shook his head, naw. Courses? No thanks mate, and he continued, talking about how he reckoned that you were either picked for promotion just after the start of your career because of how you fitted into the school you were at, or you were put down as someone who could be relied on to teach well, make the kids enjoy being at the school and so on, but no-one was going to give you anything extra to do, I'm telling you, or at least they aren't gonni give you any more money for doing it, Christjesus!

Sandwich Toaster said the reason he'd been asking, it's just, em, I had to read this article by Davis and Moore, I was, em, given it to read, em, at an education, em, course I was on, something I had to go on, part of being new in the job and such, it was compulsory.

Armpits interrupted him, see, that's what I mean man! Sandwich Toaster said what do you mean, that's what you mean? Davis and Moore, man, Davis and Moore, Armpits put his hands in the air, see, I don't know who or what you're talking about! Davis and Moore! A course!

Crossword Freak Number One put his paper down, then picked it up again when Armpits looked at him and said put your glasses back on man.

Sandwich Toaster reached into his briefcase, it's just I went on this course and got given this set of notes, and then I bought the book, it links in sociology with education and.

Jesus man, Armpits broke into what Sandwich Toaster was saying, shaking his head at him, one, I don't know how you can bring yourself to read that shite, and two, I don't know how you've got the fucking time, at least, if you're trying to do your job well!

Sandwich Toaster started to put the book away.

Armpits said naw, naw, don't do that, I'm sorry man, sorry, tell us about it, eh? And Armpits reached down and lifted Sandwich Toaster's arm back up, Sandwich Toaster's hand was still holding the book, the book was hanging, opening up so the pages separated.

Sandwich Toaster said, half-looking down at the bit of a book, with highlighter pen marks on it, hang on, let's see, here, well, em, if attainment in education, as a pupil I think this refers to, is linked to social function when you leave school, I mean, when the pupils leave school, know, and have some kind of social function, know, a job, whether they have a family etcetera etcetera, doesn't education socially stratify society, and then the brightest and best people get the best paid jobs, with the most responsibility?

Armpits looked at him. He blinked and looked straight ahead, aye, go on son.

Sandwich Toaster continued, talking about whether income could be linked to academic performance, or was it intelligence which led to status being accorded to people, that status being in relation to whatever capacity it was, intelligence or performance.

Armpits raised his eyebrows, Christjesus, I was really making the effort to try and understand you there son, but I've not got a fucking clue! I think I'm reasonably intelligent, I know, I know, I'm a fucking idiot at times, and half the things I say are just shite, but I'm reasonably intelligent when I want to be, and, but it's not just that all that stuff you're talking about bewilders me, it's that it just doesn't fucking matter! And I'm thinking that maybe it should matter and I just don't see it, but in actual fact, it just fucking doesn't, it doesn't matter! And maybe I should feel bad or guilty that I know that it doesn't, but I just don't, Christjesus, Davis and Moore!

He looked around and saw Mr Tambourine Man come in to the staffroom.

Mr Tambourine Man went up to the urn table and asked across to Armpits if he'd eaten all the biscuits, where's the fucking penguins ya fat turd! Armpits said aye, aye, I had two, but there were more than that there after I had mine.

Mr Tambourine Man laughed, and Armpits walked over to join him at the card table, pals? Mr Tambourine Man said aye, pals, sit down man, tell me about your day.

Sandwich Toaster stayed sitting where he was and flicked through the pages in his book. He caught the eye of Crossword Freak Number One, then put the book back in his briefcase.

…

My dad killed himself because of me! Marie turned round to face the girl she was shouting at across the room, and her voice rose and the tone she had been adopting changed. She stared for a bit, and turned back again.

The class was looking at Marie, nobody said a thing.

Then, or after a while, the girl said oh, Marie, I didni mean it like that, Marie, I never meant it like that, and she looked at Marie and cried.

One of Marie's eyes was watering, and she got up out of her seat and went across to the girl and said it was okay, I'm not getting at you, honestly, I'm not, and Marie put her arm over the girl, around her shoulder, I'm sorry, I know you didn't mean it like that.

The girl smiled back up at Marie and put her hand on Marie's.

There, it's alright now, said Marie, and they didn't move, the two of them, and then the girl said come on and sit down here Marie, she pulled out the chair beside her and Marie sat down, putting her head in her hands.

…

Sandwich Toaster said that he only came into teaching because he couldn't think of anything else to do.

He'd actually always wanted to go into something involving engineering, aye, not the difficult stuff, but cars, old ones and such like, or motor mechanics even, I fancied that as a college course, but my dad encouraged me to go to uni to study. I say encourage but it was more like forced, you'll go to university or you'll be leaving this house son! And I'd ended up doing English there, at uni, I only did that because I couldn't think of another subject, and I wasni bad at English at school, and then suddenly I had a degree in English Literature and I never knew what to do with it, so I ended up doing teacher training and then I was a teacher, banzai!

He sighed, and now I'm stuck, I don't like it, I don't enjoy it, and I don't think I'm very good at it. Not

405

like you, I mean, I've heard the guys here in the
staffroom say you'll make it, know, when you're not in
here they say it, and you're still a student. It's your last
week next week, yeah? The Wednesday you finish, is
it? Back at the uni for a couple of days after that, hand
in essays and things, aye, heard it.

He looked at his feet, me, I'm already a year in,
and I'm just. I mean. I'm just. It's just that they don't
say that about me, do they, they don't say that I'll make
it, do they.

…

I like my dad but. No in the same way that yous
lot like your dads though, Billy frowned, but still. He
looked around at the class and said that his dad had
always told him not to worry about school, and that
he'd got by in life without qualies or anything, know,
he got his fourth year exams, but he'd never needed
them for anything, there had never been any
requirement for them since, and he said Billy would be
the same.

Somebody asked if Billy didn't think it was a
mistake just to be leaving at Easter, just to not come
back to school at all, ever? Seeing as he'd been one of
the ones put down to actually do a few exams? Billy's
brainy sir!

Billy said no I'm no, shut up, no I'm no!

And a couple of pupils said aye, compared to us
well!

Billy spoke about what the point would be,
know, the point in saying something's a mistake, eh, he
looked at the pupil who asked about making a mistake,
I canni go back now though, can I, say I'm coming
back and all, it'd just be stupid, I'd just look stupid, and
he pursed his lips, then he said anyhow, the school

406

willni let me now anyway. He looked down, ach, exams are only for folk going to get jobs that need them, and I don't ever want a job like that, he was using his thumbnail to flick a piece of wood out of the desktop.

The class looked about at each other and at Billy, a couple of pupils said maybe Billy might change his mind in the future, and that regret might be what he felt about leaving school before doing any exams.

Billy didn't reply to them, he just said sir, sure everybody says you might as well live for the present time, eh sir? Well, not everybody, but some people eh. And he followed this by saying, it's stupid to think about what you've done once you've done it eh, regrets and that, or, em, just well, you've done it, haven't you. Eh? You never know what's gonni happen.

…

Somebody said in the staffroom, what do you expect from a child who comes from a family like that, I mean did you see the mother on the news? They were all talking about the case of William's family, though the called him Willie, there had been a few items on television over a couple of days while there had been some kind of hearing in court.

People were agreeing, saying things like yeah, what do you expect? And, the state of her, did you see! And all the hangers on behind her coming out of court, aye, disfunctional or what! It's no wonder the boy couldn't work out what he thought was right or not!

And, it's no wonder the boy turned out the way he did.

…

Scout said did you see me eh, and the people in here saying what a good man, about me they were talking, eh! He smiled and then stopped smiling. And

407

tutted, a hero, a hero I was. He sighed then, a hero for an afternoon, he was saying, and asking was that what you had to do to get recognition in this place, he shook his head, bit his lip, recognition! His lips turned up a bit at the corners, he was half-grinning, and here's me been in here longer than practically anybody else in the normal staff, there's only the deputy rector's been here longer, aye!

Scout waited a few seconds before continuing, aye, he's alright for a man him, the deputy rector, he always at least says hullo in the corridor, aye okay, he upsets a few folk, those who think he's stuck in his ways, old school tie, people who've been passed over for promotion, but then, you always get people like that, don't you, and I mean, who doesn't upset their colleagues once in a while?

And Scout continued, people still show that they know he exists though, know! He shifted on his chair, me, I'm no saying I'm nothing in here, but you see what I'm getting at, the others, their attitude to me, know. The ones in here. I suppose there's always got to be somebody who's a nobody. He laughed, and he wasn't smiling as he laughed, heh heh, and said, I guess folk in the workplace always need a spare part around, eh.

He stopped talking for a moment and looked up, then, I could tell them things, know, you know? They're interested in football, they talk about it on a Monday, know, folk have got an interest. But they don't answer me, do they, you've seen it, you've seen it haven't you, they just don't answer. They do hear me though. I think they listen.

He looked up and out of the window, that Joseph, he's nothing but a wasted talent, and there's nothing worse in a boy. Dad's on methodone I heard, hundred and twenty mills a day, aye, down from a hundred and fifty at one point. Don't think he uses anymore, but used to, big time. Mum's been on and off for years. That Joseph, he'll end up the same way, even if he does end up getting taken on by a club, and know why? Money, 'cause they'll give him money.

Aye, nothing worse than wasted talent.

…

If I was at the Palace of Versailles I'd have let the German people in, to join the meeting, Marie was speaking, wasn't it unfair that everything was presented to Germany just like that sir, was it a Diktat they called it sir?

No way, Sam intervened and said he'd never have let them in. Marie didn't reply, she looked at him and smiled when he started talking. Sam went on, aye, I mean, they'd flaming started the war, how can you let them have a say in how the treaty would get written, Sam looked at the rest of the class who looked at Marie, who still didn't say anything.

They all looked back at Sam, who said aw, you just think she's right about everything you do, and he waved his hands at the rest of the class.

Billy said well, maybe Marie is right, and maybe it wasn't fair to the Germans, because didn't sir teach us that the war started after that Austrian guy got shot, and he was Austrian and it was guys from somewhere else that shot him, not Germany, isn't that right sir? Ah, Sam! So there you are, the British could have been the bigger people about the thing and just let the Germans in eh!

Sam insisted, look, at the end of the war the British and French said that the Germans had started the

409

war, and they'd won the war, the British and French, they won the war so they must be right because they won the war, and if they were right and they said that the Germans had started the war then the Germans must have started the war, and anyway, Germany signed the treaty and the treaty said in it that they were guilty of starting the war.

The class looked at him, nobody said anything, Marie looked at her desk.

Ah see, Sam smiled, none of you can argue against that!

…

Negatives, it's all about negatives, the Phantom had his head down, sitting at his desk, you'll have looked at the American Revolution at university no?

He continued, Edmund Burke and all that, an Irishman, recognising the oppression suffered by the colonists, trying to tell the English that something dramatic was happening across the Atlantic, appealing to the Englishness of the English by telling them how English the colonists were, telling them to loosen the reins in America like the Sultan of Turkey did across his empire, loosen the reins, loosen the reins! All his political life, watching the trouble in America.

He broke off from the American Revolution for half a minute, actually I think I can remember my Joyce tutor at university saying something similar about Dubliners, any Irishness being simply a negative of Englishness, or some such argument.

He paused and then returned to America, and the colonists starting to call themselves American, defining themselves as being not English, like the Scots so many times before, aah, and, aah, yes, yes like the Irish later, just before partition, like a mistreated lover,

like a dog that's been kicked around by his owner, like
someone being passed over for promotion.

He fiddled with his glasses sitting on his desk,
enemies, without enemies what are we, you see?

The Phantom raised a fist and said the fight, the
fight! And, should we not take strength from the fight,
thwart the thwarted ambition, oh yes, aah, then he said
he realised that he had forgotten that he'd been talking
about the American Revolution, aah, or the War of
Independence as they like to call it!

He started to look at the papers on his desk, aah,
now, did I call you in here or did you come to see me?
…

It's a redemption thing, you know? Mr
Tambourine Man was staring straight at Armpits as he
talked to him, redemption, a begging letter. Armpits
said you're scaring me man! Hmmf, Mr Tambourine
Man grinned, but seriously, do you not think Back On
Board is a cry for help, or forgiveness of some kind?

Armpits stuck out his lip, em to be honest mate
it's the one song I'm not really all that wild about, I can
imagine it being a good sing-song in a concert mind,
arms waving and such, lighters out everybody, hee hee!
But that aside.

Naw naw, you've got it all wrong man, Mr
Tambourine Man waved his arm in front of his face. He
looked down at the ground.

Then Mr Tambourine Man stood up and
slammed his hand down on the table in front of him,
god sake man, can you not see past a bloody melody,
look somewhere deeper for the thing, whatever thing
you're seeking, the thing! The thing!

Armpits looked back at him and then at the two
or three people who were staring at the pair of them.

411

Mr Tambourine Man shouted, I'm telling you, it's a redemption thing, he's saying pull me up with grace! Why do people die of cancer! He slumped backwards in his chair and cried.

A couple of people got up and walked out, one of them muttering, here we go again.

Armpits signalled to the other teachers who were left in the staffroom, and they looked down and carried on with what they were doing.

Mr Tambourine Man was sobbing, Armpits approached his friend, come on man, let's go for a walk eh.

…

Armpits sat down at the end of the day. The whole thing's wrong isn't it, it is, it's all wrong, or else I'm just a sick bastard. And fuck, don't say I'm a sick bastard!

He had a pencil and he was lifting it up and down, tapping each end of it in turn on the table. He talked about how the folk round here did nothing and how he couldn't change them, I don't even want to change them, eh, but Christjesus, if they don't piss me off every day now, he waited a second, then he said, fucking teachers, it's just fucking teachers, they've only got themselves to blame.

He said there'd been a day of action the term before, it was a thing with other unions about pensions and other things attached to contracts, and you know how many came out, here, out of forty-something in the union? Fifteen! Fifteen! We've not got a clue, and therefore we do not have a fucking chance!

It was the old staff as well that came out, I don't know, all the folk who've just come in to teaching recently, they don't realise, they don't realise what's happening, they've not seen it happening in front of them. Mind how we teach about the Plains Indians in the third year? And the kids learn about how all the old chiefs went along with the treaties after Sand Creek, Wounded Knee, all that stuff? Fort Laramie and everything. But the young bucks, Crazy Horse and the like, they couldn't let it go, they didn't realise they couldni win against the government, they wanted to fight? Well it's the bloody opposite in education!

Thatcher, Blair, and the sons of Thatcher, I've said it before, fucking mark my words eh, just mark my fucking words. He sighed. Ach, it's not teachers really, it's everybody, just people, just people. And they just don't think to do anything about it, they don't know that's there's something they might be able to do.

Armpits leaned back on his chair and hung an arm over the back of it. Hmmf! It's as if everybody wants to say, listen to me everybody, but not me really!

He looked at the table. Aye, maybe it's just me who doesn't know what's happening.

He held his hands up, they go eh, sorry mate, but we're not taking part, we don't want to be political. That's all they can say to you, Christjesus, at least if they thought about things just for a second and then decided to bloody opt out then fair enough, it would irritate you, but you wouldn't mind, at least they'd have taken the matter into some consideration, but no, bloody straight out with it. We don't want to be political!

The faith I used to have, fuck. I might as well give up eh. I mean, Christ look at me, here I am, still trying to get a promotion for better pay, and all the time I'm thinking, what, do I not work hard enough as it is?

Armpits looked at the window.

And while I'm thinking about it, could someone not say I was a fucking hypocritical bastard too, going for a management position in the first place? I mean, I am, am I not?

He kept staring.

And some of they bastards who are promoted, who've actually started climbing the ladder, they actually hate kids, hate pupils, they do, they hate them! They think this place is somewhere to turn up at eight-forty-five and leave at three-thirty on the fucking dot, and they're the ones who're fucking running the show, in actual control of the thing, the whole shazam, the total thing!

And deciding if I should get an extra forty pound in my wage packet at the end of the month!

Sometimes, ach!

They can fuck off, eh, just.

10. BUT THEN I'M TIRED

Oh hi sir, hi!

Hang on, I'll just move these bags, sit down beside me, seriously, have a seat, sir!

Woops, watch yourself, this driver's a bit crazy! So.

How're you doing, how is everyone, will you say hi to the gang for me!

This gonni be your last day, really?

Aw sir!

Em, I'm just going to meet my mum in town to go shopping. I'm going to have a baby, I'm so excited!

I know, I know what you're thinking, you're thinking, she's mad, doesn't know what she's doing, no, no, it's alright, I understand.

But honestly, really, I totally wasn't upset when I found out, I was just, well. okay, I was upset!

But my mum and me talked.

I know it must look like, well, like I don't know what I'm doing, but honestly I really want this, and I know I can look after it.

Sixteen, I am, well, fifteen, fifteen, but I'll be sixteen in the summer and the baby won't be born until October, and my mum said I can stay in the house as long as I want, she's getting round to the idea now, aw, she'll be all over it when it arrives!

The father?

Och, who needs fathers!

If it wasni for him I wouldn't be in this mess!

I mean, I really want the baby, I'm just saying mess because of all the stuff I've had to do, the doctors, the forms and stuff.

I really do.

Want the baby.

Anyway, he's at another school, and he's got two wee sisters, twins, both of them have got disabilities, I think it's physical with one of them and physical and mental with the other, it's such a shame.

I've never met them though, the sisters.

But I know that his family can't afford to pay for a baby.

It's okay.

So, you're leaving the school, wow!

Well, aye, of course you weren't going to be staying, but still, I can't believe it, that's been nearly three months you've been here!

There I mean!

Did you like it?

Did you think it was a good school?

Have you been at many others?

Aye it is, it is a good school.

I've got loads of friends there, lots of memories.

Friends for life.

I hope!

Boys and girls.

Aw, there were a few boys I had got my eyes on, might land one in the next couple of years, get a husband.

If anyone'll have me, that is!

Naw, none of the Bin Brigade! Sam? Billy? Kevin's nice, but he'll never leave home.

Still, the Bin Brigade were a real hoot eh!

We had some good times eh!

Aw, the Bin Brigade.

I should never have actually joined that lot, I was a good girl in classes, hard worker too, my mum always made me do my homework.

416

Then I had to be off school for a wee while.

Em.

Em.

Look I'm not going to pretend anything, you probably know I had to have an abortion.

Then I came back to school and suddenly I'd been moved loads of classes, I was in with the Bin Brigade most of the time.

I didn't mind, I quite enjoyed it.

And anytime I told people to shut up slagging me they would stop, so.

I liked Marie, I used to think I wanted to be like her.

I told her once, and she said that was stupid and that she sometimes wished she was like me.

Isn't that funny!

I know she was just being nice though, but it was actually still nice to hear her say it.

Anyway this is my stop here, just got to get some money then find my mum, you going on to the school yeah?

Just get past you here, woops, sorry, hee hee!

Aw see you later sir, no, you enjoy your last day, don't you worry about me, just take care of yourself, all the best for the future.

Have a good life!

…

Did you ever get your essay written, the sociology one?

I could give you some of my Open University notes, that is, once I'm finished with them of course, and I'd like them back, of course.

I just mean.

I like to keep things.

417

You don't think they'd be much use?

Well, just call me here at the school if you think you may need them.

I was wondering if you had seen on the news last night when they were showing industrialists and businessmen saying that children leaving school are ill-equipped for employment, lacking in skills, the schools were missing something out.

You hear my colleagues in the staffroom saying how maybe these people are right, the industrialists, the businessmen, how education should be about skills as well as knowledge.

As if we're not teaching skills in our subjects!

All of our subjects do have something to offer in the skills area, indeed, the pupils learn about communicating with each other in Modern Languages, or in Physics there are problem-solving tasks all the time.

Quite simply, job skills are learned on the job, you know?

You know?

I saw those people on the news last night, and it's all very well to say that schooling should, what do they say nowadays?

Track?

Yes indeed track!

It's all very well to say that schools, or education, should track and respond to society's needs, and in particular last night there was some learned scholar putting an economic argument forward that schooling should reflect the economy's demands, but just because mass education has been brought about as a result of industrialisation, does that mean that industry should control education?

418

Yes indeed, mm!

Hmm.

So, have you, you know, are you commited to teaching, you feel the calling, ha ha?

I always felt I should be a teacher.

Learning, that's what life is, isn't it, what do they say, a curve, the learning curve, but do we learn more as we get older, that is the thing!

Do we learn less?

Do we try to learn more, want to?

Yes, more a learning parabola, a parabola, that is, we hit a peak!

Perhaps that is the danger we have to watch out for.

This is why I'm doing my Open University course, I need to learn as much as I can, and it informs my teaching, it really does, I can inject my lessons with general sociological observations, I don't have to tell the pupils that's what I'm doing, but I do generally feel.

I feel.

That if the pupils feel you have a good knowledge base, they will be more likely to feel that you are worth listening to, at least in relation to the subject you're trying to teach them, to get them a pass in an exam in.

So, ah well, well.

I suppose you've been doing very well here, I'm sure you don't need me to give you, ah, a pep talk.

Well if I don't see you before the end of the day, then all the best young man, that is, of luck!

…

Aw, hey sir, this is your last day, right?

I'm sorry I'm going to miss your last lesson this afternoon, I've got to go on a college visit today, part of getting ready for next year.

Yep, college, for definite, I just love thinking about it!

I'm going to go with my mum.

She's really backing me up with this, I'll get good qualifications, I'm not going to let her down.

Em.

We'll visit dad's grave at the weekend, it'll be the first time, for me.

Mum told me dad had always been depressed.

I think she told me just after he died but I wasn't listening to anything anybody was telling me at that time.

She says it wasn't me that made him, you know what.

I still think I kind of contributed to causing him to, em.

I know I must have.

But.

Have to try and deal with it.

Starting to see a counsellor tomorrow night, and every week after that.

Well, we'll see.

We'll see.

Reality eh.

Me and Ace then, nope, don't know what'll happen there, what'll happen at all, if anything.

We've been on and off since primary one almost!

He's had loads of girlfriends.

Though I've never kissed anyone but him.

Went to the cinema with a fifth year boy last Saturday but just let him hold my hand.

And I wanted to go in the afternoon and not at night, I think some boys think I'm weird!

Ace and me though, we'll keep in touch, for definite.

Don't really know what he's going to do, where he'll go.

Who knows, maybe one day when he's a famous actor he'll ask me to marry him!

Aw, he's so talented, and my mum likes him, she always has.

My dad didn't though, well he didn't like Ace's mum and dad, so there you are!

Still, perhaps I'll be a famous writer first, and then Ace'll have to beg me to marry him!

Dreams eh!

Reality.

And then dreams.

Realities and dreams.

Look at this place.

My old school, I got sent to it when I was in primary four, it was terrible, the pressure you were under to do well for your parents, the staff, the name of the school!

Everything reeked of money there, and I don't just mean the classrooms, the PE facilities, music, science labs.

All the girls there, they were all loaded with money, and they just thought that because they were loaded that meant they were better people.

It made me feel sick to be a part of it, really, I thought I was going to throw up half the time.

They should bomb the place.

Or create another world for all the people who've been to, or who go to schools like that, a city with houses and cars and jobs just for them.

They can't mix with anyone else anyway.

Girls from there, they've never talked to me once since I left to come here, they cross the street rather than say hi, and I know they all giggle at what they think I've become.

And look what I have become.

I'm proud, sir.

I'm proud of my mum, and my dad.

And I'm proud of me.

I used to look at myself in the mirror and say, imagine me, in the Bin Brigade.

Then I realised, wow!

They're the best people I've come across in my life, the best friends I've had at school.

And I don't really see any of them out of school, just say hi, or how are you in town, or on the bus or something. They have a laugh with each other, and they might fall out but they don't lie to each other and they can rely on each other.

Some days I only came into school to be with them.

They let me get on with my work at the back of the room if I have a lot to do.

I'll be okay, I know I will.

My dad, well, I know I'll carry that with me for the rest of my life.

Och, it's okay.

Och.

So, can I have a hug?

Good luck sir, you're a good teacher, stick at it!

I'll remember you when I write my
autobiography!

…

I'm doing the best I can here.

Know, try to fit in, get along with the guys.

Get along, aye, heard it.

Thing is, I think it's appalling that we have a
male and female staffroom, yet I still come in here all
the time.

I don't even tell my mates, the ones that don't
teach, about the staffrooms, that it's like this, well I do
actually, but I say I go into the neutral room.

And my wife, we've just got married, she thinks
I'm getting on great, heading for promotion and all, and
I can see how anyone would try and go about that,
achieving it, but it's just not what I want.

I don't.

I used to be in a band, a good one, I played a bit
of guitar, and the bass too, occasionally, there were a
couple of fantastic songwriters in the band, pals of
mine, and we played all over the place, all our own
stuff, the songwriters insisted that we do no covers, just
our own stuff, for artistic reasons.

Artistic reasons, ha!

Heard it, yeah, understood.

I managed to get my degree, teaching
qualification, fitting it in around the music, and we even
got offered a couple of deals in the early days, but the
songwriters wanted to hold out for something better.

Eventually I got itchy feet, wanted to settle
down, have a family.

Now they're getting more offers thrown at them,
they've asked me back, they've been really nice about
it.

They've got principles.

They're going to be something, at least for a while.

My wife's saying go for it, but I don't think she means it.

I mean, I think she means it but I don't think she understands the risk.

She says we could represent the future of Scottish music, ha!

Maybe one day those two that love Aztec Camera will be talking about us!

Or two people like them.

Maybe they wouldn't be here by the time we made it.

Anyway.

I don't know what I'll do.

I just want to be doing my best at something and enjoying it too.

Know, yeah?

So, you're the one with a future in this.

Make the most of it eh!

…

Hi sir.

Aye it's me.

Naw, that's not me back, I'm just in to pick up some woodwork.

Been visiting my dad at the prison today.

Yeah.

Yeah fine.

Are you fine?

Aye, aye, I'm still getting that upholstery job, my brother says I can still do it.

School says I can leave now.

Or the social worker fixed it, or something.

424

Can't work regular hours at the moment, dad's on remand and it's about an hour to go and visit him, so.

Stepdad's going to be in a wheelchair now.

Well, I've not really seen much of my pals, not anymore.

I'm with my big brother most of the time, the guys he works with, they're all about twenty.

Naw, mum's gonni stay with my stepdad and look after him, he'll need twenty-four hour care to start off with, once he's out the hospital.

It's not my place to tell her to do something else.

And I'm not just going to walk away.

Walk away.

Aye, he's my stepdad, or I call him that, but actually he's never married my mum.

James comes round the house still, suppose he always will.

He's my step-brother really, well in a kind of way.

James is my step-dad's ex-wife's son, James, so he is.

Aye, naw, not many folk know, but I've known for years.

He's never really talked about it, he doesn't say a lot at all, he stopped talking when his own dad died when he was five, hardly says a thing now.

Speaks sometimes though, just not so much in front of lots of people.

Some teachers know about it, and they don't ask him to read out loud in class or anything.

When James was nine, it was, that he became my step-brother.

His mum had married again when James was six, but her husband left her after three years, or something like that, and he, James's stepdad that is, moved in with my mum when she split up from my dad.

James lived with us for a year in primary seven, to be with his stepdad, then he went back to his own mum.

So, he's not a blood-relative, but still.

Mum said I should always treat him like a brother, so I do.

That's nearly five years now.

When he's sixteen he'll be able to get a job with me.

So, aye, I'm doing a few hours here and there with my brother, got a job later this afternoon.

Then the pub!

Aye!

They'll let me sit in with my brother and his pals and I'll have a half-pint, sometimes two eh!

Aye it wasni a bad school here, the teachers and everything, the teachers were good, mostly.

Shame about, em, Mister thingmy, the R.E. teacher, he was a good guy.

Aye you're all good guys, teachers here, trying to teach us lot!

All the teachers I've had were good, wouldni say a bad word about any of them.

Hope they'd say the same about me!

The Bin Brigade eh!

I never really knew how it started, why we all got put in there and ended up as a class.

Still, you don't argue.

It was just me and Billy at first, we had a fight in a French class and got chucked out, and then we had to sit in this classroom every French lesson, then a few others in the same yeargroup got put in with us, out of other subjects each week.

Then there was something happening, school inspectors, I think, and we got told to stay out of the way.

One time the deputy rector told us to move classrooms, then later the same period he came running in and told us to move again, from one building to another!

Me and Billy were at the back of the group, and when we were in the playground the deputy told us to pick up a couple of bins and go and empty them in the big skips behind the Science block.

Then after that we all got told to empty all the bins from time to time, do other things too, but bins was the main thing.

I like it, cleaning up, I do!

There isn't even a group like us in the third year, we do such a good job, eh!

We got told we'd still learn stuff and that, as well, and we do, well, we did.

I did.

Look how much you've taught us sir in, what's it been, eight weeks, ten?

You be okay yourself sir, aye look after yourself.

Thanks for everything sir, you know, the class.

I really enjoyed your lessons.

See you around sir.

Buy you a drink when I'm eighteen, hee hee!

…

Afternoon sir, thought I'd pop in a wee bit early before today's lesson.

427

Got a wee something for you, just to say thanks very much and, well, it's been a treat to know you.

Aye, open it!

You're the only teacher that's let me bring in my own films to watch in class!

There you are, just a wee postcard to put on your wall.

Stan Laurel eh, supercool for cats, that guy is.

Mum said I should get you something.

I found it in a shop in Edinburgh, think it's secondhand, but it's in good condition, not bent or anything.

The frame's just a cheap thing.

There aren't many photos of him without Hardy in them as well.

I like the actual picture, just Stan and the huge old movie camera.

They were a great double act, the two of them, but just, there's something about him, and he's affected so many people, actors, the way the present themselves on screen, the way films get made.

We went to his birthplace once on holiday, weird family, mine, eh!

I though you could stick this up in every classroom you have from now on, know, once you get a real job eh.

Mum said you could look at it and think about how what you do can have so much influence, much more than you know, and it would inspire you to inspire the pupils, eh!

Seriously sir, the way you've taken the class, you've let them do what they want and they've still just wanted to do what you want them to do, just gone along with you.

Well, most of the time!

I got a guitar at the weekend, always wanted one, played about with other people's before, and I've played the piano since I can't remember.

Started to write songs already, and they're as crap as you'd expect.

But just watch out for me, I'll get better!

If I ever do get into a decent performing arts course, I want to be able to do everything well.

I know it's a bit cut-throat though, mum and dad have told me.

Eventually I'd like to go to London, just to be there eh!

Get some acting jobs, work in the afternoons and evenings, sleep all morning, save some money, see some shows, the lifestyle, culture, get some girls, ha!

Aw, I don't know.

I really like Marie you know.

If she asked me to run away with her today, I'd do it in an instant, quit the dreams, go be a janitor, shop assistant, anything!

On Valentine's Day I bought her a card that plays that song, you know, it goes, I wanna stay with you for the rest of my life, the song starts playing when the card opens, yeah?

But I never gave it to her, just, it's too cheesy, it's not me, not like me, just, so it's still in my room at home.

Hee hee, who knows, eh?

One of these days I'll walk up to her, I'll tell myself Ace, don't not do it, do it!

Act!

Bell will go soon.

The Bin Brigade, that mad lot.

Supercool group of guys.

I don't really know whether I'm part of them or not.

Other pupils say my name gets read out on registers in classes that I don't turn up to.

Nobody seems to stop me joining the Bin Brigade.

The deputy rector came in once and I talked back a wee bit to him and he asked me if I wanted to stay there and I said yes.

I didn't expect him to just say okay and turn away!

I used to think that the pupils in the Bin Brigade were like an audience but eventually I saw them, I don't know, maybe not as friends, I don't know.

Supporters.

They really want me to do well, they tell me when they've seen me in a rubbish thing on telly like an advert, or my face poking out the side of the screen in a non-speaking part on a crap programme.

They'll always say they liked my performance.

Anyway, I'll nip for a pee while you get sorted for the class, back in a minute.

Have good times in your life sir, here's my card, look me up!

…

That it then sir, your last lesson with us, eh.

Last lesson here altogether?

Very last?

And it was with us?

Excellent.

Perfecto!

Back to uni then is it?

Aye.

430

Gonni miss us?

Aye?

Haha!

Aye well, put it there sir, it's been a pleasure knowing you.

Good luck eh, you're a star man.

Me?

After school?

'Gers game tonight, just the reserves mind, what with Scotland playing tomorrow and everything.

Getting a bus to the match with my dad in the morning, missing school again, oops!

Who knows when I'll be back!

Aw, after finishing school you mean, when I leave at Easter?

Who knows!

No idea sir!

I'll find something.

My dad knows a few people.

This guy, mega-rich, he can get me a job with the council, he's not a councillor, he builds houses, but I think he knows people on the council, he would always be able to help out with the thing.

So maybe I'll do that for a while.

Would like to do something where I'd be driving, lorry, taxi something like that.

Maybe.

Maybe haulage, I'd like to have my own business eh.

I used to be a van boy for a delivery company, just for a while, at the weekends.

But I just got bossed about by the guys there, they even punched me and everything.

Stuff that!

431

Plus, I was missing the football, so.

Who knows what I'll do.

Taking Kev to the game tonight, dad got an extra ticket and said we could take him.

Think my dad feels sorry for him, keeps telling me to include him in stuff we do, always telling me to be the bigger person, that's all he ever says!

Some dad eh!

Kev's alright though.

He used to get bullied at primary and I suppose people still think he can't look after himself, but he can, really.

Everybody worries about him, with his mum and everything, but him and his mum are pretty tight.

He takes her to the doctor and everything, sometimes has the day off to look after her if she's ill, goes with her to her wee brother's Parents' Evenings at the primary even!

My dad's never been to any of my Parents' Evenings!

My mum?

Aw, never mind.

They keep asking about him when he's off, Kev, he's usually just got a cold or something, it's nothing.

Probably nothing today, I'll see him later, I bet, he'll turn up at some point.

I'll be letting him know he's let you down by not showing up, eh.

The class think he's a poor soul.

The class, haha.

What a bunch we are, eh sir!

Got to tell you sir, I hate school, but it's funny being in that class, what a bunch eh!

The Bin Brigade!

I never really liked that name a lot but, made us sound like we were dustmen, like that's all we were good enough for when we left school.

And I bet none of us, none of them, end up as dustmen.

Or if they do it'll be because they want to, not because they have to.

It'll be out of choice.

That'll be me leaving here in a week or two as well, Easter, that'll be me, gone.

Ach, might come in for a few exams, see what happens.

Anyway.

Right then.

Put it there again sir.

Aye, don't you worry about me eh!

…

In the jingle jangle morning, och, who the eff am I kidding that I can sing!

Hey son.

Aye.

So, election tomorrow, Scotland match too, eh, quite an eventful prospect eh.

You be taking an interest in the outcomes of either eh?

Aye, probably best not to, none of it matters in the long run.

A promising rebellion against the government by party loyalists, well party normally-loyal-ists!

But something almost certainly to be overturned when it really counts at the next General Election.

And meanwhile Scotland, after scoring early in the first half, lose heroically in the end to two late goals in the Eastern European rain!

I don't know what it is.

False hope son, false hope.

Tomorrow tomorrow, two certain defeats for the price of one, know!

And really, who cares eh?

Who the eff cares!

Ah, who cares about who the eff cares eh!

Inevitability eh.

And that's not to mention a possible Day of Action vote in the near future, if it actually happens, these things have a habit of getting called off.

Maybe it has been already, I've not heard anything about it recently, it's maybe just other unions getting asked.

Day of Action!

A day.

Of.

Action!

Haha, well it'd never happen anyway, and there won't even be the hope for it, false or otherwise.

Even our good union rep will tell you that, nobody in their right mind is going to give up a day's pay to freeze their effing balls off walking down Princes Street or up Glasgow Green, or wherever, asking the government to pay a wee bit more attention to the teachers or any other public sector mugs.

Not with the public already hating us for the holidays we get, and then having to fork out for extra childminding on the effing day itself.

Public support?

Aye, right!

And half of them, over half of them wouldni even turn up on a march, except maybe for the piss-up afterwards, spending money they're not even earning

434

that day, aye I've been there, done it, souvenir mug, me.

So.

Aye, you don't need me boring you.

So.

My divorce papers come through tomorrow.

You involved with someone yourself?

Nah, don't even answer that mate, I'll only start, and who am I to.

No.

So the teaching eh, you're not gonni join the police eh!

Aye, you'll be fine son, seen you with the kids, just in the corridor, know.

Plus the kids like you, they've said.

Fair guy, good guy.

Stay that way.

It gets harder, but you stay that way, and even though the job'll get harder, you'll still be able to tell yourself, as you go to sleep after you've had the shittiest day imaginable, that you'll still have done a good thing, just turning up for work.

Then no matter what else is going on in your life, you know you're doing a good thing for at least some hours in the day.

Keep at it, keep being the best you can be son.

Anyway, the police isn't for everyone.

That's all I can tell you.

Aye, tomorrow.

Good luck, son.

Tomorrow tomorrow.

...

435

Sir, I just came back for, is it alright, can I take some of the stuff I've done in your lesson off the wall please?

Just these World War One posters eh.

I'm going at Easter, leaving school, and with you not being here anymore, someone else might not allow me to take them down.

I don't need to do my exams anymore.

The army let me know at the weekend.

I can't wait.

Joining the army at last, me!

Just take these posters, yeah?

Did you like us, sir?

I mean, the Bin Brigade.

Sometimes I didn't like the rest of them, they abused me about the army!

But.

They've not said anything since I got in.

Aye, the army'll be good for me, my mum says, she's always said it.

Her brother joined the army straight from school and it did him the world of good, used to get into bother with the police, and when he joined the army it straightened him out, stayed in for nine years, got a good job now.

I used to get into trouble at primary, got put in a wee behaviour unit here two periods a week in first year, even had a teacher to go to some classes with me.

But I never got into trouble once in first or second year.

Still, I still got put into this class early in third year, suppose the school thought I was still a troublemaker because of my primary record.

I didn't complain.

436

I knew it wouldn't prevent me from joining the army.

Yeah, the army at last then!

Thought for a while I'd never get in.

That fitness test man!

Now I just have to see school out until Easter, then leave without doing my exams.

I'll aim to make a career of it.

Officer?

Don't think so.

Maybe.

No, I'll be a soldier for a few years, might learn a trade, there's no-one better than the army for training you in the trades.

Once I've got enough money saved, I'll be able to buy myself out and get a job with other ex-army people, same regiment.

Yeah I am scared, if I think about it.

You go to the talks, see the adverts on telly, I mean you do know there's a risk and everything, death is possible.

But still, you join up looking forward to travelling abroad, building schools and bridges in places that need them, skiing, parachuting, all these things, you think about them more than the bad stuff before you actually join.

Plus, you know, if there's something you want to do, you shouldn't not do it, you should do it!

Now though.

You know that sometime you could be posted to a place where any day there's someone else or lots of other people waking up in the same place as you, same town, same country, the same morning, and they're wanting to kill you or one of your mates, and they've got a gun or a grenade or a bomb and they'll try and do it, and it might just be luck that you're still alive at the end of the day.

But you'll be alive, at least.

Thanks for the posters, I liked your classes sir, History, Scottish history and the First World War, the've been my favourite lessons in school, ever.

Even though I still think half of it's made up! Ha ha!

Sir, remember that thing I told you, about the thing the army guy told me, about the history books, well, I was remembering as well, one of our old teachers told us that he was sold a deal and bought a whole load of these text books in for the school that he taught in before this one, and when he read through the book it turned out that the writer had made up the names for all the people who were quoted in it, it was all old radio DJs, I canni remember the names of them, Lord James Saville I think one of them was, the writer was just having a laugh, he knew that people would just believe what was in the book, just 'cause the book said that it was telling the truth, it was a history book, and people believe what they read in history books!

Ach, I don't know, maybe I'm remembering it wrong, I don't know.

See you then, aye.

You can sleep sound at night sir, I'm on watch!

...

Big week boy, Scotland match tomorrow, the kids are talking about it eh, boys going mad.

Think a few of them'll nip off early to get ready to watch it!

Six o'clock kick off, what with the time whatsit between here and there, so.

438

You don't strike me as the keen sort son, football I mean.

No a supporter of anyone are you?

Kids here, some of them not bad players, aye, used to take a few teams myself.

Boys were always dead enthusiastic at the start of the season.

August training sessions, forty kids you'd have, kicking balls around, fighting to get into the team, fighting they are!

Then you'd start playing a few matches, maybe win a couple, then one week you'd get trounced six-nil then then the next it would be eight.

Heads go down, the in-fighting begins, boys bickering amongst themselves on the pitch.

You get one game where you're one-nil down at half-time, still got a chance, and then you see what the kids are made of.

Can they come back?

Not a bit of it.

Once they've played the kids from the bigger towns once, the harder areas, that's when they realise they've just not got the whatsit.

Fight.

I remember.

Ach.

Aye.

See that Joe though.

I'm not saying I would ever have been a manager of a top club.

But just.

That Joe.

He was my last chance I reckon, last chance to get back into the closed circle of the top scouts, connections to the big time, know.

Oh, I've put a few half-decent boys through to lower division sides, seen a few do okay.

But that Joe, he had the potential, I'm telling you boy.

And I would have been doing him a favour and all.

Lift him out of where he was, where he is.

When he came to this school we all got told about what he was like at the primary, distancing himself from the rest of his class in primary one and two, no talking to anyone, the other pupils, self-imposed social isolation, I'm telling you.

Wanting to be cuddling his teacher the whole time.

Then he became a bully, picked on one boy in particular, that lad, I've seen you teach him sometimes, Kevin is it?

Always wandering about the place like he's sleep-walking, that's the one, aye.

Well, apparently he got bullied mercilessly by Joe, from about primary five onwards I think, or four.

Aye, aggressive boy, Joe, even towards his teachers, at primary age and all!

Now you look at him, making nothing of himself.

I could have taken him away from all that.

Joe.

Fucking.

Fucking cunty wee creature.

He could have taken me away from all of this.

His dad, fucking cunt.

Ach.

Hmmf.

That's you then this week son, isn't it, Friday.

Today?

Oh, today?

I didn't realise it was today.

But today's only a Wednesday.

Oh well, you'll be hoping to get a job in a good school eh.

Could do worse than here, boy, could do a lot worse.

Aye I know there's a few of us just blether about in the staffroom, but there's some good teachers here.

And good pupils.

Believe me, good pupils.

Well, all the whatsit boy.

Maybe see you again if you end up in this place eh.

Keep you a seat by the window eh!

…

I say, egalitarian?

Democratic?

Are you quite sure, dear boy?

Are you going to back it up?

With evidence?

Aah.

Evidence, that's what you historians live off, eh!

But I must say.

Egalitarian!

Democratic!

Where are my glasses, this won't do, won't do at all.

Now, let me see here.

But.

Dear boy.

Dear boy, dear boy, dear boy.

What you've written here.

What you term as modern Scottish schooling is neither egalitarian nor democratic!

Do you mean to say you're being told that at university!

Well I must say I doubt whether you would find a single teacher in this school who agrees with that statement!

Who is telling you that then?

Aah, it's the history of education, aah!

I cannot believe you're getting told that during teacher training!

I'm asking myself, am I wrong?

You have to write an essay about this then, is that right?

I'm sure I could find you mine on the same subject from nearly forty years ago, what!

I'll still have it!

With all the old papers.

Everything I've written.

All the things that I have written.

Egalitarian eh, democratic!

I look around this office, and across there at the rector's office, sometimes wondering just, just what, what if it was me in there.

Would it make a difference?

Would I?

Would it make any?

Difference.

Aah.

And in my heart of hearts I know it would not.

I.

Would.

Not.

Make.

One.

Difference.

An essay on Scottish education then, I'm sorry, they call it schooling at the universities now!

Aah.

We talk about a palace revolution in here, I talk about it!

But, all of the teachers in this school would agree with me on this one point, listen to this.

If modern Scottish schooling was so egalitarian and democratic, then how is it that a school like this is fighting for funds with bigger institutions in other parts of the town, the authority, state schools just like us!

Aah!

Picking their pupils these days, that's what some of them are doing!

Nobody in education does what they think is right anymore, aah!

Virtually, em, fucking, em, fucking advertising themselves in the primaries!

Sociologically, is this where evolution has got us!

Ah!

Fuck fuck fucking!

Excuse me.

Excuse me.

Em.

I think I can safely tell you, dear boy, that as student regent I have written you a very complimentary report on your practice here.

443

Your head of department speaks highly of you, as do your colleagues in History.

Well done, dear boy, absolutely well done, splendid.

And are you looking forward to taking up your first post?

Interviews, next week?

Well, all I can say is that I hope you've learned something from our school, our small corner of the state eh!

Aah, and perhaps one day you may be in a position to make a difference.

We all make a difference, we all do.

Perhaps in small ways every day.

Goodbye dear boy.

And good luck!

Aah!

…

So that's us then son, your time in the department coming to an end today, eh.

You enjoyed yourself aye?

Aye, it's no a bad place this eh.

If you didni think so you couldni keep working here.

Tss!

There's nothing like teaching history to children.

They love the stories don't they!

That's what it's all about, getting them to enjoy their learning.

Characters, that's what they love, characters!

Ergo, if you teach about characters, they will love their learning.

Stories!

I'm saying, the Crusades, the Wars of Independence, voyages of discovery, American Revolution, French Revolution, American West, American Civil War, First World War, you could study anything really, any History department can make its choice, some of my colleagues in other schools they think the topics we cover aren't academic enough.

But these periods, they're full of characters, people.

People!

Names the kids can hang on to!

Richard, Saladin!

Wallace and Bruce, Moray!

Columbus, Magellan!

Robespierre, Custer, Lincoln, Kitchener eh!

Stories, Stirling Bridge!

Mutinies, battles!

The Crusades, the French Revolution, the First World War, turning points!

And they're all about people!

Scottish?

Does it have to be Scottish?

We do a bit of Scottish in every year, I'm certainly not saying it's not important, you won't find anyone less patriotic than me, no!

Just, it's important to have the world view as well eh?

Otherwise it's just a de facto nationalist politics course.

Know?

The Middle East, France, Europe.

So, the future of Scottish History lies abroad eh!

Sounds like a political statement, and it wouldn't be like me to make something like that eh!

Tss!

You know, when I started teaching, I thought it would be a pretty humdrum existence.

But the more you're in it.

You become taken with what you're doing, inspired.

Oh, it can be a trap for some people, don't get me wrong, a trap for definite.

But.

I can honestly say I love my job.

I love cycling into work each day, oh aye don't think I don't know a few people have a snigger at the thing, and I'm no talking just about pupils, aye.

But I don't care, and know why?

Because I love what I do and nothing anybody can say or do will change that, I love teaching History, and I tell you what, I think the pupils love getting taught by me too.

So there!

Tss, it's not about that though, it's about, just, doing a good job and going home knowing you're making a difference.

And you can do that son.

See that Bin Brigade lot, the ones you've been teaching a fair bit of?

Disengaged so they are, but still.

I used to think it was only me that they thought was the bee's knees.

But you!

Since you arrived son, what a difference, asking to work, asking to get on with stuff they've started with you!

If only the rest of the school knew what could be done with the most vulnerable children, then think

446

what an effort they'd make to get things done with the so-called best pupils eh!

So, that you off then, eh?

Well, I'll be seeing you around, listen out for my bicycle bell and get well out of my way or you'll have me over the top of my handlebars!

…

Aye, hi sir, sorry about not being in class.

Aye, I got in late again.

Anyway.

Billy said it was your last day and to come and see you, so.

What was that question?

Aye, hee hee.

Aye, sorry about all the sleeping and that eh, know, in class.

Just tired you know, the milk round.

And everything.

I wanted to be there for your last lesson, really, but.

Aye, aye, I'll stay at it for a while, something might come out of it.

The boss there says I'm a good worker, never miss a morning, and I never do.

Some of the other guys there, older than me, they have a morning off a week just not turning up, hungover or whatever.

Won't catch me hungover.

Don't drink.

Aye, naw, never will.

Boss says maybe I could be driver when I'm old enough, once I've got my licence and that.

Might not be bad.

But there's this one guy in the office at the depot, been to college and got a qualification.

Think I'd like to do that in a year or so.

It'd leave a spare place on the float but, maybe my wee brother could get a job on the morning runs then.

And I'd get a lie in, wouldn't have to start till nine!

My mum's thinking about moving but, just, a new start she says.

So everything might change.

Don't really have a lot to hold us down here.

Wee brother's got friends in primary, he'd make new ones I suppose.

Me, no, I'd go with them.

Friends, no, not a lot.

Billy.

When Joe's not around at least.

I mean, I like most of the guys in here.

Get no hassle from most of them.

They're funny!

William, man!

Aw, oh, I mean I hope he's okay.

I just mean, it was always funny with him in the class, him and James.

It was after I missed a few weeks off school once, and then a few odd days here and there, and after that I got put into the Bin Brigade.

I'd started to fail in some subjects, I thought I'd been doing okay before then and I could catch up.

But.

The school said I wasn't able to, and I had to do what work I thought I could do in the Bin Brigade.

It's okay though, I don't get teased about my mum in here.

So.

See you then sir, just going to go home and make tea for my wee brother, then meet Billy to go to Glasgow with his dad for the football.

I'm not really interested in football, but it's an evening out, eh.

Aye late night too, then up early in the morning, I'll be there but!

Aye, and sleeping in class later!

Cheers sir, what was the question!

…

What a day, Christjesus.

Here you are son, big fucking cup of coffee, do you good eh, not drink it?

Here you are anyway, have it man!

Don't not take the coffee, take it!

Ach.

Ach.

I'll just.

I swear I'm touched but then I'm tired, doo-dee-doo-dee-doo-doo, doo-doo, that's how it goes eh!

There's a song called Down The Dip, and the Dip in Down The Dip is really a pub.

Going down the dip with you means the singer was going down the Dip with a mate, know, going down the pub?

Well, so an acquaintance told me, I'm not really sure if it's true or not.

I'm not sure, I always thought it meant, know, going downhill, metaphorically anyway, on the fucking slide, getting into a run of bad luck, know.

People never really go in for the meaning of words, more the sound they make, the sound of the words, yeah?

It's an acoustic thing, Down The Dip, and after The Birth Of the True appeared at the end of Knife, you just thought young Roddy would be doing that every time.

I mean, finishing off every album with a cheeky wee strumalong, but that was the last of them eh!

For a while anyway.

I don't even know why I care.

I.

Don't.

Even.

Know.

Mind you, High Land, Hard Rain's better than Knife, but as an album closer The Birth Of The True knocks the fucking socks off Down The Dip eh, concert favourite now, you know what I'm saying, crowd liking it?

You not having a coffee son!

You never have a coffee!

And the words of songs, do they no get you either?

Or is it just melody you go for and all, ha ha!

Come on son, you got to admit the words of songs have meaning for you sometimes, they get to you yeah!

It's your last day here, you're about to leave for the last time, eh.

So that's you, you've finished your final teaching practice, you're gonni pass, dead cert, and enter into the world of education.

You happy?

You should be.

You're in a privileged position son, all of us here are.

Privileged.

Think back to when you were at school.

'Course, some of your teachers would have been pure bastards, some still are.

But listen, was there ever a time when you didn't think to yourself when you watched teachers do their job, Christjesus, I could do that!

And I don't mean, Christjesus I could do that better, but, just, Christjesus, to be able to do that, wouldn't that be fucking wonderful!

Ach, recollections, eh.

I swear, anyone could teach if they had the bottle.

You just have to know more than the kids and tell them about it, it's a simple concept.

But to actually get to do it, and do it well, Christjesus, think of the privilege it is!

Look at the kids in this school, pure gems most of them, and we have the chance to guide them, tutor them, persuade them, argue with them, all of that.

Ach, you go for promotion and you just end up doing less of what you're good at, less of what you went to uni for four, five years to do.

You end up enjoying doing things other than teaching.

So you're better off remaining a classroom teacher in the end, eh.

Which isn't to say I'm not full of bitterness and regret!

Recollections and regrets.

So, son.

451

What you gonni tell me, eh, hey, what is it, you're tired eh?

Aye, we all are.

We all are.

All tired, son.

Okay then, aye, all the best son, mind when you're a headteacher, I'll be applying for a deputy post at your school!

Or a head of department, I'll still be fucking looking for that then!

Och.

You swear you're touched but then you're tired, eh.

Aye, son, you look it.

…

The school gates were half-closed.

Some pupils who'd been playing five-a-sides, or hanging out at the chess club, they were still passing out of them.

A few teachers were walking through too, carrying books, boxes, papers.

A group of two, and then a three.

Then a three, then another two.

Three pupils, with one running up behind them to catch up, making the four.

It worked out.

A stone, that had been kicked off the ground by someone, rose from the rubble and hit the bottom of the gate, and bounced up in the air again.

A kind of parabola formed before it dropped and settled in the dust.

It worked out.

Staff drove out the gates, or walked to the bus stop, looking down the road for the next bus as they did so, or heading to the station, so they could travel home.

Home, to wives, husbands and children, empty houses, union meetings, lesson preparation, or twilight courses, Open University tutorials, marking, perhaps the thoughts of a career outside education, recollections and regrets.

Recollections and regrets.

Maybe even some time for a family life.

With the next day to contemplate, teachers, colleagues, they were all just trying, trying to do their best.

Chaplain Divine, Bicycle Clips, the Crossword Freaks.

Walks In Snow and the Dog-Catcher.

Armpits and Mr Tambourine Man.

And Shakespeare, Bastard Guy.

The Phantom, and Sandwich Toaster.

And the Joke Club, Scout.

Ex-Cop.

And tonight too, children would leave the school grounds and head off, to their own homes.

Homes, or part-time jobs.

Homes, with mothers in the houses, memories of fathers.

Or it would be homework, with the TV on across the room, maybe drunkenness in the background, the desire for love or escape.

The desire for love or escape.

With realities and dreams in their heads, the Bin Brigade, their fellow pupils, all waiting, just waiting to make something of themselves.

Or even just for something to become of them.

Billy and Kevin.

Ace and Marie.

Sam, Kelly, Joseph.

William and James.

Teachers, pupils, all living their lives apart from each other, without each other, outside school, at the end of the day.

For tomorrow, they would be with each other again, together.

And then, there would be the football to digest, and laughter to be shared, and politics to be discussed, and music to be listened to.

And difficulties to be confronted or ignored, and classes to be late for, and ambitions to speak of, and the news to disect, and friends to exist with, and teachers to work for, and children to complain about.

Stories to be told.

History, to make up.

And for me, lots of lessons to learn.

9 781784 076658